WINTER AT THE DOOR

Center Point
Large Print

Also by Sarah Graves and available from
Center Point Large Print:

Dead Level
A Bat in the Belfry

**This Large Print Book carries the
Seal of Approval of N.A.V.H.**

WINTER AT THE DOOR

Sarah Graves

CENTER POINT LARGE PRINT
THORNDIKE, MAINE

This Center Point Large Print edition
is published in the year 2015 by arrangement with
Bantam Books, an imprint of Random House,
a division of Penguin Random House LLC.

The text of this Large Print edition is unabridged.
In other aspects, this book may vary
from the original edition.
Printed in the United States of America
on permanent paper.
Set in 16-point Times New Roman type.

ISBN: 978-1-62899-581-7

Library of Congress Cataloging-in-Publication Data

Graves, Sarah, 1951–
Winter at the door / Sarah Graves. — Center Point Large Print edition.
pages cm
Summary: "Tough but haunted police chief Lizzie Snow, a big-city cop
with a mission, takes on a small town with a dark side when she moves
from Boston to Bearkill, Maine, hoping to find her missing niece. As a
blizzard bears down, Lizzie gears up for a showdown with a killer"
 —Provided by publisher.
ISBN 978-1-62899-581-7 (library binding : alk. paper)
1. Women police chiefs—Fiction. 2. Drug traffic—Fiction.
3. Eastport (Me.)—Fiction. 4. Large type books. I. Title.
PS3557.R2897W56 2015
813'.54—dc23

              2015011154

This book is for John Squibb.

WINTER
AT THE
DOOR

Carl Bogart's old Fleetwood double-wide mobile home stood on a cleared half acre surrounded by a forest of mixed hardwoods, spruce, and hackmatack trees shedding their dark-gold needles onto the unpaved driveway.

It was late October. From the black rubberized roof at the mobile home's kitchen end protruded a sheet metal stovepipe topped by a screened metal spark guard and a cone-shaped sheet metal rain cap.

No smoke came from the stovepipe. Cody Chevrier pulled the white Blazer with the Aroostook County Sheriff's Department decal stenciled on its door up alongside the double-wide and parked. Bogart's truck, an old green Ford F-150 pickup, was backed halfway into the lean-to shed that stood at right angles to the trailer.

A day's worth of fallen hackmatack needles veiled the truck's windshield. Cody got out, his door-slam loud in the clearing's silence.

"Hey, Carl?" Half a cord of white maple logs chainsawed to stove length lay in a mess of wood chips with Carl's splitting axe stuck in the chopping block at the center of them, as if he'd just gone inside for a drink of water or something.

"Carl?" At midmorning, frost still glazed the fallen leaves lying in coppery drifts in the trailer's shade, the day clear and cold now after a night that had gotten down into the twenties. There were no marks in the rime under the trailer's windows that Cody could see.

Besides the pickup truck, Carl's shed held a shotgun-shell reloading press bolted to a massively overbuilt wooden workbench, the bench's legs fastened through big galvanized angle irons to a pair of old railroad ties set parallel into the shed's poured concrete floor. Seeing this reminded Cody that it was about time for him and Carl to start thinking about lugging the shell press indoors for winter. Turning slowly, he regarded the double-wide again.

Around it, long grass lay flattened by the deer who used the clearing as a sleeping yard; Carl didn't hunt anymore himself, just reloaded the shotgun shells for others. No tire tracks were on the grass, and the hackmatack needles on the driveway had already been disturbed by Cody's own vehicle, as well as by the breeze that had sprung up at dawn.

So: no sign that anyone else had been here recently, Cody thought, unable to keep his mind from running that way even with no real evidence yet of anything amiss.

A red squirrel scampered up the steps to the double-wide's screened porch—from May through September, the mosquitoes here could stand flat-footed and look right over the house at you, and the blackflies were worse—then reversed itself in mid-leap and ran back down them again, hot-footing it across the yard into the woods.

"Carl, you old son of a bitch, get your ragged ass out here," Cody yelled, because Carl was scaring him now. This was not like the old retired ex-cop.

It was not like him at all. A low howl rose from the back seat of Cody's vehicle, where Carl's black and tan hound, Rascal, had been confined for nearly an hour already. The dog had been found way over on the old White Oak Station Road, nobody with him, and calls to Carl to come down and get the animal hadn't been answered.

Which was also not like him. Cody mounted the steps, shading his eyes with his hands to peer into the screened enclosure. As he did so, memories from years past assailed him, from back when a much younger Cody Chevrier was the newest, greenest Aroostook County sheriff's deputy imaginable, and Carl was his boss.

Back then, by this time of the morning Carl's wife, Audrey, would've had her day's laundry out drying already, Carl's flannel shirts and tomato-red long johns flapping from a line strung on pulleys between the porch and the shed. She'd have had strong coffee burbling in a percolator and fresh-baked coffee cake laid out on a white paper doily, sweet smelling in the warm, bright kitchen.

Broiled brown-sugar topping on the coffee cake, she'd have had; Cody could almost taste it. But Audrey had been gone all of ten years now, and from the porch's far corner the old clothesline hung slack on bent wheels, a few blackened wooden clothespins still clipped to it.

Cody called through the screen, heard Carl's radio playing tinnily inside. No other sound, though. And Carl wouldn't ever have left his axe out that way.

Or his dog roaming. Rascal howled dismally again from the rear of the Blazer, the sound raising the hairs on Cody's neck. The breeze kicked up another notch, chilling his armpits inside his jacket and giving him gooseflesh.

Oh, he didn't like this. He didn't like it a bit.

With a feeling of deep reluctance, he pulled open the screen door and crossed the porch he and Carl had built together one fine autumn week-end all those years ago. Rascal's predecessor, Rowdy, was just a pup at the time, Cody recalled, the young dog nosing around and getting in their way, while inside, Audrey fried ham-and-egg sandwiches for lunch.

The eggs were from her own hens, the crisp homemade pickles preserved from cukes grown in her garden. She'd raised prize dahlias, too, back

12

then, or was it roses? Cody couldn't remember.

No matter, though; once she died, Carl had quit mowing so much and let the raised beds and the cold frame go to ruin. Now in the screened porch a rickety wooden card table heaped with old copies of *Field & Stream* and *Sports Illustrated* stood beside a bent-ash rocker with a striped blanket for a cushion, a reading lamp with a blue plaid shade on a tripod stand, and a trash-bag-lined barrel half full of empty Budweiser cans.

No ashtray. Carl never smoked. He always said a cop couldn't afford to mess up his sense of smell. From inside the trailer, Cody sniffed scorched baked beans and a rank whiff of something else.

"Oh, man," he said softly.

Carl Bogart's body lay sprawled on the linoleum just inside the double-wide's entry. Cody stepped over it into the familiar kitchen, then turned and crouched to feel for a pulse in his old friend's whiskery neck.

He'd known there wouldn't be one, though. Blood stained the cabinet fronts in the kitchen and a dark pool had begun drying under Carl's head near the weapon, a .45 revolver that Cody recognized, fallen by Carl's hand.

"Oh, buddy," Cody said sadly. "I'm so sorry."

Then he went back outside to call dispatch.

ONE

TWO WEEKS LATER

This is not what I signed up for," Lizzie Snow said. "And you know it."

She gazed around in dismay at the small, dusty office whose plate-glass front window looked out at the remote northern town of Bearkill, Maine. The office walls were covered with fake wood paneling, the ceiling was stained 1960s-era acoustical tiles, and the ratty beige carpet was worn through to the backing in the traffic areas.

"You said I'd be . . ." The furnishings consisted of a beat-up metal desk, an office chair with one of its cheap plastic wheels missing, and a metal shelf rack of the kind used to store car parts in an auto supply store, plus one old phone book.

Not that sticking her in a *better* office would've helped. ". . . on patrol," she finished, trying to control her temper.

Squinting out across Main Street, she told herself that the town, at least, wasn't so bad. Two rows of small businesses and shops, a luncheonette, and a corner bar called Area 51 whose sign featured a big-eyed alien with a cocktail in its hand made up the downtown district. There was a laundromat, a flower shop, a supermarket, and an office supply place called The Paper Chase.

All were apparently doing business, though not exactly thriving; years ago in the post-WWII housing boom and for decades after, timber harvesting had supported this community and many others like it. But with the lumber industry sadly diminished, the area's agriculture—potatoes, oats, broccoli—couldn't take up the slack, and there wasn't much else here to work at.

Or so she'd read. Bearkill was one of many Maine towns she'd Googled before coming here, but this was her first visit.

Too bad it's not my last . . .

She supposed she should've liked the little town's air of brave defiance, stuck way out here in the woods with not even a movie theater or a Whole Foods, much less a museum or jazz club.

But, dear God, there wasn't even a Starbucks, the only hair salon was called The Cut-n-Run, and if you could buy any makeup but Maybelline in this town, she'd eat her hat.

"Yeah, I know the job's not like I described," Aroostook County sheriff Cody Chevrier admitted.

Six-two and one-eighty or so with close-clipped silver hair and the perma-tanned skin of a guy who spent a lot of his time outdoors, summer and winter, Chevrier was in his late fifties but still trimly athletic-looking in his tan uniform.

15

"Since you and I talked last, though, there've been a few developments."

"Yeah? Like what, a crime wave?" she asked skeptically. On the sixty-mile drive north up Route 1 from the Aroostook County seat of Houlton this morning, she'd seen little evidence of that.

Farms, forest land, widely spaced homes and small roadside businesses were the norm here, she'd seen after filling out the stacks of pre-employment paperwork Chevrier had put before her. Around the courthouse and the sheriff's office, men and women in business garb carried briefcases and drove late-model sedans, but once she'd left Houlton it was good old boys in gimme caps and women in pastel sweatshirts all the way. Nobody looked as if they had a whole lot to steal, or the inclination to steal anything, either.

"You might be surprised at what goes on in this area," said Chevrier.

"Uh-huh." She eyed him sideways. "Maybe."

And moonbeams might fly out of her ass the next time she passed gas, too. But she'd been a cop for a dozen years now, and she wasn't betting on it; crime-wise—*and otherwise,* she thought bleakly—this place was deader than Elvis.

"You said I'd be on the road," she reminded Chevrier again. "First with a partner and then . . ."

According to the Aroostook County Sheriff's

16

Department's website, there were 2,500 miles of public roadway in "the County" (locals always used the capital *C*), which spread across half of northern Maine. Eight thousand miles more of privately maintained roads belonged to major landowners, primarily lumber companies. In area the County was larger than Rhode Island and Connecticut combined; its 71,000-plus residents generated approximately 600 criminal complaints and 400 traffic incidents each quarter.

In addition, the sheriff's department served court orders and warrants, moved prisoners and psych patients, worked with the Maine DEA, the warden service, Border Patrol, and Homeland Security, and staffed a seventy-two-bed county jail; the transport detail alone logged 160,000 miles per year.

And none of it could afford to get screwed up just because she was a new deputy. She'd need an experienced partner for a while before working a patrol assignment on her own; that much she'd understood.

Eventually, though, she'd be out there solo: keeping her eyes and ears open, asking polite questions and maybe a few not-so-polite ones. Searching—

And sooner or later finding. If, that is, it turned out that there was really anything—any*one*—up here to find . . .

Out of the blue, Chevrier asked the question

17

she'd seen on his face when he'd first met her in person the day before.

"So, you will pass the physical, right?"

The Aroostook County Sheriff's Department's mandatory pre-employment fitness test, he meant. Sit-ups, push-ups, a mile-and-a-half run . . . all required in order to finalize her hiring.

"Yeah," she replied, controlling her impatience. Back in Boston, where she'd been a homicide detective until a few weeks ago—*dear God, was it only that long?*—she'd done those things religiously at the police academy gym on Williams Avenue. Six days a week, sometimes seven . . .

Usually seven. It was among the joys of being a woman cop: to the dirtbags—and to some of your coworkers, too, though they'd deny it—you were a pushover until proven otherwise. So there was no sense allowing for even the slightest chance of it being true; on a good day, she bench-pressed 220. She just didn't look like she could, or at any rate not at first glance.

Short, spiky black hair expertly cut, blood-red nails matching her lipstick, and smoky-dark eye makeup meticulously applied took care of that, as did her scent, which was Guerlain's Rose Barbare, and her high-heeled black boots rising to the tops of her tightly muscled calves, snug as a second skin.

She had no uniforms here yet, so today she

wore black jeans, a white silk T-shirt and navy hoodie, and a butter-soft leather jacket. The look wasn't fancy, but perhaps partly as a result of all those gym hours it was effective; exiting Chevrier's vehicle, she'd attracted second glances from several of Bearkill's passing citizens, some even approving.

Some not so much. Hey, screw them. "I'll do just fine," she repeated evenly, "on the fitness tests."

"Okay," Chevrier replied. *If you say so,* his face added, but not as doubtfully this time; whether it was the confidence in her voice, a closer appraisal of her gym-toned form, or a combination of the two that convinced him, she didn't know.

Or care. "In that case, you're the new community liaison officer here in Bearkill," he said. "First one we've ever had."

Gesturing at the dingy room, he added, "I'll set you up with account numbers for furniture and supplies, and we've got people on contract to get the place cleaned and painted for you."

On the way here, he'd explained that her assignment had changed because a federal grant he'd been expecting to lose had come through after all. So he had funding for this new position.

But he hadn't described her duties, an omission she thought odd. Could it be he believed that being from a big city meant she already knew the usual activities and objectives of such a job? Or . . . was she supposed to invent them herself?

Her hiring had been fast-tracked, too: a mere two weeks between the time he'd learned that she was in the coastal Maine town of Eastport—her first stop after leaving Boston—and this morning's paperwork.

It was another thing she felt curious about: why he'd been so interested in her, and in her homicide experience especially. She made a mental note to ask him about all of it if he didn't volunteer the information soon, just as a husky teenager on an old balloon-tired Schwinn bike pedaled by the big front window.

Sporting a nose stud and a silvery lip ring and with his pale hair twisted into utterly improbable-looking dreadlocks, the kid wore faded jeans and a drab T-shirt and was tattooed on all visible parts of his body except his face.

Really? she thought in surprise. So apparently not every young male in Aroostook County was a good old boy; she wondered if Tattoo Kid here was a skilled fighter, or if he survived looking the way he did by trading something other than punches.

". . . department credit card for gas, but we do repairs back at the house," Chevrier was saying, meaning that vehicles were taken care of in Houlton, she thought, likely through a local car dealer's service department.

Which as news was not earthshaking, nor was the rest of the procedural stuff he was reciting. Lizzie slipped a hand into her jacket pocket and withdrew a creased photograph of a little girl who was about nine years old.

The child had straight, shoulder-length blond hair and blue eyes, and wore a red, white, and blue striped cape of some shiny material; she held a small banner that read HAPPY 4TH OF JULY!

I'm coming, honey, Lizzie thought at the photograph, worn from frequent handling. *I'll find you. And when I do . . .*

She tucked the picture away again. It was why she had left Boston, why she was here in Maine at all: an anonymous tip, her first hint in years that she had living family after all. But she still didn't know the end of that last sentence.

When I do . . . then what?

". . . get yourself a PO box right away so we can send you your paychecks," Chevrier was saying.

She wasn't even sure that the child in the photograph was the one she sought. Her younger sister Cecily's infant daughter, Nicolette, had gone missing from Eastport eight years earlier, right after Cecily's own mysterious death.

If she wasn't a sad little pile of bones in an unmarked grave somewhere, Nicki was Lizzie's only living kin, and after a long time of believing the child was dead there'd been other hints

21

recently, too, that instead she was somewhere in northern Maine.

But Lizzie wasn't sure of that, either, and anyway, northern Maine was a big place. There was, she realized for the thousandth time, so much she didn't know.

I should have done more, started sooner.

I shouldn't have just let it go.

But she had; for one thing, she'd needed to earn a living, and there was no undoing any of it now. Tattoo Kid pedaled by the front windows a second time, his eyes meeting hers briefly and then looking quickly away again as Chevrier went on:

"I'll get a requisition going for your computer stuff, have a carpet crew come up from Bangor . . ."

She turned to him. "No."

His brow furrowed. "So . . . what, you mean you've decided that you don't want the spot?"

For a moment she was tempted; she'd have loved telling him to take his job and stick it. After all, who offered somebody one position, then waited until they showed up before informing them that it had turned into something entirely different? But . . .

"Oh, I'm taking it." She crossed to the desk, grabbed the phone book, and threw it into a corner. Who used a phone book anymore, either? "But only on two conditions. First . . ."

She aimed a finger at the front window. "You

22

want me to build friendly relationships with the people here in Bearkill? I mean, that's what a liaison officer does, right?"

She had the funniest feeling that Chevrier might not know quite what one of those did himself. But never mind:

"There's only one way I can quick-start relationships with these folks—"

At the far end of the downtown block, the office supply store was somehow still alive, while at the other end a run-down gas station survived, as did the tiny convenience store attached.

"—and that's for me to buy stuff from them."

Which was also true in Boston, and anywhere else there were cops: coffee and a lottery ticket at the bodega, an apple at the fruit stand, sandwiches at the luncheonette—you bought a little of this or that anywhere you thought you might get the chance to talk to people, hear things.

"Supplies, cleaning, painting, new tires for the squad car whether it needs 'em or not," she went on. "All of it has to get done locally. And as for computer equipment?"

She turned to face him. "Look, Sheriff, I've got my own reasons for wanting the job you're trying to foist on me, okay? So I'm not walking away even though you know damned well you absolutely deserve it."

He shrugged again, acknowledging this. "But," she went on, "as far as computers and printer paper and everything else this place needs?"

She waved a hand around the bleak little store-front. "Either that office supply joint down the street is about to hit a big payday, *and* my car gets serviced here in town, or you can forget you met me."

She expected pushback about the car, at least; regulations, routine. But instead he kept nodding at her demands, which among other things gave her an even stronger sense of how very much he wanted her here.

Curiouser and curiouser. "Okay," he said. "That makes sense. Do it however you want. You'll need purchase orders, but . . ."

"Not so fast. You haven't heard the other condition."

Chevrier looked wary—"What's that?"—as the tattooed kid on the bike rolled by yet a third time.

Briskly she zipped her jacket, settled her black leather satchel on her shoulder, and pulled the creaky front door open, waving him out ahead of her.

"Come on," she told him.

The kid with the piercings, body art, and blond dreadlocks was now halfway down the street, looking back at them. She yanked the balky door shut, then jiggled the key in the lock until the tumblers fell sluggishly.

"I'm hungry. We'll talk over lunch. You're buying."

• • •

There he is! Sighing in relief, Margaret Brantwell hurried down the canned goods aisle of the Food King in Bearkill. She'd looked away for only a moment, she was certain, and when she looked back her year-old grandson's stroller wasn't where she'd left it, parked by the frozen foods case.

Oh, if Missy knew that I'd lost track of him even for an instant, she'd—

Well, she wouldn't let Margaret take care of him anymore if that happened. But Margaret adored her daughter's baby boy, she'd be desolate if she couldn't—

"Mrs. Brantwell?" The store manager stood by the stroller. A clerk was there, too, looking worried. Both frowned accusingly at Margaret.

"Mrs. Brantwell, we were just about to call the police. The baby's been here all alone for ten minutes, we didn't know—"

"Ten minutes?" Margaret glanced around. Everyone was looking at her. And the baby was crying; she crouched hurriedly by him.

"Oh, no, I've been right here, I was—"

But then she stopped as it hit her with a horrible internal lurch that she didn't remember where she'd been, didn't recall the moment when she'd walked away from the baby in his stroller.

That she didn't know how long she'd been gone. Defensively she grabbed up the baby, cradling him against her chest.

25

"I was just down the aisle, I can't imagine how you missed seeing me. You must not have been trying very hard."

There, turn it around on them, see how *they* liked it. Poor little Jeffrey wailed fiercely, his face squinched and reddened.

"There, there," she soothed him. "Did all these strangers scare you, baby? There, it's okay, Grandma's got you now."

A red-aproned clerk hurried up pushing a grocery cart. "Oh, Mrs. Brantwell, there you are, you left your—"

Margaret drew back. "*That's* not mine!" She hugged Jeffrey closer. His cries grew louder. She felt like crying now, too, surrounded by these unpleasant strangers all trying to tell her things that weren't true.

The items in the cart—milk, lettuce, coffee beans—*might* be hers. But where did that huge chocolate bar come from, and the cheap wine? And the jug of motor oil wasn't even from this store.

They were trying to trick her, that's what it was. But it wouldn't work, because she was too smart for them. *Can't pull one over on Margaret,* her father used to say, and it was still . . .

Grabbing the stroller's handles, she whirled and stalked away from them, all the foolish people with the unfriendly looks on their faces. Outside the store, she carried Jeffrey to the car and put him in his car seat, buckling him in carefully the way she had promised Missy she would always do.

Then she settled behind the wheel and sat there for a moment to gather her thoughts, get over the awful fright she'd had.

There, that's better, she thought as her heart slowed. Even Jeffrey calmed down, sucking energetically on his pacifier, his sweet little face relaxing, so cute in his blue knitted hat.

She'd made him that hat. If she could find where she'd put the yarn, she might make mittens. Meanwhile . . .

She looked around at the busy parking lot outside the Food King, people bustling back and forth with their carts in the cold November sunshine. It was a lovely day.

Just lovely, and the drive down here to the store had been so easy and uneventful, she didn't even remember it.

She turned to the baby. "Jeffrey, we're here! We're at the store, and now we're going to go in. Are you ready?"

He grinned, waving his pacifier in his chubby fist. She got out and found his stroller waiting by the passenger-side door as if someone had put it there for her. She looked around mystified, then decided that it was too nice a day to worry about it.

Blue sky, crisp air . . . now, what exactly had

she come to the store for, again? She'd made a list but she must have left it at home. She was always doing that. *Silly. Getting so forgetful.*

"Never mind," she told Jeffrey as she pushed him across the parking lot in the stroller. Such a beautiful baby, she simply adored him, and felt so grateful that Missy allowed her to take care of him the way she did. *My grandson . . .*

At the entrance she slowed uncertainly; the store looked so unfamiliar all of a sudden. But how could it? She'd been here—*surely she had*—a thousand times before. Only—

"Never mind," she repeated, as much for herself this time as for the baby. "We'll figure it all out when we get inside."

It was the biggest slab of meatloaf Lizzie had ever seen, flanked by a mound of gravy-drenched mashed potatoes the size of a softball and a fluted paper cup of celery-seed-flecked coleslaw, the shredded orange carrot and purple cabbage drenched in enough dressing to float a barge.

"What's so funny?" she demanded at Chevrier's smile when the waitress delivered their food. He'd ordered a chef's salad, which was also enormous but not quite as artery-clogging as her own meal.

"You ever heard the old saying 'Never eat anything bigger than your head'?" he replied with a chuckle.

Lizzie dug in. She hadn't eaten since the night before, and the meatloaf was as delicious as it. looked. "You ever heard the old saying 'Don't criticize what other people are eating'?"

He nodded, chewing. "Good one."

The Coca-Cola was so cold that it made her head hurt, and the gravy on the potatoes hadn't come out of a jar or a can. They ate in silence for a few minutes.

"So," he said around a mouthful of dinner roll.

Driving out of Bearkill, he'd sped them down a rural highway between fenced fields green with what he said was winter wheat. Huge out-buildings dug into the sides of hills were, he informed her, for potato storage; yards full of machinery, from familiar-looking tractors to massive contraptions resembling some science-fiction variety of praying mantis, flanked pretty, old-fashioned farmhouses whose long, low ells linked them to massive, gambrel-roofed barns.

"That way, Farmer John doesn't have to go outside so much in winter when he needs to do chores," Chevrier had explained about the house-barn connections.

"In the blizzards we get here, you could get lost ten feet off the porch," he'd added, while she'd stared out the car window at a little girl in denim overalls riding a bike in a farmyard driveway, pigtails flying.

It wasn't Nicki, of course. For one thing, the

29

pigtails were red. And the child looked a bit too old, maybe ten or eleven. *But what if it was her?* she'd thought. *Would you take her away from . . .*

But it wasn't, she told herself again now. "Which reminds me," said Chevrier, "you got any survival gear? Winter stuff or wilderness stuff? Or to have in your vehicle?"

In Boston she'd thought of the wilderness as anything past Route 128; at her headshake he went on:

"Okay, got some items kicking around at home, I'll bring 'em in for you. Flares, emergency blanket . . ."

He shrugged. "Can't be too careful." Then: "Anyway, I guess you think I've got some explaining to do."

That, of course, had been the other condition: that he level with her.

"Yeah," she agreed, eating another forkful of coleslaw. The cabbage was peppery-fresh, the sweet dressing full of celery seed so delicious she was tempted to sip the remaining puddles with a spoon. "You could put it that way."

Coming into the restaurant, he'd been greeted by everyone they passed, and when he stopped at booths and tables to chat, he knew their names and their kids' and grandkids' names. In Maine, she recalled, county sheriffs were elected officials.

"The thing is," he went on, washing the last bit of roll down with a sip of coffee. "The thing is, I've got ex-cops dying on me. When they shouldn't be. And I've got questions about it."

He'd chosen a booth farthest from the rest of the room, a noisy spot near the cash register. She stopped chewing.

"Really." In her experience, when somebody started talking like this, you just tried not to get in the way.

You just let them know you were listening. Chevrier took a slow, casual look around the room to make sure no one else was, then went on.

"Yeah. Last year or so, four of 'em. All on the up-and-up, says the medical examiner."

"But you don't think so." Obviously, or he wouldn't be talking to her about it. "So they were all unwitnessed deaths?"

Because otherwise the medical examiner probably wouldn't have been called at all. Chevrier nodded, speared half a hard-boiled egg, and ate it.

"First one, Dillard Sprague, last December," he recited. "He was a boozer, lost his job with the Buckthorn PD over it a few months before."

He washed the egg down with some coffee. "Supposedly he slipped on an icy step coming out of his back door, late. Got knocked out, lay there, and froze to death. His wife, Althea, found him when she got home the next morning from her night shift at the hospital."

Lizzie winced. "Not a fun discovery, huh? But

if that's all there was, couldn't it have been accidental, just the way it seemed?"

Chevrier looked sour. "Right. Could've. If he was the only one. Next guy, Cliff Arbogast, a few months later. He lives right up next to the Canadian border, got let go off the Caribou force when it turned out he'd been running the family car with his department gas card."

He ate more salad. "Which," he went on around it, "wouldn't have been so bad, but his wife was an Avon lady, drove all over taking orders and making deliveries."

Lizzie loaded mashed potatoes and gravy onto her fork. From outside, Grammy's Restaurant had looked like any other roadside joint: red and white sign, aluminum siding, twenty feet of gravel parking lot separating it from the highway it sat beside.

Inside, though, it was clean as a whistle and smelled like a place where somebody really knew how to cook.

Which somebody did. She ate some more meatloaf. Then: "What happened?" she asked. "To the Avon lady's ex-cop husband?"

Chevrier dragged a chunk of iceberg lettuce through a dollop of Russian dressing and chomped it. "Electrocuted."

"Excuse me?" She'd heard him, all right. But modern building codes and wiring regulations made such accidents rare. The only fatal power mishap she'd ever seen, in fact, wasn't a household event at all.

It was after a big storm, back when she was a rookie patrol cop on the Boston PD: downed trees, live wires, standing water. Add a bunch of pain-in-the-butt looky-loos out gawking at the damage and, presto, one dead civilian.

But cops knew better. Some she'd worked with wouldn't go near a live-wire situation until the power company was on scene.

Chevrier seemed skeptical, too. "Yeah. Spring evening, Cliff's taking a bath, listening to the Red Sox on the radio," he said.

"Radio's on the sink, it's plugged into the outlet by the mirror, you know? So he reached for his razor and shaving cream and somehow he knocked the radio into the tub with him."

He grimaced. "Or that's how the story goes, anyway."

"Huh." She ate the last bite of her mashed potatoes, drank some Coke, meanwhile trying to picture all this. Just pulling a radio into the tub with you was a pretty good trick, and . . .

"Breaker didn't trip?"

Because even though it was not a good idea, in a properly wired house you ought to be able to float a radio in the bathtub like a rubber duckie, the power cutting off microseconds after the overload hit the circuit breaker.

You wouldn't like it much, but you wouldn't

necessarily die, either. Chevrier looked across the room to where a big man in a denim barn coat and rubber boots was just getting up from his table.

"Place didn't have circuit breakers," Chevrier said while watching the man approach.

"Old house, still had fuses. One of 'em had burned out some time earlier—he'd stuck a bent nail in there."

He sighed, remembering. "So the wires melted, started a fire, and that's how it got called in, originally. Dwelling fire."

"I see. So that makes two of them so far? Sprague, Clifford Arbogast . . ."

"Yeah, and two more. Michael Fontine, ex–state cop, he lived way over by the border crossing in Van Buren. And . . ."

But just then the big man in the barn coat arrived at their booth. "Hey, Cody."

The new arrival had ruddy cheeks, thinning blond hair, and a linebacker's meaty build. Twenty or thirty pounds more than he needed packed his tall, powerful frame, but on him it didn't look too bad, maybe because it was distributed evenly instead of all hanging around his waist.

Or maybe it was because he had the brightest, bluest, and possibly the smartest-looking eyes she'd ever seen, pleasantly crinkled at the corners.

"And whom do we have here?" The little ironic stress he put on *whom* was just audible enough to be charming.

She stuck out her hand. "Lizzie Snow." With a nod across the table, she added, "I'm Sheriff Chevrier's newest deputy."

His grip was warm and firm, and he didn't milk the moment by holding on for too long. "Trey Washburn. Hey, good to meet you, Lizzie."

"It's *Dr.* Washburn," Chevrier put in. "Trey here is our local veterinarian. Puppies and kittens, that sort of thing," he added jocularly.

Washburn's smile was infectious and his teeth were white and well-cared-for-looking. "Right," he said. "Also horses, pigs, cows . . ."

His hands were very clean, and a faint whiff of Old Spice came off him. "No elephants so far, but if the circus comes to Houlton this year like they're threatening to do, that'll be next."

He looked back at Chevrier. "Haven't seen you in a while. Sorry to hear about Bogart. You find a home for his hound yet?"

With a quick glance at Lizzie, Chevrier replied, "No. Might just keep him myself if I can talk the wife into it. Dog's a pain in the rear, but he's all I've got left of old Carl, you know?"

A moment of silence that Lizzie didn't understand passed between the two men. Then:

"Lizzie," said Washburn pleasantly, "I'm going out to take a look at a newborn calf later today. If the sheriff here doesn't already have you too busy setting up a speed trap or something, you're welcome to ride along."

At the invitation, her inner eyebrows went up. Could he be hitting on her? The twinkle in his blue eyes said yes, but he was a friendly guy. So maybe he always twinkled.

Before she could reply, the restaurant's front door opened and another man came in: tall, dark-haired, sharp-featured. His deep-set eyes scanned the dining room swiftly before finding her.

Then his harsh face softened. Every woman in the place, old or young, watched him cross the room; he was just that way, loose-limbed and easy in his well-cut jacket and dark slacks.

Comfortable in his skin. Quickly, she banished the memories this thought evoked: *Oh, his skin* . . .

Hoping Chevrier and Washburn hadn't noticed her reaction, she drank some of the watery Coke at the bottom of her glass to wet her mouth. But the new arrival had noticed, of course.

He always did. As he approached the booth, his lips moved subtly in a small, utterly outrageous imitation of a kiss.

Damn, damn, *damn,* she thought.

It was Dylan Hudson.

Her new place was a rented house on a dead-end street on the easternmost edge of Bearkill, a tiny ranch-style structure with a mildewed porch awning, a small plate-glass picture window, and a concrete birdbath lying on its side in the unkempt front yard.

Half an hour after showing up in the diner, Dylan eyed her appreciatively as she strode up the front walk and let herself in with her new key.

"Looking good, Lizzie," he said.

The landlord, with whom she'd only spoken once on the phone, had left the key for her in the mailbox mounted on a post at the end of the front walk; yet another astonishing difference from the way things were done back in Boston, she thought.

"Oh, shut up," she snapped crossly at Dylan, pushing the front door open. The air inside smelled stale but otherwise okay.

"What the hell are you doing here, anyway?"

She looked around, meanwhile thinking that in a moment she'd be alone in here with him, and that she'd rented the place fully furnished. And that last time she'd checked, the word *furnished* implied a bed . . .

Behind her, Dylan waltzed in without being invited. But then she didn't have to invite him, did she? He knew perfectly well that he'd been invited wherever she was, pretty much from the first moment she'd laid eyes on him.

"Answer my question, please," she told him as he bent to plump one of the cushions on the upholstered sofa: brown plaid tweed with big shiny wooden armrest knobs, truly ghastly looking.

Cheap pottery lamps, wood-laminate end tables . . . the place had been decorated out of Walmart,

37

it looked like. But it was better than nothing, and anyway, furniture shopping wasn't on her agenda.

Finding Nicki was. Dylan stood innocently a few feet away. "I mean what, did you think I need babysitting or something?" she went on.

He turned, the look in his dark eyes mischievous. The faint scent of his cologne, some very subtle champagne-y thing that was emphatically not Old Spice, floated in the still air; he'd been wearing it when they first . . .

No. No, don't go there, she instructed herself firmly.

Dylan grinned wickedly. "Babysitting, huh? That could be fun." But then his expression changed. "Come on, Lizzie. I just wanted to help you get settled in, you know me."

After she'd said goodbye to the veterinarian Trey Washburn and turned down his invitation, she and Chevrier had driven back to Bearkill, with Dylan following in his own car.

Chevrier and Hudson knew each other pretty well, somewhat to her surprise; Maine State Police detectives like Dylan worked often with the rural sheriffs here, it seemed, unlike back in the big city, where in her experience the relationship was more often competitive, to put it mildly.

"Yeah, I know you," she answered Dylan now, a pain she'd thought healed suddenly sharp in her chest. "You're the guy who swore to me that your wife was already getting a divorce."

She crossed the small knotty-pine-paneled living room and drew the flimsy-feeling dark red curtains back from the picture window. Weak autumn light filtered in, the sun at a long, low angle already even this early in the afternoon.

Dylan came up behind her, gazing out at a tiny lawn thickly carpeted with fallen leaves. The other houses on the street were just like this one, small ranches set well back in postage-stamp yards.

"Hey," he said softly. "Come on, I thought we'd settled all that."

Silence from Lizzie. She'd thought so, too.

Sort of. He went on. "Anyway, it's not so bad here. Maine's a fine place. You'll enjoy it when you get used to it."

"Sure," she replied scathingly. Right now back in Boston, the afternoon light would be on the river, turning the rowers whose shells skated like water bugs over the golden surface to slender silhouettes, their joints articulating in unison.

But no, don't think of that, either.

Stepping away from him, she went into the kitchen, which like the rest of what she'd seen of the house was outdated but clean and perfectly acceptable.

All it needs is one of those cat clocks with moving eyes and a swinging tail-pendulum, she thought before spotting one on the wall over the ancient electric stove; it had been hidden by

39

the corner of the round-shouldered old Frigidaire.

She pushed back the sheer panel at the window over the sink, wondering again what the hell she thought she was doing here; the plain, small house full of mass-produced furnishings felt like a trap suddenly. But then she drew in an amazed breath.

Dylan stepped up beside her. "See, what did I tell you? Not too shabby, huh?"

The field behind the house had been an orchard at one time, the squat, thick-trunked trees now ancient and their rough bark charcoal-gray. Set out in even rows, they bore masses of red-gold apples on their topmost banches but were nearly bare lower down.

"Oh," she breathed. Despite the late season, green grass still spread under the old trees, and here and there a thicket of deep-purple asters mixed in among stands of goldenrod.

The sun's slanting rays burnished each apple to glowing red.

"Deer eat all the lower ones," Dylan said. "They can stand up on their hind legs, did you know that?"

"No," she managed, aware of his hand on her shoulder. *And of the rest of him.* "Dylan, I really think you'd better—"

Over a year ago, they'd said goodbye; the minute she'd found out he was married, he was history. That she'd gotten the news from his wife when she'd burst in on them together had made the discovery more shocking, but it couldn't have been more painful.

Only a month later he'd learned of his wife's illness. Then came the desperate attempts to save her life, unsuccessful, followed soon after her death by his departure to Maine and a job with the state cops. She'd convinced herself she was glad—not about his wife's death, but about his absence—and had continued her own life, though there had been no one else. He and Lizzie had seen each other again for the first time only a few weeks ago; it was a meeting he'd engineered, luring her to Maine by saying that he'd found possible new clues to her missing niece Nicki's whereabouts.

That he, too, had gotten a photograph from some anonymous tipster. And although some of Dylan's story had turned out to be a lie, just part of his plan to somehow see her again, the photos themselves were not.

And now he was here. With her. She felt him watching her. It seemed she could feel his heart beat. "Dylan. I really think—"

"Look." She followed his gaze, saw the deer stepping from the thicket at the field's end. No antlers; it was a doe, plump and well muscled after a summer of good grazing. Approaching an apple tree, the animal reared up . . .

"Oh," Lizzie breathed again as the deer plucked

a red fruit with her front teeth and munched it, then picked one more before slowly lowering herself back down onto delicate front hooves.

"And see, closer in here you've got a fence. You could even have a dog," said Dylan.

He knew very well that she had no wish for a dog, never had. She might not even be here long enough to consider the idea; who knew what might happen? But his half-joking suggestion implied that he would like her to be.

And that he still knew how to push her buttons. *Oh, does he ever.*

The doe's eyes were huge, like pools of dark liquid, its nose deep velvet black. Only when Lizzie turned did she realize that Dylan was no longer beside her.

"This won't do," he said, frowning, opening cabinet doors one after another, exposing the emptiness within.

The refrigerator hadn't even been turned on yet. An opened box of baking soda stood on the narrow top shelf. Without further comment he strode past her to the living room, returned with his jacket on already.

"Come on," he said. "We'll go to the store."

He smiled invitingly, no guile in his expression, which was of course when he was the most dangerous. But in the short time he'd been getting his jacket, she'd felt how empty this house was and how garishly that fluorescent overhead light would shine down on her tonight as she sat alone at the kitchen table.

"You can tell me about the new job," he coaxed.

"Okay." She gave in, reminding herself not to talk to him about the suspicion Cody Chevrier had begun confiding, the real reason—or so she now assumed—that he wanted an experienced ex–homicide cop for his department's small-town liaison officer.

His suspicion, she mentally summed up the sheriff's fear, *that there's a cop killer way up here in the Great North Woods.*

Outside, Dylan swept open the passenger door of his beloved old red Saab sedan, recently refurbished. The Food King was just a few blocks distant; afterwards she'd have him drop her at her new office where her own car was, she decided.

Because letting him come back to the house again would be a prescription for . . .

For what you need, her mind finished; she shut the thought off brusquely as he pulled into the grocery store lot and slotted the Saab into a parking space. Then he turned to her.

"Listen," he said seriously, "I'm going to get a guy up here to sweep the house for you, all right? And that office of yours, too."

She was about to protest that they were already cleaner than they would ever be while she was using them when she understood.

"You mean for . . . devices? Recorders, phone bugs? But—"

That's ridiculous, she was about to finish, and then she got it. "He told you, didn't he? Chevrier told you about why he wants me here. In Bearkill, I mean."

Just saying the town's name made her feel like laughing. Or crying. *Night school, cop academy, street patrol, scrambling up the career ladder to detective. This is what it's gotten you.*

Your sister's dead, her kid is missing, you've quit the job you wanted more than anything, the big-city murder-cop job that you gave up everything for . . .

To get this. A grim little town miles from anywhere, junky office you'll be stuck in, and at night a crummy rental house on a dead-end street, a house with knotty-pine paneling.

There probably wasn't a killer here at all, just Chevrier jumping at shadows. Maybe Nicki wasn't here, either; maybe it was all a mistake. *I hate knotty-pine paneling.*

"About his series of dead ex-cops? Yeah, he told me," Dylan admitted. "I recommended you to him, in fact. That's how he found you down in Eastport."

He went on a little defensively. "Hey, he needs you, you need to be here . . ." He half-turned to her, spreading his hands placatingly.

"Yeah, yeah," she said tiredly, because he was

44

right. To do the kind of investigating that her hunt for Nicki required, she had to be a cop, and she had to be on scene.

In short, she had to be here whether she liked the place or not. And it had to be now, too; if she waited any longer to look for Nicki, she might as well admit to herself that she was never going to. And if *that* happened . . .

Thinking of it, she saw her future stretching before her: no family, no Dylan. And no one else, either, probably. Just herself all alone and getting older, with nothing but work to keep her warm.

Which it wouldn't. Outside in the blue shadows that were already gathering at three in the afternoon, an elderly man rode a motorized chair down Main Street, talking to himself. A squad car with the Town of Bearkill logo on it rolled slowly in the other direction, the cop slumped behind the wheel looking bored.

Dear God. She unsnapped her seatbelt, holding a hand up to stop Dylan when he began to do likewise. She did not want him trailing her around the grocery store like some hapless husband.

Or any other kind. "Okay, let them sweep," she gave in. "But I'm warning you, this whole thing better not have been just a scheme to get me up here nearer where you are," she told him, and got out, slamming the car door.

It would be just like him to lure her into his

orbit this way, she realized as she stalked across the parking lot. Cook up a story on the thinnest of evidence, get her hopes up, all to get back into her good graces—*and that's not all he wants to get back into*—now that he was single again.

He might even have faked the photographs somebody supposedly had sent, lied about hearing vague stories in Aroostook County about a little girl whose origins no one knew. The sudden thought that maybe it was all just a ruse struck fear into her . . . but no, even Dylan wasn't that underhanded—was he?

Thinking that if he was, she was definitely going to kill him, she continued to where the shopping carts stood. She had started into the store with one of them when a figure stepped suddenly from the recessed area between two soda machines.

"Hey," she said, and swung around, nerves in red-alert mode and her arms already coming up into a defensive position.

"Stay where you are," she snapped. But then she realized it was the kid she'd seen on a bike outside her office earlier:

Tattoo Kid, with a dark blue dragon twining up his neck and a stud in the side of his nostril, a ring in his earlobe. The designs on his arms were so thickly inked into his skin that it was hard to see where one ended and the next one began.

He shrugged apologetically. "Sorry. But I don't

want anyone to see me talking to you. I mean, you're a cop, right?"

"Yeah." She looked out past the store-special posters taped to the big windows. Dylan was still in the car, his back turned so he couldn't see her.

"So, d'you pay for tips?"

The kid was tall, awkward and big-boned, with unfortunate bulbous features, an oddly shaped head, and patches of purplish acne not well hidden by the skimpy blond beard he was trying to grow. The sour smell of woodsmoke drifted off him along with the reek of clothes gone unwashed for too long.

She found her voice. "Maybe I do. Maybe not. Why, do you have information about a crime?"

But this was the absolute wrong answer, as she'd known even as it came out of her mouth. The idea was to get civilians to think that you could solve a problem for them, not the other way around.

And sometimes even to actually solve it. "No. Forget it," he told her hastily. "Never mind, it was a stupid question."

He shoved past her and was gone, leaving her to wonder two things: one, would she ever get control of her own quick-flaring temper?

Because she hadn't liked being startled, and even less being hit up for cash as payment for information that decent citizens ought to be providing to the cops *gratis*. But she might've just screwed herself by backing the kid off that way.

Impatiently she grabbed her cart and went into the store, blinking in the sudden bright lights. In the vegetable section a woman in drab sweats and a scrawny ponytail looked up from the on-sale bags of mixed greens she'd been examining to eye Lizzie incredulously.

Which brought Lizzie to her second question, because here she was, slim-trousered and high-booted, wearing a leather jacket that was obviously expensive. With her spiky short hair, red lips, and elaborate eye makeup, to the people in Bearkill she probably looked more like an alien from that bar on the corner, Area 51, than anything they imagined might be a police officer. *So . . .*

Milk, bread, coffee, juice, she thought with part of her mind, as the store speakers blared out an elevator-music version of the Eagles' "Hotel California." But the rest of her brain went on puzzling over that second question:

So how'd Tattoo Kid figure out so fast that I'm a cop?

She went on wondering about it as she picked out cereal, a dozen eggs, and a jar of peanut butter, rejecting the low-fat version for the one human beings could actually eat. She thought about it as she proceeded through the checkout line, then on and off again for most of the remaining afternoon and early evening.

But its interest paled suddenly a few hours later when she found herself standing in the bar with a beer in front of her, wishing hard that she'd stayed home, and staring seriously at the wrong end of what she could only hope was an unloaded gun.

And moments later finding out that it wasn't.

TWO

He was big, he was angry, and he was very, very drunk. Also, he had his ham-sized left forearm wrapped tightly around a young woman's neck, clutching her curly blond head to his chest like she was his favorite teddy bear and he was a toddler having a major tantrum.

A toddler with a weapon. "Whoa, Nellie," said the bartender in Area 51.

"Can't . . . breathe . . . ," sputtered the woman.

"Sir," said Lizzie. "Let the lady go, please, sir, and put the gun down so we can talk about this."

She'd gotten rid of Dylan finally by telling him she was exhausted, and after a solitary meal of deviled ham and canned baked beans on toast, by seven-thirty she was alone.

Home at last, she'd told herself sarcastically, sinking onto the ugly plaid sofa. But half an hour later, she was climbing the walls; no TV, no Internet yet, and although she had a phone, there was no one she wanted to call. So a visit to the local watering hole had seemed like a good idea.

But now maybe not so much. Narrowing his small, bloodshot eyes, the drunk guy found her face. Then his booted foot shot out surprisingly fast, just missing her knee.

"Get th' hell away," he slurred. "I'm gonna . . ."

Unable to speak, the woman in his grip gazed imploringly at the bartender, who grabbed the phone with one hand while using a remote to mute the TV's broadcast of a *Hollywood Squares* rerun with the other.

The drunk man spotted him. "You call the cops and I'm gonna shoot," he threatened. "Now gimme another drink."

"Aw, jeez," the bartender complained. "Dammit, Henry, why d'you always have to—"

The trapped woman was turning blue. Lizzie got right up in the guy's face, hoping her guess about him was right.

"Henry, listen to me, he doesn't have to call the cops. I am one, okay?"

A cop with a gun, too; Chevrier had not yet issued her a duty weapon, but she had her personal piece, the Glock semiauto she always carried, tucked into her leather satchel.

There were already too many guns in this situation, though; adding a second one might just make it worse.

"Go ahead, pour him another drink," she told the bartender, not taking her eyes from the intoxicated man's face.

"A double. On me," she added when the bartender hesitated.

Because the guy had the woman locked in one arm, his weapon clutched in his other hand, and he'd have to use one of them to pick up his fresh beverage, wouldn't he?

But when the bartender put the glass down hurriedly, the man ignored it, a wild look of injured righteousness coming into his eyes. "Ain't gonna diss me no more, are ya?"

He gazed around belligerently, as a strange *gak-gak* sound clacked from the throat of the blond woman. Her hand fell from her captor's thick forearm.

"Henry," said Lizzie. "You're hurting her. Let her go."

But Henry's mind—or "mind," Lizzie thought impatiently, since if ever a word deserved air quotes it was that one, used in connection with Henry—was now occupied by the tricky puzzle of grabbing his drink without giving up either the gun or the girl.

Meanwhile the bartender babbled on the phone to someone who was seemingly not too interested in Area 51's patron-pacification problem. "How the hell do I know if it's loaded?" he was yelling.

Yeah, Lizzie thought, staring at it. And why, precisely, had she thought coming out tonight was a good idea?

"No, it ain't a domestic dispute," the bartender yelled into the phone. "It's Henry, he ain't had a girlfriend since Noah built the Ark, for Pete's sake. He just grabbed Missy 'cause she was handy, that's all. Now, are you going to—"

Behind the bar, a police-band scanner sputtered. In case *Hollywood Squares* got boring, Lizzie supposed. Beside it a huge jar of pickled eggs stood next to a Paul Bunyan bobblehead doll.

Oh, yeah, this is my kind of place, she thought, recalling her usual haunt back in Boston, a place with a weekend jazz trio, dark leather booths that were dimly candle-lit, and a chalkboard bar menu listing a dozen brands of single-malt Scotch.

Leaning over, the drunk man broke into her nostalgia trip by attempting to slurp fresh booze from the glass using only his lips. The maneuver loosened his grip on the blond woman's throat enough for her to drag in a gagging breath.

But only one. "Dammit, Henry," said Lizzie.

She didn't want to hurt him. Not permanently, anyway.

Still, he wasn't cooperating, so when he leaned over for his next sip, she stepped past him and pivoted on her left foot while kicking him very hard in the back of his knee with her right.

"Blearrgh!" he exploded, his arms flying up reflexively as the anguish of a mashed peroneal nerve suddenly took precedence over any and all other concerns.

The woman took two short, staggering steps and collapsed to her knees, dragging in great whooping breaths. The drunk's gun, a mean-looking little Raven .25, clattered to the sticky floor.

Lizzie grabbed the weapon, popped the magazine. Empty. She pulled the slide back as the bartender watched, wide-eyed.

There was a round in the chamber. *Jesus.*

"Aw, Henry," moaned the bartender, "why'd you want to go around with it loaded, for Pete's sake? Now you're in trouble."

By now the blond woman had recovered somewhat and made her way to the back of the room through a door marked LADIES.

"Call the cops back," Lizzie told the bartender sharply. "Say there's an officer in here with a suspect in custody, who would appreciate the freaking honor of their presence like right the freak now."

Her heart was still hammering. *Jesus, it was loaded.*

"They're already on the way. But he's not a bad guy," the bartender told her. "Just once in a while he gets a little—"

"What, murderous?" *Oh, Christ on a freaking cracker.*

But . . . she came to a quick decision. *This is going to come back and bite me in the ass, maybe.*

But the guy behind the bar knew Henry better than she did, and when she came out of the ladies' room even the recently assaulted blond woman looked pityingly at the man lying on the floor clutching his knee.

"Gimme . . . 'nother drink," muttered Henry, his eyes filling with tears, just as the local cops burst in with guns drawn.

Quickly Lizzie slipped the ejected round from the .25 into her pants pocket. Noticing this, the bartender nodded minutely, tight-lipped.

"Henry, you're an idiot," said the blond woman, then turned to the local officers in their dark gray uniforms, regulation black shoes, and tinny-looking badges.

"Forget it, Ralphie," she said to the younger of the pair, a red-haired, strutting rooster of a man whose lip thrust out in a thwarted pout as she spoke, and whose gaze went to her chest and lingered there a moment before it reached her face.

"Aw, Missy, you can't keep letting him get away with—" The other cop scowled disgustedly at the bartender. "You're not going to press charges, either, I suppose," he said. "Get us both here, now you're going to say it was a false alarm."

The big man on the floor had clipped his nose on the edge of the bar on his way down. The blond woman grabbed a bar towel, dumped some ice into it, and thrust it at Henry.

"I'm sorry, Missy." He yelped when the cold towel touched his face but kept it there. Then from behind it came a muffled question so dumb, it made Lizzie wish she'd kicked him harder:

"Can I have my gun back?"

The cops turned sharply to him again, the redheaded one's hand going to the baton on his belt. The Raven .25 was already in Lizzie's own belt, hidden by her leather jacket.

"He never had any gun," she said firmly.

The bartender looked away, but he didn't contradict her, and the sight of all the blood in the icy towel had startled Henry so much that for the moment he couldn't speak, either.

Fortunately. "He's just drunk," said Lizzie. She didn't know why she said it, only that this was her scene to handle.

That something was going on here and she was too new to know quite what, but in some strange way everyone in here was testing her, watching to find out how she dealt with a situation that she didn't yet understand.

A different kind of fitness test, and if she flubbed it, any hope she'd had of doing anything useful in Bearkill—for herself or anyone else— would be over before it began.

"Drunk and rowdy, that's all," she continued. "Unless you disagree?" she asked Missy. The blond woman had been the one with an arm wrapped around her throat, after all.

But Missy just nodded. "No harm done." She took a gulp of her beer, gone flat in its glass. "Go on, you guys, it's fine."

At this, the older cop made a face of disgust

and left, but the younger, carrot-topped one approached the man on the floor.

"Hey, Henry. C'mon, get up. Let's get you home, huh?"

A wet snore was the only reply. The young cop bent to shout "Henry!" in the sleeping man's ear; still no response.

So maybe the rooster act was just that, Lizzie thought as she watched the cop shake Henry's shoulder, not unkindly; maybe it was an act he put on with the uniform, and this cop was okay.

Time would tell. Sighing, the cop straightened. "Can't budge him."

"Forget it," said the bartender. "He'll wake up by the time I'm ready to close. I'll run him up to his place then."

Another surprise; back in Boston, if you passed out in a bar, you could wake up in an alley missing your wallet—or in a hotel bathtub, packed in ice and minus a kidney.

Though that latter possibility was likely just urban legend; the only "organ theft" she'd ever seen herself had turned out to be a revenge murder, not quite cleverly enough disguised.

"Okay, I'm going now," said Missy, grabbing a purse and jacket from the back of a barstool.

The clock behind the bar was shaped like a flying saucer; glancing at it, she added, "Cripes, Ma's up watching the baby. She'll be—"

The bartender made a snorting noise. "Hey,

you're just lucky your dad's not home," he said, and the girl rolled her eyes in agreement.

"Wait," said Lizzie, swallowing the last of her own beer. "I'll walk out with you."

Because maybe this was just a quiet little town out in the middle of nowhere, with—by several orders of magnitude—more wild animals than criminals. Maybe Aroostook County sheriff Cody Chevrier was spooked for no good reason over the deaths of four ex-cops.

And maybe Lizzie's search for her long-missing niece, Nicki, her dead sister's child and her own only living relative, would hit a dead end here.

But maybe not. And if not, she'd need contacts of her own. The barkeep shot her a nod and a thumbs-up; he wouldn't let her pay for the beer, either.

So she'd passed his test, apparently, and possibly now she could strike up an acquaintance with Missy, too.

Gotta start somewhere, Lizzie thought as she followed the blond woman out the door.

"Don't say it, okay?" Missy dropped the new yellow Jeep Wrangler into gear and shot away from the curb.

Lizzie had left her own car at home, opting instead for the walk, which was only about ten minutes, and now she was glad.

"Say what?" she asked. "You mean, 'What's a nice girl like you—'"

Missy joined in sarcastically. " '—doing in a place like that?' "

She went on: " 'And so pretty, too! You don't belong here, you should move to the big city!' "

But her scathing tone told Lizzie that being pretty hadn't exactly been a bed of roses for Missy Brantwell.

"Yeah, well. I did wonder," Lizzie admitted. "You're—"

In general it made no difference if people were good-looking or not, she'd found; looks were the frosting on a cake that could be moldy or stale.

Or even poisoned. But Missy wasn't just pretty. In the truck's dashboard glow, she was flat-out gorgeous, from her pale curly head to the toes of the perfectly white sneakers she wore.

"You didn't exactly get beat with the ugly stick, either, and you're here," Missy pointed out.

Yeah, but I'm not stuck here. And I'm not getting throttled by a drunk in a saloon, Lizzie thought, ignoring the compliment.

But it was too soon to say this kind of thing to Missy, who made the turn onto Lizzie's street without asking if it was the right place. She pulled up in front of the right house, too.

"Anyway, not that it's your business," she said, "but I was there picking up my paycheck. It's my cousin's place—I tend bar when it's busy on the weekends sometimes, or starting next week it'll be more work, because the season's here."

"Season?" It was only nine-thirty, but some of the houses on the street were already dark, including her own.

She'd forgotten to leave the porch light on. "How'd you know this was my place?"

Missy rolled her eyes in response. "Please. You're a new county deputy, you're from Boston, no husband, no kids. And you rented the Walsh house on Buckthorn Road, sight unseen."

She went on, making a face of approval: "Which was lucky for you, by the way. At this time of the year there's not many rental vacancies."

So much for how the kid knew I'm a cop, thought Lizzie.

"Gossip's a sport in Bearkill," Missy added. "If the whole town doesn't know your shoe size, it's only because word on that hasn't quite gotten around yet, so get used to it."

She pushed blond curls off her forehead. "As for the season, this right here is the heart of potato country and the harvest got an awfully late start, so right now there's still about fifty zillion bushels of 'em out there, still waiting to be dug."

Turning to Lizzie, she continued. "Local kids even get let out of school to do it, but there are grown-ups in the fields, too, and they're hungry afterwards. And thirsty."

"Huh." So the houses filled up and the bar got

busy. Crime went up, too, maybe. She put a hand on the Jeep's door lever.

"Interesting. Well, thanks for—"

"Quite the little power trip you were on back there," said Missy.

Lizzie stopped, peering back into the dim-lit truck. "Huh?"

Missy gestured at Lizzie's leather satchel, which now held the gun that Lizzie had told the Bearkill cops didn't exist, and the single round that had been in it.

"Back there in the bar, you wanted things to go a certain way, so you made them go that way. Just took it upon yourself to decide, no aye-yes-or-no from anybody who might know more than you did," said Missy.

"Oh, come on," Lizzie began defensively. "You can't tell me any of you wanted me to—"

Missy smiled. "Uh-huh. Fair enough. You had your mind made up about it already, is all I'm saying. To make things go whatever way they might work out best for you."

To which Lizzie had no reply, as Missy went on:

"Hey, I may be a country girl, but I didn't just fall off the potato truck, myself, okay? You're a big-city cop? Think you've seen everything, know what's best way better'n any of the hicks around here?"

She dropped the Jeep into reverse. "Fine, and

thanks for your help, but listen up: Henry's dumb when he's loaded, but when he's sober he's mean. And tomorrow morning when he wakes up to a sore leg, he'll remember who's got his pistol."

"Oh." Lizzie swung the Jeep door closed. It slammed harder than she intended. The Jeep backed out and pulled away down the street, leaving her in the dark out in front of her empty house.

O-kay, she thought, picking her way across the damp, leaf-strewn front yard to the door. Fortunately, the penlight on her key ring worked.

Aiming it at the knob with the keyhole in it, she thought, *I don't care how safe it's supposed to be out here, I need to get a deadbolt put in, and—*

The key stuck. She pushed harder, whereupon the door swung wide open, soundlessly and without resistance.

But I locked it, she had time to think, *I know I—*

The shape rose up suddenly, silently in the doorway, looming there in the instant before it burst out at her. As she went down she crouched instinctively, rolling off the step, then leapt up.

"Stop! Police!" Grabbing into her bag for the Glock, she came up first with the .25 she'd confiscated along with—*thank you!*—the single round it had held. Not hers, but it would do; popping the slug into the chamber and slapping it shut—the Boston PD's weapons-training in-services had been exhaustive, not to mention effective—she charged after the intruder.

Across the yard and alongside the house, she kept the fleeing figure in view. But then he—if it *was* a he—vanished into the gloom, over the low backyard fence, and into the trees beyond.

She held herself still, barely breathing, listening for any sound. But all she heard as she glared out into the night was the angry thud of her own rapidly beating heart.

"Lizzie? You okay?"

She turned fast, stepping into a wide stance and leveling the weapon two-handed before recognizing the familiar voice.

Twenty feet away, Dylan Hudson raised his own hands, palms out, backpedaling hastily.

"Hey, hey. It's me, all right? What's going on?"

That's what I'd like to know. "Someone was inside."

She lowered the gun. "I chased him back here, but he was gone before I could see him very well."

Dylan approached. "Damn," she said with a little laugh, "but whoever that was startled the crap out of me." His arm slung casually around her shoulders felt good, like she wasn't alone all of a sudden, like in the old days.

Yeah, like that. She pushed the thought away. "Come on in with me a minute while I make sure there's not some other dimwit still in there."

No other dimwit was, though, and as they went through the rooms, they found that none of Lizzie's few things had been taken.

In the bedroom, the bed had new sheets, a new fleece comforter, and a new pillow, all courtesy of the house's owner, whom Lizzie had decided she liked despite his dreadful taste in home decor.

Dylan came up behind her. She was nearly as tall as he was; with his breath warm against her neck she turned to slip past him, biting her lip hard as she did so. The simple comfort of his touch would be lovely right now. As it had been in the past until she found out that he was lying, that he had a wife waiting, that . . .

Never mind. She was new here in Maine but he had an already-established network of connections who could help her find Nicki.

So she still needed him. Had always needed him . . .

Shut up. She went on into the kitchen, where the furniture couldn't be reclined upon; reluctantly, he followed. "You sure you want to sleep here tonight?" he asked.

She stood at the kitchen window looking into the darkness beyond the fence where the intruder had gone.

"I'm staying down at the Caribou Inn," he said. "There's two beds," he added.

Yeah, right. "First of all, I'm not going anywhere with you. And second, I thought you'd already gone back to Augusta."

Instead of hanging around here spying on me, she thought but did not add; she hadn't minded having him show up when he did.

"I had some things to do." He opened the refrigerator. "Hung out with Chevrier for a while, and he tried talking me into going moose hunting with him."

"What'd you say?" Nothing in the fridge interested him. Of course it didn't; he'd only opened it as a stalling maneuver.

"Told him I'd as soon stand in a pasture and shoot a cow."

Then he looked at her, knowing what she was thinking as he always had; he was thinking it, too. Sometimes she wondered why she didn't just lie down with him again, get it over with.

The rest of the time, though, she remembered walking around in a daze of misery: wanting him, hating him. Another long moment passed while he waited to see what she might do. Then:

He closed the fridge. "You going to call the cops?"

She shook her head, having had a few minutes to think about it. "I'll tell the Bearkill guys in the morning, but I think I know what this was. The house was vacant for quite a while."

Thus the tall grass, untrimmed shrubberies, and the unaired smell inside. "Probably some kid didn't get the memo about a new tenant, you know? Wanted a party spot."

Pursed lips, raised eyebrow: that notion wasn't flying with Dylan. After what Missy had said about the effectiveness of the Bearkill gossip wire, it didn't with Lizzie, either; not really.

But summoning Mutt and Jeff over here seemed pointless at this juncture, and anyway she was very tired; Dylan tipped his head skeptically at her, but in reply she folded her arms.

"Look, I'll keep the Glock out on my bedside table, okay? Besides, who ever heard of a housebreaker who comes back?"

Because even if it wasn't local teenagers just wanting a place where they could drink a few beers and maybe smoke a few joints, it was something along those lines. Had to be; after all, what else was there in Bearkill?

"Okay." He gave in finally as she walked him to the door. Outside, the night was silent, no cars moving and not even a plane overhead.

People lived like this, in this stillness so huge that it felt like an actual presence. "See you tomorrow, maybe," he said.

"You'll be around?" Keeping her voice even.

"Yeah," he said vaguely. "For a little while, anyway."

Then he turned and strode off, crossing the lawn to his car.

Closing the front door, she leaned her forehead

against it in relief. Only after she turned to confront the empty house and her aloneness in it did she realize: *Dylan, you slick bastard.*

He'd never answered her question about what he was doing in Bearkill in the first place.

He waited until everyone else in the house was asleep. His mom, tired from her job as a cashier at the Food King, had gone upstairs to escape the TV, still blaring in the living room, with his dad conked out on the sofa in front of it.

What the old man might be tired from, nobody knew. The only other person at home, a fourteen-year-old cousin who was staying here this year due to various family troubles, snored in a chair.

He tiptoed down the hall toward the back door, then froze at his father's voice: "Spud."

"Yeah?" He hated the nickname, acquired when he was a baby because his head, supposedly, had looked like a potato, all lumpy and misshapen. It still did, a little, and the name had stuck.

"Where you goin' so late?" Spud didn't reply. Maybe the old man would just fall back asleep. But no such luck:

"Don't you be gettin' another damned tattoo, hear?"

Yeah, right. Bearkill, Maine, middle of the night, there'd be a place to get inked. Sure there would.

Although Spud would have done it, if there had

been. Body art and piercings had become his way of escaping everything drab and ugly about his life, which in daylight was just about all of it. At night, though . . .

"Spud!" his father yelled once more, sounding as if his mood was getting uglier. "Dammit, you get in here!"

But instead of obeying, Spud snatched his jacket and slipped out, grabbed his bike from where it leaned on the trash cans by the falling-down garage, and coasted down the dirt driveway.

Moments later he was flying along the asphalt between farm fields, bare earth on one side with the oats and the broccoli all harvested for the year, the other side thick with withered potato vines, the crop ready to be dug. The night was clear and cold with an icy sliver of moon hanging in it like a curved claw; Spud paused on a hilltop to survey the barns, pastures, and clumps of dark forest that went on all the way to the western horizon.

Beyond that lay the Great North Woods, partly tamed in a few places but mostly wild, empty of people, and full of ways to die: you could get lost and starve, sprain your ankle and freeze, or fall off a cliff and get stuck in a ravine, howling yourself hoarse.

Or if you went out there to kill yourself on purpose, you could do that, too. With, say, your dad's old deer rifle which he hadn't used for years, but which still stood in a glass-fronted gun case in the dining room, along with a box of bullets.

Not tonight, though. Tonight, age eighteen, Spud still had what his high school guidance counselor had called options. Like, he could join the army and go fight whatever war was supposed to be so important this week. Get his ass shot off while firing his weapon at other young guys he had nothing against.

Yeah, there's a plan, he thought sourly as he pushed off on the bike again. Like in a movie he'd seen in which poor kids were set to fighting each other in an arena; the winner got food, warm clothes, a chance at a life.

It was the losers, though, that he'd found fascinating. The looks on their faces as they realized: *Not me. I'm not one of the lucky ones. I'm not going to make it.*

He knew that expression. It was the same one he saw in the smeared bathroom mirror each morning when he brushed his teeth. *You gotta pull yourself up by your own bootstraps,* people said.

But he wasn't that stupid. He'd actually been on the college prep track, taking physics and chemistry and doing quite well, thank you, until the old man got nailed with that last DUI and had his license to drive the big rigs yanked.

The swishing noise heard throughout the household then had been the sound of everyone's hopes going down the drain, not just Spud's own. So: no college. Pretty soon he was going to have to find some kind of work just to help support the household.

But pulling yourself up by your own bootstraps was still against the laws of physics. A guy like Spud, without money or connections, needed a way to get one or preferably both of those things if he was going to escape the living-dead existence that was Bearkill. And now he might've found that way: the lady cop.

His first attempt to profit from her arrival, confronting her in the Food King and practically demanding that she pay him for as-yet-unspecified information, had of course not worked; too ballsy, he told himself as he pedaled. Too fast, she didn't even know him, and the way he looked—the body art, the nose stud and lip ring, plus his dreads and angry facial blemishes . . . No wonder she'd figured him for a creep. So he'd rethought his strategy.

Watch her, the guy in the van had said, coming upon Spud on the street just outside her new office this afternoon. *Watch her. And tell me what she gets up to. I'll pay.*

Spud had seen the guy around town a few times but not often; they weren't friends. So his first notion had been to tell the new woman cop what he'd been asked to do, maybe try for a reward out of it. But after the way she'd gotten right up in his face, he'd decided it might be simpler—and safer; the guy had a mean vibe about him—just to do what he'd been asked. *Watch her*—

Hey, what could it hurt? Spud pedaled hard past the grassy front yard of a farmhouse with its wide freshly graveled driveway that led to the barn and silos. A startled spaniel flew furiously down to the dark road and ran behind him barking, then fell back.

He passed Town Hall, a low yellow-brick complex that looked like a reform school; all it needed was loops of razor wire. Next came the town maintenance yard where the snowplows, road graders, and school buses were parked.

That was another option his counselor had suggested. A town job didn't pay much, but it came with benefits like health insurance, sick days, pension, and so on. She'd been gazing at him with a look of such concern when she said it that he hadn't told her what those things—along with the whole idea of plowing snow and mowing grass for a living—made him think of:

An early grave. Not for the guys who liked it, maybe, but for him it would be better just to get his dad's rifle.

Plus one bullet. He coasted into town, past the red-brick library (OPEN M-W-F 10–4 & SA 12–3), the shuttered Tastee-Freez (SEE YOU NEXT

71

SUMMER!) and the ballfield where he'd played Little League until at age eleven, he was already just too big (PLEASE NO DOGS ALLOWED!).

He didn't care, though. By then his interests had already shifted from base hits to bass guitars, veering briefly into freebase cocaine when it was plentiful for a while even way out here. But after coke came meth, so poisonous that you had to have something seriously wrong with you to partake of it.

Which many of his friends, as it turned out, did, and so of course a couple of times he'd tried it, too. He'd gone back to weed pretty quick, though; his acne was bad enough without using some chemical junk to make it worse, and there were a few meth chicks around town by then, too, whose ravaged faces were like living warning signs.

Now rolling down deserted Main Street no-hands, he pulled a half-smoked roach from his jacket pocket, lit up with a quick, deft flick of his Bic, and, while inhaling the sweet, harsh smoke, approached the turn at the potato barn on the corner.

The barn loomed huge and silent, the harsh white security light on its rickety porch casting weirdly angled shadows from the posts that held up its shingled overhang. Decades of stomping by the booted feet of laborers had worn deep cups in the granite slabs of its front steps; from its windows, tall and narrow like vertically slitted eyes, he could imagine dark watchers peering.

Then he was past it and around onto the dark, unpaved lane. Slowing, he rolled past small houses where people were already asleep in front of TVs flickering vividly behind drawn curtains, until at the end he braked his bike silently to a halt.

This last house on the street was the one the cop lady had rented; he knew because his mother had overheard it in the Food King, and mentioned it at dinner just as a matter of general interest. Now the house was completely dark, nothing moving in it or on the street outside. Standing there finishing up the roach, he thought that most of the people asleep in these houses might as well remain there, dreaming forever.

If they even remembered how. Certainly there was nothing to dream about in Bearkill, Maine. Nothing to get up for, either. Not unless you really, really wanted something.

Out, for instance.

And you'd come up with a way to get it. Turning toward the other end of the street, he spotted a familiar van sitting under the corner streetlight by the hulking shape of the potato barn.

Watch her.

THREE

Lizzie's office in Bearkill looked no more encouraging the next morning than it had the day before. But she'd already decided what to do about that.

Getting the hell out of Dodge would be my first choice, she thought wryly, but instead, after switching on the lights for an even better view of the drab space, she went back outside again and walked down the chilly street to the Food King.

Paying for a coffee from the deli in the store, she met the cashier's curious gaze. "Do you happen to know anyone around here who does chores? Cleaning, painting?"

The clerk blinked twice. "You stay right there."

The woman in line behind Lizzie wore an oversized U. Maine sweatshirt, pink flannel PJ pants with the silhouette of a black cat and the phrase BAD KITTY repeated on them, and pink plaid sneakers.

"Hey," she protested at the delay.

The cashier held a hand up, the register's phone to her ear. "I don't know what it pays," she said into it in tones of strained patience. "You'll need to work that out with her."

The woman in the pink PJ pants tapped her

wrist impatiently with an index finger, then seemed to notice Lizzie.

"Terrible service in here," she confided. "I can remember when it was much better."

The cashier hung up. "Christ on a crutch, Cynthia, you're so old you can remember the animals lining up two by two."

She thrust change at the woman, who hurried out with her purchases. Then the cashier turned back to Lizzie. "Okay, my kid's coming down here to work for you."

And before Lizzie could protest that she'd meant an adult who had some skills and experience, someone who could do painting and carpet laying and maybe even a few repairs, the woman added:

"He's smart." She said this like it was something Lizzie was going to have to make allowances for.

"But he's big, he can lift stuff, and he's got nothing on his record, not even any points on his driver's license."

"I just need him for chores, not to be a getaway driver," Lizzie joked. But humor wasn't the cashier's strong point.

"Whatever. I'm just telling you he's honest, mostly. You won't have to worry about him ripping you off or anything."

On that ringing endorsement, Lizzie agreed to at least talk to the kid, who flew up on his bike out in front of her office ten minutes later, and who turned out to be Tattoo Kid.

Or Spud, as he informed her that he was called.

"He was as surprised as I was," said Lizzie a few hours later, following Cody Chevrier up a long dirt driveway.

It was just after noon, the pale blue shadows of the big old trees already beginning to lengthen and the tannic-scented air out here growing even colder.

"Yeah, well," said Chevrier over his shoulder. Ahead of him a huge black and tan hound that the sheriff had brought with him ambled along, sniffing. The dog had long, glossy ears and great big black-toenailed paws. Drool hung gleaming from its lips.

"Spud's different. Kind of a misfit, all that stuff stuck in him, the jewelry and piercings, and the tattoos. Feel sorry for the kid, tell you the truth. I think he's got a brain in that big head of his, somewhere."

Chevrier paused, considering. "Old man's a prick, I can tell you that much. But Spud's never given anybody any serious trouble that I ever heard. You could do worse."

The dog scrambled up onto the screened porch of the mobile home at the top of the drive, nosing the screen door open as if he'd done it before and slipping eagerly inside.

"I hear you had some excitement in town last night," said Chevrier.

Area 51, he meant. She still had the little gun. "Yeah. Is there a problem?" They followed the dog in to where a bentwood rocker and a wicker chair faced a table with magazines on it.

"Nope. Henry's pretty ticked off, I saw him in the diner this morning. And his knee hurts, I had to talk him out of visiting you about it."

Missy had predicted as much. "Yeah, well, he's lucky it's just his knee. But seriously, do I need to . . ."

Hey, a citizen had been injured, Chevrier could very well be getting flak from somewhere about it.

But he shook his head. "You're fine. Missy Brantwell's a good friend to have. Her dad's an important guy around here, has a big farm and he keeps a lot of people employed on it."

She absorbed this without comment. For one thing, she wasn't sure Missy felt the least bit friendly. And anyway:

"Do me a favor. Next time, don't talk Henry out of visiting me, all right? He's got a quarrel with me, I'll deal with it."

She pulled Henry's little gun out of her bag. "Meanwhile you might want to find a reason not to give this back to him."

He took it, looking pleased at the discovery that someone had managed to disarm Henry. "Fair enough. He's got an old felony record, no big deal nowdays, but he's not supposed to be having one of these at all."

But he clearly didn't want to make an issue of it any more than she did. "Anyway, this is Carl Bogart's place."

Chevrier looked around the screen porch. "He was the sheriff before I got the job, then his wife, Audrey, died not long after he retired. Started reloading shotgun shells and repairing guns for people, putting sights and scopes on them, and so on."

He stopped, frowning. "And then about two weeks ago he put a bullet in his head. Supposedly."

"Supposedly?" No one had touched the house, or at least not out here on the porch. On the table lay a pair of men's trifocals with tortoiseshell rims and lenses as thick and distorting as the eyepiece in a security peephole.

She glanced questioningly at Chevrier, who nodded. "Yeah, he had the cataracts pretty bad. S'posed to get 'em out, but he kept putting it off. Then—"

He made an explosion gesture with his hands. "Kerblooie. His weapon started looking like a better solution to him. So sayeth our county medical examiner."

"Only you don't think so." She sat in the wicker chair. The dog padded around the porch, sniffing, then came and dropped his head heavily into her lap, still drooling.

The dog's name was Rascal, and he smelled worse than any dog she'd ever met, like old socks mixed with tuna fish.

"Nope," said Chevrier. The rocker creaked as he sat.

"In fact I know he didn't. Try telling that to anyone else, though," he added, reaching out to smooth the dog's long ears.

"What do you mean?" Lord, but the dog reeked: his breath, mostly, she realized. Lifting the animal's upper lip with a finger, she exposed his reddened gum line and his teeth, brown with tartar.

Chevrier sighed. "I mean he wouldn't have done it, that's what," he replied, clearly tired of having to say it.

Especially when no one listened. It hit her that maybe he was a little nutty on this topic, that maybe he'd gotten her up here to support him in a theory that everyone else had already written off as unbelievable.

Unbelievable and also wrong, the first not necessarily being the same as the second, in her experience. But: "Why?"

The dog dragged its muzzle from her lap and sank to the floor. Outside, afternoon crept over the clearing, the silent shadows lengthening across the grass freckled with fallen leaves.

A breeze rattled the bare branches nearby. The dog's warmth felt good on her feet. "How can you be so sure he didn't . . ."

"Insurance." Chevrier sounded certain. "He had all the usual benefits, including the life insurance he'd had since he came on the job. But about a year ago he called me, asked me to drive him to a doctor in Montreal."

She turned in surprise. "His doctor was in Canada? Why? And why couldn't he drive himself, was he that sick?"

Chevrier shook his head. "We're pretty close to Canada, you know. People go back and forth all the time. And no, he wasn't sick that anyone knew. But on the way up there he swore me to secrecy and then he dropped a bomb on me. He thought he had lung cancer. He'd been suspecting it for a few months."

The sheriff sighed. "So first he'd bought himself a big new policy, got it all set up and squared away, then he waited a few months before getting his suspicions confirmed so the insurance company couldn't get out of paying benefits on account of a preexisting condition."

"Which he had? He was right about the cancer?"

Chevrier nodded again, grimly. "Yup. He'd done his homework about it, too—doctor in Montreal turned out to be one of the top guys for that kind of a tumor. But there wasn't a whole lot that even he was going to be able to do for old Carl."

"Because he'd had to wait," she guessed. "So as not to have that preexisting condition problem . . ."

"Yeah." Chevrier stuck his hands in his pockets, recalling it. "And while he was waiting, this big tumor of his was growing, getting even bigger until it was blocking off half his windpipe."

She got up, zipped her jacket, and shivered inside it. "That kind of thing can get ugly. It must've been hard for him."

"Yeah. He was uncomfortable. Struggling, not to put too fine a point on it. But I'm telling you, the guy was determined."

Not to kill himself, Chevrier meant. He saw her getting it. "Yeah, because if he committed suicide, the insurance wouldn't pay off." He went on:

"Bogie had a grandchild with birth defects, see? Her care's very expensive. The death payout on the policy would've given his son and daughter-in-law a break. On the money angle, anyway."

"But not anymore." She sniffed at her hands; not only did the dog stink, but now so did she: hands, clothes . . . everywhere that Rascal had touched radiated the stench of Eau de Mutt.

Chevrier got up. "No," he said glumly, shoulders slumped. "I talked to the son. They're probably going to lose their house and move

81

here, the kid'll have to quit her special school and therapy."

He looked around at the roughly furnished porch and the unkempt yard outside, frowning as if trying to imagine how a disabled kid would cope in it. "He would never have let that happen."

Probably this place could be cozy at night with the lamps on, but now in the bluish light of a cold autumn afternoon the porch felt lonely and discouraging.

"How long did he have?"

Rascal got up, stretched, and padded to the screen door, where he stood watching a squirrel race back and forth on the driveway. The dog's tail kept time with the squirrel's activity.

"To live?" Chevrier laughed without humor. "To look at him, you'd still have thought it might be forever. But he told me the doctors said a month, maybe a couple of weeks. Said it would be fast, once it really all started to go south. But the insurance company investigators said the pain made him put a bullet in his head instead."

He made a face. "Course they did. It's in the company's own interest to think that's what happened, isn't it?"

Getting up, he pulled open the screen door. Rascal scrambled out, ran to the tree where the squirrel had taken refuge just in time, and stood there gazing up yearningly at it.

"So they don't have to pay out. And it's true,

he did try to commit fraud on them, I'm not denying that part. But I'll tell you what," said Chevrier with sudden fierceness, his eyes on the dog.

"I knew Carl Bogart a long time. I know what kind of cop he was and what kind of man he was, and I know for a fact that he could have done a whole damned year with a red-hot poker stuck in him if it meant his family would be better off afterwards."

He turned toward her, his eyes gleaming moistly in the light filtering in through the porch screen. Behind him, Rascal tipped his head as if inviting the squirrel down.

"And I'm telling you that Carl didn't kill himself, no matter how well someone set it up to make it look like he did."

He sighed heavily. "Anyway, I just wanted you to see Carl's place, get a feeling for what kind of guy he was."

So that was it. Neat, sweet, and complete, as her old Boston patrol partner Liam O'Donnell used to say. Chevrier thought that somebody had killed his friend.

Just not *completely* complete. "There are," she said slowly, wanting to be sure she understood, "three others like this? Cops dead, you don't like the explanations?"

Three of them now that he'd told her about, and one more. He nodded slowly and with appreciation for the unlikeliness of it. "Yeah. You've been thinking about it, huh?"

She had. It had been running along in the back of her mind ever since he told her the real reason he'd hired her here. An experienced murder cop was about as useful as a fish on a bicycle in Bearkill—

Except when she wasn't. "I figured it might take a while for it to sink in," he added.

"Well, it is unusual. I mean it's a big number." She tipped her head at him consideringly. "Four of them," she repeated.

"But all part of one crime," he agreed. "Only I can't seem to figure out what they had in common, why they . . . Hell, that's really the problem isn't it?"

Yeah, that was the problem, all right: why? Because if you understood that, the rest opened up: the who, how, everything.

Without the why, though, you could have all the other stuff and more: arrests. Convictions, even. With enough of the who and how, you didn't necessarily even need a motive in the court-room.

But without one, if it had been your case, it would still all be like ashes in your mouth.

Lizzie got up, crossed the porch, and opened the door into the mobile home, averting her eyes from the dark brown smears and spatters of what she knew must be Carl Bogart's blood.

"You left it like this?" she asked. Chevrier stood in the doorway behind her.

"Yeah. Sorry, I know it's ugly. But when it happened, that's when I finally decided to try getting somebody up here, somebody who could—"

"—have a look," she finished for him, moving past the sink with its dish drainer holding one cereal bowl, one juice glass, one cup with a spoon in it. Bogart had been a tidy widower.

"Yeah, I get it," she added to Chevrier. *And then I turned up, a homicide cop looking for a job in Aroostook County.* "Hudson told you about me?"

A three-piece living-room set plus end tables, a coffee table made from the highly polished cross section of an enormous tree trunk, and a large flat-screen TV furnished the next room.

"Yeah," said Chevrier, following her. "I went through here after it happened, by the way. Nothing missing. Nothing even out of place."

"And no note." A tall, glass-fronted gun case held a quartet of lovely old rifles. A mahogany breakfront displayed some framed photographs, including one of a smiling silver-haired woman.

"No note. That's Audrey, his wife." He went ahead of Lizzie down the hall to three bedrooms, one a catchall and the next set up like an office with framed cop commendations and commemorative placards on the wall.

The third room was Bogart's: lamp, chair, bed.

85

A cell could hardly have been plainer. A braided rug with some blankets heaped on it showed where Rascal had slept.

"I took the dog's dishes back to my place," said Chevrier. "But I knew better than to try bringing those blankets into the house past my wife."

The place did smell pretty doggy. More to the point, though, there was nothing even slightly odd or unusual about it. Back in the kitchen, she paused over the spatter evidence.

"You checked his hands?" For evidence that Bogart had fired a gun recently, she meant. But Chevrier shook his head.

"I did, but he fired weapons all the time, and handled the powder for reloading shotgun shells, too."

"I see." She could still get a scene specialist up here, she supposed; there were favors she could still call in, in Boston.

But this long after the fact, she doubted it would do any good. The insurance company could simply say that any aberrations from normal splatter patterns were from degrading of the evidence over time.

And Chevrier seemed to understand this. "Anything occur to you, though?" he asked as she walked back out onto the porch.

"Not yet." Her boots made a hollow sound on the pressure-treated pine steps leading down to the yard. "I'm sorry about your friend."

They got into his vehicle. Time to go; you wouldn't think fresh air could feel so smothering, but it did. Right now, it definitely did.

On the way back to town, the road crested a hill, then ran flat along the top of a ridgeline. "So what's this Brantwell guy like? Missy's dad, I mean?"

Chevrier glanced at her. "Last night in the bar," Lizzie explained, "Missy's cousin said something about how she was lucky he wasn't home. Because she was getting in late."

Across the valley the sun was already thinking about setting, the distant treetops sharply cut out against a glowing red sky.

Chevrier's lower lip pursed judiciously. "Like I said, he's got a lot of workers on his farm. Pays good, treats 'em fair as far as I've ever heard. Well spoken, decent looking. He's on the county board of commissioners, belongs to the Chamber of Commerce, and so on."

In the shadowy valleys between the ridges, lights in houses and yards began going on. "That's where he is now, in New York at a meeting on milk prices," said Chevrier. "He's kind of like the County's unofficial ambassador for stuff like that."

"Travels a lot, then, does he?" The relief in Missy's eyes last night when she was reminded that her dad wasn't at home had been impossible to miss.

Chevrier shrugged. "Pretty often. Once a month, sometimes more, he'll be away a few days. He's got a good foreman working for him, Tom Brody, manages the farm."

He shot another glance sideways at her. "Why, you think he might make problems for Henry about last night?"

"No, no." It wasn't as if Henry was related to Missy, or—heaven forbid—married to her. Henry was just a local screw-up of the small-town variety as far as Lizzie could tell. She leaned back in the seat. "I doubt he'll even hear about it. I just wondered."

They drove on in silence until Rascal thrust his flop-eared, foul-breathed muzzle between the truck's two front bucket seats.

"The dog needs his teeth cleaned," she said. "And a bath."

"That reminds me," said Chevrier. "Got a favor to ask you."

"No," said Lizzie at once, knowing what was coming. The dog liked her, and she'd heard Chevrier say his wife didn't like it.

Nevertheless, when she got out of Chevrier's vehicle on Main Street, Rascal got out, too, and could not be persuaded back in.

"Thank you," Chevrier said sincerely. He'd be airing his vehicle for a week. "It'll only be until I find someone else."

"Yeah, yeah," Lizzie said sourly, still thinking

about Carl Bogart and the others. But Chevrier couldn't stay to talk about that now, either; he had a meeting with drug enforcement guys from Bangor to get to.

It occurred to her, though, that even if she didn't want the dog for company, she could use him for an alarm system. Also, when Dylan Hudson started hinting around about staying overnight again, as he inevitably would, she'd be able to point out to him that she already had one mutt. *Ba-da-bump* . . .

Meanwhile she had one more chore on her to-do list, so once she saw that the lights were still on in her office—

She'd given her new helper Spud his instructions and left him to it; if there was disappointment coming in that department, she'd deal with it later, she decided as she crossed the street with the big hound keeping a surprisingly calm pace beside her.

He hopped into her Blazer as if he'd been doing it all his life, too, and moments later they were heading back out of town. "Good dog," she told him, and he eyed her gravely in reply; then she turned her attention back to her errand again.

When she'd mentioned her plan to Chevrier, he'd told her she wouldn't be able to miss the Brantwell place, and as it turned out he was right. The long, well-maintained driveway was fenced on both sides with posts and barbed wire, and at the top a sizable complex of farm buildings spread away on both sides of the large, well-maintained, white clapboard house.

Big farm is right, she thought as she pulled up alongside two cars, Missy's yellow Jeep and a newish Cadillac Escalade. As she got out, a man came out of the nearest barn, wiping his hands on a rag.

"Help you?" Smiling but businesslike; introducing herself, she saw his eyes register the official car and the fact that she was a cop, but not with any concern.

"Roger Brantwell?" she asked, not thinking he could be; his face, while friendly, was thin and ferret-like.

"Oh, hell, no," he said, laughing in reply; a *pleasant* ferret. "I'm Tom Brody, I'm just the hired man around here. Or one of 'em," he added. "Place is crawling with 'em, as you can see."

He waved a flannel-shirted arm around the neat, organized-looking barnyard: wood crates stacked here, farm machinery parked there, nothing random-appearing. And Brody was right, the place bustled with men—no women, Lizzie noticed—busy hammering or painting or hauling or fixing big pieces of equipment she didn't recognize, in the bluish late-afternoon light.

As she watched, Missy came out onto the broad porch that ran along the side of the house. A wooden porch swing on heavy chains hung by a window full of red geraniums; she stopped by it.

"What's up?" she asked, gently jouncing the baby she held in her arms and not sounding any more friendly than she had the night before.

"Got something I'd like to run by you," Lizzie said. It had occurred to her earlier, but she'd wanted to ponder it.

"See, I've got this kid Spud working for me," she began when Missy had invited her inside and sat her down in the kitchen.

Not enthusiastically, but she'd done it. And not just any kitchen: new ceramic tile, stainless steel, polished granite, and a door leading out to a sunroom with wicker and ferns, a fountain trickling prettily in the corner, made this one look fresh out of a decorating magazine.

"Spud?" Missy responded skeptically. "That freak?"

"Yeah, well." Lizzie spread her hands. "He doesn't seem so bad. Why, should I know something?"

Missy had put the baby, a handsome and placid little boy about a year old, into a crib in the lamplit sunroom, where he'd promptly fallen asleep.

"No," she said, "I guess not. I don't know how anyone stands looking at all that body piercing of his, though. That nose stud, ugh."

Which was what Lizzie had thought, too, but judging people on their style choices didn't seem right, and after what she'd seen on the streets of Boston, it wasn't even especially exotic.

Also, the kid had seemed very eager; pathetically, almost.

"Yeah, well, maybe you can keep me from having to look at it so much," she told Missy. "I was hoping I could get you to come work in the office for me."

She needed someone so she could have regular office hours without being stuck there herself, and for that Spud wouldn't do at all. But Missy had begun shaking her curly head even before Lizzie finished.

"Oh, no. I couldn't. I've got the baby, and—"

"But I thought your mom took care of him?" As Lizzie spoke a young woman wearing an apron over blue jeans and a sweater came through the kitchen, carrying a can of Pledge and a dust rag.

"And it's not like you're stuck here doing the cleaning," Lizzie added when the girl had gone. The Brantwells' program of hiring help went for inside as well as outside, apparently.

"It won't make you rich, just twenty hours a week—"

Not that Missy needed the money, obviously. Every surface in the place glowed with what Lizzie recognized as the effect of plenty of cash: new, clean, shiny, not a speck of dust or smudge of a fingerprint anywhere, and the cars outside were new, too.

"—but at least there won't be drunks trying to strangle you," she added, and at this Missy did crack a smile.

But her mind was made up. "Thanks. But it wouldn't work, I'm afraid. My dad's got some really rigid ideas. It's only because it's family that I even talked him into the bar thing."

Lizzie sipped coffee. It was intensely pleasant, sitting in the bright, clean kitchen like this with the fountain trickling in the background; she got the feeling that if a person lived here, everything would be taken care of for them.

That there'd be a safety net, and that it might begin to feel a little tight after a while, as Missy had—well, she hadn't said it, exactly, had she?

She hadn't needed to. "I see. You mean he doesn't want you working? Because you're his daughter, or—"

Or because he's a control freak? The whole place wasn't just neat; it was aggressively so. There was that handsome baby in the sunroom now, too, the circumstances of whose birth might not have been what Mr. Brantwell had wanted for his daughter.

Missy wasn't wearing a wedding ring and there didn't seem to be any baby daddy around. *Don't assume,* Lizzie told herself, but still, she was getting the strong sense that Roger Brantwell might be a little . . . *Oppressive* was the word she wanted, actually.

But Missy only looked more stubborn. "Dad's protective, is all." She rinsed her cup at the sink. "So thanks, but—"

Disappointed, Lizzie got up, too. Anyone who could stay as cool as Missy had with Henry's arm around her throat would've been good backup in the office. But . . .

Just then a pleasant-looking older lady came in, wearing tan slacks, a matching sweater set, and pearls. Her short graying hair was well cut and her pretty, softly made-up face provided a lovely preview of what Missy's would look like years from now.

At the moment, though, that face looked . . . worried. Panicky, even.

"Honey, where's Jeffrey? I thought he was still upstairs in his crib." The woman glanced anxiously around the kitchen.

"No, Mom, I brought him down. He's in the sunroom." Missy smiled indulgently as her mother hurried to where the baby slept.

"She's just nuts about him," the girl confided when she and Lizzie were back out on the long porch. "Loves him to bits."

Dusk had fallen and work lights had gone on in the buildings and around the yard. "That's great. She must be a huge help. And does your dad love him, too?"

Missy glanced sharply at her. "Of course he does. Why ask me a silly thing like that?"

94

Across the yard, three guys in gloves and jackets helped a fourth hoist a piece of machinery onto the bed of a pickup truck. Lizzie turned back to Missy.

"Yeah, sorry, it was a dumb question, wasn't it? Anyway, if you change your mind about the job . . ."

"I won't." A car turned in and its headlights started up the long driveway; another Escalade, Lizzie saw when it got closer, brand-new like the other vehicles.

It pulled in by the shed at the far end of the drive, and a man in a tan sports jacket and slacks got out, hefting a canvas overnight bag and turning to send a searching look at Lizzie.

"Help you?" he asked crisply as he crossed the porch.

Well, he was a businessman, and this was after all his place of business, Lizzie thought. She smiled and put out a hand. In a businesslike manner. "Hi. I'm Deputy Snow."

Close up, Roger Brantwell was a tall, well-built man in his late fifties who looked like he'd probably been a quarterback in high school. Now his curly blond hair was receding and his strong, square jaw had a pouch of softness under it, to match the one over his belt.

He took the hand Lizzie offered perfunctorily, then dropped it. "Is there some trouble?" His quick glance at his daughter suggested that if there was, she'd better not be the cause of it.

"Not at all," Lizzie replied quickly. "I just stopped by to say hello. And to say thanks," she added. "Your daughter helped me out."

"I gave her a ride home last night, Dad," said Missy, and he nodded, accepting this.

"I see. Well. Nice to meet you," he said, and Lizzie could read his thoughts about Missy on his face: too-short hair, too much makeup . . .

She got the strong sense that to Brantwell, any makeup at all might be too much. "I know what you're thinking," said Missy suddenly when he'd gone inside. "That I should go somewhere, do something. Away from here."

Lizzie turned back to the girl. "I never said . . ."

"You don't have to." Missy gazed flatly at her. "I know he seems . . . a little unfriendly. But he's got a lot on his plate. All this—"

She waved a hand, indicating the house, yard, and buildings, and the men working among them. "It can be a lot of pressure. He didn't get anything handed to him, and it's hard, making a go of this place."

She took a breath. "And a woman like you who went to college and even graduate school, probably, I know what your type tends to think about someone like me, too."

My type? Lizzie thought a little defensively.

Missy went on: "But I live here, Lizzie, okay? This is my home, right here in Bearkill, and

96

I don't want to go anywhere," she declared.

From the sound of it, she'd made this speech before. *Fine, but is that because you do love it?* Lizzie wondered.

She looked once more through the geranium-filled window at the kitchen with its arched doorway into the pretty sunroom.

Or is it because it's so safe, familiar, and comfortable, and you don't know what you'd do otherwise?

"Of course," said Lizzie, putting her hands up placatingly. "I never meant to imply any other thing."

Thinking, *She's quick on the uptake. She'd have been good to have in the office.* "Anyway, see you in town," she finished. "And by the way, that kid of yours is really cute."

"Yeah," Missy relented with a faint smile. "He is, isn't he? And . . . look, thanks again for your help last night."

"Don't mention it." The flannel-shirted fore-man, Tom Brody, crossed the yard and got into the Escalade that Brantwell had just driven up in, pulling it across the wide graveled area toward where Missy's new Jeep sat gleaming in the yard lights.

Hey, at least the benefits here are good. As Lizzie started the Blazer, Brantwell came back outside again; then he and his daughter went in together and the door closed behind them.

• • •

It was only just past four in the afternoon, but the cold sky was edging toward dark when she reached Bearkill, the sun's last thin gleams fading behind the treed ridges to the west. Parking the Blazer across from her office, she noted in dismay that her new helper had hung blue plastic tarps at the windows, concealing whatever was going on inside.

Dope smoking, probably, she imagined. Or beer drinking, or both. God, what had she been *thinking* when she—

She shoved open the door. The kid looked up. "Hi."

"Hi, yourself." All ready to blast him with verbal fury, she found herself at a loss for words. "What're you doing?"

The answer, though, was clear. It was just that it was all she could think of to say, confronted by the prospect of a space so utterly changed that it might as well have been transported from some other solar system.

The planet Whitewash, maybe. The walls and the ceiling were now devoid of the many tack holes, bumps, scrapes, and gouges that the previous surfaces had possessed. The ceiling tiles had been painted and new fluorescent fixtures, shedding bright light that somehow managed to be pleasant yet forcefully illuminating at the same time, had replaced the old, dim, flickering ones.

"Well, I—" He got to his feet, a big, plump, dreadlocked teenager with piercings and tattoos everywhere, wearing a pair of black jeans, black high-tops, and a ratty black sweatshirt with the sleeves cut out of it.

He gestured around. "I did what you said. Today I got the place ready. The furniture's coming tomorrow. Oh, and I'm having the communications stuff done by the sheriff's people, okay?"

The floor covering, which had been cruddy beige rug, was now gray indoor-outdoor carpeting, not quite professionally installed but still pulled acceptably tight under wooden furring strips; he'd nailed them like floor trim at the carpet's edges.

"Because I know you said try to use locals," he added.

She had said that. But she'd had no idea he would get this far, this fast. She went on looking around wonderingly as Rascal paced the room's perimeters and lay down yawning on the new rug.

"But I think you want stuff nobody can hack, right? I mean, for your phones, computers, all your—"

"Yeah." She looked at him. "You sprayed it?" That was what the drop cloths were all about, everything covered if it was not supposed to get painted. Then . . . *pssssst!* the spray painter came out, and presto, pretty soon it was done.

Again, maybe not quite the way a professional would have approached it. But it was nice, and the smell was already fading.

Seeing her reaction, he looked smug, as if he'd known that she hadn't expected much from him. "Anyway, about the computers? I arranged for the big items, but you can get the peripherals and accessories here in town, okay?"

At the little office supply store on the corner, he meant, just as she'd planned. Meanwhile he'd picked up the annoying verbal tic of ending all his sentences on an up note, as if they were, like, you know, questions?

"But for, you know, security's sake?" he went on. "The comms office in Houlton is bringing in your hardware tomorrow. They'll hook it all up for you, too."

She kept looking at him. Telling him he could clean up the office, make it habitable, had been more in the way of throwing the kid a bone. She'd still meant to find adult help.

He, however, had taken it extremely seriously and he hadn't done badly at all, even thinking about the security angle and doing something about it.

"So now I'm going to be your office manager and maintenance guy?" he went on.

She peeked into the washroom: spotless. Paper towels in the dispenser, check; toilet paper, ditto. A small bottle of mouthwash, a new wrapped toothbrush, and a comb were on the sink; also, the linoleum floor tiles shone.

"I mean, you'll need someone for that, right?" he added hopefully. "Part-time, at least? In the beginning, anyway?"

He was practically rubbing his hands together in appeal. She looked around once more: the front windows sparkled, dust bunnies had been chased from between the radiator vanes, and was that—

It was. A single carnation stood in a small florist's vase on her desk. She didn't like carnations, but . . .

He waited expectantly. "Yeah," she said, turning slowly. She'd planned to spend a week or more on this place, hiring out some of the work, doing the rest herself.

She had not, to put it mildly, been looking forward to it. "Yeah, part-time to start is fine."

There were things at the house that needed doing, too, once the office got squared away. Then something else occurred to her.

"Don't you go to school?" There'd been kids in the grocery store as well, she realized, during the hours when they should've been in classrooms. "Doesn't anyone around here go to—"

He was already nodding. "Oh. Yeah, you wouldn't know, would you? I'm eighteen, I graduated already. But it's potato time?"

Not waiting for a reply, he hoisted a black plastic trash bag crammed full of spray cans, used paintbrushes, crumpled newspapers, and wadded-up plastic drop cloths, and dragged it to the doorway.

"Here in the County, they let kids out of school to work the potato fields," he went on. "See, a machine comes along and digs potatoes, the kids grab 'em up, throw 'em in baskets? Takes about two weeks to get 'em all, the kids make money and the taters get picked. They've been doing it here for, like, a couple centuries?"

He stopped. "But you probably don't want to hear about that boring stuff." Then, looking down at Rascal, "Want me to walk him for you?"

"Oh, no thanks," she began. But it was a thought; also, the animal would need food, and maybe a bed, and . . . what else did dogs need, anyway?

Spud grinned. It didn't make him attractive, precisely, but it went a long way toward diluting the effect of the dreadlocks and piercings; not much could be done about the tattoos, she supposed, other than long sleeves. But hey, it wasn't like she'd be sending him to conferences of law-enforcement professionals.

"That's Carl Bogart's dog, isn't it?" Spud went on. "You've got him now? That's great, it's a good place for a dog where you live, way out there on the edge of town."

"Yeah, well, in Bearkill that's only a ten-minute walk," she began jokingly, then recalled suddenly the dark shape that had barreled past her the night before, out of her place.

It struck her also that the tattoos covering Spud's arms and neck weren't hearts with the word *Mom* inked in them, drawings of nude women, or other such traditional decorations.

Lightning bolts, blood-dripping daggers, screaming skulls . . . Spud went for the violent end of the body-art spectrum. Even the jewelry in his piercings looked like weaponry: bent silver nails, spikes twisted into gleaming spirals.

"Really, you're sure you don't want me to take him out?" the boy persisted, crouching by the dog.

What she wanted, suddenly, was for Spud to go away and leave her alone to think. "Thanks, but I haven't gotten any supplies for him yet, and you'd need a leash to—"

But Spud was undeterred. "He won't run away. Only reason he took off when Bogart died was that Carl couldn't call him back."

He hefted the trash bag. "Why'n't you go on and pick up the stuff you need for him at the Food King. I'll meet you back here so you can take him home."

Not waiting for an answer, he went to the door with the dog right alongside him, then turned back a final time. "It's nice of you to take Rascal," he said seriously. "Old Carl loved that dog. And I'll bet he's really going to like your backyard."

Right, she thought as he vanished with the trash bag and the dog. *My backyard, yet another thing you know about . . . how?*

But then the smells of woodsmoke and clothes needing a wash wafted from him again and she realized: if it had been him running past her at her house last night, she'd have known it.

And he knew where she lived because everyone did, of course, and about the yard, too. Probably the whole town knew her blood type and her bank balance, in fact; all grist for the rumor mill that Missy Brantwell had warned her about.

Besides, Spud had grown up here. He knew everything about the place. *So don't get paranoid, Lizzie,* she instructed herself, and let her new helper take Rascal for his evening walk while she went to the Food King, where it turned out a king's ransom was about what it cost to get ready for pet ownership.

Counting out the bills at the cash register, she hoped that hiring Spud wouldn't turn out to be similarly expensive, or if it was, that money wasn't the only thing her own snap decision to go along with his wishes on the matter ended up costing her.

She was still thinking this, meanwhile loading bags of dog kibble, biscuits, a leash, and a synthetic chew-bone the size of a brontosaurus femur (its packaging said Bacon! Flavored!) into the car's back seat when from the shadows at the rear of the store's parking lot came a yell of distress.

And then a whole lot more of them.

"Help! Help! Help!" Just the one word, wailed over and over again in a voice that was high and ragged, left no doubt in her mind that this was not a joke.

Vaulting a concrete Jersey barrier, she jogged sideways to avoid a stray shopping cart and raced across the asphalt. Under the lights by the store entrance, she swerved around to where the compressors, the trash bins, and the loading dock stood, casting deep shadows that hid . . .

"Help!" At the far end of the lot where old shopping carts and trash lay scattered . . . "Help! They're killing me!"

Finally she spotted him, sprawled on the ground beside what looked like another cart. But instead it was one of those motorized power chairs, the kind they advertised on TV to give frail and elderly people their mobility back.

She thought that in this case the chair might've made a little too much mobility possible. As she crouched by the victim, someone drove a car up and shone its headlights on him. "Call 911," she yelled, then assessed the old man rapidly.

By the book: airway, breathing, circulation, all present and operating, no blood obvious anywhere. Next, check state of consciousness: "Hey, buddy, it's okay, I'm a cop. What's your name?"

The old man looked up pleadingly. In the headlights' glare his face was bone white. He was wearing a cotton T-shirt, loose drawstring trousers, and tube socks.

No shoes; he'd come out here in his night-clothes, by the look of it, maybe from home but more likely from some kind of care facility; those loose trousers looked institutional. And—yep, there was a plastic ID bracelet around his bony wrist.

"Help," he said again, but confusedly this time, whispering it while glancing around in puzzlement. "How . . . how'd I get here? Which son of a bitch got me in all this . . . Help!"

He struggled to sit up. "Oh, I'll be in trouble now. They'll fire me for this, I've got to—"

No bones were sticking out, and the pulse in his wrist was strong and steady. The palms of his mottled hands were scraped, maybe from where he fell when the chair overturned, and there was a bruise just over his right eyebrow.

But nothing suggested serious injury; he was more scared than hurt. She looked around, but there was no sign of who might have attacked him . . . if he'd been attacked at all, she realized, squinting into the surrounding shadows.

A sharp grassy slope ran uphill past the parking

lot's edge; if she'd had to guess, she'd say he had tried to climb it in that motorized contraption but the grade had been too steep.

So he'd rolled his vehicle, basically. Her hand, which at first had gone automatically for her radio—*old habits die hard*—came to rest instead on his bony shoulder, as somewhere in the distance that 911 call she'd asked for began paying off with the welcome sound of a siren.

People from the parking lot at the front of the store began wandering over, staring or squinting suspiciously. Then a man pushed his way up, his voice familiar before she glimpsed the face: Trey Washburn, the veterinarian she'd met the day before.

"Hey." He hunkered beside her. "What've we got here, a one-vehicle accident?"

She laughed, partly out of relief at the sight of someone she knew, but more at the accuracy of the description.

"Yeah. I think he tried to climb that hill on the scooter."

A boxy ambulance arrived. Four techs jumped out and began wrangling the scene, the victim, and their own emergency gear so efficiently that Lizzie felt free to stand back.

"Dan," she heard one of them say to the victim, "did you go out without your jacket again?"

Which was when Lizzie realized she'd left hers in the car.

Washburn pulled off his down-filled parka, draping it around her.

"Here," he said, and when she protested: "Don't worry about it. I've got a good layer of blubber to protect me."

It wasn't blubber; when his arm had been around her, she'd felt its solidness. Meanwhile, over his protests, the old man got lifted onto a gurney and then hoisted up through the bay doors of the emergency vehicle.

"Call my son!" he yelled. "Call my son, he's the lord of the forest!" The old man could still be heard yelling from inside.

Then the bay doors closed, the vehicle rolled away, and moments later nothing remained to show that anything untoward had happened except the scooter, lying there with its underside up in the air like a turned turtle.

No one had asked her anything, and it seemed as if the techs knew their patient. "Maybe he does this often?" she hazarded.

She walked with Washburn back toward the lit area of the parking lot, the vet carrying a brown paper shopping bag. In it she spied three baking potatoes, a couple of steaks, and mixed salad greens; her stomach growled hungrily.

"Yeah," he answered her question. "Old Dan's a well-known escape artist from the nursing home, a couple blocks thataway."

They reached his car, a shiny black BMW X3

glittering in the parking lot's lights. Flipping up the hatchback, he stowed his groceries, then came back around to where she stood admiring the vehicle.

Veterinarians made decent money here, apparently. "No, keep it for tonight," he said as she began pulling off his jacket, but she was already pushing it toward him.

"Thanks, but I have one. It's just in my car. Really, I—"

Smiling, he allowed her to press it into his hands. Then he paused, lifting it to his face.

His bright gaze met hers. "Smells better than it did."

Foolishly she felt hot color rising to her cheeks as he put the jacket around her again. "It's Lizzie, right? Lizzie Snow?"

"Yes," she managed, furious with herself. Had living way out here in the boondocks already turned her into a woman who blushed when a man spoke to her, especially one that she didn't even find attractive?

Except she did, sort of. He was so . . . so friendly, simple, and normal without being the least bit simpleminded. The opposite of that, actually, and she always found the opposite of simpleminded very attractive, indeed.

His cell phone burbled; holding up an apologetic finger, he took the brief call, and when he'd hung up:

"Listen, that was a buddy of mine. I was supposed to cook for the two of us, but he's tied up. So it's either I eat all that food I bought by myself, thus adding even more meat and potatoes to my already sturdy frame . . ."

He was sturdy, too; the kind of person that another person could lean on, and why in the world was she thinking that?

". . . or I could make dinner for the two of us," he finished.

"You mean you and me?" she managed, then realized how dumb that sounded.

But he only laughed. "Yes, and I broil a mean tenderloin."

Her stomach growled again. And he was . . . not cute, really, but pleasant. More substantial than the word *cute* had room for.

Still . . . "I can't. I've got a dog waiting." And Tattoo Kid waiting also, she realized suddenly.

At Washburn's inquisitive look, she explained about Rascal; to her surprise, he knew the animal. *Of course he does, you dope, he's the veterinarian.* "Glad to hear he's found a home," said Washburn.

"Well, I'm not sure I'd put it that optimistically. Foster care, maybe." Chevrier had been urgently persuasive and she had succumbed, but now she wondered how she would even have time for the creature.

Washburn went on. "You know what, though? I

seem to recall old Rascal being due for his rabies shot. Couple of other things he might need, too, maybe? You could kill two birds, et cetera."

He smiled coaxingly at her. "You bring the dog over, let me cook up a nice meal, and meanwhile my vet tech can do Rascal's shots and so on, okay? That way, you won't need to—"

Again with the insistent "feed me" sounds from her famished midsection. This time she was pretty sure he heard them.

"Got a good burgundy waiting. Goes fine with rare steak," he added persuasively. "Yum yum."

He rubbed his own middle. It made her laugh, and she liked the feeling. She liked it a lot. "Okay, you sold me. But if that mutt's got fleas, you have to promise to get rid of those, too."

"Deal," he agreed swiftly, following up with directions to his place.

"Five miles out." He waved down the street past her office. "Big white sign says 'Great North Woods Animal Care.'"

He climbed into his snazzy SUV. "See you soon."

Then he drove off, leaving her there with doubt rising in her; what had she just done? Still, she really was starving, and as she glanced back at the Food King, she saw the store's lights going out and a clerk putting the CLOSED sign on the door; they rolled the sidewalks up early around here, apparently.

Besides, she was still wrapped in Washburn's jacket. So she'd have to return it.

". . . and that's the story," she finished a few hours later.

The den in Trey Washburn's sprawling ranch-style house was a haven of dark mahogany paneling, rugs in rich, dark jewel colors, and big, softly upholstered chairs and sofas. A fire in the huge stone fireplace flickered warmly; two liver-spotted retrievers occupied twin plaid dog beds, one on either side of the hearth.

"Wow," said Washburn. She'd said more than she'd planned to. "Guess you've got your work cut out for you, then."

She laughed, not with amusement. "That's an understatement." It was the first time in a very long while that she'd confided in anyone; maybe it was the wine, which had in fact been very good, a California burgundy several cuts above what she usually drank.

She hoped she wasn't making a mistake by having a second glass. But Washburn was a good listener, smart and sympathetic without trying to seem to understand too much, too fast. She'd wound up telling him about quitting her job in Boston when Dylan Hudson got a series of tips, accompanied by a mysterious set of photographs, suggesting that her niece might be here in Maine.

She hadn't said any more about Dylan; you

didn't tell a guy who had just broiled you a good steak about your once-faithless, now-back-in-your-life-again ex-lover. Nor had she mentioned the assignment Chevrier had given her.

"Bottom line, I think my niece might be in the area. I want to find her and—"

She stopped, brought up short for the second time in as many days by the question of *What then?*

Washburn sipped his wine, set it aside. "And see what action turns out to be required? Or what's possible?"

"Yes," she said, relieved at hearing it put that way. "I don't know why I've been having such trouble articulating that."

He got up to stir the fire. "I know the feeling. Sometimes when I'm really close to a situation, it helps me to hear someone else describe it. You know, minus all the drama?"

He turned from poking a log back into the orange flames. "Not that I think you're over-dramatizing anything," he added hastily.

But she understood. "No, I get it. And you're right, my problem is I don't like all the *what thens* that might come up."

"Cody tell you about Carl Bogart?" He changed the subject abruptly. "The sheriff before Cody got the job?" He smoothed one of his dogs' ears. "He was Cody's mentor, you might say. But more than that, he took Cody under his wing."

Washburn looked up. "Back in the day, Cody was a wild kid. I see now what old Carl must've liked in a teenage hellion. But in those days, and for quite a while even after he got hired on as a sheriff's deputy, nobody else did."

He got to his feet. "And then a few weeks ago, Carl Bogart died. Shot himself; it tore Cody up pretty bad. Course, Carl was an old man. But . . ."

"But Cody's more upset than you expected?" She put it out there carefully.

"Yeah. Thing is, Cody keeps it all pretty close to the vest. But if there's anything I can do to help him . . ."

She thought about telling the truth, that Chevrier had added four dead cops together and come up with murder. But . . .

She put her glass down. "He hasn't said anything about it to me. It's always hard when people leave you, though. Or anything you love. But you know about that, too, I guess."

She gestured at the dogs, now peacefully snoring, "You do your best as a vet for them, I'm sure, but you can't control all the—"

"Right," he said, letting her change the subject this time, but she got the strong feeling that he was backing off deliberately.

That if she didn't want to talk more about Cody Chevrier's state of mind—*or about Cody's suspicions,* she thought suddenly—he wouldn't force the subject. She wondered abruptly who else around here had questions about Chevrier, or had the big vet only been making casual conversation?

It didn't feel like it. But maybe that was merely the wine she'd drunk. Washburn stood, all six feet of him, and smiled down at her where she'd curled her stockinged feet up into the chair.

Which was when she realized that looking straight at him was fine, but being smiled down at by him wasn't half shabby, either.

"What say we go check on old Rascal?" he said, and she told herself she wasn't disappointed as she slid her feet into her boots.

"Yes. Thanks so much, it's been lovely. But you're right, I should probably . . ."

She glanced around for a clock, didn't find one among the rustic lamps, woven wool throws, and plump cushions in the den.

It struck her again that he seemed to do well for himself, caring for animals way out here at the back end of beyond.

They collected the dog from the kennel area, connected to the house by a slate-tiled breezeway. His clinic technician, a pleasant young woman named Bonnie who'd apparently stayed late just for Lizzie, had done a thorough checkup and shots on the dog, cleaned his teeth, clipped his huge, jet-black nails, and bathed him.

Thanking Bonnie profusely, Lizzie followed

Washburn out, Rascal padding behind with Eau de Mutt no longer radiating from him.

"The place feels more like a hospital for people than a vet's," she told Washburn, impressed by the modern, clean-smelling facility with its fresh white paint and antiseptically gleaming surfaces.

"Thanks. We try." On their way back through the house, they went down a hall lined with photographs of prize horses, some massive draft animals with shaggy hooves and bulging muscles, yoked four across and pulling carts or farm equipment; others tall, blond beauty queens or sturdy ponies looking as if they belonged on the Russian tundra.

"Some are mine," Washburn said when she asked about the horses. "Some patients. It's not just house pets around here, you know?"

So maybe fancy-horse upkeep paid the freight on this outfit. They passed through a kitchen bright with copper, slate polished to a shine, and an elaborate gas stove with six grated burners, a griddle, and a warming oven. He was the only person she'd ever met who owned such a thing, and he knew how to use it, too; for dessert he'd made crème brûlée, wielding a flame over the sugar expertly.

"There's dairy farms, sheep, and some people will keep a pig or a steer even if they don't live on a farm," he went on, "for a meat animal. The 4-H kids and the FFAers, too. Future Farmers of America," he added at her questioning glance. "So I have a pretty sizable large-animal practice, one way and another. I drive all over the County visiting farms, besides keeping my hours here."

Outside, the hound Cody Chevrier had foisted on her waited as Washburn held her jacket. Stepping out over the threshold, she realized with a pang that she wanted to stay. Because—

Because he's nice, all right? Because he seems like a decent guy. A sweet, smart, non-law-enforcement human being.

And—oh, why not admit it? she thought as they reached her car and he wrapped her in an affectionate bear hug—*because I've been alone for a long time.*

She stepped from his embrace reluctantly, knowing that the smile on her face must be sheepish. "Thanks again. For dinner and—"

He shrugged shyly, suddenly reminding her of a bashful kid. "My pleasure. Come back in daylight, I'll show you around more."

From where they stood on the wide pea-gravel driveway, he waved at the hills rolling away under a moonlit sky, the streams gleaming between sloping pastures, square plowed fields, and the vast, black expanses of forest, looking now like huge shapeless holes that all the rest was in danger of falling into.

Or being devoured by; much more forest than anything else. A city street could look ominous, too, whether emptily menacing or full of trouble. But it never looked . . . implacable, as if it would do whatever it wished with you without explanation.

As if once you were in it, you'd be just another specimen of prey, engaged in the age-old dance of the hunter and hunted. Trey spoke, breaking the spell.

"Yeah, huh?" he said as he gazed over the dark landscape. "Quite the view."

"Indeed." He'd put his arm around her. She let it stay. "It must look even more amazing in the daytime. How do you ever get any work done? With that to look at, I mean. Or do you get used to it?"

"Huh. Good question. No, you don't. Or I don't, at least." He took his arm away, waving to take in the entire scene.

"In a way, though, I'm obliged to pay attention to it. I own," he confessed, "about half of it. Forty years ago my old man owned the whole thing. All you see."

She turned, amazed. "You're kidding. That must be . . . well, I don't even know how to guess how many acres. How did he ever get so much—"

Washburn laughed. "Won it in a poker game? No, I'm kidding. His great-grandfather got some in one of the original land grants after the Treaty of 1842. That's when the Canadian border got put smack in the middle of the Saint John River."

He took a breath. "All the settlers who'd been on their land since before 1836 got to keep it, basically, whether they'd gotten it from the British or from the U.S. of A. And some who were really only squatters stayed, too."

His voice grew enthusiastic. "See, until then nobody could agree on a border. They even almost had a war, the Aroostook War, with troops marching here and plenty of fighting words, but—"

He stopped suddenly as, with a deep sigh, Rascal lay down to wait some more. "But you're tired and freezing out here, aren't you? I'll tell you the rest of it another time."

He let Rascal into the car's back seat. "About the war, and my dad and his many thousands of acres," he finished as she slid behind the wheel.

She looked up at him, noticing the wry twist his voice put on the final words; wry, and something else that was considerably less pleasant. *So. More to the story,* she thought.

"I'd like that," she said. Rascal stretched out with a whining yawn of satisfaction, ready to ride. "Good night."

"Oh, and listen, one other thing."

He bent and leaned into the car, his voice still casual but with something else in it now, something different. Something important.

"If you ever want to meet one of those ponies in the pictures"—from the corridor between his office building and the house, he meant—"there's a woman just outside of town, she's got a couple of really nice ones. Althea Sprague, her name is. If you stop in, you can tell her I sent you."

The name pinged a memory. "Sprague? Was her husband by any chance an ex-cop?"

He was already nodding, like maybe it was a connection he'd wanted her to make. Behind him, the crescent moon low in the sky was pale silver, the color of a knife blade.

In its faint glow, the distant tree line stood sharply in silhouette, the fir tops like pointy teeth. "Yep," he confirmed, and went on:

"Althea's a widow now. Since nearly a year ago. I'd say it was a shame, but I can't help thinking her life's a lot easier as a result. Anyway, good night."

She backed the car around, heading out, saw him wave from the porch steps in her rearview mirror as her tires crunched down the white, beautifully maintained gravel driveway.

A lot more to the story, maybe. With the trees rising up on both sides, the empty, curving road back toward Bearkill was like a lightless tunnel with a broken yellow stripe running down the middle of it.

"You know, Rascal," she said, unexpectedly shaken by the enormity of the darkness, the utter completeness of it. A low "wuff" came from the back seat as if the dog understood what she was saying, although of course that couldn't be.

"You know, now that you don't smell bad, I've got a feeling you're going to be mighty welcome company around here, once in a while."

No lit-up signs or other hints of life pierced the night, just here and there an isolated farm driveway with a yard light, barn doors, and shed fronts harshly illuminated like stage sets for a play that might turn violent at any moment.

More to the story. Like how, after he got his thousands of acres . . .

God, but it was *really* dark out here. An animal scuttled into the road; startled, she hit the brakes and horn together and barely missed it. But the creature, some lumpily gray-furred thing, seemed oblivious in its calm moseying across the pavement, unaware of the bloody fate it had barely escaped.

A mile later she reached the slightly larger highway leading into town. By then her thoughts had returned to what the country veterinarian had said, his hints—were they deliberate?—that he knew why Cody Chevrier had hired her.

That Chevrier might be . . . well, not unhinged. But maybe not entirely reasonable, either, about his old mentor Carl Bogart's death. That Lizzie should perhaps meet one of the other dead ex-cops' widows, Althea Sprague.

And—*admit it,* she told herself, pulling at last into the driveway of her dark little house and shutting off the ignition—that they should see each other again, and not only because there was more to tell of the story of his dad's thousands of acres.

She sat there in the darkness as the engine cooled, the dog waiting patiently in the back seat.

Like how, after he got them, he lost half of them.

Which I will bet any money is quite some story, indeed.

Watch her . . . Spud hunkered yet again across the street from her house in a dark side yard, waiting for her to get home. The people who lived in the house he crouched beside were out at the high school honors dinner and would be for another hour.

Their son, Brett, was the star of the senior class and was going to U. Maine next year. *Yeah, good old Brett,* Spud thought with savage envy. But then his attention snapped back to the present as in the darkness across the street she got out of her car, finally. *There* . . .

Her slender shape, glimpsed for a moment in the light from the open car door, nearly made his heart stop. Everything about her just knocked him the hell out; he might have watched her even if he hadn't been hired to by the guy in the van.

He stared, pierced by an awful longing . . . *But no, don't think about that. Or about what ends up happening to the girls you watch, either.*

The thought came unbidden; he shoved it roughly from his mind again. She wasn't one of them, and besides, he didn't like thinking about that stuff. Silencing his mind, he went on gazing hungrily until the car door slammed and the light went out.

Might as well go home . . . But then the car's back door opened and a dog jumped down. A *big* dog . . . Rascal, of course.

He'd forgotten about the dog. But she'd brought him with her. And now—*Uh-oh.*

As if hearing this, the dog's enormous head turned. But of course it wasn't hearing him. It was *smelling* him, snuffling up his scent.

Panic seized him. *Now what do I do?* If he stayed where he was, the dog would uncover him and she wouldn't even have to call the police, would she? She *was* the police.

But if he ran, she'd hear him, probably see him, too; and the dog might chase him.

Closer . . . As the dog reached the end of the driveway, Spud tensed; if he jumped up and ran, she might not see him clearly. He readied to leap. But in the instant before he made his move—

"Wait," she said. "Sit." The dog lowered its head mulishly, its eyes like two coals staring through the darkness. Only when she seized the nape of its neck did the creature obey, turning to follow her reluctantly.

Christ. He let out a breath. Across the street a

123

flashlight flared briefly; a key snicked in a lock. A tall, narrow oblong of light with her shape in it showed; she urged the dog through.

The door closed, and very soon the lights inside went out.

Margaret Brantwell. Margaret Brantwell. Margaret . . .

Lying in the warm, sweet-smelling straw of the cow barn, Margaret recited the name over and over the way she'd written it in her notebook at school. Seeing how it looked, how prettily it flowed from her pen, and it was just as pretty when she said it.

And soon it would be her name. She wouldn't be Margaret Allen anymore; as soon as she graduated from high school, she and Roger would be married and then they would have a farm of their own, even bigger and better than this one, the one she'd grown up on.

In their stanchions, her father's cows breathed peacefully, giving off the smells of silage and milk. Margaret snuggled down deeper into the clean straw, content. She was young and in love, just seventeen years old and with her whole life just waiting for her out there, and—

"Mom?" A voice came from somewhere. A light went on, making her blink painfully. "Mom, are you . . . ?"

The voice sounded worried. She sat up

reluctantly. "Who is it?" She peered around in confusion at the tractor, its massive tires bulking in the gloom, and at the long, flat wagon loaded with potato boxes, ready to be hauled out into the field.

No cows. No straw. No . . . "Mom, what're you doing out here?"

A blond girl in pajamas and robe crouched before her, a look of concern on her pretty face. "Mom, I looked all over for—"

Who is this girl? She was lying, Margaret realized, not on straw but on burlap sacks. And this barn—

Not seventeen. I'm fifty-nine. I'm in my husband Roger's barn, not my father's. And this is—

"Mom, it's me." *Missy. My daughter.*

"Oh, honey." She managed a laugh, took the hand her daughter offered, and let herself be helped up. "Oh, this is so silly."

She didn't remember coming out here, lying down. But Missy wouldn't understand that, wouldn't—

A pang of fear pierced her. *She didn't remember.* "Mom, you aren't even wearing a coat. What are you—"

Or slippers, either. What had she been thinking? "Oh, honey, it was so pretty outside, I just came out for a minute and then I guess I . . . I must've fallen asleep."

Inside, she took the robe Missy held out for her, accepted the cup of hot, sweet tea. "You must think I'm very silly."

Yes, that's what it is. Silly. Not—

Her daughter shook her blond head indulgently. But there was a look in her eyes that Margaret didn't like.

Not anything worse. "I love this place so much I just wanted to go out and look at it a little while, that's all."

She smiled reassuringly at her daughter. "You'll understand when you're my age. Now you hop on up to bed. You may be . . ."

Sipping her tea, she went on. "You may be Jeffrey's mom, but I'm still yours, remember?"

Finally Missy smiled, relenting. "Okay. Probably when I'm your age I'll want people to cut me a little slack, too, huh?"

"Probably you will." Then: "Honey, I know we've talked about this before. But about Jeffrey's father, I—"

It had been on Margaret's mind lately, maybe because she'd been spending so much time with the baby now that Missy worked part-time at her cousin's bar. Missy had never revealed who the baby's father was, probably because she thought opening the subject would make her own father so terribly angry again.

The months that Missy had spent somewhere away from home—she had never revealed where, either—had been hell, the fact of her pregnancy little more than a postscript by contrast. Now they were a family again, baby Jeffrey a beloved addition.

Still, it was hard to see Missy alone. Families should be together. "Honey, don't you think the baby's dad should know . . . ?"

That his child exists, that he has a son, Margaret meant to finish. But Missy's face closed stubbornly as it always did at the mention of this subject. "Mom," she protested.

So Margaret gave up again, just as she always did. "Okay," she relented gently. "You probably know best about that. Sleep tight, honey," she added, then waited until she heard Missy going up the hall stairs to let the smile on her own face fade.

Jeffrey. The baby's name is Jeffrey. And mine is . . .

Biting her lip, she set her cup in the sink and waited for it to come to her. Then, keeping a sharp ear open in case Missy came downstairs again, she got a pen from the utility drawer in the pantry and inked it in tiny letters on the inside of her arm.

Margaret, she wrote. *Margaret Brantwell.*

So she wouldn't forget.

FOUR

H ey, Lizzie!" It was Dylan, calling from down the street.

"No time!" she called back, jiggling the damned key in the office door lock and hurrying in, meanwhile hoisting her bag and urging Rascal along.

It was just one week today since she'd breezed into town, thinking the place couldn't possibly offer her any challenges and that a dog would be no help. But in the days since, she'd brought Old Dan back to the nursing home twice, both times hearing about his son the woodsman but never meeting this legendary personage; she'd also hauled Henry off another Area 51 patron, delivered Missy Brantwell's mother home after she'd forgotten where she'd parked her car, and right now she was being urgently summoned to find a pig, a task for which Rascal at least was well suited.

"What?" she demanded, rummaging through her desk drawer as Dylan came in.

What she hadn't done was find out any more about Nicki or solved Chevrier's ex-cop murders . . . if they were murders, an idea she found less and less convincing. In her spare time, she'd dug into each of the supposed victim's histories but found no common thread among them. Except of course that they were dead . . .

"I think I found something. About Nicki," Dylan said.

"What? Where?" She grabbed the elusive folded sheet of paper from the drawer and slammed it.

"Allagash. I'm on my way there. A guy, a hunter out in the woods, he got lost and while he was out there he saw—"

"Come on." She rushed back out again, this time with her map of Bearkill and the surrounding area in hand, to her car.

Well, not *car*, exactly; *behemoth* might've been a better word for it. The department vehicle she'd been issued was a white Chevy Blazer just like Chevrier's, big and ugly as hell but with the full Interceptor package.

"If you're a bad guy and it's chasing you, you'd better have a rocket ship," said Chevrier when he'd driven her to Houlton to pick up the vehicle.

And this had turned out to be true. Bad guys, however, were not the problem this morning; bad farm animals were. She shot out of her parking spot; past the Food King, she put on her flashers and beacon.

No siren, though. No sense scaring people for a pig. At the corner she swung onto Route 223.

"What else?" she demanded, meanwhile scanning both sides of the road for a renegade porker. It

129

was too soon to see it, though, she realized after a moment; from the directions she'd been given and her sense of the map, the farm was still a dozen miles away.

And it's a pig, not a racehorse . . . Half a mile outside Bearkill, they were in a logged area. A buffer of trees had been left standing on either side of the road, but now in late fall with the leaves gone, you could see through to the clear-cut beyond: chainsawed stumps, stacks of forty-foot tree trunks, chewed-up earth, and a litter of branches churned together by the massive tires of big machines.

"Allagash," said Dylan again, but he might as well have been speaking Urdu.

"I don't—" More clear-cut sped by. Then the logged-off tract ended and a series of pastures began: fenced, with surfaces lumpy from years of hooves treading them. A watering trough made from an old bathtub flanked a salt lick whose dusty surface had been whitened by cows' tongues on one side.

They must be getting close now, but still no pig. Seven days ago, she wouldn't have understood what was so urgent about finding what amounted to a few hundred pounds of bacon. But now—

"Allagash," said Dylan, pushing Rascal's imposing snoot out of his collar, "is a town. A very," he added cautioningly, "*small* town. Smaller than Bearkill."

To be smaller than Bearkill, you'd need a negative number of people, she thought, then realized that wasn't fair. Everything here looked small by comparison with Boston. "And?"

More fields. No pig. "And it's also an area. The Allagash wilderness area. No people at all, or hardly any."

"Really. That's starting to be my theme song, isn't it?" But again it wasn't really; the town of Bearkill, she was beginning to understand, only seemed thinly populated by contrast with the big city she'd left behind. It was, she reminded herself again as the terrain grew hilly once more, all relative.

"Hey, what's this?" Dylan asked, plucking a small electronic device about the size of a pedometer from the Blazer's console.

"Personal locator beacon." Winding around and down, the road bottomed out along a stump-studded swamp, darkly murky with wisps of mist on it where the sun's low rays slanted through the mossy boughs.

"Chevrier gave it to me. You push the button, it signals a satellite so rescuers can find you. All the deputies have one. Anyway, Dylan, what about—"

"Get stuck in the snow out there," he said, eyeing the device, "that thing might come in pretty handy."

"Uh-huh." Not that she expected deep snow

any time soon. "Dylan, do you not *have* any more information for me, or are you just . . ."

After a chilly start, the last few days had been warmer, like a false spring, and now the warmth brought a sick-sweet reek of rotting vegetation drifting up from the swamp. And—

"Damn," she said abruptly. A gravel turnout flanked the swamp at the road's lowest point. A boat-launch spot? Or maybe it was a picnic area?

Lizzie didn't know, but she did know with sudden urgency that she'd drunk way too much coffee this morning, and hadn't hit the ladies' room in her rush to get out of the office. She swerved into the turnout; the pig—and whatever Dylan had to say, which she was convinced now couldn't be much or he'd have already said it—could wait.

Dylan, she groused mentally as she made her way down to the swamp toward some bushes, knew that even the hint of news about Nicki was a reliable attention-grabber. But if he thought that he could yank her chain just by saying the child's name . . .

There. A low, flat spot, not too weedy and out of sight of the road . . . Quickly, she completed her task and stood. A highway department trash barrel had been thoughtfully placed not far off.

Beside it, she watched a huge bird, long-beaked and stick-legged, step deliberately along the swamp's edge. Dimly aware of a low hum coming from somewhere nearby, she caught her breath as the bird's beak flashed, then came up gripping a shiny minnow.

The hum was getting louder. Puzzled, she glanced around. The mist seemed to be rising, not just up off the water but from the weedy patches and reed thickets around it.

Rising, and surging toward her. The hum rose to a whine as the first sting caught the side of her face, the next inside her collar. *Mosquitoes . . .*

Slapping and flailing wildly, she raced for the Blazer, lunged in and slammed the door, gasping. Some made it in with her and she swatted at them, killing some but missing others, while Rascal's droopy bloodhound eyes followed her jerky movements worriedly.

Dylan, by contrast, was laughing so hard he could hardly breathe. "If you could've seen yourself . . ."

"Get them *off* me." Even though she'd gotten most of them, their whining drone still sang in her ears.

"Okay, okay. Here, hold still, there's one on your—"

"Where?" Panic pierced her, which was ridiculous, they were only mosquitoes, for heaven's sake. But that huge cloud of them, rising up from the reeds like some alien monster . . .

A shudder seized her. "Hold still." Dylan leaned close, his hand cupping the back of her head to steady it. With the other hand, he delicately plucked something from her left eyebrow and drew it away between thumb and forefinger.

Then he squished it. "There," he said, not releasing her. "I think that's the last one."

"Thank you." The warmth of his hand on her hair sent a pulse through her, sweetness and pain mingled so thoroughly she could hardly tell one from the other.

Their eyes met, and for a moment he seemed about to speak. Or possibly to kiss her, and if that happened—*oh, if that did happen*—what would she do?

But then his face filled with understanding, a kind she'd never had from him back in Boston; back when they really were lovers, when . . .

He drew his hand back. She wanted to take it in both of her own and never relinquish it. But—

"It's okay," he said. "I get it, Lizzie, I really do. If I were you, I wouldn't trust me, either."

She sat motionless behind the wheel of the Blazer, still feeling his touch. "Yeah, well." Her pounding heart slowed.

She started the engine. "Rascal's got dibs on the back seat, anyway," she added, trying to make light of what had happened.

Dylan didn't reply, busying himself wiping the remains of the insect off his hands with a tissue from the box she kept on the console.

Soon they were on the road again, and the

moment passed, or nearly so. "What else about Nicki, anyway?" she asked, trying to think of something to say and only coming up with that.

Climbing out of the ravine, the road wound around several sharp switchbacks, then leveled out on a high ridge. Off to the west spread the White Mountains, impressively high and massively solid-appearing even at this distance.

White snow patches surrounded the highest peaks. "Okay, the thing is, a while ago I put a word in a guy's ear," Dylan replied.

He'd put his sunglasses on, aviator spectacles that made him resemble a bush pilot. Now he took them off again to polish them with another tissue as if wanting something to do with his hands.

*I can tell you what to do with them. Exactly what to—*The thought surfaced, unbidden; she shoved it back down yet again.

Knowing he was thinking it, too. "Guy up in the Allagash, he's a Maine Guide," Dylan went on. "Has a business there; he takes people hunting and fishing in the area—you know, they come up from the city for a wilderness adventure."

While he spoke, he fiddled with the personal locator device.

Too bad the pig hadn't been wearing one. "And?" Driving, she kept watching for the animal; they must be getting close now.

"And he called me last night," said Dylan, "told

135

me a client of his had gotten away from him. City fella, up here to bag a moose, guide took him out before dawn and left him sitting in a blind."

Here, piggy-piggy. Sloping away from the road on both sides, the land on this long, high hill was thicket-dense and studded in the bare spots with immense dark gray granite boulders.

"So?" No pig. It occurred to her again that maybe Dylan really didn't know anything new at all, that this was just a ploy so he could be alone with her.

The idea was thrilling and deeply infuriating at the same time. And confusing . . . *Oh, just sleep with him, for Pete's sake. Who would it hurt?*

His wife, after all, was dead. But that way lay disaster, a sure route back to the kind of heartache it had taken her way too long to break out of, last time.

So no more. Here, piggy—

Dylan went on: "So like I said, the guy got lost. Instead of staying in the blind, which in this case was a tree platform—see, you're supposed to sit up there out of sight and wait for the animal to come along—"

Which to Lizzie sounded about as entertaining as toenail clipping, only with less useful result. "Make your point, Dylan, will you? Because seriously, I'm getting old, here, waiting for you to—"

A pig crossed the road. Lizzie hit the brakes,

swung the Blazer over onto the shoulder, and stopped. The pig, black and white with a round, pink snout, had tiny black hoof-tipped trotters too small for such a large beast.

Dylan stared bemusedly as the pig made its way down into the ditch running along the high side of the road. According to the call she'd gotten about the lost creature, the animal—an exotic breed, though how a pig could be exotic, Lizzie didn't know—was pretty tame.

Also, though, it was pretty *big*. "Now what?" Dylan asked.

All she was sure of was that she couldn't let the thing out of her sight. "You call," she instructed Dylan, "the owner." She gave him the number. "And I'll—"

Climbing out of the Blazer, she still wasn't sure. If the escapee had been a robbery suspect, say, or even a . . . But then it hit her: a *tame* pig. From a farmyard, where they probably had—

She opened the Blazer's rear door and waved encouragingly at another animal often found in rural farmyards. Rascal looked up doubtfully, then brightened as he got the idea. By now the pig's corkscrew tail was disappearing into a thicket.

"Okay, Rascal." She waved the big, massively snouted hound down out of the Blazer. "That's right, boy, go get 'im!"

The next ten minutes were an interesting

exercise in hound following, rough-terrain walking, shallow-stream fording, and a tricky bit of fallen-tree clambering over, followed by a sudden, briefly terrifying exercise in not-quite-as-tame-as-advertised pig confronting. Then the pig turned back toward the road.

She'd known pigs were smart, but this one was smart looking, too. Catching sight of her, its small, calculating eyes narrowed into the not particularly friendly expression one might expect in an animal prized mostly for the tastiness of its flesh.

Like, not friendly at all. Also instead of sloping gently as it had where she first pulled over, the ground here ended in a sharp drop. Fifty feet, maybe, she estimated when she eased over to the edge of it, and it ended on a thin, razorish-looking jut of granite.

Not *quite* sharp enough to impale you, but—

The pig looked at her, then back over the edge of the cliff. Out in the high distance, a hawk sailed, outspread wings unmoving, rising and falling on the unseen thermals. The land spread below in patchwork, green and brown, thinly dotted with farm buildings.

This, she thought, standing there covered in mosquito bites she didn't dare scratch for fear of scaring the pig, *is crazy.*

Snork! the pig pronounced irritably. By then, Rascal had caught up to the animal and stood implacably before it, big head lowered and massive, black-toenailed paws planted stubbornly.

"Come on, pig," she said softly. "Come on, I just want to take you home. Nobody's going to hurt you."

Not yet, anyway, she added silently, because of course that bacon, those chops.

The pig, apparently, thought the same, all four hundred or so pounds of it. God, did pigs really grow so big and—

The pig glanced over the cliff, then turned its unsettlingly intelligent small eyes—*yep, those are piggy little eyes, all right*—on her and the dog once more.

After that—

Snork! it said very clearly again. Defiantly, looking right at her.

And then it jumped.

For a while it seemed as if pig levitating might have to become part of her skill set. But almost immediately after the animal's leap, a pickup truck skidded to the side of the nearby road and a lot of teenagers jumped out.

Looking as agile as if they belonged to that circus Trey Washburn had mentioned, they wasted no time in scrambling over the cliff's edge, down to where the pig quivered on a narrow ledge.

There they snugged a rope harness around the

animal's midsection, tying him in so he looked as if he wore a homemade skydiving harness.

But they couldn't take the pig down; the descent was too steep. And they couldn't bring it up; the animal was too heavy and uncooperative. So they were stuck until another truck pulled in, a new red Ram 1500 with a heavy chain winch on the back and Trey Washburn behind the wheel.

"They called you, too, huh?" he greeted Lizzie. Then, sizing up the situation swiftly, he backed to the edge of the drop-off where the animal had seemingly attempted to commit pigicide.

Whining, the winch on the truck lowered a heavy metal clip down to the teens, who fastened it to the creature's makeshift harness. Moments later, the pig rose through the chilly air, its little piggy hooves pawing unhappily.

The only hitch came when the airborne farm animal abruptly transferred some of what had been inside it to a location outside of it. But the kid standing just below jumped sideways out of the pig's target area in the nick of time, and after that—

"Thanks," Lizzie said inadequately as Washburn helped lead the animal up a ramp to the youthful crew's pickup bed. Swatting the pig's rump to urge it along, he slammed the tailgate shut.

"Hey, no problem. Glad that's all you turned out to need," he responded as the teenagers' truck pulled away. "You go on up the road a little ways, though, you can meet the lady I told you about, Althea Sprague."

"No kidding. That's her pig?"

A dozen yards off, Dylan busied himself getting Rascal back into the Blazer. If he recalled meeting Washburn, he gave no sign of it.

"Sure is, and I'll bet she'd like to thank you," Washburn said. Then, "So when can I get you back to my place again?"

He really did have the brightest, smartest eyes, and the way he'd handled the pig problem was nothing short of masterful.

"Get there before sunset, I can show you around outside. And not to brag, but steak's not the only thing I can—"

"Hi," said Dylan, coming up from behind them with a smile. A *pleasant* smile, that only someone who knew him well would realize was not a bit pleasant.

"Lizzie, I don't mean to rush you—"

He looked at his wristwatch. There was no reason he had to rush. But he wanted to send a message, apparently; glancing over at Dylan, Washburn got it loud and clear.

"I'd better get moving, too, I've got a rabies-shot clinic scheduled at the office later," he said, hopping into his truck with the ease of a much smaller man and pulling away.

But not before catching Lizzie's eye and

shooting her a wink that was, if not suggestive, certainly friendly in the extreme.

"Guy thinks he walks on water," Dylan groused when they were back in the Blazer, "just because he knows how to hoist a pig."

Which was pretty funny, and so was the sight of Dylan Hudson being made jealous by a back-country veterinarian.

A pleasant, decent-looking, intelligent, and very *effective* member of the profession, too, she couldn't help thinking. That he could cook was just a side benefit.

"Yeah," she said. "He thinks well of himself, all right."

And so do I, she thought but didn't add, surprising herself; she wouldn't have said Trey Washburn was her type. Still, the crooked grin that had accompanied his wink stayed with her, sweet as a blown kiss.

Absolutely so do I. "Listen, I want to talk to that woman, Althea Sprague. You want to drop me off, take the Blazer? Come back in half an hour, maybe, and we'll talk some more?"

Because she still had to hear the rest of what he had to say about Nicki—*if anything,* she thought skeptically—but sitting and waiting for her had never been his thing, and he agreed. When they got to the farm with *Sprague* on the mailbox, though, and he saw Washburn's red truck in the yard, he changed his mind.

142

"I'll wait," he said when she'd parked. He settled himself in the passenger seat. "Don't be too long," he added, eyeing the veterinarian's vehicle.

"Yeah, right." Letting Rascal out of the back seat, she made a face at Dylan, then turned her back on him and went in.

"Oh! You wonderful woman, you!" cried Althea Sprague. "Thank you so much for finding Mister Wiggle!"

Lizzie looked at Washburn, who was having trouble holding back a laugh. "That," she ventured, "is the pig's name?"

"Well, of course it is, dear, what did you think, it was one of our names? Now sit right down here, dear, and let me make you a nice hot cup of—what did you say she liked, Trey, should we give her coffee or would she rather have a real drink?"

Althea Sprague, a small, wiry woman with a puff of hair like a gone-to-seed dandelion on her head, darted around her farmhouse kitchen with such relentless energy, she was hard to focus on.

"Coffee's fine, please." *You're the one who could use a drink,* Lizzie thought when she saw how nervous the woman was, and why would that be? But then a possible reason occurred to her.

Outside the kitchen windows, the kids who'd brought the pig home were back to raking leaves, cutting firewood, and hauling feed for the animals in the penned yards. Lizzie saw sheep, goats, more spotted pigs, and a couple of bony-looking horses.

"Our new arrivals," said Althea, looking out over Lizzie's shoulder. "We'll fatten them up soon enough."

This was, Althea went on to inform Lizzie, a rescue farm for creatures whose previous owners could no longer feed them.

"Trey helps me tremendously," she added to the veterinarian, who bowed shyly at the praise. But a few minutes later when Trey had gone, Lizzie cut through the small talk.

"I'm sorry about your late husband." Dillard, his name had been.

Chevrier wouldn't have confided his suspicions to the widow. But she was nervous about something, Lizzie guessed she knew what, and when Althea spoke, she confirmed it.

"I didn't kill him," she said. And rushing on, "Oh, I know Cody thinks he's keeping it close to the vest, his worry that Dillard was murdered. But I've known Cody all my life, he doesn't ask questions for no reason. And," she added, sounding a little desperate, "now he's got you here, a Boston homicide detective."

She made it sound like such a thing was unimaginable, or nearly. "And you're worried that maybe I'll think you did it?"

"Yes," Althea admitted reluctantly. "Dill was a son of a bitch when he was drunk, and at the end he always was."

She inhaled shakily. "That's why everyone thinks I'm better off without him. Except," she added, "me."

"You do seem to have landed on your feet," said Lizzie. "If that's not too awful a thing to say."

"Of course I have," retorted Althea. "It doesn't mean that . . . I mean, what was I supposed to do, crawl into a hole and—"

Interrupting herself, she tapped hard on the window with the small but nicely cut diamond of her engagement ring, which Lizzie noted she was still wearing along with her wedding band.

"Those kids," she explained of the youths rough-housing just outside, "they're from a community service program in Houlton. I get them to work here and they get school credit in return. And mostly they're great, but sometimes you have to—"

"Refocus them?" One teen straddled a fence rail, pretending it was a bucking bronco, while the others tried dragging him off. But at Althea's window-rapping, they got back to pitchforking hay.

"Right." Althea bustled back around the kitchen. Unlike the Brantwells' place, her establishment hadn't seen fresh paint in a while, or any Cadillac Escalades in the driveway, either.

But in the kitchen the old black woodstove radiated warmly, and the kids running in and out for tools, drinks, and snacks all had happy looks on their faces despite their much-patched, faded sets of outdoor clothes.

"I bought this place with Dillard's life insurance from his job as a cop," said his widow. "And I can't say life's not easier without him, because it is. A lot," she emphasized, looking back out the window, "easier."

Past the haystack, the view was of the pigpen; Althea smiled at the sight of one large spotted porker—Mister Wiggle, or possibly some other very fortunate creature—plunging his snout delightedly into a trough of what looked like potato peels.

"But I loved him," Althea said. "Even at his worst, I got awfully mad at him and all, but . . ." She turned from the window. "Do you know what I mean? That a person can make you so angry, but the fact is that you love them and that's all there is to it? You just do?"

Outside, bliss spread on the pig's face. "Yeah. Yeah, I do know about that, actually," said Lizzie, "but—"

"Well then, you understand. So tell Cody I thank him for his concern. But he's got it all wrong about Dillard," Althea said. "I think it's even messing his mind up a little."

She looked around the old farm kitchen with

its bare wooden floor, beat-up white metal cabinets and sink unit, and wheezing, ancient refrigerator, then went on:

"He got loaded that night the same way he did every night. Dillard did, I mean. And our septic pipe had frozen the way it did every winter, and he'd put off fixing it the way he had every winter."

The tiny woman with the dandelion fluff of brown hair sighed heavily as she remembered. "So what I suppose is, he went out the back door and stood on the back step and peed off the side of the porch the way he'd been doing since the pipe froze. And then he must've stepped *off* the porch. For a cigarette, I guess."

Lizzie tipped her head questioningly.

"He didn't want to get the smell inside 'cause he'd promised me that he'd quit," Althea explained, rolling her eyes to show how serious that idea was, coming from her husband.

Lizzie imagined the next part. "And there was a frozen patch on the ground, wasn't there?"

From peeing off the porch the way he'd been doing. "An icy patch, from all those nights before where he'd been . . ."

Hearing it, Lizzie could see it: the feet hitting the slick spot, flying up in the air in an instant, and the head coming down, *thud.*

"That's right," Althea said softly. "Must've been early in the evening when it happened, too,

147

because by the time I got home from work and found him, he was already frozen nearly solid."

Her eyes sparkled with tears. "He was good company when he was sober, Dillard was."

"Yeah." They stood there together a minute watching the pig eat his potato peelings. "Yeah, I'm sorry for your loss."

Lizzie walked to the door. "So, let me get something straight, though. You don't think there's anyone else, either, who might've had anything to do with your husband's death?"

Althea shook her head sadly. "No. I mean for one thing, why bother? The way he was drinking, he'd have been gone soon anyway."

"I see." In the yard, Rascal romped with Althea's dogs. "Well, listen, for what it's worth I really don't think you have anything to worry about."

Althea's face brightened. "I appreciate that. It's just that when I heard he'd hired you, I was afraid that . . ."

Yeah, thought Lizzie, *and I wonder who else drew their own conclusions about Chevrier bringing me on?* Maybe the sheriff's suspicions weren't quite as close to his vest as he thought.

"Don't think of it anymore," she said. "As far as I'm concerned, I was just out here to find a lost pig."

"Thanks," said Althea again, her smile now so relieved that when Lizzie walked back to the

Blazer, calling for Rascal, who galloped cooperatively along behind her, she felt she'd already done all she needed to for today. Find a pig, then eliminate an anxiety for someone—

"Hey, back in Boston I could go all week without doing that much good," she told Dylan as they headed back toward Bearkill. "But now, about this lost hunter of yours . . ."

Still thinking, *So some fool got lost in the woods, so what?*

Dylan just wanted her attention, that was all; it was a risk she hadn't considered before, that he might take advantage of the situation. But this was Dylan, after all, so how likely was it that he wouldn't?

A silence, then: "She's here," Dylan said finally. "Lizzie, I think Nicki's in Allagash, or near it."

For an instant she thought she might lose control of the vehicle. Then her vision cleared and her hands steadied.

"I figured you'd better finish catching your pig before I told you," he said, ducking away when she made as if to swat him.

"No, really," he added, "my guy, the hunting guide, he's not going to be ready for us for a couple of hours anyway."

Why not? she wondered immediately, always the suspicious cop. Back in Boston she'd told civilians when they were meeting and where, not the other way around. But before she could ask:

"The hunter I told you about, while he was out there," Dylan said, "he saw a little blond girl. After the guide lost track of him, he wandered around, stumbled into an encampment, and—"

"Could it have been just someone's house?" And by extension just someone's kid, not the child Lizzie was looking for at all.

Dylan shook his head. "Guy didn't think so. Said it was some kind of a weird situation, really way out there in the forest and not a normal house or—"

"Can he find it again?" Suddenly the rural landscape, only a backdrop moments before, shimmered with possibilities.

With hope. "He doesn't know. I was on my way to see if I could get anything out of him, that's why I swung by to check in with you. Want to come along?"

"Oh, do I," she replied, preparing to turn south at the highway intersection, back toward Bearkill. "Where are we meeting him, at the diner?"

Grammy's, she meant, but Dylan stopped her before she made the turn. "Oh, no, he's not coming down here. He's got a camp to run, hunters coming and going. He can't just up and leave." He pointed north on the highway. "I'm going to him. Seventy miles or so, way up thataway."

"Oh," she said. "So that'll take like . . ."

"Good chunk of the rest of the day. He's on an island, takes a boat ride to get there even after the drive, but . . ." He looked impatient. "Why, you got something to do? Go help give rabies shots, maybe?"

"Oh, stop it," she retorted. "I just—"

There was no reason, really, why she shouldn't go, but she should let Chevrier know; she was still new here, after all, and if he tried to find her and couldn't, he might become alarmed.

On the other hand, if she did tell him, and he objected . . .

"Lizzie, it's already nearly noon and it gets dark early, remember?" Dylan persisted. "And I don't know when that visiting hunter is leaving the camp."

To go home, Dylan meant, and if that happened, then she might never get the chance to ask the hunter about what he'd—

"Okay," she decided abruptly, and turned north; almost at once they were in thick forest again, with massive evergreens and hardwoods crowded up to the road like eager if not particularly friendly spectators. Chevrier, she convinced herself as she drove among them, would probably not even notice she was gone.

Spud rolled on his bike up to the front of Lizzie's office in Bearkill just as her Blazer pulled away from the curb; as her taillights flashed at the stop sign on the corner, he let himself in. A couple of days earlier he'd watched a technician sweep the space electronically for snooping devices and come up empty.

So now was Spud's chance. He pulled the items he'd ordered online, specifying overnight delivery, from under his jacket:

The microphones, smaller than dime-sized, that he fastened to the desk and phone. The wireless camera, no bigger than his thumb; stuck to the ceiling, it would be invisible unless you looked hard.

Which she wouldn't. There was nothing up there to look at; in his fervor to make himself indispensable, he'd turned the place into a clean, bright space with new furniture, fresh carpeting, and light beige grass-patterned wall covering to hide the old fake-wood paneling.

Still, he might not have much time to do this. Glancing out the front window nervously, he hurriedly got the stepladder from the utility room and scrambled up it to stick the tiny camera in next to the edge of the lighting fixture over her desk.

He'd been told what to order online by the guy in the van and given access to the PayPal account he was supposed to use to order it. And he'd followed his instructions explicitly.

The camera. The microphones. For this office, and for her house, too; that part would be a trick.

A shiver of apprehension went through him as he thought of it, clambering down.

What he was doing was big-time crime; she was a cop, after all. And considering what else they'd probably find out about him if ever he got arrested for anything, he had to be careful.

Very careful. But when the guy in the van had told Spud that there was five hundred bucks in the job, Spud hadn't argued. Five hundred up front and the same again when the tasks were done.

What the guy hadn't said was why. But now, as Spud returned the ladder to its place in the utility room, he decided again:

Not my business. He'd barely glimpsed the guy's face in the van's dim dashboard glow, but what he had seen had not reassured him. Young, slim, coldly impassive, with eyes that seemed to glitter unpleasantly even in the gloom of the van's front seat . . .

No, Spud didn't want to know any more about that guy at all. He'd be perfectly content not meeting him again, in fact, even if it meant not getting the other five hundred.

Still, he knew he would get it. That had been the scariest thing of all about the guy, the vibe he gave off of being someone who always did what he said he'd do. And what he'd said was:

"Screw this up and I'll kill you."

Then he'd driven off, leaving Spud with no

doubt in his mind whatsoever that the guy really would.

I did what he said, though. I'm doing it now. The tiny camera by the light fixture was invisible. *So he'll pay me. And he won't kill me. And the rest . . .*

The rest was none of his business.

"Big bust coming up soon," said Dylan. "Major cop doings in Bearkill."

They'd been driving for an hour through thickly forested wilderness so remote that there wasn't a cell phone signal.

"Yeah?" Lizzie watched for deer crossing the road—and, God forbid, moose—although luckily they hadn't met any.

Dylan nodded. "What I hear. That's what the meeting Chevrier went to was about, give him a heads-up that the drug enforcement crew is on the way. I hear it's a bunch of meth freaks."

"Not my department." Or if it was, she'd hear of it when she needed to. Right now all she wanted was to get off this endless ribbon of blacktop snaking through the remote north woods.

"So," said Dylan after another little while, "any progress on that thing of Chevrier's?"

"No. Dylan, I'm trying to—" A big truck had appeared from around a curve, an eighteen-wheeler hauling God knew what to God knew where. Straight at them, but the driver got it back over into his own lane in time.

"—drive," she finished, gripping the wheel. The Chevrier thing, as Dylan called it, was shaping up to be just that: his theory, based mostly, she feared, on his feeling that his friend Bogart wouldn't have killed himself, that four ex-cops had been murdered. And Althea Sprague had only cemented Lizzie's opinion.

"Different guys, different jobs, different deaths," she told Dylan now that the big truck had blown by. "None of them lived near each other or had any cases in common. I can't find anything to link them at all, in fact . . ."

They weren't related, and neither were their wives. They hadn't owed money to anyone, and none had cases pending that they needed to testify in, or perps they *had* testified against getting out of jail or prison recently. Nothing at all to—

"There," said Dylan suddenly, pointing at an arrow sign as they came up on a crossroads; five minutes later, they'd arrived in front of a tiny convenience store with two pumps, one gas and one diesel.

She got out and looked around, stretching her legs. *And you thought Bearkill was a small town . . .*

But compared to that busy little metropolis with its own police force, the Food King, and even a bar and an office-supply store, for heaven's sake,

Allagash was little more than a wide place in the road. Lizzie gazed around at its few small wooden houses, all clustered around a crossroads as if fearing to get out any farther into the woods than they already were.

From the trees a few last maple leaves waved like tattered orange rags against a blue sky. The silence was complete. Dylan frowned, tracing his finger across a map.

"Okay, I think it's—"

The old gas pumps still rang up gas in ten-cent increments, and you didn't have to pay inside first. While Dylan continued puzzling over his directions, she filled the Blazer's tank.

Past the pumps, under a sign that read MAINE REGISTRATION TAGGING STATION, a man hoisted a dead deer on a tripod scale. The animal reminded her unhappily of the ones in her backyard.

"What's that all about?" she asked, meaning the scale.

Dylan looked up. "What? Oh, when you get a deer, you tag it and bring it to the station to weigh it and register it. That's how the Fish and Game division knows how many animals are being taken. There's stations like these set up all over the County, at little stores, gas stations, and so on."

"Huh." She replaced the gas nozzle thoughtfully. "So if you wanted to get word out to every hunter in the area . . ."

But Dylan had gone back to his map. Inside the store, a boy of about twelve dressed in forest camouflage and a blaze-orange vest bought drinks and snacks, then went outside again.

"Well, hello there," said the clerk pleasantly to Lizzie. He had a bushy gray mustache and eyebrows to match. With a glance out at the Blazer, he added, "I'll bet you're the new deputy, ain't you?"

He pronounced it "deppity." "Heard about you," he said, "and ain't you just as pretty and smart looking as they told me, now?"

"Smaht," the Maine way of saying it. *And the gossip wire works even way up here . . .*

On the wall behind him ranged tins of chewing tobacco, Slim Jims, and fishing bobbers, phone cards and rolls of lottery tickets. Beer, soda, and bottled water filled the wall coolers, and the shelves offered a few canned goods, cereal, and coffee.

Only the cooler's selection of premade sandwiches was a disappointment, the labels differing but the fillings all looking like the same unappetizing mystery meat.

"Take care," the clerk advised kindly as she paid for the gas and returned to where Dylan had gotten his bearings at last.

"That way," he stated, pointing down a small side road on the map, "three miles. Supposed to take us right to the lake."

157

"You've been here before, though, right?"

She steered the Blazer the way he said, noting that the road was narrow, unpaved, and generously furnished with spine-jangling ruts and bumps.

"Dylan? I said, you've been here?"

"Mmm," he replied, studying the map once more. "Not exactly. But up here there ought to be a—"

"Dylan!" She slammed on the brakes; he looked up, annoyed.

"Oh, come on, Lizzie, just because I haven't done this route before myself, that doesn't mean—Oh."

He looked through the front windshield, then once more to make sure what he saw was really there, and sat back nonplussed.

"You know," he said thoughtfully, "I don't think I've ever been this close to a live moose before."

And I, Lizzie thought grimly, *don't ever want to be this close to one again.*

Slowly the moose turned his head. His dark, round eye was as big as a pie plate, or it looked that way, anyhow. And those antlers—

They were as wide as the Blazer. If he turned his head fast, he could smash that massive rack of branching bone right through the windshield and—

Chewing, the moose regarded them. Lizzie touched the horn lightly. The moose *scowled,* his fleshy lower lip thrusting out. It was not at all the sort of look she wanted to see on a—

"Hey!" Dylan's head was stuck out his lowered window. "Hey, you big galoot! Get along now, or I'll—"

She turned, unable to repress a smile. "Dylan, where in the world did you learn to use a word like—"

The moose *blatted,* spraying half-chewed vegetation onto the Blazer's windshield, where the wiper's sprayer struggled to remove it. But then, as if taking Dylan's order to heart, the animal turned and plodded up the road ahead of them thirty yards or so before sidling off into the brush; moments later they'd reached the end of the dirt road, pulling up into a grassy area.

"Well, this is a fine mess you've gotten us both into," said Dylan, and of course she did not punch him in the head.

"Kidding, kidding," he added, holding his hands up in mock surrender. They got out of the Blazer.

"Hunting camp, eh?" she said in disgust. In the grassy area was a picnic table, a rough stone fire pit, a green metal trash barrel, and a small painted sign reading OUTHOUSE with an arrow pointing down a path into the woods.

"What do they hunt for here, sandwiches?" she demanded.

Speaking of which, she could use one. It was way past noon, and except for the prewrapped horrors she'd seen in the general store, there probably wasn't any lunch material for miles.

Dylan pushed cautiously through the brush at the far side of the clearing, then vanished entirely into it. His voice came out of the tangled undergrowth: "Hey! Hey, Lizzie, look over here!"

Grousing, she pushed in after him, then blinked in surprise. Past the thickets, a sandy beach spread to the left and right. Straight ahead, a blue lake glittered.

Two kayaks rested side by side on the sand; Dylan crouched to peer at a note taped to one of them.

"'Camp is directly across lake. Paddle toward flag. Regards, Herman Nussbaum,'" he read aloud. "That's the guy that I told you about," he added, straightening, "the hunting-camp guy who—"

In the kayaks lay black plastic paddles and bright orange life jackets. Dylan eyed them speculatively, frowning.

"I thought he'd come get us. In," Dylan added, "a motorboat. But if this is the way over there . . ." He lifted a paddle.

"Oh, no." Lizzie backed away. This must've been what the guide meant about getting ready, she realized; towing these tiny deathtraps over here for them to use to get to the island.

Or as he probably put it in his hunting-guide brochures, "Arranging water transport."

Of which, she had already decided, she was having no part.

"No, we'll call this guy. I'm not an outdoors-woman, Dylan. I've never been in a kayak in my . . ."

Because first of all, what would a little girl be doing at a hunting camp reachable only by boat? Or by small plane, maybe. Which was yet another large messy can of remote backwoods worms she had no intention of opening, or at least not without careful research on the aircraft and its operator first.

And maybe not even then. "Come on, Lizzie, it's less than a mile," Dylan said. "Don't you want to talk to the guy in person?"

Dylan was already donning a life jacket. But the kayaks were so small and precarious looking, and how in the world did you get into one of them without getting drenched, anyway?

"Dylan, for all I know, this is all a complete false alarm. And anyway . . ."

"Here, put this on." He took her arm, eased one side of the jacket up onto it, then did the other. "Worst case, you'll get a scenic boat ride."

That was not her idea of what the worst case might be. He finished fastening the jacket's straps and snugged the sliders up tight across her front. "There. You look right out of L.L.Bean."

Which was not, to put it mildly, among her ambitions. He seized her shoulders gently and turned her to face the water.

"Look. Just look and tell me you don't want to . . ."

The sky overhead was paint-box blue, the water so clear she could see straight down through it to the pale green plants swaying on the rippled sand. As she watched, a huge hook-taloned bird hurtled down, struck the water with a great splash, and rose again, gripping a shiny fish.

"Lizzie. Come on. The guy's not going to be there forever."

"Well," she said doubtfully, "I suppose with life jackets at least we aren't going to . . ."

Finally, at his continued urging, she gave in and lowered herself inexpertly into the kayak. Dylan gave it a push, sliding it smoothly out onto the shining water.

"Paddle," he called, so she did, clumsily at first, but soon they were skimming across the small, bouncy waves together, the paddling an easy, intuitive motion.

"Oh," she said happily, and Dylan smiled sideways at her. A loon called from somewhere up the lake; a fish jumped.

This could be it, she thought. *In a little while, I might be talking to someone who's seen Nicki and—*

Then they heard the gunshots coming from the island.

Pop. Pop-pop-pop-pop-pop. Too fast for a standard rifle—

"Shit," snapped Dylan, recognizing the sound at once just as she had. It was automatic-weapon fire coming from just beyond the line of trees marching along the island's rocky shore, thirty or so yards distant.

Paddling hard toward the skimpy cover offered by the rocks—more like boulders, really, they were at least half her size, but Gibraltar wouldn't be enough right now—she was acutely aware that her chest was protected only by the layer of foam in the life jacket.

In other words they were sitting ducks out here. "Maybe just somebody target shooting?" she called hopefully.

But then a round whizzed by her ear with an ugly *zzzt!* and Dylan's arm came up abruptly, shreds of his jacket sleeve flying.

Bloody shreds. Fright pierced her, and she couldn't shoot while she paddled. "Dylan?"

No answer. He kept paddling, too, but when they hit the beach between the boulders, he hauled himself from the kayak and fell.

Jesus . . . Jumping from her own boat, she crab-walked clumsily, keeping her head low and scanning the tree line until she reached him. There was blood in the water and on the sand. She pulled the Glock from her bag, fired twice over the rocks, then twice more.

"Dylan?" He already had his phone out; if she hadn't been so pumped with fright and fury, she'd have wept at the sight. *No signal* . . .

But then she saw that it wasn't a phone at all.

It was Chevrier's locator beacon; Dylan must've grabbed it from the Blazer.

"Gotta get someone out here," he managed as he activated it, "gotta let 'em know we're . . ."

Good old Dylan . . . Of course he'd grabbed it. On the Boston PD, they used to say the only way he'd ever stop thinking was if you cut off his head.

"Fine." *If it works . . .* She eyed his bleeding arm, then poked her head up to scan the trees again. The gunfire had stopped.

For now. Hauling him up, she helped him stagger toward the tree line. Her face pressed his rough cheek.

"A little farther," she urged him. The shooter might still be back there, but on the beach, they were ridiculously easy pickings.

They reached a massive blowdown, some ancient tree that had lost its rooted hold long ago and fallen outward toward the lake. Gasping, she let him down as gently as she could, then pulled his jacket off, followed by his shirt, and ripped the shirt swiftly into strips.

The wound in his upper arm was a small round mouth spitting gouts of dark blood. She wrapped a torn strip of cloth around it, then several more, twisting them all together tightly by winding a length of fallen branch through them and turning it like a crank.

"Hold that," she ordered. "Can you?"

Because if he couldn't, she couldn't leave him; the wound was arterial, she knew from its regular pulsing. He'd bleed to death.

"Go on. I'm fine." His feeble smile said otherwise, as did his color, now nearly as pale as the remains of his white shirt. He angled his head at the woods. "See if . . ."

Right, if there were bad guys in there that she could find, seize, and smack the living shit out of, if possible.

Better yet: *Sorry, Judge. But the perpetrator was resisting arrest and his head accidentally hit my bullet.*

Or Nicki might be there . . .

She knelt by Dylan. The tourniquet was holding. His grip on the stick that held it tight seemed firm . . . for now.

"Do *not* lose consciousness, do you hear me?" Her voice broke and she let it. "Dylan?"

His eyelids fluttered open; his lips pursed in a kiss, then formed a word: *Go.*

Rising, she ran, scrambling up a short, grassy path into the woods, weapon at the ready and her heart full of a clear, urgent purpose:

To kill the next son of a bitch she met. But moments later, when she burst through into a shaded clearing surrounded by huge pines, it was obvious.

Someone had taken care of that already.

FIVE

The *whap-whap* of an approaching helicopter broke the silence in the bloodstained clearing. Through the trees, Lizzie could see two med techs hustle beneath the turning rotors toward Dylan. The next man out of the craft was Chevrier. "Here!" she yelled.

He stopped when he reached her, his eyes widening just as hers had. The smell of gunfire still lingered in the clearing, ringed by a half-dozen small pine-log cabins, where two men lay dead, their blood staining the pine needles under the old trees.

One victim, clad in a fancy, multi-pocketed suede hunting coat and expensive-looking tan boots, had a single hole in his forehead. With his arms flung out and his legs together, boot toes aimed at the sky, he resembled a child making a snow angel.

Only there was no snow, and if angels existed, it seemed he was right now meeting them. "Aw, hell," said Chevrier quietly.

The second man lay in a mess of the bloody feathers that had exploded out of his down jacket when the barrage of gunfire hit him. His body lay twisted and crumpled, one leg underneath him and one arm bent at the wrong angle, the way it would be if a lot of bullets slammed different parts of it in different directions.

Lizzie had seen it, once, that herky-jerky dance. Once had been enough; she swallowed hard, then spoke.

"He heard the first shot and came running out, maybe, to see what's what," she told Chevrier, who nodded.

"Yeah, he would. That's Harold Nussbaum, he's been guiding up around here for forty years." He eyed the body sorrowfully but didn't approach it.

There'd be a scene team; this was state police investigation material, not the county cops'. His job and Lizzie's, too, was just to preserve the evidence as best they could.

"You know the other dead guy?" Chevrier asked.

On the beach, the med techs were hoisting the stretcher with Dylan strapped to it up toward the chopper. Her heart caught as his good arm fell limply off to one side.

But then, turning his head, he waved it in a weak salute, knowing she'd be watching if she could. *Dylan* . . .

Tears blurred her eyes; she blinked them away grimly.

"No," she pronounced firmly, turning back to Chevrier. "We had . . . that is, Lieutenant Hudson had heard that a little girl had been sighted by a lost hunter back here in the woods somewhere. I accompanied him to check it out."

"Yeah, huh?" Chevrier rubbed his chin thoughtfully, gazing around the clearing.

The helicopter took off with a roar and a rush of wind that sent the pines swaying, foamy whitecaps scudding across the lake. Lizzie had a moment to wonder how she and Chevrier would get off the island.

Not that she cared much. Hell, if worse came to worst, there were those kayaks, although even at only a little before three in the afternoon the late-autumn sun already nearly touched the tops of the purplish-black line of pointed firs to the west.

Chevrier's lips pursed consideringly. "So, you hear a rumor about some little kid and the first thing you do is, you get a wild hair and come flying up here, don't check in with dispatch, just think you'll charge right in and find out what's going on."

She steadied herself, then spoke. "Sheriff Chevrier, my understanding was that the hunter was from out of the area. He might leave at any time, go home and be out of our jurisdiction, maybe even not be locatable, and we might not be able to—"

But Chevrier wasn't listening, instead staring again at the body of Harold Nussbaum, whom he'd probably known. "Yeah. Yeah, what the hell, that's what I'd have done, too," Chevrier said.

Whew, she thought. So maybe she wasn't going to get chewed out for—

But then he aimed a stern index finger at her. "If I had a good reason for wondering about it all in the first place, that is," he added. "Difference is, I'm the boss and you're not."

He took a breath. "So I'll tell you what's what. I need you for my own reasons, so I've been cutting you some slack on your private motivations, okay? But when we get back to town, you're gonna tell me what the hell you're up to, haulin' your city-girl butt all way up here to the boonies in the first place."

The chopper's sound faded. Chevrier's anger didn't. "And *if* I like your explanation, I won't *bust* your butt right the hell off this job. *And* maybe I won't put the kind of recommendation in your file, anybody reads it you'll be lucky if your next one's working as a grade-school crossing guard."

By now he was toe-to-toe with her. "Agreed, Deputy?"

She nodded. "Yes, sir. Absolutely," she said.

Thinking, *Somebody saw Nicki. That dead hunter there, maybe, and he was already talking about it.*

So to stop him, whoever has her came here and killed him.

• • •

"Hey." The van, an older but unrusted gray Econoline, pulled up alongside Spud as he pedaled through the early evening.

He'd hung around all day in the office waiting for Lizzie Snow to get back. He needed to know absolutely and for sure that she wouldn't notice the devices he'd placed, or he wouldn't be able to sleep tonight for worrying about it.

But the morning and then the afternoon wore on and she hadn't arrived, and the waiting had worn him down. At last, when it got to be past five o'clock, he'd decided to go—

"You do it?" the guy demanded from the van's driver's-side window.

The snooping gadgets, he meant. He looked twitchier than usual, his gaze dancing from Spud's face to the van's rearview mirror and back again.

Like something frightening had happened to him recently. Or something bad. Then Spud noticed the long, groove-like wound on the guy's jaw: like a deep, blunt claw mark.

Or . . . a gunshot wound? Spud found his voice. "Yeah, I—"

It was the first time Spud had seen the guy clearly: tan, clean-shaven, good-looking in a strange, faintly forbidding way. His eyes looked old, but the rest of his face was smooth and oddly unlined, uncreased by emotion. Like nothing could make him smile.

Or weep. The guy had long dark hair that he wore in a thick braid. He had on a fringed suede jacket with beadwork on the fringes, but the beadwork was fake; Spud had seen the jacket at Walmart.

"Get in." His hands on the steering wheel were slim and strong looking, oddly long-fingered. Without wanting to, Spud imagined them gripping a knife.

"I said, get in." His voice was low and calmly compelling.

Spud glanced up and down the rural road: no one coming in either direction. The guy in the van waited, expressionless.

Then: "You want your money or not?"

Still no one. There would be, though. Spud didn't want to be seen with this guy, but he also didn't want to get in the van.

Not at all. "That's okay," he said, "you can just—"

Hand it to me, Spud was about to finish. But instead the guy's hand shot out the open window, seized a fistful of Spud's laboriously twisted dreadlocks, and pulled.

The guy spoke. "Dude. Don't make me come out there. Just put the bike in the back, hop in, and chill. You read me?"

"I . . . I read you," Spud managed, seeing stars and tasting the blood leaking from his split lip where the ring in it had hit the van door. The next thing he knew, he was inside the vehicle, his bike stashed in the cargo compartment along with what looked to Spud like guns: a half-dozen long ones and a shorter, bulkier one, all wrapped up individually in blankets.

Soon he was riding beside the guy, with no idea where he would end up or if he would be alive when he got there. The guy had a bone-handled knife in a scabbard on his belt; once he'd seen it, Spud couldn't take his eyes off it.

Amusement curved the guy's lips. "It's just what you think it is. And I use it for just what you think I use it for."

The guy wore jeans and a pair of moccasins. Leather, like the jacket, Spud thought. But not factory made; too rough.

"Look in the glove compartment." The guy turned down the old White Oak Station Road, roughly rutted and little used now that a shorter way into town was paved.

Fenced fields lined the road, dark and lumpy with plowed-up earth and the remnants of withered cornstalks. In the chill air, Spud could smell the sweet-sour perfume of the corn heaped up and fermenting in nearby silos, food for local cows over the coming winter.

Spud opened the glove box, wishing he were inside one of those silos, alone in the corn-mash-perfumed dark.

Emphasis on the *alone* part. Inside the glove

compartment lay a rubber-banded sheaf of cash. "Take it out. Count it."

The inside of the van was very clean and quiet except for the crunching of the tires on the rough dirt road.

Trying to keep his hands from shaking, Spud counted out the money: a thousand in tens and twenties. "This is too much. You said—"

The guy's head turned slowly, reminding Spud of wild animals in nature movies, tracking their prey. He smiled finally.

It was not an improvement. "I mean, you already gave me five hundred, so—"

His voice died. The guy kept looking at him. Spud calculated rapidly. He was out all night often enough so that no one would get worried about him until morning. So he was on his own here. His gaze went from the guy's knife to the van's door handle and back again.

"Chill, punk. How come you're so nervous, anyway? You some kind of a nervous Nellie?"

The guy looked back at the road again. But he wasn't smiling anymore, and the question didn't sound friendly.

The knife's handle was carved in intricate patterns. Spud thought it resembled human bone. Although how he'd know that, he couldn't have said. It reminded him was all.

The guy spoke again. "I've got another job for you and I'm paying you in advance again, okay?

Half now, half when it's done, just like before."

He shoved a paper bag at Spud as they reached the old tumbledown garage that the Station Road was named after. Flanked by a huge, flat tree stump as wide as his mother's dining room table with all its extra sections put in, forty years ago the garage had been a gas station.

Spud looked at the bag. "What . . . what d'you want me to do?"

Saplings grew up through the buckled pavement between the collapsed garage building and the two rusted skeletons of old gas pumps out front. The bent metal tops of the pumps, their glass long ago shotgun-shattered but the round frames still in place, looked to Spud like a pair of smashed heads.

That bag's just a trick. He just got me out here to kill me. So no one will know, I did what he wanted so now he—

The guy slid the knife from its scabbard, so fast that Spud didn't have time to react. "Hey!" he shouted, shrinking away in sudden fright.

The guy looked casually up from paring a shred of cuticle from the edge of his left thumb. "Relax."

He put the knife away slowly. "You really are a nervous guy, aren't you? A little pussy, with all your jewelry and your ink."

He regarded Spud evenly. Spud couldn't speak, fearing that if he didn't get out of this van soon,

174

he might throw up or wet his pants. There was just something about the guy . . .

"So are you hiding something, little Miss Nervous Nellie?"

No words came from Spud's mouth. Instead a surge of bitter fluid threatened to erupt from his throat. "N-no," he managed.

The guy sighed, seeming to believe the lie. "I didn't think so. You're a disappointment, you know that?"

Spud thought that this question probably did not require an answer . . . fortunately, since right now it was all he could do just to catch his breath.

"Seemed to me you might have more stones."

Spud's chin lifted resentfully. He felt that under ordinary conditions, his supply of stones was adequate. More than, even.

"But maybe I'm wrong," the guy said, watching Spud from beneath lowered eyelids. "Am I? Do you have stones?"

The answer to this question seemed suddenly very important to Spud, as if his life depended on it. Clearing his throat, he mustered what little voice he could summon.

"Yeah," he muttered. "Yeah, maybe I do."

The guy's lips curved upward again in what served him for a smile. Nodding, he appeared to come to some conclusion, one Spud hoped very sincerely did not involve the knife.

"Why are you doing this, man?" he asked.

Dumb, maybe. But he thought he deserved to know.

The guy didn't answer, pulling the van out onto the road again. Spud glanced over his shoulder at the ruined gas station, the broken gas pumps, and the skeletal trees.

"So," the guy said as they turned onto the paved road and started back toward town. Now that he'd scared Spud half to death, he seemed more cheerful, almost human.

Almost. "So, open the bag."

"I don't get it," said Trey Washburn. "For one thing, how'd whoever was shooting at you get off the island? That's where he was, right? The shooter?"

By nine that evening, her own bed was the only place Lizzie wanted to be. Several hours of debriefing in an office at the sheriff's department in Houlton followed by a small mountain of paperwork had taken all the energy she had. But Washburn had been insistent, and after all, she'd had to eat something.

"Nussbaum had boats on both shores," she told him now. "The hunting clients used them to get back and forth. Anyone could've taken one."

Washburn's chicken cutlets in champagne-mushroom sauce were as delicious as his steak had been. She made a mental note to save a morsel for Rascal, who'd waited patiently at the office for her all day; luckily, Spud had been there to care for him so the dog had been fine when she finally picked him up.

"As for why the shooter stopped, I was shooting at him. Maybe I hit him."

A dark, roiling desire for vengeance rose in her as she said it. *Between the eyes would've been good.*

"But all I really know is that the locator beacon worked," she added, "or Hudson might be dead now."

Washburn nodded, digging into his own dinner. "Yeah, I've got one of those myself. They're great for hunting—the signal bounces off a NOAA satellite, so it's fast. Lucky there was a med-flight chopper in the area, though."

It had been on its way back to Houlton from a training run; lucky, indeed. Washburn drank some wine. "And you and Chevrier, what, paddled back in the kayaks?"

"Uh-huh." This time they were eating at the kitchen island with the fire in the cookstove's side-mounted firebox radiating warmly and the radio tuned to a French-language jazz station out of Canada. She drank some more wine, too, hoping to obliterate the mental picture of blood erupting from Dylan Hudson's arm.

And of the dead men in the clearing. "Anyway, thanks for the meal. I feel like I used up one of my nine lives this afternoon."

She looked across at Washburn, who'd dropped whatever he'd been doing when he heard what had happened. "But this helps," she added, sipping the good Riesling. "It helps a lot."

"I'm glad." When they'd finished, he got up and began clearing some of the serving things, rinsing them at the sink.

"Stay there," he told her when she tried to get up, too. "I like doing this stuff."

Clearly he did, moving around the elaborate kitchen with the ease of one accustomed to being at home in it. Outside the window looking out over the long valley to the mountains beyond, an icy moon was setting behind the jagged trees, the sky a moon-washed indigo spattered with prickly stars.

"So what did Chevrier say when you told him the whole story?" Trey Washburn wanted to know when they'd carried their coffee into the living room.

She'd turned down the cognac. "He was pretty good about it, actually. My having other interests here wasn't a big surprise; Hudson had filled him in before I ever came. After what happened this afternoon, though—"

That violent red splash again, slashing across her vision; she blinked it away, settling into the luxuriously soft sofa as Trey sat beside her.

"—he was very clear on what he wants the ground rules to be," she finished.

No going off alone without letting someone know where she was. No solitary meet-ups with people she didn't know unless she had backup. And most of all, in the event she did locate Nicki, no freelance tries at removing the child or confronting whoever had her, no matter what.

"But overall, I think I can live with what he wants," she finished.

The music had changed; now from the excellent sound system a duet from *The Phantom of the Opera* began floating through the fireplace-scented air. One of the spaniels came over and licked her hand tentatively.

A clock struck ten somewhere; behind the brass fire screen a log popped and settled. And then, without any warning at all, she began to weep.

Not sobs, just tears streaming. *Damn. I'm a cop, dammit, that stuff isn't supposed to affect me—*

But of course it did. It had to, and the ones who didn't let it were the ones who ended up sitting alone with a bottle and a gun, trying to decide which one to put in their mouths this time.

"I'm so sorry," she said, managing a little laugh as she rummaged for a tissue. "After this whole nice dinner and—"

"Don't be." He slung a solid arm around her, drew her close. To her surprise, she let him. "You think you're immune?"

She sighed shakily. "I guess not. Or even if I am, something was different about today."

"Yeah. Today it wasn't some civilian, someone you could put over *there*. In *that* category, you know? Far away."

She nodded against him. His shirt smelled like laundry soap and some other sharp scent, something bracing and medicinal.

"And it wasn't your usual scene," he added as the spaniel settled itself on her stockinged feet. "Big city, lots of other cops around."

I could get used to this, she thought, even through a pang of disloyalty to Dylan.

Right, her mind retorted instantly, *because he's been such an honorable guy to you.* Still, she couldn't escape the feeling as Washburn went on:

"That big woods up there is no joke, Lizzie, so don't think it is. It plays by different rules, it doesn't have any mercy at all, and it doesn't give any warning, either."

He settled his arm more closely around her, his voice softly reflective. Probably it was only her own imagination that made it sound more warning than consoling.

"It just takes people. Sometimes on its own, sometimes with help," he said. The fire popped loudly with a flare of red sparks, startling her.

But then she settled back against him. "What do you mean?"

"I mean there are people out there. Little

groups, some are survivalists, end-of-the-world nuts, tiny religious sects."

She listened carefully; no one else had said this to her.

A weird place, the lost hunter had reported. But now he was dead, so she couldn't ask him any more about it.

"You get back far enough into those trees, you could make nuclear weapons with no one figuring out what you're up to. And I've heard stories about guys who live all alone like wolves out there. Not many, and not often, but—"

"You think that's what happened? The lost hunter ran across someone who didn't want to be seen?" *Or who didn't want someone else to be seen . . . like a little blond girl.*

But Washburn shook his head. "I don't, actually. Not now. In summer, maybe, but now it's just getting too damned cold."

The fire in the huge stone hearth had fallen to glowing embers; the dogs snored softly.

"My best guess is that some local punk tried robbing Harold Nussbaum. It's well known he had wealthy clients at that hunting camp," Washburn said.

"With an automatic weapon?" she objected. Also, she hadn't seen any punks like that around here. But she was too tired to debate, so when he shrugged a "who knows?" she didn't argue.

Instead she sat up. "I guess it's too late to have

that tour of the property you promised me. And I'm pretty tired . . ."

It was not, she felt sure, his own acreage that he had been hoping to explore tonight. But if he was disappointed, he was too gentlemanly to show it. At the door, he held her jacket for her and switched on the yard lights.

"Hey." He caught her in an embrace. "I like you a lot, you know that?"

Drawing her in, he held her just tightly enough. The moment lengthened as almost against her will she relaxed into him; at last he released her, steadying her as she stepped back.

"There," he said, smiling. "Maybe that's enough affection for one evening."

She laughed in spite of herself. "How'd you get so smart?" She really did like him. It was just that she couldn't shake the thought of Dylan, recuperating from a gunshot wound tonight.

His injury, once the nicked artery got sewn up, had proven to be fairly minor; when she called the hospital after her long session with the state cops, she'd been told he'd already signed himself out against medical advice.

Which was typical Dylan, she thought as Trey Washburn zipped her jacket for her, snugging it up to her chin.

"A vet has to learn how to get close," he replied lightly, "without getting bitten. There, now you won't freeze."

"Thanks, Trey," she told him. "My turn to cook next time, okay?" *Assuming there is a next time,* she thought as she pulled the Blazer out of the veterinarian's driveway.

"I mean, rushing out like this isn't exactly a compliment," she told Rascal, who sprawled on the back seat.

The dog yawned hugely in reply and settled again. Having him had turned out to be a blessing instead of an inconvenience, especially since Spud was walking the dog daily; another living creature, one she could hang out with and bounce her thoughts off of without fear of contradiction, was comforting.

Or fear of romantic complications. Or any other kind . . . But as she turned onto her street, her headlights reflected off a car parked in front of her rented house.

A state cop car. For a moment she was puzzled; she'd spent the afternoon with state homicide investigators, explaining how and why she'd been on the island near Allagash that afternoon when the shootings happened.

So what did they want now? And . . . why didn't she see them? Dousing her headlights, she drove slowly past the empty car to the end of the street. No cops . . . but her house lights were on.

When she'd gone out earlier, she'd left only one lamp in the living room burning. Negotiating the turnaround, she headed back up the street. *What the . . . ?*

Follow-up questions from one of the Staties was one thing; even at this hour they were probably still working. But entering her house while she wasn't home was . . .

She pulled into the driveway and parked, then told Rascal to sit tight, still puzzling over her unexpected company.

She could have left the door open. It had a way of seeming to lock without really doing so. She swung her legs out of the Blazer just as it flew open.

Two men emerged, one pushing the other ahead of him. *Dylan.* And—

Dylan shoved his captive off the front step, then seized him by the neckline of his sweatshirt again. It was Spud, his face flushed and his eyes bright with tears.

"You know why this young man might be in your house all by himself?" Dylan demanded.

He was angry, his lean face hatchet-like and his lip curled in fury; from experience she recognized the delayed reaction of a guy who, if a bullet had zigged instead of zagged a few hours ago, would be dead now.

"Honest," Spud pleaded, "I know I probably should've waited, but you said a guy already hadn't showed up to do it, so I—"

"Right," Dylan drawled, giving Spud a one-handed shake. For a guy who'd been shot today, he was feeling pretty peppy.

Or maybe that was part of the reaction, too. She'd taken a round once, just a flesh wound, nothing major at all, and that night she'd cleaned her service weapon, both her personal guns, and all the closets in her apartment before falling into bed at dawn, her eyes wide and her heart hammering.

"Dylan, let go of him." Spud sniffled, dragging his sleeve across his face. Then:

"Hey!" She got up in the kid's face. "Talk to me, bud, or I'll hand you back to that guy."

The kid cringed. "All right, okay? I'm going to, just let me . . ."

Dylan couldn't take any more. "Let you what, think up some fairy tale to lay on her? Forget about it, Lizzie, I already called the local cops, but I'm taking him into custody myself, he can get a lawyer and—"

"I've got a new lock for you, okay?" Spud shouted. For the first time, she noticed the paper bag he was clutching; Dylan snatched it from him.

"I should've waited. I know that, I apologize." Spud rushed his words nervously. "But I wanted to . . ."

The Bearkill patrol car pulled up just as from the bag Dylan withdrew a new lockset, still in its plastic packaging.

The redheaded officer Lizzie had met in the bar got out and came up the walk. ". . . surprise you," Spud finished miserably.

Eyeing the kid in disgust, Dylan shoved the lockset at her. It was a heavy-duty one, the kind she'd have chosen herself.

"I was going to leave the new keys in the mailbox and a note on the door so you'd be able to get in," Spud pleaded.

And so would every junkie burglar for miles, Lizzie thought automatically before remembering they didn't have those around here. Or anyway not nearly so many of them as in Boston.

"He's got some tools inside," Dylan offered, not the least bit apologetically. But she could tell he was cooling off some.

"The tools are yours?" asked the redheaded cop.

Spud nodded. "My dad's. He used to do a lot of handyman stuff, before . . ."

His voice trailed off. "Anyway, I'm sorry. I'm *really . . .*"

The kid looked freakish, but he'd been a real straight arrow for a week now, nothing hinky about him. She came to a decision.

"Okay, big misunderstanding here. Dylan, why don't you go take Rascal down the street, okay?"

Grudgingly he obeyed; his gunshot arm was in a sling, but he looked okay otherwise. She watched him go with relief, the big dog loping

186

cooperatively along beside him, and the Bearkill cop also departed, grumbling about more false alarms.

Then she turned back to Spud, whose bike lay in the bushes nearby. Surely if he'd been up to something nefarious, he would have hidden it better. And he hadn't yet taken out the old lock, she saw; yet more small favors.

Life was just brimming with them tonight. Sort of. "Go home. Leave the tools," she added when he turned first toward the house instead of the bike.

The despair on his face changed to dawning hope. Christ, the kid was a bowl of jelly inside; it struck her that this was what all the piercings and tattoos were about.

Covering the soft inner parts; another reaction she knew too well. "The job'll be a lot easier in the daylight, right?"

He couldn't quite believe it, scanning her face closely for signs of a cruel joke. But when it didn't come:

"Yeah. Yeah, it sure . . . Thanks, Miss Snow," he finished.

She'd asked him to call her that, not wanting first-name familiarity; the phrase "Deputy Snow" was a mouthful for him, around that ring in his lip.

"Really, I hope you don't think I'd ever do anything to . . ."

"Just get lost before he comes back." She glimpsed Dylan's shape and Rascal's, approaching out of the gloom.

Dylan still looked ticked off, his sharp features pushed forward aggressively. One thing about Spud, though: despite his ungainliness and general air of being perhaps the biggest doofus on the planet, he could move fast when he had to, so that by the time Dylan and the dog arrived both kid and bike were gone.

"Here," said Dylan, handing the leash over. Rascal turned his jowly face upward and cast his droopy gaze from one to the other of them.

"I'm sorry I jumped the gun," Dylan said. "I was driving by, and all those lights were on—"

"Oh," she said evenly. "Just driving by. Why not in your own car?"

"Left it in Bangor. Exhaust system sounds funny, I dropped it at the mechanic's and took a car out of the motor pool."

Sure. Or he wanted a vehicle she wouldn't immediately know was his; if, say, she happened to catch sight of it. So she wouldn't know he was keeping an eye on her.

A closer look at his face, though, showed it pale and drawn, pinched with pain he wasn't admitting. And even aside from whatever else they had once been to each other, he was still a fellow cop.

"You'd better come in with me," she said.

SIX

*O*h, *man.* He'd rushed into the job, wanting to put it behind him, figuring that if she came home, she'd believe him, that he was only trying to help. Which in the end she had, because she trusted him, as over the past week he'd worked hard to make sure she would.

But Spud hadn't figured on that suspicious friend of hers showing up just when he did. *Man, that was close . . .* Pedaling fast on his bike toward home through the icy night, Spud wondered what the guy in the van would say if he knew.

But then he stopped wondering, because the answer was that the guy probably wouldn't say anything. He'd just *do* something.

And Spud wouldn't like that thing.

He wouldn't like it at all. Cruising past the high school with its dark, silent windows and empty athletic field, Spud felt a pang of hopeless longing go through him, for the days when he thought "getting good grades" and its equally hopeless partner in his ambitions, "being popular," were all he had to worry about.

The first so his dad wouldn't bitch at him and his mom would smile weakly at him in that sad, already-beaten-down way she had, like having a kid who got As in geography was all she had ever dreamed of back when she was his age.

And the second so he wouldn't be so god-damned lonely all the time. He'd had a friend once; back in grade school a kid by the name of Ty Weston had been Spud's constant companion.

Just not by Spud's choice. Kinky red hair, a bad lisp . . . Ty had hung around, day in and day out, trying to ingratiate himself with a Super Soaker squirt gun.

Spud cringed recalling the lengths he had gone to, trying to shed the little loser.

Like me. Still a loser. In high school he'd started getting the tattoos, holding back some of the money he earned digging potatoes each fall—

And God, you want to talk about back-breaking? Little kids did it, got out there in the fields and waited for the machine to come down the row. Once the potatoes were unearthed, the kids scrambled over the hills, pulling them out and tossing them into baskets. Up and down, grab and lift, turn and drop . . .

Stupid work, his father called it. *That's why you're so good at it.*

Which Spud had been. He'd earned decent money, even after turning some over to his mom. The tattoos and the piercings he'd gotten in Bangor would finally make him cool, make him popular, or so he'd thought; instead, they'd merely made him notorious.

At last he rolled up into his own driveway. Riding made him feel better, like he could get away from whatever he needed to. But once he got off the bike, it all crashed down on him again: *Caught.* Or nearly. The house was dark, his mom asleep and his dad most likely passed out in front of the TV. A loose strip of aluminum siding tapped rhythmically against the side of the house in the icy breeze; it had been doing that all Spud's life.

Inside it was going to smell like socks, TV dinners, his dad's never-ending chain of the thin, brown cigarillos called Swisher Sweets, and the cheap sherry his mother thought nobody knew she nipped at, morning and night.

Plus maybe a whiff of Spud's own marijuana; he tried only smoking it outside, but now that it was getting colder that was becoming problematic. And anyway, what were they going to say, be substance-free like us?

Leaning the bike against the garage, he plucked a joint from his jacket's inside breast pocket and fired that sucker up. But the smoke didn't quiet his head's busy hum as it usually did for him. Instead, he felt worse again, much worse.

Like he might have to *do* something. Something . . . forceful, so he wouldn't feel so weak, so . . . *caught.*

Something like he'd done before. Spud pinched the roach end out and dropped it back into his pocket; waste not, want not, and weed could be hard to get around here if you hoped it would stay a secret. Luckily he could hitchhike to Bangor for that as easily as he could for . . .

The wreckage of tonight's plan cut harshly into his musings again, the memory of his humiliation jaggedly painful. At first it had all gone smoothly; he'd been checking the house out, just riding by as he often did, when he noticed she was out. Pushing on the front door, he'd been stunned when it swung open.

He hadn't been able to resist a look inside. Luckily, he'd had the lockset with him. And she had asked him to do the work, so his explanation had sounded true. What he hadn't said, of course, was that he'd meant to have the new key copied so the van guy could get in whenever he wanted.

To do what, Spud had no earthly idea. He doubted it would be good. Not much he could do about that, though, not unless he wanted the guy doing something to *him* . . .

But there was no sense thinking that way, harshing his own mellow, what there was of it. Standing there in the frigid dark, he let his head loll around on his neck, working the kinks out.

But on his last head rotation, he spied out of the corner of his eye the familiar van slowing down on the road. No headlights, just the vehicle stopping there.

Waiting. At the foot of the driveway, the van just sat there: silent, malignant. Spud wished he wasn't stoned, that on top of everything else he wasn't going to reek of weed once he'd gotten into the vehicle.

Which, of course, he was absolutely going to have to do. Even now, his reluctant feet carried him down the driveway. The van's passenger-side door swung open, the interior lighting up to show the guy waiting.

Face forward, hands resting lightly on the wheel. Spud got to the open door and halted, wishing he'd stopped to pee on his way home.

Because wherever he was going now, he didn't think there would be any rest stops. "Hey," he said.

The guy's index finger tapped the steering wheel lightly. All the rest of him was as motion-less as a snake readying itself to strike.

Suddenly Spud's own house with its socks-and-TV-dinner smell, its fusty old carpets and cheap furnishings and the jerry-rigged shower forever dripping into the rusty bathtub . . .

As he climbed into the van, all that he was leaving whirled vividly before him in a kaleido-scope of longing: his mom's pink foam hair curlers. His father's undershirts.

His own safe bed. But climb in he did, because he was . . .

Stupid. Dumb kid, good for nothing but stupid

work. Anything else, he screws up. Which he had, and the guy must know it. So now . . .

The guy turned slowly. His eyes were like two black stones.

Now he would have to pay.

The wound under the dressing on Dylan's upper arm was hot and tender, the suture line angry looking. They'd given him a pair of orange plastic prescription bottles at the hospital, one with painkillers and the other with an antibiotic.

"You take any of these pills yet?"

He stared stoically ahead. "No. Couldn't drive with the dope on board and they dosed me at the hospital with the other stuff, so it wasn't time yet."

She shook tablets into her hand. "Yeah, well, it's time now."

Give it overnight, she thought, for the antibiotics to show some effect. She grabbed a washcloth out of the bathroom and soaked it in cold water at the sink.

"Here," she told Dylan, holding out the pills and a glass of milk. That he didn't argue told her how awful he felt.

Antibiotics, do your stuff. The wound itself didn't look bad enough to go back to the hospital immediately, but if it wasn't better tomorrow . . .

She laid fresh gauze four-by-fours on the suture line, held them lightly with her thumb while she wrapped the gauze bandage once around his upper arm. "That too tight?"

He shook his head. She wrapped the gauze around a few more times, cut it, and secured the end with a swatch of tape.

"There." In the kitchen, the coffee finished brewing; she brought a cup for each of them to the living room, where she'd set him up on the sofa with blankets and a pillow.

Because nobody, she'd already decided, was going anywhere tonight if they didn't have to. "Dylan, when we were up there in Allagash today . . ."

He drank deeply. Dylan without caffeine was like a car with no gasoline. "Yeah?"

An unexpected shiver went through her as she remembered her first thought at the sight of his sleeve flying bloodily apart. *I'll have to swim to him, get him in a lifeguard's carry, and—*

But he was fine. He was going to be—

"Dylan, the shooting didn't start until we were out on the water, more than halfway there in the kayaks."

He frowned, wincing as he reached to set the emptied cup on the end table. "So? Hell, I'm just glad we didn't pull up on shore right when—"

"Yes, I am, too," she interrupted. "But you're missing something. Don't you think it was a little too coincidental?"

"Huh." He leaned back against his pillow.

"Maybe you've got a point. Like someone staged the whole thing for our benefit. But how did they know we'd be—"

Staged, she thought, but with real people as actors. Real people who bled . . . and died. "Somebody went there to kill those two men."

Maybe somebody who didn't want the story of a child spotted deep in the woods getting any further than it already had.

"Which means," she went on to Dylan, "someone followed the hunter, overheard him telling the guide his story, and . . ."

A new thought struck her. "This guide fellow, Nussbaum, he called you from there? On what, a cell phone?"

Dylan shook his head. "No cell signal on the island. He's got—had—a ham radio setup. That's part of the experience he's selling the city guys, a real remote getaway."

Color was coming back into his face. He'd discharged himself from the hospital, then suffered the consequences. But she'd fed him scrambled eggs and gotten the pills into him; now he yawned.

"Dylan, stay awake a minute. How'd you get Harold Nussbaum's message? Who'd he radio to and who called you?"

Because someone had known they'd be there, and roughly when; the more she thought about it, the more she was sure the point had been not only to kill those men, but for her and Dylan to *see* it.

"Chevrier," Dylan replied. "Harold radioed the sheriff's department, Chevrier called me. Couple more back-and-forths, we had it set up I'd be there by midday or a little after."

"So it was maybe twenty-four hours between the time the lost hunter got found and . . . Dylan?"

But it was no use. He snored softly, his face smoothed in sleep. Injury, pain, and exhaustion plus the pills . . . never mind one cup, a whole pot of coffee wouldn't have helped.

Still, he'd told her enough. Chevrier had heard the radio messages from the guide whose client had seen a child deep in the woods. But so, perhaps, had a number of other people.

Anyone could. You could listen in to ham radio on a scanner, the way they did at Area 51. Plenty of people had them and tuned them to police and fire department transmissions as well as to ham radio messages; for some, like the guide Harold Nussbaum, they were a necessity, while for others they were entertainment.

But that wasn't the point. Dylan slept on while she let Rascal out into the yard and waited for him to return. After that she undressed, removed what was left of her makeup, and brushed her teeth before climbing into her chilly bed.

With a soft whine, Rascal sank to the rug beside her. Poking her hand from beneath the covers,

197

she reached down to smooth his silky ear. "Yeah. I'm lonely, too, bud."

Which wasn't the point, either. Lying there wide awake, she saw the crime scene again unreeling in her mind's eye, but this time she didn't dismiss it. Instead she tried to bring an elusive detail into focus, the thing that made the scene . . .

Wrong. Something flat-out nonsensical about— And then, just as she was dozing off, it came to her and she sat up abruptly. *The clothes, brand-new looking, that the dead hunter had been wearing . . . and the shiny new boots.*

But he'd been lost in the woods. Staggering through swampy areas, clambering over logs, shoving his way in and out of the brushy thickets. So how'd he stay so pristine? He might have put on a clean shirt since then; pants, too. Probably the camp even had hot showers.

But the boots had looked expensive, possibly handmade. He wouldn't have had a spare pair of those along. Also, now that she thought about it, if she'd been lost in the woods that long, she doubted she'd stay another night in the wilderness if she could help it.

The nearest hotel with a hot tub and a bar that could mix a martini or three would've been her next stop. All of which added up to . . .

Rascal lifted his head. Then he hauled his big body up and padded to the window, his nose making a weird snorkling sound as he sniffed a strange new scent into it.

"Hey, boy. It's okay. Lie down, fella." She snapped on the lamp on the bedside table, saw by the blood-red numerals on the clock that it was nearly 3 a.m.

All of which meant that the dead hunter was . . .

Rascal planted his paws, opened his drooly mouth, and let out a howl that the hounds of hell would've envied.

All of which meant: wrong hunter.

The dog bayed again, trotting anxiously from the room. In the living room, Dylan muttered sleepily, then called out.

"Lizzie? There's someone—"

She shot up, cursing when she remembered Dylan had her robe on, then grabbed her long raincoat from the closet, pulled it on, wrapped its belt around her waist, and tied it. Striding fast down the dark hall, she recalled that her weapon was in her bag, and her bag was—

She hit the living room at a run, Rascal ahead of her baying like a crazed banshee. Half off the sofa, Dylan grabbed for his own gun, on a chair with his clothes. But he'd forgotten his bad arm and as he yelled out in pain the front window exploded.

The rock flew in with a crash of glass, tearing its way past the red curtains to land with a thud on the floor. She rushed to the front door, yanked it open, and hurried outside, Dylan's weapon gripped in her two hands.

But there was no one there. Halfway down the front walk, she stopped, swiveling left and right with the weapon but seeing no fleeing shape, not even departing taillights.

A dog barked distantly; not Rascal, who stood stock-still by her side, growling into the gloom. A light went on in one of the houses nearby. Moments later a siren shrieked; someone had called the cops.

Good, she thought grimly, staring into the night, because this time it wasn't a false alarm. An edging stone was missing from the ones lining the front walk, and the whole front window's pane of glass had collapsed inward, leaving a jagged, shard-edged frame like a mouth full of shining teeth.

Inside, she found that the hurled missile was indeed the absent walkway stone, half white-washed long ago from the look of it and the other half dark with earth and crumbly leaf mold.

Also, there was a note rubber-banded to it. Seated on the sofa, Dylan unfolded the note, a sheet of ordinary lined paper torn from a note-book.

Outside, the Bearkill squad car pulled up for the second time that night. Glancing at her, Dylan read the note: " 'Go home. Don't mess with him. Please.' "

He stared at it a moment. Then he began to laugh.

"What's so funny?" she demanded as, outside, the squad car's doors slammed. A sputter of radio traffic came from the car, the sound so familiar that a pang of homesickness shot through her.

Go home. Yeah, that sounded good. Only—

Dylan was still laughing, holding his bad arm and shaking his head as the cops came up the front walk and pounded on the door.

Lucky I'm not a bad guy with a shotgun waiting in here, she thought acutely. "I *said,*" she demanded of Dylan, "what's so—"

More pounding on the door; she grabbed Rascal's collar. No sense getting the dog shot.

"Coming!" she called, just as Dylan finally got control of himself and spoke again, still looking down at the note.

"'Don't mess with him.' 'Go home.' Oh, Lizzie . . ."

With her hand on the doorknob, she glanced back at him once more as he explained what he thought of the implied threat that had been stuck to the rock hurled through her window.

"Lizzie, they don't know you very well here, do they?"

The guy drove silently, and he drove for a long time. Spud hadn't noticed the police scanner on the dashboard before. But now he did, its faint

201

sputtering and bursts of garbled words in the cab's dim interior like messages from outer space.

From some other universe, one where I'm not going to be dead pretty soon. Because that, he felt sure, was the guy's plan, never mind what he'd said about showing Spud *why.* That promise was just to keep Spud cooperative.

But the truth was, Spud hadn't done his job. The guy had known, maybe because of the scanner—*that Bearkill cop,* he thought now—and this was the result: headlights stabbing ahead onto a narrow, rutted track between the trees. No lights or houses, not even any of the hand-painted signs put up by the snowmobile clubs or ATV riders on well-used routes.

Just nothing. But sooner or later they would stop. Then Spud was certain he'd be marched even deeper into the woods, until—

Bam! A rock scraped the van's underside, startling Spud so badly that he nearly passed out. A couple of miles later, the guy slammed on the brakes.

His smooth, expressionless face turned to Spud. "Get out."

Spud's throat closed with fright. Afraid not to obey, he fumbled the van's doorhandle with fingers that felt as thick as clubs. Half-falling once he'd managed the van's door, he hit the ground on legs like pillars of Jell-O, stumbled, and fell.

Crawl. Crawl like a crab, doitdoit getaway-getaway . . .

But the guy stood over him already. "Get up."

Somehow Spud managed it. "Listen, I can try again. I can—"

The guy snapped a flashlight on, waved Spud ahead of him. "Walk."

Spud hadn't seen a gun out, only the ones rolled up in the van's cargo area. But there was that knife the guy had on his belt; that would be plenty. The flashlight beam drilled through the darkness to a path ahead, like a tunnel into the woods.

"I gotta pee," Spud managed. The guy waved the flashlight again, jerking his head toward the side of the faint trail.

Run, Spud thought as he zipped up, but once more the guy was right behind him. "Look," said Spud, trying hard to sound as if he were being reasonable.

Instead of pleading for his life. Begging . . . any minute, he knew, he was going to start sobbing like a little kid.

The guy sighed. "Just walk," he said patiently. Because of course he could afford to be patient, couldn't he?

He knew where he was, and he had the van keys. Also, he had that knife. "Go on," the guy said, gesturing out ahead again with the flashlight. "You wanted to know. Now you'll see."

So Spud did, having no choice; one foot in front of the other, down a path that grew narrower and less discernible with each step. Soon he was pushing through thick brush, long thorns needling his hands and clawing at his face.

After that came head-high saplings slapping him whiplike, then a bog that threatened to pull him down with each sucking step. Gasping, Spud struggled forward, wondering if the guy meant to march him to death.

Although when he glanced back, the guy seemed to be moving along quite easily. *Because he knows the way, where to step.*

Because he's been here before. Burying his victims, maybe. Another harsh hiccup of fear made Spud's gut clench, just as a low branch hit him hard, square in the forehead.

He felt the ground hurtling upward at him, then the guy's hand catching the neck of his T-shirt and twisting it, hauling him up by his throat with Spud too scared and exhausted even to flail effectively. God, it was cold out here. On his feet once more, he just stood dumbly gasping into the darkness.

Because at night, more than anything else that it was, the forest was *dark*. Like a cave.

Or a grave. "Can't," he whispered, distantly amazed at how quickly he'd been brought to this condition of helplessness, of utter not-caring about anything. It was the fear, he knew, that had done this to him. "Kill me or whatever. Just . . . whatever."

Behind him the guy paused as if acknowledging this, Spud waiting for the knife with his head bowed and his arms at his sides. The guy stood close behind him, pushing him up against a curtain of dark spruce branches. *Come on, come on . . .*

Get it over with, he thought. But when the blow came, it was not the sharp knife thrust Spud expected. Instead—

"Get in there," the guy said, then reared back and kicked Spud hard, hurtling him through the spruce-bough curtain into a clearing lit by a small campfire.

A clearing with a little girl in it.

As Spud burst through into the clearing, the child sat up. A woven hammock suspended between two posts held her, wrapped in a zipped-up sleeping bag. Her head rested in a rough fur-lined hat.

She was, Spud guessed confusedly, about nine years old: taller than a little kid, shorter than a teenager. In the orange flickering firelight, her gaze searched the clearing and found him still windmilling his arms to stay upright.

She did not make a sound, only looked past him to where the guy now came through easily, slipping between the spruce boughs as if they weren't there at all.

Or as if *he* weren't, as if he were some kind of ghost or bad spirit, haunting these woods and . . .

Stop that. Cold and scared, Spud felt his mind beginning to play tricks on him, making up a story that explained it all.

No matter how impossible the story was. Because this . . . this was *more* impossible, wasn't it? The guy crossed to a second hammock.

Behind it stood a small tipi-style structure covered in bark and evergreen branches. To one side, an open lean-to held tarp-draped shelves filled with canned goods, jars of what looked like rice and other things Spud couldn't identify.

As his eyes adjusted, he saw that the tops on some containers were bulging, the contents leaking. But before he could think about what that meant, the second hammock moved.

A woman sat up from it, swinging her thickly stockinged legs over the side in a practiced motion. Spud stared as the woman crossed the clearing and ducked into the lean-to.

A moment later she emerged with some items on a rough wooden tray: mugs, a loaf of dark bread, a jar of instant coffee. She kept her head turned as if she didn't want him to see her face.

Still, he began to feel hopeful. Probably the guy wouldn't kill him in front of these two. *But, man, this is so . . .*

With a jerk of his head, the guy summoned Spud closer. "Sit."

Spud obeyed swiftly. For one thing, relief was making him feel faint; once he got moving, if he didn't sit down by the fire he thought he might topple into it.

The child's pale blond hair shone from around her hat's brim as she turned over in her hammock. The woman set the tray down, keeping her face averted, then recrossed the clearing and got back into her own hammock, all without a word.

The guy broke the bread, thrust a chunk of it out at Spud. He poured steaming water from the kettle hung over the fire into the mugs and spooned in instant coffee. "Drink it."

The hot liquid felt scalding going down. But it warmed Spud from the inside, and when he'd dunked the dark, coarse bread into it and eaten some, he began to feel almost human again.

The guy ate steadily as well, consuming his food in small, even bites. When it was gone, he drained his cup, rinsed it with more hot water from the kettle, and crossed the clearing to toss the rinse water out.

The water made a shining arc, sparkling in the firelight, then hit the darkness out there and was gone.

Swallowed up . . .

The guy went to the lean-to, came out with a blanket, and threw it at Spud, then returned to the fire and dropped to his haunches. The way he bounced lightly on the balls of his feet, freshly energetic even after their long hike, told Spud that any ideas he might be having about escape strategies were not only foolish, they would probably be fatal.

That is, if this whole escapade didn't end up being fatal, anyway. "So," he ventured.

He'd finished his coffee. Maybe, he thought, he should rinse his cup, too, and toss the rinse water out. That seemed to be the drill around here.

The guy eyed him steadily, like a cat waiting for a mouse to try making its move. *Nah, probably not.*

He cleared his throat and spoke again. "So, am I, like, your prisoner here or what?"

The guy shook his head. He had what was almost certainly a knife scar under his left eye. It did not, Spud noted acutely, make the guy any friendlier looking.

"Listen, I'm really sorry," he went on when the silence had lengthened uncomfortably. "I screwed up. I was trying to change the lock, I didn't know that the other cop was going to show up just when—"

The guy's face stayed emotionless. He looked down at the fire, its faint popping and crackling the only sounds in the forest darkness, its flickering in the low evergreen branches over-spreading the clearing like some ancient dance, full of strange light and shadow.

You see it and die, Spud thought very clearly as

a shiver that had nothing to do with the cold night air went through him.

"I've been thinking about you." The guy changed the subject. "Who you are, what motivates you."

Great, Spud thought dismally. *Life lessons from some whacko with a Daniel Boone complex.* But the guy's voice was low, sort of hypnotic in a weird way, and Spud was tired.

"Yeah?" he muttered. Tired and scared, though the Jell-O-legged terror had gone. A passive, frozen-in-place kind of fright had replaced it deep in his bones like some icy infection.

The guy regarded him. "Yeah," he said at last. "And what I think is, you're smarter than I thought."

Well, duh, Spud thought. But silently. The guy went on:

"In fact, now that I know you better, I think maybe you've got a few dirty little secrets of your own, hmm?" The guy peered intently at him.

No. No, Spud thought, and then, *How could he know?* It was a part of his life that he kept locked up, buried safely away. *No one knows, so how could—*

"Also," the guy went on smoothly, "I think you work best when you understand why you're doing things. Besides knowing I'll gut you like a fish if you don't do them, I mean."

A small smile twitched his lips briefly. Then:

"So here's the deal. I'm just a person like anyone else."

Uh-huh. Spud kept the skepticism off his face.

"That's my woman." The guy gestured at the second hammock, while Spud noticed: *Not "my wife," or "my girlfriend."*

"My woman," like he owns her or something.

"When I found her, the kid was with her. So now I take care of both of them. And that's all I want, to be left alone, live my life the way I please. That's my right as a man and a citizen, wouldn't you agree?"

Clear, simple . . . *My right as a man.*

"Yeah," Spud said again, but less sullenly this time because who could argue with that?

"Right now, I want to move out of here. It's getting cold, the food is starting to freeze . . . maybe to a place in town for the winter, somewhere with heat."

Also perfectly understandable. The frozen fear in Spud's own veins melted a little, so it no longer felt as if his heart were pumping ice chips with each pounding beat.

Still crouched easily on his haunches—Spud got the feeling the guy could've stayed that way for hours—his captor added:

"But I can't, because the woman you've been watching wants the kid."

The kid in the hammock, he meant. Spud felt

his face wrinkle into a puzzled grimace. "What? Come on, why would she . . . ?"

At the same time, he got a strong, strange feeling that the woman in her own hammock was listening to all this; that her stillness at the edge of the firelit clearing wasn't of sleep.

As if to prove it, at the guy's last words about the little girl, the woman sat up and turned anxiously.

That was when Spud got his first real look at her face, and at the thick, purple scar that ran from the corner of her mouth all the way to where her hair covered her ear.

That's why she stays with him, Spud thought clearly.

The guy didn't notice, or didn't seem to. "No one is allowed to mess with them. But the cop wants to. And that can't be. See?"

He got to his feet, reminding Spud of a snake uncoiling itself. "It's as simple," he added, "as that."

"But h-how?" Spud managed, clambering up himself on legs that were suddenly shaky with fright again. "How d'you know it's what she wants?"

The guy gazed flatly at him. "The dark-haired guy she hangs out with, that state cop? He's been around here before, asking a lot of questions about a missing kid. A little blond kid. I heard he's even got a picture."

"So? That doesn't mean—"

"And now all of a sudden *she's* here, and they're tight as ticks, those two. They even came up-country looking for the kid."

Up-country; it was what people around here called the woods far beyond the towns. Like here, for instance.

"So what would you think?" the guy went on. "Coincidence? Or would you figure maybe now they're both in on it? Trying," he added, his tone turning icy, "to take what's mine, just like—"

"Yeah," Spud agreed hurriedly. "Yeah, you're right."

Never mind whether it was true. Agreeing with the guy was his best chance at getting out of here. "But . . . why don't you just leave, then? Go far away? I mean, you've got the van and—"

"I'm a businessman, that's why," the guy snapped back. "And I'm not giving up on my business just because—"

Business? Spud thought. *In what, sticks and pinecones?* But then it occurred to him what else might be in the lean-tos.

"Anyway, never mind," the guy said. "I've got enough on my plate right now, things are happening and I've got to stay on top of them. So all I want from you is to do what I say, when I say it. And now you know why. Have you got that?"

"Y-yes." Biting his lip, Spud averted his gaze,

then saw, with eyes now adjusted to the dark, that there was another of the low structures just beyond the clearing's edge.

Another lean-to, one with more shelves in it, and on the shelves were small bundles rolled up in . . . what was that, plastic wrap?

The guy's hand gripped his shoulder, viselike. "Curiosity killed the cat, buddy. Don't forget that."

Spud jumped startledly. "I-I won't. Really, I—"

The guy spun him around, seized both his shoulders, and held him for a moment, long enough for Spud to see what the guy wore on a leather thong around his neck, small and shriveled and fixed to the leather by a thin silvery wire.

"That's good," he said, releasing Spud and at the same time giving him a little shove—

Not hard, just enough to make Spud shuffle clumsily and step unseeing nearly into the campfire while he tried not to vomit.

"I'm very glad you understand," said the guy, catching Spud before he could stumble into the flames. "Because I've got a big assignment for you. And it would be a shame if you messed it up."

His grip was still strong, his voice still smooth, almost friendly—*almost!*—and that *thing* . . .

"Your friends in town need a distraction, something else to think about."

Spud closed his eyes, but he couldn't stop seeing it.

"So here's what you're going to do . . ."

That *thing*—

The thing on the guy's necklace was a human thumb.

SEVEN

The screech of the brakes and the blare of the car horn outside her office the next morning were bad enough, but the silence that came after the thump was horrifying.

"Dylan, what are you doing here? I mean, still here?" she'd just that moment asked, and he'd smiled wisely at her but hadn't replied, hunched over his coffee.

Moments later they were charging out the front door of her office. "I mean seriously," she persisted as she ran, noting with surprise that he was not only keeping up, he was ahead of her.

It was just one day after he'd been shot, helicoptered out of the wilderness site, and patched up in surgery. After that, the rock through her front window had ended any hope of a night's sleep for either of them.

Not only that but Trey Washburn's truck had been passing by her house just as she and Dylan came out of it. On the dead-end street, it couldn't have been an accident; he'd been stopping by to see her, no doubt, and had seen something else instead.

A quick wave, a tight smile, and the veterinarian was gone, almost certainly drawing absolutely the wrong conclusion—

And now here Dylan was, sprinting along as if he hadn't had a hole blown through him less than twenty-four hours earlier; it was infuriating sometimes, this wiry resilience of his.

"Over there." He pointed at a white sedan with its hazard lights on, stopped in the middle of the street with its driver's-side door open and people gathering around it.

"I'm doing what you're doing." He answered her original question as they reached the scene, civilians crowding around it.

"Okay. Step back. Coming through." She took control, amazed as always by the wonders an authoritative tone could work.

And by the fact that once she'd learned it, she was pretty much golden in the telling-'em-what-to-do department. "What?"

The victim lying in the street was Old Dan from the nursing home, and this time it seemed he'd driven his motorized chair right out in front of a car. She assessed him swiftly while Dylan started directing traffic one-armed, his only concession to his wound that Lizzie had seen all morning.

"I'm looking around," Dylan went on, coaxing a timid Jeep from behind the stopped sedan, then urging an old station wagon in the other direction. "Okay, keep moving," he called, waving at the next car in line.

"That's not—" she began, and then Old Dan seized her hand.

"My son," he whispered, "is king of the forest."

"Right, Dan," she responded reassuringly. "I know. Listen, we need to get you—"

The standard phrases came out automatically, and Old Dan seemed okay, though his motor chair looked totaled. The driver of the car that had hit him seemed in worse shape:

"Oh my God," he kept saying. "Oh my—"

But he'd be okay. Meanwhile the question that had woken Lizzie before dawn: What *was* Dylan still doing here, anyway?

He wasn't on vacation, the shooting at the lake wasn't his case, and there was no case—at least, not yet—concerning the dead ex-cops Chevrier was so concerned about, so that wasn't it, either.

Yet he was still hanging around in Bearkill, and the only other explanation she could think of was . . .

He glanced at her, meanwhile expertly choreographing the flow of traffic around the accident site. "Lizzie, I know what you're thinking."

She felt a flush climb her neck; of course he did. And it was yet another infuriating thing about him. *Infuriating and—*

"But it's not you, okay?" The Bearkill squad car arrived; gratefully, she got to her feet, but not before Old Dan grabbed her hand once more.

"He tells me," the elderly man said, bright-eyed. "He tells me about . . . his *packages!*"

"Okay, Dan," said the local cop. Behind him

two EMTs with a neck brace and a stretcher pushed in impatiently. Straightening, she left it all to the cops whose job it was.

"I'm here in Bearkill talking to folks," Dylan said as she hurried to catch up. "Getting impressions, asking questions. You know," he added as they headed to her office again.

"You mean you're . . ." Did he mean he was working a case? Exasperation flooded her, that he hadn't told her about it, and—*admit it*—the tiniest pang of disappointment, too.

He shrugged, winced as his wounded arm reminded him not to.

"Maybe. There's a thing. I'm not sure if it means anything or not."

They walked in together. Spud hadn't come in yet this morning, too embarrassed maybe by his performance the previous night.

"See, there were a couple of girls down in Bangor. They went out partying and never came back. Bodies found soon after. One last spring and another one about a month ago."

She pushed open the office door; still no Spud. "Dylan, you really think somebody from here might've . . ."

Inside, Rascal lay chewing his brontosaurus femur. Dylan shook his head. "Don't know. One of the dead girls had mentioned to one of her friends that she'd met someone from the County."

Which was what people here called Aroostook County, as if there could be no other.

"And that's all we've got," said Dylan. "Can't say I'm getting anywhere with it here, either."

He sank into her office chair and she let him, still too wired up by seeing Old Dan nearly pulverized to relax. And there was something else still bothering her, too.

"Listen, sorry about your case. But closer to home . . . I think maybe our shooter yesterday blew away the wrong hunter."

He looked up interestedly. "Yeah, you know, that bugged me, too. The boots, huh?"

"Uh-huh." She'd described what she'd seen to him, as thoroughly as possible. "So try this on. First guy, the lost hunter, sees something he shouldn't out there in the woods. And once he gets back, his time at the camp is up and he's supposed to go home. So . . . he does?"

"And then a new hunting client shows up," Dylan supplied.

"Right, but the shooter doesn't know that. He thinks he's killing the guy who saw . . . whatever he saw."

"A little girl," Dylan agreed. "That's what Nussbaum said his client had seen. So basically the shooter kills the second hunter instead of the first one by mistake?"

"Uh-huh. Unless . . ." She went on to the other thing that was still bothering her.

The scary thing. "Dylan, what if it was no mistake? Like we said last night, what if whoever it was knew somehow that we were coming?"

He frowned puzzledly; she went on. "I mean, what if the first guy left and our shooter *did* realize it?"

Then he got it, his dark eyes narrowing. "So when we get there, the shooter's waiting. Maybe he heard radio traffic and that's how he knew when to expect us. We get close, he attacks us, then kills the new hunting client and Nussbaum, too—"

He stopped. "But why? He's got to know shooting cops is a good way to bring the hammer down."

"Yeah, maybe. But what if no one found out? Way out there in the woods . . . Dylan, if he'd gotten both of us, we might not have been found for a long time."

In the city it would be nearly impossible. But here where the trees outnumbered people . . .

"He gets my keys, he weighs down our bodies in the lake, he puts the kayaks back where they were and hides my vehicle. Maybe the other bodies, too. Presto, we've vanished without a trace."

And just like that, anyone who'd seen a child or heard the story of one would be . . .

"One problem," Dylan objected. "The original hunter. The cops looking for us would track him down and—"

220

From Nussbaum's records, he meant; surely he kept some. But: "So what? He can't lead them back to where he was when he saw that camp or whatever it was. He was lost, remember?"

She shook her head decisively. "And he doesn't know anything about us at all. Case," she finished, "closed."

Dylan looked thoughtful. "Yeah. Yeah, maybe." He pulled his phone out and punched numbers into it.

"Toby?" he said. "Yeah, it's Hudson. Listen, the hunter who was at Nussbaum's before yesterday's shooting? I need to talk to him. You got names and numbers from a . . . What did Nussbaum have, a guest book, maybe? Yeah? You got that handy?"

He waited, pulling out a pad and scribbling on it. "Newton. Andrew Newton . . . Yeah, thanks," he said, then punched in another number and asked for Nussbaum's previous hunting client.

The one who hadn't been shot, who'd left before . . . But then a frown creased his forehead. "Really. I'm so sorry. It happened when? I see."

He glanced up at Lizzie, shook his head minutely, scowled at the phone again. "I'm sorry to hear that. My sympathies. Sorry to trouble you."

"What happened?" she demanded when he hung up.

He grimaced. "Well, our guy has apparently

221

gone from being the luckiest hunter on the planet to the unluckiest."

He tucked the phone away. "Seems he flew out of Bangor to Teterboro, took a cab home, and got hit by a car outside of his apartment late last night, in Manhattan. Hit-and-run. The cops are looking but there were no witnesses."

She couldn't speak. Finally: "So she's out there. Nicki's out there in the woods, Dylan, he saw her and . . ."

Searchers, she thought. *The warden service can help. Dogs, Border Patrol officers. We'll put posters up at the deer-tagging stations—*

And she'd go out there. Had to. "Get Chevrier on the phone, will you?" she snapped. "Tell him I'm closing up this office for a little while, I've got to—"

Nicki. Her throat closed convulsively. *Honey, I'm coming, I'll make it up to you, I swear I will.*

But Dylan didn't obey, instead seizing her shoulders to gaze down into her face. "Lizzie, it's not that easy."

She shoved him away. "Easy? What do I care? You think it's been easy for her, all these years in who knows what kind of a mess?"

She rummaged in her bag. *Weapon, ammunition, phone.* All fine, but not enough. Before she left, she'd have to find out what else a person needed for a long trip into the—

"*Lizzie.*" Dylan grabbed her again, this time

222

wrapping his arms tightly around her so she couldn't free herself.

"Listen to me, dammit. You—we—can't just go charging out there. We still don't know where she is, or even if it's her for certain. And we don't know who has her."

Imprisoned in his embrace, fists clenched against his chest, she gasped for breath, so full of emotion and urgency that there seemed no room for air. "Let . . . me . . . go. I've got to—"

"Yes. You do. But not like this. You could get her killed, Lizzie, don't you see that? You saw Nussbaum and the guy with him, and now the other hunter's dead, too, just like we'd be if that weapon he was using had any kind of accuracy at distance."

He held her more tightly. "What do you think, that was just a convenient accident, that hit-and-run, some kind of coincidence?"

She stopped struggling. "No." *Of course it wasn't, that was why she had to . . .* "No, I—"

He relaxed his arms. But he kept them around her, and to step away from him now seemed . . . well, it was too much to ask of herself, that was all. Just too much.

"This is no local yokel, Lizzie. Or if he is, he's a yokel with some unusual connections. Now, it could've been a coincidence, the hit-and-run."

"But you don't think it was."

He hesitated. Stranger things had happened

and they both knew it. But then he shook his head.

"No. Or at any rate it's not safe to assume that. Because it's possible that after the shooting, someone else got a look at that guest register of Nussbaum's, too, and realized he'd made a mistake."

And then made a phone call to New York, to someone who could correct it. Which of course implied knowing someone there who could and who would want to.

"But let's not get ahead of ourselves," said Dylan. "Because if we're not wrong, we need a plan. We need to find out more, starting with exactly where this camp that the lost hunter saw is, how many people are there, how many weapons . . ."

She nodded again. He was right, of course. And she'd step away from him in a minute; she would. But for right now . . .

"I've always known I'd have to do this," she whispered into his shoulder.

"Find her, no matter what. But I put it off, made excuses, I told myself she was probably dead," she went on. "I told myself that and somehow the time went by until—"

Until I couldn't stand it anymore.

"I know. I knew back when we were together." He moved her gently away from him, his hands on her shoulders. "You're an open book to me, kiddo. Sorry, but that's just how it is. And I'm on your side, whether you like it or not. Got it?"

She got it, and for a moment she was tempted yet again, remembering how it had been between them: everything she'd wanted and more.

Much more. "Oh," she said, which was when Trey Washburn came through the door, head down, not seeing them until he was inside.

But then he did see, and he understood, too. "Sorry, I—"

Confusion and hurt clouded the big veterinarian's gaze. "Lizzie, I just wanted to say I heard about the trouble at your place last night, wondered if there's anything I can do to help."

He glanced at Dylan, then at Lizzie again. "But I see you've got all the help you need," he finished with a last, terribly communicative look at her.

Wordless. It didn't need words, did it?

Way to go, Lizzie, she thought. *Way to go.*

"So I guess I'll be leaving now," Washburn said evenly, and went out again, closing the door very firmly behind him.

Then Dylan spoke. "Lizzie? Look, Lizzie, I'm sorry if I—"

She whirled on him. "Shut up, Dylan, okay? That right there, what just happened? Him coming in? That was luck."

Because Dylan was a heartbreaker; he'd done

it before and if she let him, he'd . . . She stalked to her desk.

"Like a jumper getting yanked back off a ledge," she went on cruelly, seeing him flinch.

"We might be working together—you've got connections I need so I don't seem to have a lot of choice about that."

Or about some other things, either, her still fast-beating heart added wickedly.

She told it to shut the hell up, too. Just . . . "But don't touch me anymore. And no more of your meaningful little looks. Stop—"

"Stop what?" he inquired innocently, and from the mischief in his grin she knew she might as well have been shouting into the wind. But at the moment, she wasn't being carried away by it, anyway, and for that she felt almost grateful.

Almost. Meanwhile her search for Nicki had just taken a sharp turn, hadn't it? A ninety-degree swerve into who-the-hell-knows-land.

"I'm calling the warden service," she told Dylan. "Because you're right, we need more info, and to get it, we need to find this guy and check out his whole setup. Weapons, personnel . . ."

"Might be hard to hold off the bod squad," he warned, "if the wardens deliver a solid fix on their suspect."

The homicide guys, he meant. They'd be hot to make their collar, grab up a shooter who'd already killed at least two and maybe more, and who'd attacked her and Dylan besides. And if there ended up being a little blond girl in the crossfire . . .

Well, if there *was* crossfire, they'd try to avoid her, of course. They'd try as hard as they could. But—

"That's where you'll come in," she told Dylan. "You know them, you're on the same team. So you're going to exert what I'm sure is your considerable influence, when needed."

For right now, though . . . She punched numbers into the phone.

"Hi, yeah, this is Lizzie Snow, deputy with the Aroostook County Sheriff's Department. I need to get a bulletin out to the deer-tagging stations. Is that possible?"

She waited while Dylan eyed her in surprise. Probably he'd thought it would take a while for her to be able to get things done. But when she hung up the phone, she'd extracted the promise that the tagging stations would post the flyer she'd be emailing, pronto; now all she had to do was assemble it.

So: scan in the Nicki photograph, specify the general area where she wanted the wardens to keep their eyes open, write up what she had of a campsite description . . .

She was pressing Send on the computer's fax function when Cody Chevrier burst in, his face furious.

"Come with me," he ordered her. "Now. You, too," he added to Dylan, either forgetting or not caring—the latter, she saw from his expression—that Dylan Hudson wasn't his subordinate.

Not until they were in his Blazer, speeding out of town with siren howling and roof lights blazing, did he explain. Even then it was in a voice so taut with anger he could barely speak.

"Another one," he grated out through clenched teeth.

Trees and fence posts flashed by. Cars, too, Chevrier passing with ferocious abandon. Lizzie clutched her seatbelt and grabbed the hand-grip over the passenger-side door, while in the back seat even Dylan held on, looking taken aback.

"Another *what?*" she demanded as they screamed around a slow-moving potato truck.

Chevrier hit the horn, swerving back into his own lane just in time to avoid an oncoming motorcycle. The look on the biker's face was horrified, like he was witnessing his own death.

Which he nearly had been. But that wasn't the death Sheriff Chevrier was so exercised about this morning.

"Another ex-cop," he said, stomping the gas in response to a sign that read SLOW. The rural countryside flew by in a blur.

"Dead," he said. "And this one—"

He yanked the wheel hard, avoiding a flock of

228

ducks waddling across the road only by the length of a single feather.

"I don't care what *anyone* says—"

In the side mirror, an aproned farm wife ran down the road behind them, shaking her fist.

"*This* one," he snarled furiously, "was *definitely* murder."

At the top of the driveway cut roughly through the leafless trees, the small, log-cabin-style house had a low-roofed porch running the full length of its front. A couple of wooden rockers flanked a bentwood table on the porch, next to a large gas grill, a metal shelf unit loaded with grilling equipment, and a picnic table spread with a red-checked cloth.

None of it had been touched in a while, the gas grill's top littered with blown-in leaf bits and the tongs rust-edged. An electronic bug zapper hung from one of the porch posts, and on a wooden chair by the post, a woman sat stunned.

"Hi, Cody," the woman said, looking up incuriously as they crossed the lawn. From the deadened expression on her slack face, it seemed that she might never be curious about anything ever again.

"I came to ask him if he wanted firewood from us this year." Even her voice sounded distant. "I guess not, though."

She smiled eerily. Her eyes did not participate.

Lizzie was not even sure those eyes were focusing on anything, their pupils dark pinpoints and their gaze flitting this way and that.

"She's in shock," Dylan told Chevrier. He crouched by the woman in the chair, speaking to her gently.

Yeah, you're good at that, Lizzie couldn't help thinking.

At making women, especially, think things are going to be okay when they're absolutely not.

But in this case, at least, the talent was useful; she put the thought away as Chevrier came back, his face tight with repressed emotion.

"Hudson, put her in my car. Give her some coffee out of my thermos. Go on, Hannah, go with him."

Obediently the woman got up, looking as if she'd have jumped off a cliff if someone told her to. As if, after what she'd just seen, she really didn't care what happened.

Then Chevrier brought Lizzie inside. "You need to see this. Because later they're going to say that he did it. That he did it to himself. You need to know why they will."

She followed him through neat, knotty-pine-paneled rooms filled with the same kind of oversized, plaid-upholstered furniture that was in her own rented house, ugly but comfortable.

Whoever lived here had health problems, she saw; by the recliner in the living room stood a

230

small oxygen tank with tubing and a vaporizer of some kind connected to it.

The bedroom, small and plain, held the usual furnishings plus three more small tanks: two solid green ones like the one in the living room and one more, solid brown. In the kitchen, a large old-fashioned cookstove featured gas burners plus a wood-burning firebox to one side.

A percolator on the stove had boiled over sometime in the recent past, spilling coffee grounds into the burner. In the sink stood a rinsed plate and cup, two spoons, and a knife and fork.

"This way." Chevrier jerked his head sideways. She could already see through the doorway from the kitchen into the small bathroom.

The walls, floor, and fixtures in there were all splattered with blood and brain matter, so she guessed already what she was about to confront: a small tiled room, a tub or shower enclosure, and a shotgun, fired by pushing the trigger with a yardstick or some similar tool, or by pulling on it with a string looped back around the gunstock.

Only a shotgun made that kind of a mess. Steeling herself against the thick, nauseating smell in the room, Lizzie stepped in and stood by the sink to take in the details:

Shaving things on a shelf. A wastebasket containing a few used tissues. Tooth glass and toothbrush. And in the tub a man's body, fully dressed in a pair of blue jeans, a flannel shirt, and a pair of sneakers, but no longer possessing anything that could even remotely be said to resemble a head.

He'd chosen the string-around-the-gunstock method. "Okay," she said. "Anything special I should notice?"

Chevrier shook his head. "That's his shotgun. I've been out hunting with him many a time. But this," he said, "isn't how he would do it."

Dylan looked in. "Cody, you want me to drive Hannah Dodson home? She walked over from her place, but it seems kind of harsh to let her just . . ."

"Yeah, Dylan, thanks. Make sure someone's there with her, all right? And we'll wait here for you," said Chevrier.

"I wanted you to see it," he told Lizzie when Dylan had gone. "So when you hear later about how it's open and shut—"

Something struck her; she glanced back into the bathroom. "How sick was he?"

The collection of pill bottles on the windowsill consisted of at least a dozen small orange plastic containers with white printed pharmacy labels.

"As bad off as Carl Bogart, maybe worse," said Chevrier. "Hey, guys get old," he added sadly. "Anyway, he had pancreatic cancer, couple of months left. Another reason they'll say it was suicide, besides the method."

And besides the fact that it was hard to fake a

thing like this, she thought, because despite the chaotic first impression it made, blood spatter came in recognizable patterns. You could drug a man, lay him down, shoot him, then pose him as if he'd done it himself, taking care to get all the details just right: the angle, the point-blank distance, the powder tattooing, even.

You'd still have a telltale hole in the back-splatter, though, caused by your body being smack-dab in the bloody middle of it when the gun went off.

"You think somebody talked him into it? Or threatened him?"

That way, the evidence would look right. And a guy dying of cancer might not be hard to persuade.

On the other hand, though, what could you threaten him with that was worse than his own near-certain imminent fate?

She followed Chevrier back out onto the porch. "Why are you so sure he *didn't* kill himself in there?"

Chevrier turned to her. "Weren't you listening? Terminal cancer, already it was painful, and he was expecting worse. A lot worse."

The lightbulb went on: those pills. "He had another method planned? Something not so . . ."

In her experience suicides were of two kinds: the ones who didn't want to hurt someone on their way out and the ones who did. A self-

233

administered dose of shotgun shell argued strongly for the latter variety.

Just ask that poor woman who found him . . .

"Bingo," Chevrier replied sarcastically. "All those bottles in there on the windowsill? They're full. Pain pills, sleeping medications, he'd been saving them up. Got a supply of anti-nausea medicine, too, the kind that really works, so he wouldn't puke 'em all back up after he . . ."

He stopped, sudden tears coming into his voice. "He was a good guy, Wilson Sirois was. Game warden all his life, loved being out there, knew the woods way up along the Canadian border like his backyard."

Chevrier kicked at a clod of dirt left by one of the cops that had been in and out of Sirois's house. "He was gonna go out there when the time came, had his spot all picked, a nice little glade by a stream we used to fish. And I . . ."

Lizzie waited, looking out across the valley from the long front porch. Far to the west, the northern Appalachian mountains shone white with snow at their tops, the endless forests below a greenish-black charcoal scribble.

"You know all this because you were going to go with him," she finished for Chevrier. "To help him, and stay with him?"

He nodded, starting down the porch steps. "Yeah. That was the plan. He said he would let me know."

Dylan pulled the Blazer back up into the yard and sat behind the wheel waiting. "But I guess that won't be happening now. He did it without me. Yeah, sure he did," he snarled sarcastically.

Chevrier spat on the half-frozen ground, looked around in bleak misery. "Freakin' epidemic of it around here, wouldn't you say?"

They climbed into the Blazer. "What if the weather got too bad, though?" The weather forecaster on the radio this morning had been hinting at snow, and there'd be more of it soon.

And it didn't sound as if Sirois was going to last until a spring thaw. "Or he was too sick to do it."

Or, she didn't add, *if it all just went south too fast for Wilson Sirois to swallow his pills.*

"Or if something else went wrong." Sirois could've ended up in an ambulance instead of by his stream in any number of ways. "And anyway, as a method, pills are iffy."

No need to go into detail. But she'd seen pill overdoses back when she was on patrol, many of them deliberate.

She had not, however, seen very many successful ones. The human gut tended to rebel before enough of the substance had been absorbed, or at least that was how it had been explained to her by a Boston emergency-room resident, one long-ago midnight just before Christmas. Even anti-nausea meds might not help.

Chevrier understood. "Sirois knew everybody

235

and they knew him. There wasn't an ambulance tech or ER doc in the County who'd have resuscitated him."

He took a breath. Dylan drove carefully and well, keeping thoughtfully quiet. Not until they got to the highway and turned toward Bearkill did he speak up.

"The woman who found him says he was a retired game warden," he said. "Does that mean he'd have been able to help find someone in the woods? Or a campsite way off the beaten track? Sick as he was, could he have gone along, or maybe at least helped out with suggestions from home?"

Nice one, she thought about the connection he'd just made. *Some hidden place that a lifetime in the woods might've made the game warden aware of . . . a place where someone might be hiding a child?*

Coming toward them, a boxy red and white emergency vehicle flashed its lights at the sight of the Blazer. No lights or siren running, though, and they weren't racing anywhere, either.

They'd been told what awaited, no doubt, and who the hell would be in a rush to confront that?

"Yeah," said Chevrier when the ambulance had passed, another county car with a deputy at the wheel right behind it.

"Sirois could've done that. Out in those woods,

236

there, he was the man. Everyone around here knows it, too."

His voice grew reminiscent as he recalled his dead friend; his second loss in a month, she realized.

"Yeah, you needed somebody located up there, he was the one you wanted out hunting for them. People said Wilson Sirois could find an eyelash in the Allagash, and it was true."

At first, Margaret Brantwell thought she must simply have made some kind of mistake. Things had been noisy around the house all morning, what with the hired guys outside trying to get the last bales of hay under cover before the snow got here and the dogs barking in their pen, trying to get at the hired guys.

Also, the baby had been crying, fussy and not wanting to go down for his morning nap. But finally he'd quieted; she'd left him in his crib in the sunroom, a peace lily shading him and the small mechanical fountain she'd had put in when the room was added onto the house trickling pleasantly.

And then . . . She remembered very well thinking how lovely it all looked, and how glad she was to have time with her grandson even if he could be a little fussy now and then.

For a while she had thought she might never make peace with Missy again. Missy's father was a proud man, and he'd taken his daughter's pregnancy—and her refusal to name the baby's dad—very hard. Margaret had been sorely torn, caught between her husband's anger and her daughter's obdurate stubbornness.

But little Jeffrey had won his grandfather over at last, as Margaret had been pleased to recall when she'd finally put the child down for his nap . . . or had she?

She looked around, not frightened yet but only perturbed at herself. *Silly. That must've been some other day.*

Which unfortunately was not out of the question. She knew she'd been forgetting things— losing thoughts, she called it to herself when she dared think of the mental blurry spots she had been having lately—and she must have misremembered this.

Of course she had. The baby would be up in the guest room that she had fitted out for him with such pleasure, once Missy started letting him stay for the whole day while she worked.

Returning to the kitchen she took such pride in, all tile, granite, and stainless steel with new white cabinets and a center island, Margaret paused to grab a pile of clean cloth diapers still warm from the dryer and press her face into the sweetness left by boiling hot water and Ivory Snow soap flakes.

Then she went on upstairs, wondering distantly

what it was that she'd been so worried about only moments ago. Humming, she placed the diapers in the hall cupboard now given over to baby things, the terrycloth onesies and tiny socks and the sweater she had knitted for him. *I should find that yarn and knit mittens . . .*

Next she went into what had been the guest room. The crib, a white-painted maple one bought brand-new in a Bangor department store, came recommended for safety by *Consumer Reports* and held a properly firm baby mattress with a blue sheet and a blue fleece blanket; stuffed toys, plush bedding, and anything else a small child could smother in were forbidden, naturally.

Even the baby quilt she'd stitched for little Jeffrey was not allowed in there, so she'd draped it over the raised railing where its bonnet pattern showed prettily, appliquéd in gingham. Oh, how she loved being a grandmother, she thought, crossing to the baby's crib and peering in.

And finding it empty.

"So, let me get this straight," said Chevrier. "You think both hunters got killed, and Nussbaum, too, because one of the hunters was in the woods out there and saw someone? A little girl?"

They sat at a booth in Grammy's Restaurant, their lunches barely touched. "Yeah. Sounds unlikely, huh? But that's it," said Dylan.

239

"And my guys, Sirois and Bogart and the other three, you think their deaths might be also hooked into it all somehow?"

Another nod, this one a good deal less certain, from Dylan. He'd ordered a seafood plate but looked as if chicken soup with saltines might suit him better.

"Maybe," he said doubtfully. He picked up a french fry, ate half of it, and put the rest down, swallowing more Coke instead.

"If Sirois really could've helped find that campsite, that's a possible connection. For the rest of them, though . . ."

He sighed, leaning back uncomfortably as Lizzie got up from the booth. As she crossed to where the waitress was filling a tray full of water glasses, she heard Dylan add tactfully, "Let's just see where it goes."

She slid back into the booth in time to catch the tail end of Chevrier's reply. ". . . so what do you suggest? 'Cause I can tell you right now, a search party that doesn't know where to search out there might as well just—"

"No." She picked up her sandwich, looked at both men over it. "Not a search. A tip line."

She bit in and chewed industriously. If the sight of a guy in a pool of blood had been enough to ruin her appetite for very long, she'd have been dead of starvation by now.

"For the hunters, trappers. Loggers, too, maybe,

as well as the game wardens. People who spend time out in the woods might see something."

Watching her devour her meal, Chevrier slowly picked up one of the fried shrimp he'd ordered and put it into his mouth. It went down, and he took another, but not eagerly.

"Huh. Not a bad idea. You started on it yet?" he asked, and when she answered in the affirmative, he looked grimly impressed.

"Good. Way to take the initiative," he said as the waitress arrived with the milk shake Lizzie had ordered for Dylan.

Then, seeing how rocky the detective looked with the sweat glistening in his hairline and his eyes pain-pinched, Chevrier paused in scarfing up his shrimp.

"Get a little of that down if you can," he advised, "and take a pill, for God's sake. You look like a damned ghost."

He turned back to Lizzie. "But we don't have to say why we want to find this place, right? Just tell guys, when they're out in the woods, keep their eyes open. We just want them to call if they see anything and—"

"Right. All that's under control," said Lizzie, pleased that the move she'd made was meeting with the boss's approval. She was about to say more when the diner's front door swung open, letting in two patrons:

The veterinarian Trey Washburn was having

lunch today with a pretty brunette wearing a short, silver-colored down jacket, slim jeans, and a pair of red cowboy boots. It was the veterinary technician she'd met a few nights earlier, Lizzie realized, but she hadn't noticed then how attractive the girl was.

Looking over the room, Trey spotted her and waved, his face looking a lot friendlier than it had a couple of hours earlier.

Or maybe just smug. But then another new arrival hurried in: Missy Brantwell. Scanning the room swiftly, she rushed over, nearly colliding with a waitress in her hurry.

"Oh, thank God you're here," she babbled to Chevrier. "I saw the Blazer outside and I—"

Wiping his lips, Chevrier got to his feet as the room went silent, Missy's frantic voice suddenly the only sound in it.

"Cody, the baby's missing. Jeffrey was with my mom, but now he's gone. We looked everywhere and he's just not there."

A sob escaped her, but she pulled herself together enough to choke the rest out, her eyes imploring.

"Cody, I think maybe Jeffrey's been kid-napped!"

EIGHT

O h my God. Ohmygodohmy—
Spud pumped his bike up the driveway, jumped off it, and threw it under the porch. Slamming up the front steps, he flung himself into the house, where the fresh tobacco smoke and reek of beer said that his dad was home.

Slumped before the noon news on TV, the old man barely stirred as Spud rushed by. "Wha's yer hurry? Cops after you?"

A boozy laugh punctuated this witticism, followed by a fit of coughing. Not for the first time, Spud wished his dad would just smoke up a couple of cartons all at once, get it over with.

Then, still seized with the enormity of what he had done—*ohmygodwhatI*—Spud headed for the stairs and the safety of his own room.

But the old man wasn't done yet. "Where you been all day, anyway?" he wanted to know. "Out robbin' banks?"

His hand already on the banister, Spud paused. It wasn't any worse than a lot of other things his father had said to him. The litany of foul names he'd endured being called over the years would fill a book. But somehow . . .

Slowly Spud turned and walked back into the living room. Leaning down, he plucked the beer can out of his dad's hand, enjoying the look of injured surprise that filled the old man's bleary eyes.

This is what I'll be someday, Spud thought. *Never mind what I read, what I think, what I want, or even what I try—stupidly, clumsily—to do to get out of it. This:*

Drunk, dumb, addicted, and sick. Hooked by the eyeballs to the goddamned TV set, sucking up game shows and soap operas and "reality TV," shows about other losers, just with nicer clothes and plenty of makeup.

"Gimme that," his dad whined, reaching up for the beer can, too lazy to get up and try taking it. "What the hell do you think you're doing, you little pissant, you—"

Spud held the can, a nearly full twenty-four-ouncer, just out of reach. He wasn't sure what had come over him, only that it felt good. "This? You want this?"

He danced back a couple of steps, whirled, and flung the can hard at the TV, whose screen exploded in multicolored sparks and flames before going entirely dark.

"There. There's your goddamned beer. Whyn't you crawl in there and get it, you want it so much?"

Fury replaced shock on his father's face. Pushing his veiny hands into the couch cushions, he charged up at Spud, undoing his belt as he advanced.

"Crazy as a shithouse rat, you are, you know that? Your mom's way too soft on you, but I'll fix you. I'll smack the crazy right out of your—"

Spud put a hand up, closed it around that stringy throat to stop the sounds coming out of it. "Shut up."

Step by step, squeezing because it felt good, Spud pushed his dad backward until the old man's legs hit the couch cushions and he sat down again, choking and flailing.

Spud didn't let go. Instead he leaned forward, squeezing harder, enjoying the sight of his dad's eyes bugging out. *This is for the belt, Dad. And the switch. And the yardstick.*

And your fists. His dad's face was turning purple, hands weakening in their useless attempt to loosen Spud's grip.

"You're mistaken," Spud said softly. "I haven't been out at all. I've been here all day, up in my room. And you know it, you know it 'cause you've been here, too . . . right?"

His dad's leg shot out in a badly aimed attempt at a kick. In response, Spud kicked back, aiming his boot at the old man's kneecap and connecting with a sick crunch. Then he shoved his dad's throat so hard back into the couch that it nearly vanished into the upholstery.

"I said, am I *right?*" Then he waited. His dad was stubborn. But eventually it sank in: something had changed between them.

This was a new Spud. The whippings and beatings were over and the litany of foul words . . . done. *Because after this morning . . .*

Spud hung on a moment longer just to make sure of it. Then, with a last contemptuous shove, he let go, stepping back quickly as the old man lunged forward, vomiting.

"Jesus," Spud said in disgust. When the gasping and puking ceased and the old man sat catching his breath, Spud spoke again.

"Ma's gonna be home in an hour. Better make sure this shit's cleaned up and the TV gone, too. You can figure out what to tell her about that."

His dad glowered malevolently. But he didn't say no.

He'd better not. "And remember what I told you. I was here all day. Understand? Otherwise, next time you're passed out—"

He put both hands around his own throat, squeezed, and stuck his tongue out sideways, letting his eyes roll around unfocused in imitation of being strangled.

His dad looked away. Spud went on upstairs, where he washed his hands and face at the rusty bathroom sink, then changed his clothes. The guy in the van, he had noticed, was clean and clean-shaven, and he lived out in the woods, for God's sake.

When he was done, Spud went back down for a snack, Cheetos and a liter of Pepsi he found in the fridge. He didn't enter the living room, but as he went by he could hear sounds from in there: the clanking of a bucket and the swishing around of water in it, and now among the rank odors he also smelled soap.

Muttering curses, the old man was cleaning his mess up. Spud felt confident that his dad would do the other thing, too:

Keep his mouth shut, or if he had to speak, then say what Spud had told him to. The look of true fear in the old man's eyes as he was being choked had left little doubt of that.

Good, Spud thought. Then he returned to his own room, where he spent the rest of the afternoon playing Grand Theft Auto. Not until much later, after dinner—his father did not appear—and after he'd gone with his mom to the Walmart in Presque Isle for a new TV, paying for it with his own money—*because I did it, I did what he said*—did he lie wide awake in bed.

Staring at the ceiling, starting up at every sound, sure that it was the cops coming for him. Thinking—

Oh my God. Ohmygodohmygod—

I did what he told me to do, I—

The task itself had been unexpectedly easy. None of the many obstacles that he had imagined had in fact arisen:

Roger Brantwell hadn't been home, for one thing, or Missy Brantwell, either, and for another the Brantwells' whole place had been swarming with hired help, getting trucks and tractors ready to harvest Brantwell's potato acreage and getting the hay indoors.

Keeping his knit watch cap pulled over his hair, his arms covered, and his head down, Spud had just walked up the driveway like he belonged there, and no one had even looked at him. And inside had been as simple:

No one around, the whole place shimmering with new paint and cleanliness, full of a sense of order and domestic routine that Spud didn't have time to stop and wonder at. Once he heard a woman upstairs humming to herself, and he froze, but she didn't come down and the vacuum cleaner that was running at the other end of the house never approached.

He'd found what he wanted in the sunroom, grabbed it up, and run outside, then forced himself to walk slowly back down the long driveway again, certain that at any moment there would be an outcry.

But there wasn't one. The van came along as he reached the road, the guy's face impassive. He'd handed over his burden as he'd been instructed to do.

And that had been that. *Done . . .*

The trouble now, though, was that he couldn't stop reliving it. He jerked bolt upright in bed, trying to get it out of his head.

Only it wouldn't go. It was real. Not like all the computer games he played, not even like the girls that he went out to find sometimes, girls who were real but not *really* real.

Not real like he was. That was why he could . . . *do* things to them. And he would do those things again soon, he knew; find one, leave her where she fell. Then for a while he would feel better, almost human once more.

All that he knew just as surely as he knew that the day became night.

This, though. This was different, this was—

Oh my God, I stole a goddamned kid.

"Missy? Honey, you've got to stop crying, baby, they need you to help."

Roger Brantwell had just arrived in New York for a New England marketing association meeting when he learned that his grandson was missing and had flown home at once, leaving his Escalade behind in the city.

Now, though, bending over his weeping daughter, he seemed more frustrated by her refusal to listen to him than worried about any danger to the vanished child.

Lots of people did that at first, not wanting to let the truth in. Lizzie decided to cut the guy some slack, at least for now.

But he sure didn't make it easy. "Missy," he repeated insistently, "they need—"

His daughter jerked her head up from the long table in the conference room at the Aroostook County Courthouse in Houlton, her haunted eyes makeup-smeared and her face a tear-streaked horror.

"Need me to do what?" she gasped through her sobs. "Answer more questions, give more descriptions? How many times, a hundred or a million? Until you understand that *I don't know?*"

She glared around furiously at the collection of cops in the room: local, county, and state, all hoping for some scrap of new information that would tell them where a missing child might be waiting for them.

A staffer from social services was there, too, silent and grimly narrow-eyed. Lizzie wondered if Missy had any idea what she was in for, even after the child was found.

If he was. "Go through it again, Missy," said Chevrier patiently. "I know you think you've already told us everything, but you never know. Any new detail you come up with could be the thing that—"

She hadn't been accused of anything—not yet—and there was no point in upsetting her even more than she already was. But he knew, and so did everyone else in the room with her, that when a kid went missing the first ones you looked at were the parents.

And that too many times, even though you went

250

through the motions, in the end it turned out that you'd never really had to look any further than the kid's own home.

"I told you, I was at the bar. It got really busy this week, Jimmy needed me to help restock, so I left Jeffrey with my mom. I knew he'd be fine, I've left him hundreds of times, and—"

She stopped, seeming to realize how that sounded. "I mean, not literally hundreds. But he was fine with her, he . . ."

The social worker's lips tightened. Dylan leaned in to where Lizzie stood listening. "She doesn't know yet, does she?"

Lizzie shook her head; how bad it would get, he meant, the questions and insinuations that were coming. They weren't there yet, but soon every news outlet in the state would be pestering for updates and interviews: with Missy.

Or her relatives or friends. Anyone would do; compared to the media, the hounds of hell were merciful.

"No." Lizzie sighed. "Anything from the volunteers?"

Every all-terrain vehicle in town was out searching, every scout troop and church group, everyone who could walk, ride, or crawl through the fields and forest around the Brantwell home had come out of the woodwork to say they'd help. A missing kid just seemed to summon up the good in people, it seemed.

Or the desire to be a part of the excitement, she added to herself sourly. Some of the faces she'd seen in the volunteer groups had looked more avid than concerned.

But that didn't matter. The more ground covered, the better, and if somebody found that child alive, Lizzie would gladly allow them their fifteen minutes of fame.

"Uh-uh." Outside it was dark. "They're shutting it down for the night. The Amber Alert's up on the interstate flashboards—they've expanded it to all of New England. There's posters at all the border crossings and a flyer on every squad car's dashboard."

"Great." But as they both knew, getting the word out wasn't the same as getting the kid back. Ninety-eight percent of the tips that came in on the hotline would be obviously worthless; or worse, they'd look good but then prove to be misleading, wasting time and resources.

Lizzie knew this. She'd learned it when her own dead sister's child was on those posters.

Now Missy was crying again; she'd been tough all day, but she was starting to despair as the hours wore on.

"Missy," said Roger Brantwell, "please."

The social worker had watched grim-faced, taking occasional notes. But now: "Has anyone talked with the child's father?"

At the question, Missy stiffened. "No. He has nothing to do with—"

The social worker was undeterred. "Perhaps so. But you must understand that we'll need to speak with him. My department, and the police, as well."

Straightening, Missy turned, fixing the social worker in a gaze Lizzie felt glad not to have leveled at herself. *Girl's got a spine,* she thought with reluctant admiration.

"Lady, get the hell out of my face," Missy pronounced. "I don't even know what you're—"

"Let's go," said Lizzie to Dylan. "I'll find out about it when she finally names him."

Missy wouldn't win this battle; if the social worker didn't win it, then the cops would. But it was obviously going to be a knock-down, drag-out.

"Until then, though, I don't need to hear any more of the back-and-forth." Too predictable, too sad . . .

The courthouse halls were paneled in dark wood wainscoting, with matching ornate wooden trim around the doorways leading into the courtrooms. The banisters, stair trim, and everything else that was not either highly polished linoleum or freshly painted plaster were also heavy, gorgeously carved wood, gleaming richly.

It was a far cry from the old brick and cinderblock public buildings she'd gotten used to back in the city; the place even smelled clean, and the ladies' room was like a hymn to scouring powder and lemon-scented disinfectant.

Still, she was glad to step outside, through the crush of reporters in the lobby—no network trucks had arrived yet, but they'd be here next, Lizzie supposed tiredly—into the icily fresh night air.

Dylan blew a breath out. "Man," he said, rubbing his hands together in the chill. "Bad scene. You think she even knows who the dad is?"

"Maybe. Probably," Lizzie amended, recalling the look of pain in Missy's eyes at the question. "Yeah, I think she knows. Just doesn't want him back in her life again, probably."

Or maybe having people know who it was would humiliate her; the Brantwells, after all, were well respected, according to Cody Chevrier. Lizzie could imagine Roger Brantwell's reaction if he found out his grandson's dad was some drugged-out local loser.

In a little park behind the jail entrance to the courthouse stood a hot dog cart, shuttered for the night. She paused by it while Dylan caught up. Under his black topcoat, his shoulders were hunched against the cold, his hands jammed into his pockets.

"You okay?" He looked terrible, his lips tightened to a thin line of misery.

"Yeah." He grimaced. "Damn pain pills screw up my stomach, though." Neither of them had eaten since lunch, and at this hour even in Houlton everything was closed; she pictured him alone and making do on cheese crackers out of a vending machine.

"If you want to come back with me, I could make eggs again," she said. "You could crash on the couch," she added, regretting it as soon as the words were out.

The smashed window at her house was fixed, courtesy of some guys Chevrier had sent over from the department's maintenance division. But every cell in her body was tired . . . *and it's a bad idea, anyway,* the sensible part of her brain reminded her.

He seemed to think so, too. "No, I'll go back to the motel," he began, but then he stopped, his face under the streetlight bone-white and exhausted.

"You know what? Okay." He gave in abruptly. "I'll bring my car, though—I'll need it. You go on, I'll be along shortly."

Which made sense. Of course he'd need his car. And despite the long drive back to her place, the idea of leaving his beloved Saab on the street overnight would be unacceptable to him.

But something in his voice set a mental alarm bell ringing. That he would want to linger here by himself first . . .

For what? As she got into the Blazer a suspicion struck her, but she squelched it at once; if he needed to call someone and he didn't want her to know about it, then she didn't want to, either, she told herself. That's not what they were to each other now.

Then she concentrated on driving; Houlton's downtown crisscrossing of one-way streets seemed as confusing as Boston's, for a new-comer. Still, at the corner by the courthouse, she turned left before realizing it was the wrong way; the Route 1 intersection headed back to Bearkill was in the other direction.

"Damn." From the back seat, Rascal tipped his head at her, his sad hound-dog eyes inquiring.

"Don't worry, though, fella. We'll just go around the block and try again." To get back where she needed to be, it was up one side of the park, then across, and—

Glancing across the tree-lined quadrangle to the red-brick courthouse with the lit-up clock tower and tall, columned cupola perching above it, she noted that it was after midnight. Late, but not terribly; at least 6 a.m. wouldn't come as a disaster.

But then she saw Dylan still sitting in his car with his phone out, the streetlight's gleam lighting him from the side. Calling someone, just as she'd thought . . .

She thumbed the radio as she drove. Dispatch

256

gave her the number she wanted; she punched it into her phone one-handed.

"Hi, can you put me through to Dylan Hudson's room, please?" she asked the motel clerk where he was staying, and waited.

Hoping she was wrong. Knowing she was a jealous, suspicious person, one who had, moreover, no right whatsoever to be snooping into—

The line was busy. She kept driving, hitting Redial every so often until she was nearly to Bearkill, passing the darkened Tastee-Treet and the high school. Then the phone in Dylan's motel room rang.

It was answered at once. A woman's voice. *Of course it is. Suspicions confirmed . . . again.*

"Hello?" the woman asked a second time, then hung up.

Lizzie looked down at the phone, considered throwing it out the car window, and then after a moment's reflection pressed the Off button instead.

Hey. He's got a right. You don't own him, you've let him know you have no intention of—

Yeah. Sure she had. Probably that was why she drove the rest of the way home with her hands clamped so tightly around the steering wheel, she could see the whites of her knuckles through the skin.

"So, what do you think now of Chevrier's thing?" Dylan wanted to know when he got to her house twenty minutes later.

He looked like hell, so worn and in pain that she nearly—

What? Took pity on him? He's lucky I didn't poison the eggs.

"His ex-cop murder theory? Too many victims," she replied, shaking her head. "I could see if it was just one or two. But so many?"

She set plates in front of them both. "I like Chevrier, I think he's good. But so far, I just don't believe it."

"Yeah, hard to figure." Dylan dug tiredly into his eggs. "I mean, if there was a motive, maybe. But I can't come up with one that covers them all, and neither can he."

"Or me." In off moments she'd researched more of the dead ex-cops' pasts—military service, marriages, debts—and come up yet again with zero in common among them.

"On the other hand"—he broke off a piece of toast, dipped it in fried egg yolk—"the high number does make it—"

"Right. Funny looking. I mean, what are the chances?" She drank some orange juice, wishing intensely that she had never invited him here tonight.

But it was too late now; she decided just to try to get through it as best she could.

"There's one I haven't even had time to find out much about yet," she added. "Guy named Fontine, lived over somewhere on the Canadian border."

Dylan nodded tiredly. "For a total of five. That's a lot of dead guys in a year, for sure. I can see why Chevrier's upset."

"Right." Beyond that, though, neither of them could come up with any more useful ideas on the subject.

"Good eggs," said Dylan after they'd eaten in silence for a while; tired as they both were, she doubted he'd take her subdued manner as anything but a need for sleep, and he didn't.

"Thanks, Lizzie." He sat back from the table, his eyes dark-ringed.

"You're welcome. Go on now," she told him, thinking that she might as well at least be kind.

It was all that was left between them. Expecting anything more had been worse than foolish. She managed a smile.

Fool me twice, shame on me. He'd taken a pain pill before eating, and now his eyelids drooped.

"I'm going to run the dog out once more, but you should get some sleep if you can. Take the bed, okay? I'll probably be up for a while."

Besides, that way she could at least get him out of her sight. He nodded exhaustedly. "Yeah, okay. Lizzie knows best."

Make that just "Lizzie knows," she thought. But she let him go off to her room with no more than another insincere smile for a good-night, and if he noticed, he was too tired to say so.

"Come on, Rascal," she said five minutes later

as she finished changing into her sneakers and pulled her jacket back on.

Outside, the night was as still as a held breath on her dark dead-end street. At the corner she paused, looking past the huge looming shape of the potato wholesaler's barn with its long low porch. When she'd left for work early that morning, day laborers had already been waiting outside, bundled against the cold as they lined up for a shift of potato harvesting.

But now it was deserted, and downtown Bearkill was quiet as well, even the big-eyed, white-faced alien on the Area 51 sign gone dark. Turning her back on it all, she let her feet fall into a slow jogging rhythm on the cold pavement, the dog keeping pace.

Minutes later she was well out of town, the last cross street far behind and the road curving lazily uphill. Her legs fell into the familiar motions, the day's stresses pounding out of her each time the soles of her shoes met the road.

But it was very dark, with no streetlights to show her and Rascal to passing vehicles, of which to her surprise there were still a few, and the road's shoulder let off sharply into a loose scrim of sand and pebbles.

Maybe this wasn't such a great idea . . . The last straw came when an oncoming car flashed its brights and then left them on, blinding her, and even worse, hit the horn as it went by, so that

Rascal jumped and nearly leapt out into its path.

"Okay, that's it." Back in the city, a late-night run had been almost as well lit as midday; here, though, she was going to need reflectors, maybe a hat with an LED light, and for the dog a reflective vest and collar.

She reversed course, making her way carefully back along the curving highway into the grid of Bearkill streets. Here were some streetlights, at least, but gloom lay between them, too, and the spruces and pines that had been allowed to remain as ornamentals years ago now loomed in the tiny yards, great dark behemoths.

She stopped suddenly, not quite certain all at once of where she was, exactly. Rascal stopped, too, aiming his big head at something in the darkness, sniffing suspiciously.

"Wuff," he uttered, backing up to stand beside her, his eyes fixed on whatever was hidden in the darkness among the trees.

Her hand went to her weapon as she backed away slowly. There was a streetlight not too far behind her, flakes of snow swirling down through it, and houses beyond that.

But here it was very dark. Rascal moaned, a sound that was half whine, half growl, and all the way miserable. She took a step backward and then another, but the dog wouldn't budge and his leash was too short for her to go any farther until he gave in.

"Rascal, *come,* dammit." The dog's eyes widened, his growls now a constant mutter and his hackles stiff.

And then . . . nothing. Gradually the dog relaxed. At the end of the street, a vehicle started up, pulled out, and came toward them; an older Econoline van, she saw as it passed by.

Nothing to worry about. Just someone headed for a late shift somewhere, probably. She wasn't even sure the guy in it saw her and Rascal standing there in the dark.

She let a breath out and after a moment broke back into a jog. And this time the release she'd hoped for from the exercise and the cold, fresh air actually came; by the time she got back to the house where Dylan slept, she felt weightless, the events of the day sliding off her tired shoulders, at least temporarily.

Inside, she showered, put on clean sweats with the Boston PD logo on them, then fell onto the sofa bed and slept, deeply and dreamlessly, until the phone jangled her awake at 3 a.m.

He should stay home, stay inside. He knew that. But—*I stole a kid!*—the unholy agitation that seized Spud that night was like a lit match sizzling in his brain.

A hit of weed didn't help, nor a second one. By just after ten, with the rest of the house already asleep, he'd been jumping out of his skin.

Ohmygodohmy—He knew what would fix it, though. He knew it from experience. The thought had been building in him and now . . .

Abruptly he slapped his laptop shut and jumped up from his bed, peering between the slats of the venetian blind at his bedroom window to where thickening snow filtered through the yard light onto the front lawn.

Nobody around, no cops waiting to pounce; none that he could see, anyway. Best of all, there was no van sitting at the end of the driveway . . . *or waiting for me to deliver a year-old boy* . . .

His bike stood right outside, though of course he wouldn't have to ride it the whole way to Bangor. Even this late at night, there would be some trucker or lonely traveler who would stop for him if he stuck his thumb out.

He knew that from experience, too. Swiftly he dressed for the trip, covering his tattoos with a long-sleeved sweatshirt and a scarf around his neck and popping his nose stud and lip ring out, dropping them into his jacket pocket to put back in later.

Finally he unbraided his hair, brushing it flat and covering it with his watch cap again, then slipped outside for his bike and pedaled through the night toward Route 1, where in the thickly falling snow he shoved the bike off the pavement into some trees, then stepped back up to the road's edge and waited.

As he'd expected, he didn't have to wait long. It was a good ride, too: The car that slowed for him belonged to a housekeeping worker on his way to the night shift at the hospital in Houlton; with a bottle of Allen's Coffee Flavored Brandy in his hand and a loose, half-in-the-bag grin on his face, the guy wouldn't remember he'd picked anyone up, much less be able to describe his passenger.

After the janitor let him out, Spud trudged up the on-ramp of I-95 headed toward Bangor, and had just reached the merge with the travel lanes when his next stroke of good fortune hit:

This driver turned out to be a college kid on his way back to school, his eyes caffeine-bright and his iPod blaring out headbanger stuff, metal music that filled the little junker the kid drove with a defiant roar.

With no jewelry or tattoos showing and his hat snugged down, Spud doubted he could be described accurately by this kid, either, and the joint he'd brought to share during the ride plus the beers the kid had with him made it even less likely.

He got the kid to let him out in downtown Bangor, where the snow had stopped and at nearly midnight the streets were as dark and ominously empty as the opening scene of a zombie movie. He walked past the tattoo shop where he'd gotten most of his ink and piercings, the comic book store, and the video games arcade.

In daylight he might've lingered at one or more of these. Now, though, he was on a mission and soon he reached Blackie's, which from the outside looked like any other hole-in-the-wall bar: dim neon sign in the hazy window, a sand-filled bucket for butts by the front door.

Inside, however, despite the lateness of the hour, the joint was jumping. "Gimme a Bud," he told the bartender.

No one checked ID in here, one reason he liked the place. Another was the number of single girls it attracted. He didn't know why; the music was awful, just a garage band playing Nirvana covers, and the decor was worse, cheap tables and metal chairs.

Still, somehow the place was catnip for chicks; a dead man could probably hook up in Blackie's, Spud thought as he drank some of his beer and surveyed the action, patiently waiting.

Soon his patience was rewarded. "Hi!" said the girl with the little mole on her cheek, smiling brightly. "You wanna dance?"

Spud put down his beer, smiling back. She was just his type: young, female, and already pretty drunk.

"Well, I don't know." He glanced around. Most of the tables were empty, the dance floor packed with bouncing bodies. Flaring strobe lights keeping time to the music's thudding beat turned faces into unrecognizable masks, and the noise was stunning.

He leaned down, noting her glassy eyes and her loose-limbed state of inebriation. Lipstick stained her plastic beer cup.

"You with somebody? I don't want to get in trouble with your boyfriend. Or even your girlfriends."

She let her head loll back, giggling. "Naw, no one's with me. I'm a big girl, I'm allowed out by myself."

Myshelf, slurring the word. "I'm Alison," she added.

Alishon. Spud chugged his beer, glanced around once more. But of course no one was watching; you could fire off a cannon in here and nobody would notice.

Alison took his arm, her smile slackly dreamy. "C'mon, big guy," she said, putting her face up for a kiss.

He bent to comply and saw that she'd bitten her lip sometime during the evening.

She tasted of blood and Juicy Fruit.

The cop cars' flaring cherry beacons stained the falling snow blood-red in the predawn darkness by the side of Route 1 just outside Bearkill, where the wrecked car's glowing taillights peeked up over the edge of the embankment.

It was snowing hard; the two long tire tracks at the side of the road were already filling up again. The guys with the gurney huffed and puffed, straining to haul the victim strapped to it back up the steep slope.

When they got near, Lizzie smelled beer even out here in the open air. "Empties on the floor, lots of them," one of the EMTs reported.

He thrust the victim's wallet at her. Inside she found a State of Maine driver's license and a college ID.

"Looks like somebody's going to miss a few classes," Cody Chevrier said sourly, reading over her shoulder.

"Yeah." She handed them back to the EMT, who zipped them into the property bag. Someone at the hospital would be calling this kid's parents. "He say anything?"

The pair of EMTs hoisted the gurney into the boxy emergency vehicle's lit-up interior. "Nope. Out for the count."

She'd set up flares and a row of orange flashers to warn oncoming traffic. Now the wrecker from the little gas station in Bearkill backed slowly across the deepening snow and the driver hopped out, scrambling down to attach the towing cable to the wreck.

"What was he doing out here at this hour?" According to the home address on his license, the victim's obvious route would've been this way, along Route 1, so he was in the right place.

Just at the wrong time. The wrecker's winch engaged with a metallic whine, pulling the mangled vehicle up from the ravine.

From the rear, the car looked fairly normal.

But from the look of the older sedan's demolished front end, it was anyone's guess whether or not the crash victim would be able to tell them why he had chosen to drive through Bearkill so late.

"No idea," said Chevrier, shaking his head.

The tow truck's driver leaned down from his window. "I'll put it in the lot out behind my place, okay?"

Since arriving in town, her purchases at the Bearkill Gas-o-Mart had included a set of tires and one of windshield wipers, several tanks of gas, and an air freshener; Rascal's Eau de Hound had returned soon after his bath at Trey Washburn's place and now battled a pine-scented cutout Christmas tree dangling from the Blazer's rearview mirror.

"Yeah, thanks, Bradley," she began. The Gas-o-Mart's owner-operator was so glad for the steady patronage, he'd given her a free set of floor mats.

But then she thought again. "Hey," she yelled as he pulled away, "Brad, wait. Run it down to the impound yard in Houlton for me, will you?"

Ordinarily, leaving the wreck in Bearkill

overnight would be no big deal. It wasn't as if the vehicle had to be secured as evidence. But—

"Problem?" Chevrier asked, hearing the exchange and coming up beside her.

"Excess of caution, that's all," she said, not ready to admit she didn't know why she wanted the car in custody, only that there were still questions about the accident.

And if the car sat out in an open lot, all chance of getting them answered—or using the answers in court, should that be necessary—would be gone.

After the wrecker departed, Chevrier helped gather the flares and flashers and scan the travel lanes for debris. One of the other deputies left for the hospital to finish writing up the accident; a third headed to Houlton to check the injured driver's record from a nice warm office instead of out here in the snow.

She aimed the flashlight, making her way through the piled snow to the edge of the embankment. Below, a massive old spruce had taken a direct hit, a deep gash in it marking the place of impact.

Maybe the kid had simply been visiting a buddy around here and got started back to school late. But in that case . . .

She frowned back up the embankment. In that case, he'd been going in the wrong direction. She blinked flakes from her lashes, peering down the steep slope again, then caught a glint in her flashlight beam at the base of the big tree.

"Lizzie," Chevrier protested as she started down the rest of the way. He'd only called her out here, she knew, so the other officers wouldn't imagine her home in bed and get resentful.

But even the deputy in charge of the scene hadn't slid down to slop around in the slush, so why should she? The driver had smelled strongly of beer; maybe he'd just been drunk and/or asleep.

Case closed, probably. But chewed-up grass and muddy ruts marked the trail the errant car's tires had cut through the snow, and at the end of it something—

Twinkled. Crouching to reach for the object in the snow, she stopped herself. Small, metallic, with a round, shiny ball at one end and a thin metal stem at the other . . .

"Hey, Cody?" she yelled back up the embankment. He stood at the top. "Got any evidence bags?"

She waited while he vanished for a moment, then made his way down to hunker beside her. "What?" he demanded irritably, holding open the plastic bag.

She plucked it up with the plastic tweezers from the kit and dropped it in. "It's a nose stud. Like the kind for pierced ears, you know? Only you wear it in—"

There were millions of them in the world, probably. But her new helper Spud Wilson had one, didn't he? And Dylan Hudson had a case, the one about the dead girls in Bangor . . .

And one of the victim's friends had mentioned that some guy from the County might be involved, Dylan had said.

"You wear it in your nose," she finished. "And I hope that I don't know who it belongs to."

NINE

When she got back to the house, the sky was getting light, the overnight snow diminishing to a sprinkle of flakes tiny and dry as salt, and Dylan was gone.

A rumble from the utility room unnerved her until she found he'd stripped the bed, started the sheets in the washer, and put on fresh ones. A pot of coffee waited in the kitchen.

Thanks, he'd scrawled on the notepad by the phone.

She tore the page off and crumpled it into the trash; no time now for any worrying about Dylan Hudson or who might've been waiting for him at the motel or anywhere else.

That was his business, she instructed herself. Hers was figuring out how Spud's nose stud got into a drunk driver's crashed car . . .

If it really was his, a question she considered answered an hour later when she arrived at her little storefront office on Main Street to find him already there.

No nose stud. Without the bit of jewelry, the hole in the crevice of his right nostril was a tiny dimple, unnoticeable if you didn't already know about it.

"Spud," she began. She could just ask him

about it, of course. But then on impulse she decided not to; if he lied, she'd have no way to prove any different. And—

Don't spook him, she thought, again out of an excess of caution. But you didn't get do-overs on these things. "How was your evening?" she asked instead.

He'd come in to put up bookshelves; she'd decided to store her library of textbooks and other law-enforcement reading here at the office.

"Not great," he replied. His face looked drawn and tired, as if he'd been up all night, but his hair was freshly washed and no longer twisted up into those silly-looking dreadlocks.

"Had a big fight with my dad," he said. "I threw," he added, "a beer can at the TV."

He sounded sheepish. "Busted it. Had to go out with my mom and get a new one."

"I see." The rest of his jewelry was all in place: a lip ring, a silver loop through his earlobe, and a small silvery eyebrow ring she hadn't seen before. "That must've been inconvenient. Was your father angry about it?"

Bent over his lumber—she was going with painted planks laid on brackets fastened to the wall studs, and he was measuring the planks' length—he grimaced dismissively.

"I guess. He started it. They find that missing kid?"

"No." By now the whole town probably knew

about the baby vanishing from his crib. "Why, do you have some insight to offer?"

It came out more sarcastically than she'd intended; she didn't like the uncertainty she was suddenly feeling about this young man. But he just shook his head.

"Uh-uh. You want these second-coated?"

The shelves with paint, he meant. "Yes, please."

She'd heard enough alibis in her life to know that he'd just given her one for the early part of his evening. The later part, though, was still anyone's guess. She found cash in her wallet.

"Here, you can use this to pay for the extra paint."

He nodded, meanwhile drawing a thick, dark pencil line on the plank with the aid of a carpenter's rule. She wondered what he'd say if she asked what he'd done after buying the TV.

Instead: "So listen, remember when you approached me in the Food King?"

Just over a week earlier, but it felt already as if months had passed. "You asked if I paid for tips. And I was wondering, what did you mean by that?"

Probably he had nothing to do with Dylan's case, himself. What were the odds, after all? But he might know someone who did, might have been in that little car with them last night before it crashed and lost his jewelry item in it.

Spud looked up warily. "Yeah, well. Just forget

274

about what I asked you, okay? It was stupid. Sometimes I'm a real dumb kid."

He lumbered to his feet, absently shoving his sweatshirt sleeves up over his tattooed forearms, then hastily pushing them down again. It was as if he hadn't wanted her to see the twining dragon, eyes bright with yellow ink and scales deep green, that wrapped sinuously around his flexor and snaked up to his biceps.

Or the livid red scratch that ran through it, from his elbow nearly to his wrist. As she considered this, the Bearkill squad car pulled up outside.

"Hey, Lizzie." The redheaded officer's name, she had learned, was Ralph Crandall; the other one was Fred Willette.

And Crandall was indeed a decent cop. "Hey, you want to ride out and see a meth lab bust? DEA's gonna bring the hammer down on 'em—"

He glanced at his watch. "Any time now."

Spud kept his head down, intent on his work. Lizzie thought about staying, noodling a little more at the kid.

Because that scratch bugged her. She'd seen a few like it in the past, mostly on people who'd been in fights.

You clutch your attacker's forearms, he pulls away . . . but it was Dylan's case, she decided finally. She'd tell him about all of this and let him decide what he wanted to do about it.

It was what she'd want if their situations were

275

reversed, and Spud wasn't going anywhere, after all. He never did.

"Sure," she told Crandall.

In the past couple of weeks, she'd seen some of the best that Maine had to offer: good food, decent people, pretty scenery, and weather that yet hadn't turned quite as viciously wintry as she'd feared, though she supposed it still would.

Grabbing her jacket to follow Crandall out, she figured she might just as well also get a load of some of the worst.

Unmarked sedans with beacons on their dashboards lined the road outside the suspected meth lab, which from the look of it as Lizzie made her way up the dirt driveway was no longer merely suspected.

"Aw, man," complained a weedy-looking little guy as he was escorted downhill past her. Then as he caught sight of Crandall:

"Hey, Ralphie, come on, man, can't you do something for me here? I thought we were pals!"

"Yeah, we're pals, all right," Crandall muttered, keeping pace with Lizzie. "If you want to call arresting someone about a million times being *pals*."

They continued up the driveway until they reached a sort of compound laid out on a rough lot. Kids' plastic toys, a fifty-five-gallon drum overflowing with charred trash, a rusting car up on cinder blocks, its doors hanging open and stuffing spilling out of its torn seats.

Most of the mobile homes she'd seen here in Maine were just that: homes, with well-kept yards and interiors. This was way out of the ordinary, and so were the people now being escorted from various outbuildings:

Six in all, they marched glumly in single file, not one of them wearing any kind of warm clothes; the two girls wore fuzzy bedroom slippers, and one of the guys was barefoot.

Lizzie looked away, spotted Cody Chevrier across the trash-strewn yard, and picked her way through it to join him.

"No hazmat?" she inquired, not seeing any hoods or suits on the technicians swarming the place. Meth labs were toxic waste dumps of chemical by-products; a site where the stuff had been cooked could be unsafe to live in for years.

He shook his head. "Not making it here. Packaging went on in the house and out back. Christ, there were kids living in there."

A final occupant emerged from the trailer's front door, her arms firmly in the grip of two female officers. Small, elderly, with matted gray hair and wild eyes, she appeared confused as she allowed the officers to help her down the concrete-block steps.

"That's the mom," said Chevrier. "The sons

moved in here and took the place over. We found her locked in a back room. Skin and bones," he added in disgust, kicking at a sodden Elmo doll on the ground.

It was snowing again, the sky dark and featureless, the color of lead. "They took the kids out first," he added.

Two federal officers in DEA jackets waved a white van up the driveway, backing it toward a metal shed. Techs hopped from the van, clad in hazmat lite: paper shoe covers, zippered suits, hair covers, latex gloves, and goggles.

If it had been a manufacturing area, they'd have worn moon suits and respirators. "How's the Brantwell thing going?" she asked, watching the techs pick their way through the litter.

Those paper shoe covers were just about useless in snow, she noted. "Nowhere," said Chevrier succinctly.

"Or on your shootings in Allagash, either," he added before she could ask. "They've got the shell casings in the lab."

To see if they could match them with any other crimes, he meant. "But there's no other evidence. And listen, that hunter from Nussbaum's camp who went back to New York? Turns out he got it with a thirty-eight, cops down there are running it all down, but—"

"What?" She stared at Chevrier. "I thought that was a—"

"Hit-and-run?" He grimaced sourly. "Yeah, well, there's a new twist on that. They did the postmortem, big surprise, they found a bullet in him. Someone shot him, then ran him over."

"Oh, man." She exhaled dispiritedly for him. "Ballistics?"

He shook his head. "Not yet. And I'm not holding my breath."

"Right. Not like on the TV shows, is it?" There, the killer always made a mistake or left a clue that some crazily perceptive lab tech or computer-nerd-slash-genius picked up on. Science, logic, and an insane amount of dedication won the day—possibly aided by a few thrown punches or well-aimed bullets—and did it before the final commercial, too.

But not in real life, where most of the time working a case was more like trudging through glue-laced quicksand.

They turned back toward the Bearkill squad, where Crandall was on his cell phone. He looked up as they approached.

"Cody, my wife wants to know was Izzy Dolaby in there with those other jerks."

Chevrier rolled his eyes. "Yeah, Izzy was there. Tell your wife her no-good cousin needs a kick in the nuts, maybe he won't leave any more of his spawn all over the County."

Crandall sighed. "Yeah, honey, he's here," he

said into the phone, then held it, wincing, away from his ear until the outraged squawking stopped coming out of it.

"Crandall's wife was a Dolaby before she got married," said Chevrier as they walked toward the metal shed where the suited-up techs had gone in. "Still is one, you ask me," he added.

Just then one of the techs came out. "Sheriff, you gotta see this," she said, shaking her head. "You can go on in, nothing's spilled or leaking. Just the opposite, actually."

She waved at the van, which had been idling in the driveway, signaling it to come on back, also. Lizzie let Chevrier go ahead of her, heard his whistle of astonishment, then stepped in, too, and saw the reason for it.

"Wow," she said inadequately. Shelves like the ones Spud was putting up in her office lined the walls, from the rough plywood floor to the ceiling. Long fluorescent fixtures, their faint hum the only sound, lit the windowless shed.

A vent fan turned slowly at the structure's far end. In the center, a plywood table held a stack of cardboard box flats ready to be assembled and filled.

Some already had been, with ziplocked plastic bags. Inside the bags were tinier bags packed with bluish-white crystals.

She turned to Chevrier. "They were packing these in the trailer?"

"Nope. Not enough room. This here is a storage facility."

He glanced around. "Looks like a lot of small-time cooks just lost a hub in their distribution network. Somebody bought from them. Izzy must've been warehousing the stuff here and then someone picked up from him, sold it on to someone bigger."

Despite the exhaust fan, the place still stank faintly of ether and ammonia. They stepped back outside, the fresh air a bracing relief, as from the end of the yard Dolaby's harsh whine cut through the falling snow. "Come *on,* man!"

His wrists were in plastic cuffs. One of the DEA cops lit a cigarette and stuck it in his mouth like a pacifier, whereupon he shut up and let himself be helped into the back of another van that had pulled up while Chevrier and Lizzie were in the shed.

"Shouldn't be too long before they get the next rung up on the ladder ID'd," Lizzie observed. "Just let Izzy get a nicotine jones going, sounds like he'd give up his mother."

"That is his mother," said Chevrier, meaning the pathetic older woman now seated in the Bearkill squad car. Lizzie waved at Caldwell to let him know he should go on without her.

"Yeah, that Izzy's a little pissant," Chevrier went on when Wally had gone. "And he's gonna find out those DEA folks are not as tenderhearted as we are down at the jail in Houlton. I give him maybe an hour in custody before he flips."

And then they'd know who the courier was. "You have any idea this was going on here?" she asked as they climbed into his Blazer.

Just then Trey Washburn went by in his big pickup with the winch on the back. Taking in the scene, he raised a finger off the steering wheel in brief greeting.

Chevrier waved back, then flipped on the wipers to brush a half inch of fresh snow off the windshield. "Nope," he said in answer to Lizzie's question. "And I guess the DEA crew didn't trust me with that little item of info, either."

His voice conveyed how he felt about that: one part ticked off, two parts what-else-is-new. "We've got a few tweakers, you see 'em around town, and once in a long while some goofball gets a bright idea, tries making the stuff."

He took the turn toward town, onto the rural highway that an hour of snowfall had whitened again after an earlier plowing. An orange town truck went by the other way, scattering sand.

"But mostly they stay a lot farther out in the sticks, where they can keep out of sight better," he added.

They drove in silence for a few miles, the passing landscape transformed by the snow squall. Plowed fields, earth-colored the day before, now sported brown and white stripes; tree trunks were glazed on one side, charcoal on the other, and the dark green spruce trees were white-frosted as if decorated for holiday cards.

Nicki, thought Lizzie. Any time now, the Christmas wreaths and other holiday decorations would start going up. She'd sent a crocheted dress to her sister's baby that first year; after that, there'd been no one to send anything to.

"Pretty, huh?" said Chevrier.

"Yes. Yes, it is."

A pastured horse wearing a red plaid blanket looked up from behind a fence, his dark muzzle sporting a wisp of straw. As they passed, a boy in a denim jacket ran down to the horse from the nearby farmhouse, carrying a leather harness.

"I bet Boston's good-looking sometimes, too, though."

She turned, surprised, as they came into town past the Food King. Area 51 sign's glowing alien shone over the entrance to the bar, its black, slit-eyed stare unblinking through the snow.

"You've never been?" she asked as he pulled to the curb. In her little storefront office, the lights were on and the shelves were all up and painted, but Spud was not in sight.

Chevrier chuckled. "Oh, yeah. I'm not a complete rube."

Embarrassed, she protested, "That's not what I meant."

But he just grinned. "I've been to conferences

283

there. Just never saw any of the good parts, that's all."

Then he frowned. "Look, not to be nosy. But I was talking to Washburn earlier and . . . did you two have a falling-out? Because he's a nice guy but kind of sensitive. Easy to get crossways with him, I mean, if you don't know him."

Or if you say you're going home alone and then he sees you coming out of your house the next morning with another man, she thought acutely.

But of course she didn't say that. "No. No, we're fine, I just . . ." She stopped, flustered.

"Say no more." He put up his hands in acceptance. "None of my business, anyway."

She glanced up and down the street: still no Spud. "Trey told me a little about that big place of his the other night. I guess his father left him, um, financially embarrassed?"

Chevrier made a face. "Financially and every other way. Guy gambled his life away, lost his land, got in debt, the stress put his wife in the grave. Trey even wound up in foster care for a while. Gotta give him credit, I've never seen a man haul himself out of a hole by his bootstraps like he has."

"Wow," she said, thinking about all those acres, the house, and the modern vet clinic. "Those are some bootstraps." Then:

"Listen, I've still got nothing on that other thing."

Chevrier's dead-cop case, she meant, wondering if she should confess her growing doubts about it. It would be only fair. But:

"Yeah, well, I never thought you'd just grab it up for me like a rabbit out of a hat," said Chevrier.

"When things quiet down, we'll take a ride over to Van Buren, over on the Canadian border," he went on. "Where Fontine lived."

The dead ex-cop she hadn't had a chance to find out about yet, he meant. He glanced in the rearview mirror as she readied herself to get out.

"Meanwhile, just . . . you know. Pay attention," he said. "You come up with anything I should hear, give a holler, that's all."

He glanced in the rearview again with a small frown; she turned to see why and caught sight of Spud climbing out of a gray van in the parking lot of the Food King.

The van pinged her memory somehow; she put the thought away for later examination. "So you want me to work on the Brantwell baby for now?"

But Chevrier shook his head. "I've got people on that. And the whole rest of the world's on it, too, now it seems like, though I'm pretty sure it's a local thing . . ."

Which made sense, she realized, since otherwise how would anyone have known there was a child in the house at all?

". . . and you don't know much of anyone around here yet," he added. "So . . ."

Right, so where would she even start? And anyway, the cops whose case it was wouldn't like her butting in, any more than she would if it were hers. Chevrier's radio spat static and then a dispatch voice reported that a snowplow had clipped the fender off a vehicle outside Bearkill and needed assistance.

Leaving Lizzie on the sidewalk, Chevrier took off, the Blazer's light-bar whirling yellow in the snow, which was once again falling thickly. The van she'd seen in the Food King's lot was gone.

And so was Spud. Though she stood outside peering around a minute longer in the swirl of fat, white snowflakes, in the few seconds she'd been turned away from him he'd simply vanished.

An hour later she was still in the office, going stir-crazy. She'd driven back to the house to get Rascal, walked him and fed him, then brought him here, but the big dog couldn't settle down any more than she'd been able to.

And Spud hadn't returned. Probably he'd decided to go home before the snow got any worse. *And maybe I should, too . . .*

The weather outside continued and the silence in the office went on, as well, while Rascal paced unhappily. *So much for your great plan,* she thought. *Come up here and get a cop job, be an insider so you can hunt for a kid who might not even be here.*

And now here she was with nothing to do, just twiddling her thumbs. *Liaison officer, my great-aunt Fanny.*

She should've waited for a real job to open up, she thought, turned her back on Cody Chevrier's half-assed switcheroo from full-fledged deputy to boondocks benchwarmer. Then at least she'd be out there doing . . . what?

She didn't even know. There didn't even seem to be any leads on the Brantwell baby, or none that anyone had confided to her. The meth distribution operation was a state case, or would be soon; the shootings at the lake were state cop material, too—

And Dylan was gone, almost certainly back at his motel by now with the woman who'd been waiting for him there.

Not that I care. And anyway . . . oh, the hell with it. Maybe she should wander over to Area 51, see if she could save another patron from another drunk with a gun.

It was just her speed, lately. "Come on, Rascal." Leashing him up, she went out into the swirling snow.

But when she got to the bar's entrance the smell of stale beer drifting from it was so dispiriting, she couldn't face going in. Missy Brantwell's truck wasn't around, either.

Of course it's not. She's probably home waiting for a ransom call, or being cross-examined by social service workers. But if you sit on your hands for much longer, Lizzie, they're going to attach themselves to your butt.

Thinking this, she turned abruptly away from the saloon's front door and strode back across the street, with Rascal prancing beside her, grinning. *Are we going somewhere?* his face asked eagerly. *Huh? Huh?*

"Yeah, buddy." She opened the Blazer's passenger door; he leapt up as if this was what he had been wanting all along.

And she had, too, she realized. So . . . *You want to investigate something?* a defiant little voice spoke up in her head. *Blow the dust off those red-hot detecting skills of yours?*

Because there was still one thing she could work on, wasn't there? Climbing in, she fired up the Blazer's engine, the heater, and the super-storm-fighting windshield wipers she'd had put on when she bought the new tires. After a quick call to the cops in the town of Van Buren, which Chevrier had said was east of here near the Canadian border, she pulled out onto the street, feeling the DuraTracs bite into the snow with a decisive crunch.

Moments later she was headed out of town on Route 227, her map on the seat beside her. Fenced fields and farmhouses lay silent under a fresh snowy blanket; once they had thinned out, her only companions were the trees thick on either side of the road, their branches already bending under a load of fast-accumulating flakes.

Everything in her wanted to charge back to Allagash and Nussbaum's lakeside camp, to start asking questions, examining evidence, making suggestions for how the investigation should go.

But in this snow, going there would be worse than useless; better to let the system collect and plow through what evidence there was, see if any of it might offer a lead. And *then* she could go off half-cocked.

At Presque Isle she came briefly out of the woods into an area of divided highway flanked by fast-food places, then turned onto Route 1 North toward Van Buren. This part of the state, along the Canadian border and the Saint John River, would've been turf most familiar to the last dead cop on Chevrier's list.

Her cell phone rang. Dylan's number . . . she let the call go to voice mail. Let him wonder where she was—*and with whom,* a small voice in her head added vindictively—for a change.

After that, she just drove. Fifty miles to the small town of Van Buren, on the border between Maine and New Brunswick, was an easy ride from Bearkill when the weather was good, probably. But now it felt endless; first more deep forest, then swamps with the skeletal remains of drowned trees jutting up from them, and then more forests went by. With ten miles still left to go, she found herself regretting her impulse.

Probably this would all be a goose chase, anyway. The house that Chevrier's dead ex-cop friend Michael Fontine had died in was still vacant, the Van Buren cop she'd talked to had said.

Although that didn't mean there'd still be anything in it to confirm Chevrier's suspicions. The phone chirped once more; there had been no coverage for most of the drive, but now it was back.

Dylan again, though, and she ignored it again as the reassuring shapes of a Rite-Aid store and a Qwik-Stop materialized through the blowing snowflakes. A block later, past street signs posted in English and French, a red-brick church with a bell tower and an elaborate rose window marked the edge of the business district.

There was a border crossing somewhere in the vicinity, but she didn't see it or a police station, either. She pulled into a gas station/convenience store; in a small town like this, surely people would remember the retired cop who'd died.

Inside, the smell of sweet drinks mingled with the aroma of the hot-dog-grilling machine, the red sausages sweating as they turned under hot lights. She chose a Coke from the cooler, then went up to the counter and asked the clerk if he could help her find her late uncle Michael Fontine's old place.

No sense broadcasting why she was really here if she didn't have to. If Chevrier's suspicions were right, she didn't want to start any alarm bells ringing about a possible investigation.

The old man with twinkling dark eyes and neat mustache smiled pleasantly and replied, but his English turned out to be so heavily interspersed with French, she could barely understand it.

"*Oui*," he said when she'd finally gotten her message across. "*Je suis désolé pour ton oncle.*"

"Right. I mean *merci*. But . . ."

Trey Washburn had said this part of Maine, and the area of New Brunswick, Canada, that lay beyond it, too, were deeply French. She searched her memory for her high school French lessons.

"Ooh at-son mayson?" she managed—*where is his house?* Or at least she hoped that was what it meant.

The clerk smiled kindly despite her butchery of his language. "*Près de la traversée. Maison jaune, petit.*"

He moved his slim, well-kept hands to show how small the yellow house near the bridge was; near the border crossing she'd missed seeing, she realized.

"*Merci*," she told him again, turning to go.

"*Bonjour, êtes-vous un policier?*"

She understood that, all right. *Are you a cop?*

Just then a younger man with a broom and dustpan came from the rear of the store, as the clerk behind the counter spoke again. This time, though, he wasn't smiling.

"Votre oncle était un bon homme, il ne s'est pas suicidé."

Not a suicide. She stood speechless. Finally, "How do you know?" *That I'm a cop. A* flic. *And—*

The younger man spoke, angling his head affectionately at the older one. "He was a cop himself in Montreal. Retired now. And he knew your uncle, they went to Saint Rose's up the street, they were ushers together at Sunday mass."

The church with the rose window . . . The youth's speech was heavily French inflected, too, but understandable. The clerk at the counter spoke again, his eyes no longer twinkling.

Professionally serious. *"J'ai dit à la police, quand ils sont venus, 'Il ne l'a pa fait. C'est un péché mortel, et il voulait aller au ciel. Après la mort de sa femme, il vivait pratiquement dans l'église, il voulait être avec elle. Pourquoi s'enverrait-il plutôt en enfer?'"*

Seeing her helplessness, the younger man translated. "He says he told the cops your uncle practically lived at the church after his wife died. All he wanted was to be with her once more, why would he send himself to hell instead?"

She turned back to the older man, who was watching her with a look she recognized: cop to cop. And he'd left a job behind, too . . .

"Do you miss it?" she asked. "Montreal, *la grande ville? Les grandes . . .*"

"*Les enquêtes des grands*," he corrected with a smile. "The big investigations? *Non.*"

He went on in French again, too swiftly for her to catch, "*Et de toute façon, c'est la même chose ici. La nature humaine, l'obscurité et la lumière. Le même partout.*"

Human nature . . . the dark and the light. Another smile, still kindly, but this time tinctured with unmistakable warning.

"*Bon chance, mademoiselle. Prenez soin.*"

Good luck, and be careful. She pondered the words as she drove out of the parking lot, wondering if they were mere French politeness or if there was more to the retired cop's warning. And why *would* a religious man give up eternal life in favor of ending his earthly one, anyway?

For herself, she believed that information about a possible afterlife would be provided, if at all, on a need-to-know basis. But for the people who worshipped in the church with the big rose window, suicide was a mortal sin.

You went to hell for it, lost all hope of seeing your loved ones in heaven. And from what she'd just heard, that hope was all a certain dead ex-cop had been living for after his wife died.

A block back the way she'd come, she spied the sign for the border crossing and turned left, braking lightly on the downhill grade. At the foot of the hill stood a red-brick customs station and a guard's box with stop signs in French and English; beyond that stretched the low concrete bridge over the Saint John River.

A car with Canadian plates pulled up to the booth and the driver spoke briefly to the officer inside, then proceeded onto the bridge. Brake lights flashed again as he slowed for Canadian customs on the other side.

A border crossing, she thought. With guards and passports. And . . . a customs station; she hadn't considered what that might mean before.

But now she did. So maybe, she thought as she found her own turnoff just before the entrance to the bridge and took it—

Maybe this trip wasn't really such a goose chase—an *oie chasse*, as her *flic* colleague might have put it—after all.

The narrow road along the Saint John River was little more than a path, two snowy ruts leading to a handful of small houses half hidden by overgrown bramble thickets. It ended at a pile of dirt with a sign stuck into it: NO SNOWMOBILES!

To the left a weedy verge overlooked the river, which she had imagined as rushing and wild; instead, the wide, flat expanse of moving water was dotted with low, sandy islands, and looked almost shallow enough to walk across.

Not that she meant to try. Beside her, Rascal whined his wish to be allowed out of the Blazer.

She eyed him doubtfully, holding up his leash as she opened his door. "I don't know, buddy. I don't have time for a long—"

Walk, she was about to finish as he leapt past her, his big, muscular body nearly bowling her over in his hurry to exit. Then, before she could even call him, he took off, up and over the dirt pile and down the snow-choked trail on the other side of it.

By the time she had clambered up the pile herself, he was nowhere in sight. Damn, damn . . . "Rascal!"

She followed his trail, aware that it was still snowing, so his tracks wouldn't remain visible, and that although it was only just before noon, the cloud-darkened sky was growing darker.

Much darker . . . then she heard the sounds. *Crunching* sounds . . .

Pushing through clumps of reed in a half-frozen boggy area, she found the source. A girl in a green jacket looked up from a canvas ground cloth where Rascal sat chewing what appeared to be the world's largest dog biscuit.

The girl got up and approached. "Hi, I'm Marie. Is this your dog? Nice boy."

She had dark curly hair, dark eyes, bright

cheeks, and a confident handshake. She waved at the river. "I'm making pictures of the birds down there, you see? I do it very often."

A camera stood on a tripod, aimed at the river. "But the light is going now, so I was, how you say, wrapping it up?"

Her smile belonged in a toothpaste ad, and her French-accented voice was musical. Rascal got up and nudged the girl for another biscuit; Lizzie snapped his leash on.

Gathering her stuff up with practiced swiftness, the girl trudged with Lizzie back toward the Blazer. Past the dirt pile that marked the end of the drivable part of the trail, Lizzie spotted the yellow house.

The *maison jaune* . . . The girl followed her gaze. "Oh, you were looking for that house? It's why you're here?"

She sounded troubled, suddenly. Smart as well as pretty, Lizzie thought.

"Poor Michel," the girl went on. She pronounced the name the French way. "He was a nice man. I used to see him in the yard. All alone. I tried to be friendly to him, but then last September he died very suddenly."

She turned to Lizzie. "You want to go in, yes?"

No, Lizzie thought suddenly. She'd thought she did, but now that she was here . . . *Not even a little bit.*

The cramped-looking bungalow, its yellow

paint not quite negating the impression of darkness from within, glowered at her. The blank, empty windows piercing the facade reminded her of the multiple eyes of some malevolent insect. No one would want to go in there.

No one. "How did you know I wanted to see inside?" she stalled.

The girl smiled. "I watch people's eyes. When I take their picture, when they look at my pictures."

She smoothed Rascal's ear. "Yours, they look at the house like they want to . . . like they want to *invade* it."

I've come all this way, Lizzie told herself, still eyeing the place reluctantly. Really, it looked . . .

"And I have," the girl offered brightly, "the key!"

"Okay," said Lizzie reluctantly. She was a cop, after all. An experienced *flic* who could take care of herself. "Lead on."

Inside, the house smelled of dampness, of rooms unheated and sink traps with water standing too long in them. A front hall held a coat tree with a blue cotton jacket hung on it, a table bearing a jug of long-dead flowers, and a wicker basket full of sympathy cards.

On the loss of your wife . . . The cards' front illustrations were of somber skyscapes, lone doves, and funeral-tinted blooms, purple iris and marine-blue roses. The house had been empty for months, yet no one had touched them or anything else, it seemed.

"This way!" the girl called from the front parlor; Lizzie followed to where a worn brown recliner, a large, not-very-new TV, and a red velvet settee made up the furnishings. On the walls, framed cross-stitched portraits depicted various saints; a white china statue of the Virgin Mary's veiled head rested in a nest of spun glass on the mantelpiece. On the hearth sat a grate-fronted propane heater.

Rascal sniffed uneasily, then sat, plopping himself down on the tan rug with a resigned groan. *You and me both, buddy,* Lizzie thought. In the kitchen, more evidence of a solitary life: one plate, one cup, one set of cutlery on the drainboard.

A saucepan on the stove held the gray powder residue of water heated a cup at a time, morning after morning, likely for the instant coffee a jar of which now held a solid, blackish lump that stuck to the glass like hardened molasses.

The bathroom: no shade on the lightbulb over the sink, a worn-down toothbrush, and a single towel. It struck Lizzie that if she had to live like this day after day, she might start thinking of a way out, too. Only not if she thought the act would condemn her to a fiery eternity . . .

Or if it meant I'd never see Dylan again. The thought caught her unprepared, showing her the painful truth of what she'd been trying so hard to ignore: that he'd been lying to her again, that he'd been looking her in the eye and lying.

By omission, at least. And that it was killing her. Grimly she turned from the thought, back to the business of today.

"How did he do it?" she murmured. "How did he—"

The girl looked up from the counter's sad kit of dishware. She'd been eyeing it with calculation; for a photograph, perhaps.

"He hung himself. In there." She angled her dark head at the only room they hadn't entered. "From the bedroom door."

The girl hadn't asked why Lizzie wanted to come in here. Too young to be suspicious of others' motives, she was so curious and eager about everything herself that it probably didn't occur to her that not everyone else was.

Or that their motives might be other than artistic. "How come you have a key?" Lizzie asked, approaching the door from whose knob Fontine must've suspended the rope.

Then he'd have thrown the looped end over the other side, stood on a chair, and—

The victim's feet only had to be a couple of inches off the floor, she knew from unhappy professional experience. She stepped into the room.

"He gave it to me," the girl replied. "He just

299

wanted someone to have one, for safety's sake, he said. In case he was ever away and needed someone to go in. He had my phone number to call, if that ever happened," she said from the kitchen.

"So you haven't been in here since he—"

Since he strangled himself to death instead of taking his planned trip. It was another thought worth turning away from: a long, fast drop from a height was one thing. With any luck, the sudden stop would kill you instantly.

But kicking away a chair was something else again.

"No" came the girl's voice, along with the sound of cabinet doors opening and closing; very curious, apparently.

"No one has. He had no one. I wanted to come in, but I was afraid to, alone. Or—not afraid, exactly. Just . . ."

Yeah. Just. In the bedroom all the dead man's things were where he'd left them: Shoes. Belt. A black leather-bound prayer book lay on the bedside table next to a long-silent windup alarm clock.

She turned, taking it in: A small deckle-edged mass card was tucked into the prayer book to mark a place; a rosary lay beside it. A ceramic crucifix with a dried palm frond stuck behind it hung over the head of the bed.

On the dresser lay a manila folder. Inside: a set

of papers for new federal employees. From what Lizzie could gather, the man who had lived here had just become a U.S. border crossing guard. But two weeks before the start date noted in the paperwork, he'd decided to put a rope around his neck instead.

A cry of surprise came from the kitchen. Closing the folder, Lizzie hurried out to where the girl stared into an open utility closet whose door had been camouflaged by the faded wallpaper.

The door covering matched the walls, and the door itself fitted so closely that no gap had showed. Lizzie had walked right by it, not even realizing it was there.

And except for the dead man, no one else had, either, at least to judge by the amount of weaponry in it. Two shotguns, a rifle, several handguns, plus boxes of ammo on shelves . . .

"Oh," the girl murmured. "I had no idea of this . . . No idea at all . . ."

An ex-policeman might very well keep such an arsenal, Lizzie supposed, especially if he hunted for sport, as so many Maine men seemed to. The shotguns for birds, the rifle for deer . . .

And since he had lived here alone, perhaps he saw no reason to lock his guns up. But . . .

"Go on outside, okay?" she told the girl, whose dark eyes were now full of worry. "It's all right, you're not going to get in any trouble. Take the dog, too, and put him in my vehicle."

Looking relieved to have something to do, the girl obeyed while Lizzie pulled out her cell phone. What she needed, she supposed, was the Van Buren cops to come and take possession of all these weapons; they couldn't be left in an unsecured house.

Punching in 911, she described where she was and what she had found. What she did not say, however, was that as far as she was concerned, Cody Chevrier's suspicions had just been proven correct in at least one instance. Michael Fontine had not killed himself with a rope, a doorknob, and a kitchen chair.

No one with all those guns would decide instead to torture himself to death. Nor, at least as far as she was concerned, had he done it by any other method; he was just too deeply religious.

But that wasn't the point. Michael Fontine had ended up hanging from a rope, and to her mind, someone else had almost certainly put him there.

Thinking this, she was about to tuck the phone away when it thweeped at her; probably that 911 staffer calling back, she thought, and punched the answer key without looking.

But instead a familiar voice spoke. "Lizzie? Don't you ever answer your phone? I've been trying to call you all—"

"Get to it, okay?" she snapped. "I'm a little busy here."

A patrol car pulled up out front. Through the

kitchen window, Lizzie watched two officers begin the trudge up to the house.

"Anyone in there?" The first officer reached the front door, yelled in through it, then pounded on the frame.

A garbled sputter came from the officer's radio. "Yes, in here," she called back. Then into the phone:

"What? Say again, please, Dylan, I—"

"Lizzie, I think Nicki might've been found. This time for real."

TEN

What's happened? Are you sure it's her? Is she all right?"

It was nearly three in the afternoon, the snow-filled sky already beginning to get dark, when she got back to Bearkill and found Dylan and Chevrier in her office.

They didn't look happy. And Dylan hadn't said they'd found Nicki *alive* . . .

Dylan got up. "Hey. Good to see you're in one piece."

But that was all; no smile, no warmth. She looked a question at him; no response. "What's going on?"

They had a DeLorme map book open to the page detailing the area just north of Bearkill. "Maine DEA had a plane up there in connection with the meth bust this morning," said Chevrier.

"Meth cook operations make heat, so they use infrared cameras to look for heat sources that shouldn't be there," he added.

She frowned. "Wouldn't the flyovers alert people, defeat the purpose?"

Chevrier shook his head. "There's quite a few airfields in the area, some municipal and some private. Small aircraft traffic is pretty common."

He put his index finger on the map. "And they

got a signal right about . . . here." He pointed at a circled area. "Maybe half an hour, forty minutes away in good weather? More, though, on a day like today."

Dylan took up the story again. "But what the flyover picked up doesn't look like a meth cook, or a grow operation like you'd see with marijuana. The heat signature for either one of those is pretty recognizable."

He turned to her. "This was hotter. Like, say, a campfire."

She felt her shoulders slump, fatigue washing over her. But with it came a pulse of anger; they'd rushed her back here for this? "So what? Somebody's out there hunting or—"

"No." Chevrier sounded certain. "The flyovers started last week, getting ready for this morning, and they've gotten the same kind of signal in the same place every time."

He looked up at her. "This is no hunter, and it isn't any temporary camp for a backwoods hiker out there, either. Somebody is living there."

She sank into a chair, unconvinced. "Fine. I still don't see why you're so sure a child is—"

Dylan pulled photographs from a manila envelope. "These are why. Flyover photographs of the site."

He spread grainy blowups in front of her: bright human shapes, like glowing ghosts. From their relative sizes, it was clear that two adults and two children were at the camp, the smallest one being held in the arms of one of the grown-ups.

"I sent that down to Augusta, they can fine-tune the detail in photos like this. They take an unsub"—unidentified subject, he meant—"run algorithms to get a pretty accurate read on the subject's height, weight, and so on."

Chevrier took up the recital. "The Brantwell baby had a medical checkup last week, and a lot of those measurements were documented. They wouldn't have changed much in a few days, and after comparisons, it looks as if that's him in the photo."

"And the other child?" she managed, her mouth suddenly dry. After all this time, could it really be—

"Uh-huh," said Dylan. "They can't be certain, of course, but it sure looks to the techs like that's a little girl out there, from her size maybe nine or ten years old. Lizzie, it could be that we've found her."

She couldn't speak. Chevrier went on into the silence. "And d'you see that little rectangle there?"

He pointed out a bright spot. "That's a solar panel. It means whoever it is has power, maybe not a lot but some. He could be monitoring radio transmissions, maybe Internet, too."

He pulled on his heavy jacket. "Right now the state police, warden service, and Border Patrol . . . they're all waiting to go in. But there's more snow forecast, getting dark. So they're waiting for daylight. Safer that way, I guess."

He snapped the strap of his fur-lined hat under his chin. "Personally, I'd be going now. Not that far, snow hasn't had a chance to pile up too bad . . . and hey, maybe it'll slow down."

"Nope," said a new voice from behind them. "I just saw the radar on TV a few minutes ago. It's going to snow like hell."

It was Missy Brantwell, and from the look on her face she had been listening for a while. Long enough, anyway:

"He's out there, isn't he?"

She took a shuddering breath. "My baby's out there," she took another breath, "and you're *not going to go get him?*"

She advanced on Chevrier. "You're just going to *leave* him there? In the *woods,* with that . . ."

Dylan stepped quickly between Chevrier and the young woman, her eyes wild and her face blotchy with weeping.

"Look," he said, "it's not impossible now, but it is nearly dark, it is snowing, and if we go at him the wrong way, whoever he's got there could get hurt, even the baby might be injured."

Or killed, he didn't say. He didn't have to.

"We don't even know who the guy is out there, what he wants or exactly where they are," he went on. "The aerial shots narrow it down, but we'll need to pinpoint—"

Missy's expression became one of wretched amusement. "You don't, huh?" She let out a ghastly chuckle. "You don't know who he is. Or where he is."

She was wearing a thick black down jacket, a red wool hat, black quilted ski pants, and thick laced boots. "Well, I do. Who he is, what he thinks . . ."

"How would you know all that?" Lizzie demanded.

Missy stared back. "Because he's Jeffrey's father."

Steeling herself, she went on. "Two years ago I spent three months with him out there at his camp."

She peered at the map. "Yep, that's it. A summer playing house in the forest. True love, you know?" she asked bitterly.

Yeah. Yeah, I do, thought Lizzie as the girl went on: "So I know him. I know all about him. I just didn't know *he* knew I'd had Jeffrey . . ."

"Because if he did know, he'd try to take the baby?" Lizzie guessed. Since after all, it seemed that he had.

Missy nodded. "Daniel—that's his name—he wanted a child. Boy or girl, it didn't matter. He wanted a kid to raise up in the right way, he said. To live off the land, be independent."

But at the thought, her composure deserted her. *"God,"* she cried, "what kind of idiot thinks a baby can *live off the land?*"

That explained why she didn't want to tell anyone who her child's father was, Lizzie realized; so the father wouldn't learn about the baby, himself. But now—

"How do you think he found out?" Lizzie asked.

"Or maybe he did know," Chevrier put in. "Are you sure he never saw you with Jeffrey? Does he ever come into town?"

The girl nodded miserably. "He does. I guess he could have seen me and figured it out. At first I was really careful, but then as time went by and nothing happened . . ."

Chevrier nodded. "Sure. You quit worrying so much. It's just human nature."

Then he turned to Dylan and Lizzie. "But Missy's right, an infant in the wilderness would be a hard project. So maybe he was waiting. Let Missy do the difficult stuff, let the kid get a little bigger, you know? And easier to take care of?"

Missy laughed bitterly in agreement. "Sounds right to me. He waited until it was *convenient* for him to—"

"I don't know," Lizzie interrupted, unconvinced. "If he was going to wait until it was easier, why not wait until spring?"

She looked around at the others. "I mean, what if he has a reason to want the baby now? Some reason why he *can't* wait? If he is planning to leave the area, for instance. He could be getting ready to go right this minute, before the snow really gets cranked up."

"Maybe," Chevrier allowed. "But we don't know that. Missy," he added, "we're going to sit you down with some—"

Detectives, profilers, maybe a sketch artist, too, Lizzie thought. Kidnapping was a federal crime. But the girl jerked away.

"Don't you touch me," she snarled at Chevrier. "You think I'll sit around answering questions while you leave my baby boy out there?"

She backed toward the door. "Well, forget it. I'm going to get him right now. Daniel might think he can take care of a baby out there in the woods in the middle of a snowstorm, but I'm not sitting around waiting to find out if he's right."

"That's really his name?" Lizzie asked, trying to stall the girl. "Daniel?"

"Yes, that's really his name, as in Boone. Perfect for a wilderness enthusiast, huh? The kind of person who prides himself on being able to live out there in the deep woods without modern conveniences."

"I see," Lizzie replied, thinking, *Keep her talking.* "So he really can live off the land, then?"

The girl nodded. "Uh-huh. And off a few scavenged things now and then. He's actually kind of brilliant at it."

Great, a brilliant kidnapper, just what we need. But as long as Missy was still here talking, she wasn't out there freezing to death in the woods.

Or getting killed by her ex-boyfriend. "And," Lizzie said, "this Daniel, he was a nice guy? Or he was at first, anyway?"

Missy's face softened. "Uh-huh. At first he was wonderful. But . . ." Her expression said that later, things changed, big-time.

"I left as soon as I thought I might be pregnant. He got so intense. He thinks he's the lord of the forest out there."

"He said that?" asked Lizzie, the odd phrase—*lord of the forest*—pinging her memory.

A jagged laugh escaped the girl as outside the front windows snow gusts blew horizontally. A plow went by, its orange lights flaring and its blade sending up a white cascade.

"No. His father did, actually." And in explanation, "You know Old Dan, the man who gets lost or tips over his motor chair all the time and has to be taken back to the nursing home?"

"Oh," Lizzie exhaled, remembering now. "That's . . . ?"

Missy nodded. "Daniel's dad raised him; his mother died a long time ago. And Daniel visits his dad sometimes. Or he did. That's how I met him—after high school I volunteered there."

"Does he visit anymore?" Because if he did, maybe they could wait. Let him visit his dad, then they'd know right where he was; they could move on him when he—

"No," said Missy. "He'd stopped doing that around the time I left him. Quit doing anything normal, really. He'd gotten some kind of a job, using his van for something. I don't know what it was, though. He never told me anything about it except that now he had some money where before he hadn't."

"A van . . . you mean like he was moving something?" Dylan mused aloud, and in response Lizzie turned to Chevrier.

"Your guy from the bust earlier today, Izzy Dolaby . . . if they were storing all those meth packets at his place, someone had to be delivering them to him, right?"

There'd been no decent vehicles on the Dolaby property. "And someone had to be picking them up, moving them along. So could this guy Missy's talking about have been doing it?"

"Transporting them? Sure," replied Chevrier. "DEA's got no info on that yet, it's why they were doing those flyovers, trying to find somebody to flip."

He made a sour face. "Izzy Dolaby's turning out to be less talkative than they were expecting. He's holding out for a walk. DEA says he's looking at time inside no matter what. And if the DEA won't cut him any slack in exchange for info on their own case, they're sure not going to do it for ours."

Then something else seemed to occur to him.

"He did say one thing, though. One of the DEA guys threatened to stick him in a cell, see if he'd change his mind by morning."

"And?" By now Lizzie was pretty sure she had no interest in Dolaby, who probably was just dumb enough to keep his mouth shut when opening it might help him, and vice versa.

But her opinion changed abruptly when Chevrier replied, "He said by morning it wouldn't matter. That by then there wouldn't be anything or anyone for them to find."

And that did it; Missy was done talking, her hand finding the doorknob. In another moment she'd be outside, and then . . .

Then when the snow stops, we'll be hauling another body out of the woods. Obviously, the minute she got away from here, Missy meant to take off, go find her kid.

Or die trying. *And Nicki might be out there, too.* The words came out before Lizzie could stop them. "Missy, wait."

Halfway out the door, the girl turned, her retort already on her lips. "I'm going, and you can't stop me."

"Lizzie," Dylan began, putting a hand up, "don't . . ."

She waved him silent. On her way out the door, she heard his cell phone warble, heard him answer.

". . . like the other two?" she heard him saying

into it, and from his tone she knew it was bad. His case in Bangor, maybe; the two dead girls. Or were there three now?

Spud, she thought as the closing door cut Dylan's voice off; where the hell had the kid gone?

But she couldn't do anything about him now. Not when outside, the wind pushed her sideways, snow whirling in it. She was out of her element here, in the wild, brutal weather and the coming night.

Nicki. I've come so far to find her, left so much behind.

She caught up to Missy, who turned with defiance on her face. "Don't try to stop me," she began again warningly.

"I'm not trying to stop you," Lizzie replied, then took a deep breath.

"I'm going with you," she said.

He'd lost the stud. From his nose, he'd put it in his pocket yesterday and then somehow he'd—

Jesus. Oh, Jesus.

He'd tried telling himself it didn't matter. Maybe on TV a little mistake like that would get you caught, but not in real life. Even if it got found, there was no way to link it to him.

But then she'd *looked* at him. In the office, his nose empty of its usual jewelry for the first time since she'd met him. She had *looked* at him. *And she'd known . . .*

And now it was snowing. He sprinted across the slushy street toward the Food King, its lit-up parking lot crisscrossed with dark tire tracks in the deepening snow. Cars pulled in and out, their occupants hurrying to stock up before the roads got bad.

Although they wouldn't be *completely* impassable; another plow rumbled past behind him as he hesitated on the lot's landscaped verge. Stormy weather never stopped any self-respecting northern Mainer from getting around; if all else failed, there were snowmobiles.

But he didn't have one. So he'd have to hope those plows were doing their stuff. He'd hung around until dark, hiding in a shed behind the potato wholesaler's barn, not wanting to chance being seen walking or biking toward the interstate.

He hadn't reckoned on the storm, though. And now he'd spied them in her office: Lizzie, Chevrier, and that other cop. Talking about him, probably, so he had to get out of town before . . .

Taking a deep breath, he waited until a woman in a hooded parka got done loading her bags of groceries into a back seat. Once she was in her car and pulling away, he ducked from behind it and began running again between rows of cars, keeping out of the lights as best he could.

Thinking, *How?* How had it all gone so disastrously bad, and so *fast?* Like an avalanche of disaster:

First the guy ordering Spud to get the kid, hand him over, and keep his mouth shut about it or—

Or I'll cut your freaking head off and I'll mount it on a stick, the guy had said while his hand stroked the knife on his belt meaningfully.

Spud had believed him, too; oh, he definitely had. Then came the lost nose stud, its absence somehow betraying what he'd done to the girl last night, though he still didn't understand exactly how . . .

And now the storm had arrived, as if even the weather was out to get him. He scanned more cars; the next one had a barking dog in it, the one after that a kid. *Come on, come on . . .*

A snow gust slapped him, shoving him back a step. But he hurled himself forward again, blinking away the tears and the melting snow.

Because he had to. Just the way he'd had to take the baby. And what he'd had to do to the girl last night, too, it was all the same, things he got forced into or that he couldn't help.

But if they found him, they'd blame him. That much he knew for certain. Gasping, Spud flung himself into a little Ford Fiesta sedan, the keys gleaming like treasure in the ignition.

Turning the key, he felt the still-warm engine firing to life, the heat coming on strong right away. Hitting the gas, he tore out of the parking lot, praying no one had seen him.

But on the street, he slowed abruptly, peering

nervously past the windshield wipers for the Bearkill squad car, puttering along though his heart's racing urged him to go, go, *go!* Not until he passed the potato barn, its porch lights glowing dimly through the snow, did Spud slam his foot down onto the accelerator.

Ahead, the road vanished into a curtain of white. A plow loomed up suddenly, then vanished in the rearview mirror. *If you come back here, I'll kill you,* the guy had said after taking him to see the forest encampment.

But now Spud had nowhere else to go. The wipers slapped open dark wedges on the windshield.

Enough to peer through, out into the night. The wipers flapped, and the snow went on falling, and the car he had stolen went on racking up the miles, due north.

After a while he felt tears leaking down his cheeks, the salt stinging his skin, but he didn't bother swiping at them.

Maybe he won't kill me. Maybe . . .

Maybe he'll let me stay.

Half an hour after agreeing to accompany Missy Brantwell on a mission to get Missy's son back, Lizzie was in her office again, finishing up last-minute preparations for the trip.

Gloves, flashlight, water bottle . . .

Dylan and Chevrier had tried to dissuade her,

of course. But in his heart, it was what Chevrier had wanted, too, and once he'd caved, Dylan did as well, so now all four of them were going.

Scarf, earmuffs . . . The path in to the camp from the road, Missy had told them, was a half mile, maybe a little longer. She wasn't sure about weapons, remembering only that there were some at the camp: a crossbow, a pistol, maybe some long guns as well, she'd said uncertainly.

Which wasn't great news. Still, he was only one guy. And he could probably only shoot one gun at a time, she told herself as the office door swung open and Trey Washburn came in.

"Hey," he greeted her, taking in the gear on her desk.

"Hey, yourself," she replied, surprised. Washburn looked ready for anything in a red-checked hunting cap, voluminous down jacket, and hunting boots, and the shotgun on his shoulder only increased this impression.

"Whoa," she said, eyeing the weapon. Pump-action, double-barreled . . . with its carved stock and gleaming engraved steel, the thing looked expensive.

And deadly. A grin creased his face, which was pink with cold. "Yeah. It was my dad's. Just one of the many things he had to sell when he went broke. I bought it back at an auction."

"Good for you." She smiled briefly at him, then went back to organizing the backpack. She'd gone home for more warm clothes and to walk Rascal, get him situated for the evening; now Chevrier and Missy were getting baby supplies, communications gear, and weapons and ammunition together.

And Dylan was Spud-hunting; she'd told him briefly about the nose stud she'd found at the accident site last night, and he had wanted to talk to the boy himself before they left, if he could.

Now: "Looks like you're getting ready for an expedition," Washburn commented.

"Just making sure my go-bag is all in order," she lied, controlling her impatience.

It was fine that he had decided to make friends again, but now wasn't the time; this trip was nobody else's business. Also, she was late; they'd be leaving in five minutes, but she still had to get her personal weapon out of the locked Blazer, check it, and stow extra clips for it in her bag.

She hadn't even had a chance yet to confer with Chevrier about his friend in Van Buren: the suicide that wasn't. But that, too, would have to wait.

"Pretty intense for routine prep work," Washburn observed.

"Yeah," she replied, not looking up. "Guess I'm kind of an intense person."

Thinking, *Please go away.* Rummaging in her purse, she found a pack of tissues and a lip balm, fished them out and stuffed them into the pack.

"Listen, the truth is, I ran into Missy Brantwell just now," said Washburn. "In the Food King, and in a big hurry. Just like you."

"Is that so?" she replied distractedly, thinking, *First aid kit, extra socks.* They were going in two vehicles in case one got stuck somewhere or had mechanical troubles.

Which, she thought, would be just her luck on a night like this. Then it hit her, what Washburn had just said.

And that he was carrying a shotgun. She looked up. "She told you." About the campsite, about where they were going and why—

"Uh-huh," he said. "I asked if I could help. She's with Hudson and Chevrier now, she'll be riding with them. To give me," he added, "a little time for a private conversation with you."

"I see," she replied lightly, wondering suddenly again how a man whose father had lost every-thing he had, putting his wife in an early grave and his son in foster care . . . how that man paid off school loans, bought the lost farm back, built a new, modern veterinary clinic, and paid for expensive horse upkeep, all on what he made as a rural animal doctor. Not to mention that fabulous house of his . . .

Darn, she thought sadly. *Just when I was really getting to like him, he turns out to be a—*

"Mmph," Washburn uttered softly, his knees buckling.

As he dropped to the floor, the man who had opened the door silently behind him dipped quickly to catch the shotgun Washburn had been carrying. In his other hand, the man gripped the brick Spud Wilson had been using to prop the door open when he brought things in and out: carpeting, shelving material.

Tools and so on. The brick's deep red hue was now darkened further by smeared blood from the back of Washburn's head.

"Old Trey here wasn't the only one who saw Missy in the store," said Roger Brantwell. He was, Lizzie noticed again, almost as big a man as Washburn.

And there was a look in his eye she didn't like. "We had a disagreement back at the house; she drove off all furious," he went on.

Sounding reasonable. Almost. *Keep him talking.* "Because you were at her again to tell you who Jeffrey's father is?"

Brantwell nodded. "But she wouldn't. She told me to mind my own goddamned business for once," he added. "Can you imagine, a girl saying a thing like that to her father?"

Depends on the father, Lizzie thought as he went on. "She has no idea what it's like trying to keep that place going. Food on the table, roof over her head. Keep my guys working, their jobs are on the line, too, you know. And it's all on me."

She glanced past him out the windows to the street, where the snow seemed to be intensifying by the minute. "So you followed her. She drove off in a huff and you—"

He nodded. "Into the store. I thought at least she wouldn't yell at me in front of other people. I just wanted to talk."

Talk now, Lizzie thought. *Keep talking, long enough for Dylan or Chevrier to wonder what's keeping me and come back to find out.*

"But instead you heard her in conversation with someone else," she said. "Trey Washburn."

Brantwell's face darkened. "Yeah. They were at the end of one aisle, I was right around the corner at the end of the next one. So I heard it all."

He kicked at Washburn's unconscious form. Washburn moaned and shifted a little, then was still again.

"The whole plan," Brantwell went on. "Where Jeffrey is. And who's got him. His father. *Daniel,*" he snarled, as if out of the whole awful situation this was the worst part.

As if he already knew Daniel, but that couldn't be right . . . could it? Lizzie dared another glance to the street outside. But she spotted no Chevrier. No Dylan, either. And now Brantwell had Washburn's shotgun, which he handled easily, as if he knew how to use it.

"I don't understand," she said. "Why's it so especially bad that he's Jeffrey's father?"

322

But then she did understand, or she began to, anyway: Brantwell had money troubles. He traveled often to New York, in a Cadillac Escalade whose cargo area had plenty of room. And if Daniel was one link in the meth-moving scheme—

"You're in business with him," she said. "He picked up the product from the individual meth cooks. Izzy Dolaby did the packaging. And you . . ."

Brantwell made the big-shipment deliveries, the next step up in the distribution system in New York. Once upon a time, that wouldn't have been profitable; the Mexican manufacturers had been well established and well funded.

But nowadays with immigration a big issue and the southwest border getting much more enforcement attention . . .

He saw her getting it. "Yeah. I bet Daniel thought it was real funny, too. I bet every time he saw me, he thought about how funny it was, that he'd been screwing my daughter."

He hefted the shotgun. "Now turn around." When she did, he touched the back of her neck with the end of the gun barrel, then took her duty weapon from its holster.

"Empty your pack."

Once she had, showing him there were no other weapons in it, he made her fill it again, aiming the shotgun at her, keeping the barrel out of her reach.

"Come on," she said as she obeyed, "you aren't going to blow me away with a shotgun right here in town, are you?"

"Good question," he replied. But he had an answer for it:

"Accident. Terrible thing. I saw Washburn with the gun, he seemed to be threatening you, and I hit him. That's when the gun went off."

He looked down at Washburn. "Killing you," he added. "And I must've hit Trey too hard with that brick."

Washburn lay motionless except for his breathing, which was hitching and too slow. Lizzie had seen blunt-force head trauma victims before, and this one didn't look merely unconscious.

He looked comatose. "Although," Brantwell went on, bending fast to snatch up the brick again, "it could be I was forced to hit him *twice.*"

"They'll be back here," Lizzie said quickly, "Chevrier and the others, they'll come looking for me any time now and—"

Brantwell lowered the brick grudgingly. "You're right. And he never saw me, so even if he does wake up . . ."

Which without swift medical attention was unlikely, Lizzie thought. She'd seen it happen; accidents, assaults. Even with the proper care, a severe blunt-force head injury could be . . . *Trey,* she thought sorrowfully.

"Come on," Brantwell snapped. "Turn the

lights out. Lock the door. You're going to go around to the Blazer's passenger side and get in that way, then slide across. I'll be right behind you."

Which he was, the gun under his right arm, ready to drop into his hand. From the easy, practiced way he handled the weapon, she knew he wouldn't fumble it or drop it. For a brief instant in the Blazer's cab, she thought she might get the glove box open—

His hand clamped hard around her wrist. "Ah-ah," he warned pleasantly, punctuating this with a nudge from the gun barrel.

She settled as best she could in the driver's seat while he watched approvingly. "So listen," he said. "I realize it must come as a shock to you, all this being out of your control all of a sudden."

You, she thought clearly, *have a big shock coming to you, too. I don't know how yet. Or when. But—*

But I am a freaking cop, dammit. And somehow, I will find a way to wipe that smug look off your face if it's the last freaking thing I do.

Right now, though, all she could do was hope hard that it wouldn't be.

An hour after he'd stolen it from the parking lot and aimed it north, Spud nosed the car off the road, gunning it hard until it stalled in a snow-clogged ditch.

He wouldn't need it again. One way or another, for him this was the end of the road. The dead girl, the lost nose stud . . .

Lizzie Snow's current suspicions were bad enough. But once the authorities got their act together and figured out that he'd killed the girl last night, they'd find out about the other ones, too. His only hope was to get back to the campsite, throw himself on the guy's mercy, convince him that a person like Spud could be useful, good to have around.

That despite their superficial differences, they were really just alike. Outlaws, men of freedom . . .

A freedom that Spud was in danger of losing, maybe forever. The thought urged him out of the car. Around him, in utter silence, the snow kept falling, piling up on branches, coating the trees, so white that even in darkness there was enough light to see by once his eyes had adjusted.

Trudging away from the car, he looked back to find it snow-covered already, the tracks he made filling up even as he stepped out of them. The driver of a passing plow—or, God forbid, a squad car—might not even see it, and anyway, investi-gation of it would reveal only that it was stolen, not by whom.

So he still had a little time. From deep in the forest came a sharp, crackling *snap!* as a snow-laden branch broke off, then a long, crashing chain reaction of thuds and further snappings as the branch fell through other trees to earth.

That gave him pause. The entrance to the trail they'd been on the first time he'd been here, hidden in a clump of barberry if he recalled it right, was . . . there. He was just about to cross the road toward it when headlights appeared from around the curve.

Panicked, he hurled himself headlong over the plow-heaped snowbank at the road's edge, burrowed himself deep into a drift, and lay there barely breathing. The car slowed; he held still.

Not a cop . . . the engine ran too roughly for that, and a loud belch from the vehicle's muffler only reinforced the impression of an old, unhappy car or small truck, forced out on this awful night by some guy's persistent hankering for beer and cigarettes, plus maybe a pack of Ring Dings and a Powerball ticket.

The car stopped. Spud unburrowed himself, readying to run, then heard the emergency brake engage with a *clunk!* The glow of the guy's flashers—*red-red-red!*—seeped through the fluffy top of the snowbank, diluted cherry pink.

Go away, he thought. *Go away, go—*

"Hello?" A man's voice. He'd gotten out of his vehicle, the guy had, some goofball Good Samaritan type. "Anybody in there?"

Spud peeked over the snowdrift as the man stomped through the snow to the stolen car, wiped at the window. "Hello?"

Melting snow iced Spud's thighs and seeped down into his collar as he lay there, trying to think what to do. The man might go home, call the cops. He might even return and wait for them.

That might turn out to be the kind of idiot he was, and *if* he was, then the best thing for Spud to do right now, in fact the *only* thing—

The stolen car's door creaked open; the man must be looking inside. Then: "Anybody around here? Somebody need help? Holler out if you can hear me!"

Lit up by his own headlights—it was an old Ford pickup with a jerry-rigged cap over the bed—the man slogged back toward the road, muttering to himself.

Good, thought Spud. *Get in your truck and—*

The man stopped suddenly. His hands went to his chest, clasping themselves there. He dropped to his knees, a wide-eyed look of startlement coming onto his face.

He'd begun toppling forward when Spud realized what the stain was, spreading on the gray sweatshirt.

Blood . . . Something yanked Spud by the collar. Falling back, he saw the trees towering high above him, snowflakes swirling down thickly through them.

And then the guy's face: flat, slit-eyed, his braid tucked up into a rough skin cap made from the pelt of some furry animal. The guy looked down at Spud, then dragged him to his feet.

The fallen man did not move. He wasn't going to, Spud knew from the amount of blood darkening the snow all around him.

And from the arrow shaft sticking out of his back. The guy let go of Spud, shoving him away sharply. "Stay," he commanded.

Like I'm some kind of dog, Spud thought, resentment flaring in him, but his legs felt watery-shaky and he couldn't quite get his breath, so he did stay. The guy crossed the road—

On snowshoes, Spud realized. *I should have brought . . .*

The guy rolled the dead man halfway over with one hand, put the other around the arrow shaft protruding from his chest, and pulled. The arrow slid free; the guy wiped it in the snow, then thrust it into a long pouch strapped across his chest.

The bow was nowhere in sight. Spud didn't feel like asking about it when the guy came back.

"Why . . . why did you do that?" The dead man's truck still stood idling in the road.

The guy seized Spud, shoved him. When Spud took a step, the snow came up to his kneecap; at the next, it reached his thigh.

Spud felt a prickle between his shoulders where the arrow might go. Behind the barberry thicket, some pines made a shelter, the snow-clogged boughs bent down like tent flaps.

"Wait." The guy vanished back out into the weather, leaving Spud sitting anxiously on the pine needles under the trees, cold and terrified.

He waited for ten minutes or perhaps for an hour; he didn't know, only that somewhere during that time he stopped hearing the truck's engine. Soon after that the guy returned.

"Up." Spud obeyed. "Walk." The guy pointed.

Spud obeyed once more, his numb, frozen feet clublike as he lifted them, hauling them agonizingly up from the deep snow and plunging them in again.

Again and again, the guy right behind him, silent.

ELEVEN

Lizzie pulled the Blazer into the lot by the potato barn on the edge of town. Chevrier's nearly identical vehicle was already there, pale vapor-puffs chuffing from its exhaust in the cold.

She watched Dylan get out and approach, shoulders hunched against the blowing snow. Someone had lent him a parka; as she put the Blazer's window down, he peered from deep in its hood.

"You okay?" he asked, his eyebrows going up at the sight of Brantwell. No friendliness in his voice, though; there hadn't been back in the office, either, she realized suddenly.

"I'm Missy's dad," Brantwell said before Lizzie could reply. "Tell her I'm coming along to help."

He'd put the shotgun down once they were in the Blazer, producing instead a pistol, which he had hidden under his jacket now, leveled at her.

"Okay," said Dylan, not seeming to think anything was wrong with this, and why would he? And since Missy knew the way, she was in the lead vehicle with Chevrier, while Dylan . . .

Dylan hadn't wanted to ride with her, Lizzie realized as she watched him sprint back to Chevrier's vehicle.

"Nicely done," said Brantwell approvingly. "Make sure you keep it up when we get there."

"Or what, you'll blow my head off?" she retorted, pulling out behind the first Blazer. "How do you think you'll get away with that in front of witnesses? And let me remind you that 'the devil made me do it' is not a legal defense."

The road, plowed but snow-glazed, stretched ahead, white gusts blowing almost horizontally across it. Brantwell didn't reply, which gave her the answer she didn't want: that he wasn't planning for there to be any witnesses to what he did tonight.

But there was still one person she didn't think Brantwell was planning to sacrifice. "Missy's not going to go along with this."

To the murder of three cops, she meant, and the concealment of their bodies so that with any luck, they might not ever be found. Because as Washburn had warned her, the Great North Woods was a big place. A person could get lost in it.

Especially if they were dead. "Missy's going to stay out of it. She's going to wait by the road, in Chevrier's Blazer."

Lizzie blew a contemptuous breath out. "Yeah, right. She's ready to walk through fire for that baby, you think she's going to just—"

He whipped the gun out, aimed it unwaveringly. "Missy," he grated out viciously, "will do what

I say. When I tell her that I know everything, that all is forgiven. That I love Jeffrey and I don't care who his father is, and that I love her."

His voice softened. "And especially," he finished, "when I tell her I'm going to bring Jeffrey back. When I swear it, and tell her she needs to be safe and well to take care of him, once it's done."

All of which was true, Lizzie realized sinkingly. It would work; he'd be saying exactly what Missy wanted to hear.

"And if when we get there I jump out of the Blazer yelling for them to take you down, what then?"

On either side of the road, wide farm fields lay under rising drifts. Occasional access lanes for mechanized farm equipment bridged the ditches between the white-frosted fence posts and the pavement.

"You can't shoot three cops with one shotgun," she added. "And even if you could, Missy would see."

The ditches, she recalled, were perhaps two feet deep, and the plows had thrown up high ridges over the access ways. The Blazer, even with new snow tires, would never make it.

"You do that, the jig's up," Brantwell admitted. "So I'll tell you what. You do what you said, and I'll just shoot that dark-haired cop, the one who stuck his head in the window just now before we left."

Dylan, he meant. Brantwell continued: "I saw the look you gave him. You like him pretty well, I think, and he's ticked off at you, isn't he?"

He chuckled unpleasantly. "You open your mouth when we get there, I'm done for. And you're right about me not being able to shoot everyone, too."

As he spoke she felt Brantwell's gaze on her in the dimness of the Blazer cab: gloating, triumphant.

"So I'll just shoot him," Brantwell said.

She managed a laugh, not wanting him to see how the threat affected her. "Well, then, you might want to adjust your target. Heck, I've wanted to put a bullet through Dylan's head myself."

No answer from Brantwell. Ahead, Chevrier's taillights pulled swiftly away. He had much more practice on snowy roads than she did, and tonight was a hell of a night to be learning, but she was going to have to keep up, like it or not.

She stepped on the gas and felt the Blazer surge forward.

The handgun Brantwell had chosen, she'd noticed when she glanced at it, was an HK P30, and she particularly did not enjoy thinking about the external safety indicator the weapon possessed; the red stripe showed a round in the chamber.

The silence lengthened. *Let it go on,* she told herself. *Wait for him to—*

"I know what you're thinking."

—*talk.* "Yeah? You mean how'd a guy like you get into a mess like this? You're right."

He wasn't. But she might as well let him believe it. Maybe he'd say something to give her an edge.

"Missy's mom is sick," he said. "Pretty soon she's going to need care. Expensive," he added, "residential care."

Another puzzle piece slotted into place. "The forgetfulness Missy mentioned? You mean she's—"

Brantwell nodded, staring ahead. "It started a couple of years ago. Not Alzheimer's. But like that. Nothing bad, little things she'd forget. But the doctors said it would get worse."

He paused, then went on. "And now it has. Just in the past few weeks, she leaves the stove on, she's wandering at night. Now this thing with Jeffrey, I'm sure that's how it must've happened. She just lost track."

His voice thickened; he got control of it again. "We don't have long-term care insurance. Once she had a diagnosis, it was too late, we couldn't afford it. But pretty soon she's going to need twenty-four-hour care, either at our home or in a . . ."

He stopped, went on. "A facility. They say eventually she's going to forget how to swallow food, how to . . ."

Another silence. Then: "So I needed money. I

needed it soon. Laying off help, selling acreage, that wouldn't be enough."

"Have you talked it over with Missy?"

Twenty miles out of town, no more ditches lined the road. Instead, short upslopes led from the pavement to the forest's edge, where white-clotted scrub trees and thickets of brush inter-mingled with old, wide-trunked evergreens.

Brantwell shook his head. "I should have. But I wanted to protect her. And anyway, what could she do about it?"

"So you had to find a way yourself."

"Yeah. No choice. I started skimming off the farm's books, putting money away. But that wasn't enough, and it couldn't go on forever. My foreman sees those books, too, and sooner or later he'd put two and two together."

Outside, the dark night went by, the storm hurling snow at the windshield and the wipers slap-slapping it away while Lizzie forced the speedometer upward, trying to keep pace with Chevrier.

Brantwell continued: "And then, out of the blue, right after Jeffrey was born, this Daniel guy pulled up alongside me one day in his van and just . . . I didn't know about him and Missy. I don't even know how he knew me. But he just laid it all out for me, what he wanted."

"And what he would pay. For you to be a drug courier."

This last silence was the longest of all. Finally: "Yeah. It was a lot. And then it got to be more. The New York people, they wanted things moved, too. Connecticut, Massachusetts—that I-95 corridor, you know—I was on it often anyway. So I made stops."

Made deliveries, he meant, or pickups. She squinted ahead; by now the snow was nearly blinding, Chevrier's vehicle appearing between gusts and then vanishing again.

"So how d'you think Daniel realized you'd be open to his—"

The words caught in her throat as something big bounded all at once from the side of the road, loomed huge in the Blazer's headlights, and missed the bumper by inches. Reflexively her foot went for the brake pedal, touching it before she could think.

A deer. "No," Brantwell said urgently, "stay off the—"

The barest touch of the brakes sent the Blazer sideways on the iced roadway, the rear end fishtailing as she gritted her teeth and forced herself to steer into the skid. *Wait. Hands on the wheel, but lightly, easy does it . . .*

Just for an instant, the Blazer was crossways in the road, aimed at the woods. But then it straightened seemingly on its own with a liquid-feeling glide, the front end swinging around back into its own lane.

She let out her breath. Ahead, Chevrier's brake lights came on very briefly; so he'd seen it in his rearview, the deer in her headlights. But then he rounded another curve and was gone.

"You do that again," Brantwell grated, his ugly side back in control, "I'll—"

"What?" she snapped. "Shoot me? Hey, put a lid on that crap, okay?" She peered ahead. "You clip me while I'm driving, I'll be dead, all right. Or as good as, maybe. But you might be, too."

They'd been on the road nearly an hour now; it couldn't be much farther. "Or maybe you'll wind up paralyzed, huh? Neck down, hooked to a respirator for the rest of your life."

Chevrier's taillights appeared again. And here the roadway was protected somewhat by the big trees, so the snowplow drifts on either side of it weren't very high.

She could ditch them here, throw him off balance and get the gun—she hoped. On the other hand, once she got off the road, she'd have to *miss* the trees . . .

But that was a chance she'd have to take, and if she was going to do it, she didn't have much time.

"Yeah, that'll be you. Just a head in a bed, and how will you care for your wife then?" she said, and yanked the wheel hard left, hitting the gas and slapping on the Blazer's high-low siren switch at the same time.

"Hey!" yelled Brantwell as the Blazer spun into

338

a 180, slid sideways, then shot off the road, ramming into the fresh snow heaped up there and straight through it.

It happened fast, but it seemed to take forever: Brantwell's head flying back, his gun arm sailing up; the exploding airbags blocking out his snarl of mingled fury and alarm.

Yeah, you'll shoot me, all right. At the last instant, a tree trunk loomed up in the windshield; yanking the steering wheel, she prayed those new tires would catch traction somewhere, hearing the Blazer's siren still howling bloody murder.

Yeah. You'll shoot me. But first—

The Blazer's right side panel scraped the tree with a sound like a giant tin can being torn open. The bouncing stopped. The pounding stopped. The Blazer stopped, clouds of steam rising from its crumpled hood.

And then . . . nothing. A thick coating of airbag powder made her cough, but nothing was bleeding or broken as far as she could tell.

But Brantwell wasn't so fortunate. He'd disdained the seatbelt; now he groaned, half-conscious. Meanwhile, the gun—

The gun, dammit. Clumsily unbuckling herself, she shoved aside the limp remains of the passenger-side airbag, scrabbled around on the floor by his feet, and—

Got it. Straightening, she tucked the thick,

blocky little weapon into her bag and zipped it. *Yeah, you'll shoot me.*

Now that he no longer had the thing aimed at her, anger washed over her. *But first—*

First you'll have to get your head out of your butt.

Chevrier's Blazer roared up outside. Moments later, someone began pounding on her window, shouting something at her, but she couldn't hear through the strange howling—

Howling. Oh, yeah . . . As she snapped off the siren, her door opened and she half fell out, into Dylan Hudson's arms.

"Lizzie? You all right?" He set her on her feet. Briskly, professionally. No embrace. "I'm . . . fine." Dazed, roughed up a little. But nothing worse. "Really, I'm absolutely—"

Her legs went out from under her as Missy Brantwell and Chevrier came running up. "Dad!" Missy cried. "Are you okay?"

"Sit Lizzie down, Hudson," Chevrier ordered sharply, turning back toward his vehicle. "I'll call the—"

Paramedics: an ambulance ride, an ER checkup. "No!" She sat up. "Go look at Brantwell, I think he hit his head."

Too bad it wasn't on a baseball bat, she thought. *Or maybe a brick.* "And send those EMTs to my office in Bearkill. Washburn's in there and he's hurt."

Missy bent to her father. "Dad?" But he only turned his face away, the girl peering up uncomprehendingly as Lizzie went on.

"Cody, cuff him up, will you? He's a collar."

"But he didn't do anything, you can't just—"

Brantwell turned back to her. "Shut up, Missy," he said tiredly. "You don't know what you're talking about, and that's my fault. But just shut up, okay? It will," he finished as Chevrier bent over him, "be easier for me if you do."

The girl stared, shocked silent. Meanwhile Dylan crouched by Lizzie.

"So you've got him cuffing people now, just on your say-so? Guess he's starting to trust you a little bit."

No concern for possible injuries; no warmth in his voice, either. *The hell with you, buddy.*

"Great. My heart's desire achieved." She made her own voice light, dug around in her bag for a tissue, and touched it to her cheek where the airbag had hit it. Her nose felt punched, too.

But she was okay. "Brantwell was a meth courier," she said. "And this Daniel guy that Missy's been talking about, he's in it as well, just like we figured."

Dylan looked thoughtful. "So . . . Brantwell believed that if we got to Daniel, then Daniel might flip, rat Brantwell out?"

"Maybe." She touched the tissue to her lip. It came away bloody. "But there's a twist.

Brantwell didn't know until now that Daniel is the baby's father."

"Oh, I get it." Dylan nodded. "Now, besides shutting the guy's mouth, maybe Brantwell wanted a little payback."

But then he frowned. "So then why didn't Brantwell just keep his own mouth shut? Come with us to find Daniel, act like he's on our side until we do, then shoot Daniel before Daniel could talk? Brantwell could say he panicked or—"

Lizzie shook her head. "Because he already had. Panicked, I mean, or at least I think that's what happened."

Getting up, she only felt a little bit like she'd been hit by a truck. "When Brantwell got to my office, Trey Washburn was already there. Brantwell must not have stopped to think. Not that he's been thinking straight for a while, anyway. But he reacted by hitting Trey from behind with a brick."

She winced at the memory, made worse by not knowing if Trey Washburn had survived the attack.

Dylan laughed without humor. "So you didn't need detecting skills after that."

"To figure out Brantwell wasn't one of the good guys? Yeah, I guess not. Especially when he aimed Trey's shotgun at me."

They trudged to Chevrier's Blazer, where Brantwell sat behind the perp screen with his hands cuffed in his lap. One side of his face was swollen and already showing a bruise, deep red darkening to purple; those airbags packed a punch. *Good,* she thought.

"And it wasn't just Daniel he was after. Once we got to that campsite, I think he was planning to kill us all." She turned to Missy. "Except for you, of course. And the baby."

Missy shook her head in disbelief.

"I took a pistol off him," Lizzie said. "HK semiauto, ten-round clip. And on the floor by his feet I found three more."

Missy frowned. "What, three loose bullets?"

"No. Three more clips. Forty bullets in all. So I guess," Lizzie added, "either he thought it was going to take a firefight to get your baby home again—"

She looked back at the wrecked Blazer. Its headlights carved white paths into the woods. But around them the forest was dark.

Dark and deep. And very soon she would be going into it.

"—or he figured ten bullets apiece would be enough to get the four of us," she finished. "Us, and Daniel, too."

Chevrier was in his Blazer; now he got out. "Okay, I've got a guy coming. Deputy, doesn't live too far. He can do transport. Assault with a deadly okay with you?" he asked Lizzie.

For the charge against Brantwell, he meant.

343

"That'll do for a start. Missy, I'm sorry," she added. "I'll explain it all to you later, I promise. But for now you've got to trust me."

In the gloom, the girl's face was haggard. But the disbelief in it was beginning to fade, maybe because her dad wasn't doing any of the things an innocent man might do: telling them they had it all wrong, for instance. Telling his daughter that there had been a mistake, that everything would be all right.

Or even talking about a lawyer. Instead he just sat there in the darkness behind the perp screen, staring at his cuffed hands.

Oh, yeah, this guy was toast and he knew it. Missy gazed at him in appeal. "Dad?"

No response. She waited a moment longer; still nothing. Then she turned. "Okay. I guess . . . Let's go, then."

She strode away from the vehicle without looking back, and Lizzie followed.

As she passed him Dylan put a hand out. "Lizzie, are you sure you're . . ."

"Up for it?" She spun away from him. "I'm fine, okay? Don't worry about me."

Because there was a time and place for everything, including confronting Dylan Hudson about his lies. *And his moodiness, too; what the hell was the matter with him?* But this wasn't it.

Ten minutes later the deputy Chevrier had

called arrived to take custody of Brantwell, and soon after that they were on the road again, heading deeper into the woods.

Spud staggered into the clearing and fell. The guy stepped around him, bent down, and unfastened his snowshoes. By the fire, he pulled off the thick fur wrappings and cap that he wore, letting his braid fall. Then he returned to crouch by Spud.

"Get up."

Spud moaned. He was cold, wet, and exhausted beyond anything he'd even known was possible.

The guy gazed impassively at him. From the other side of the blazing fire, the woman stared, too, huddled under a fur blanket.

The child Spud had seen the last time he was here was not in sight, and neither was—

Spud turned his head and puked, ejecting a thin stream of sour liquid. The guy straightened and went away, Spud didn't see where. A little while later he returned with a steaming mug.

"Drink this."

Spud struggled up and took the mug in both hands. "Thanks," he whispered, trying for a smile and failing.

The guy didn't smile, either. His face was like well-tanned leather, youthfully smooth and yet oddly old in its expression. Or the lack of one, like nothing had ever fazed him.

Like nothing would. Spud sipped from the mug,

nearly puked again at the bitter taste. Some unfamiliar herb, as aromatic as pine tar but way more repulsive, plumed up into his sinuses and burned down his throat.

But the next sip was better, setting up a glowing warmth in his face and chest. He drank the rest, its heat spreading in him.

When he looked up again, the guy had a gun aimed at him. "I want you to tell me why you came here," the guy said evenly. "If you don't, I'm going to shoot you on the count of three."

Spud stared, dumbfounded, the stuff he'd drunk threatening to return. Promising, even.

". . . two . . ." The guy's smooth, slim hand was unwavering.

Spud jumped up, hands out, palms forward. "Okay! Okay, I . . ."

The words tumbled out. "Look, I need to stay here. I'm just like you, man," he pleaded, "free and independent, you know? But now the cops are after me, and—"

As the words left his mouth he realized it was the wrong thing to say. But instead of just chasing Spud out into the cold forest, the guy laughed.

"Well, you've come to the wrong place, then."

As he spoke, a child's fretful wail came from one of the lean-tos. Spud nearly fainted at the overwhelming wave of gratefulness that washed over him, that the kid he'd stolen was still alive.

But this wasn't going at all the way he'd hoped.

The guy went to the lean-to, brought back an open laptop, the device looking strange and out of place here in the wilderness.

Spud turned puzzledly to the guy. "I don't get it. How'd you . . . ?"

The guy pressed some keys on the laptop and the screen lit up. "Remember those little cameras you bought for me, and those microphones? And stuck them up in—"

Her office. And he did remember, but when he was here before, he'd seen no power source, no way to view what the cameras saw and recorded, storing it online so it could be seen later. So he'd forgotten about it.

Now, though, Spud recognized the scene. In it: Cody Chevrier and Lizzie Snow. Then Missy Brantwell burst in, looking upset.

Sound came from the device's tiny speaker. Arguing, protests from Missy. Then a revelation; Spud looked up. "That's . . ."

The guy nodded. "Yeah. It's my kid you took. His mom had him and that was okay for a while, when he was so little. But now he needs a dad. And it's time for me to go, so he's coming along."

Go? thought Spud. *Go where?* The guy shut the laptop. "As for you, though . . ."

He tucked the laptop under his arm, leaned down, and gazed into Spud's face. The guy's own eyes were dark, like deep pools of the bitter liquid Spud had drunk; under their examination

Spud felt his secrets being picked through, his shames uncovered.

A flash of contempt mingled with pity showed in the guy's face briefly, then vanished. He thrust the gun at Spud, urging him to take it. "Here."

Nervously, Spud fumbled the thing, then finally got hold of it. "What's this for?"

"For when they get here." The guy paused on his way back to the lean-to. " 'Cause I don't know what you were thinking of, coming here," he added. "But those cops are right behind you."

Spud looked around the campsite, eerily firelit, sheltered from the snow by the evergreen canopy spreading above. Only a bit of sky showed, thin smoke spiraling up into it.

The kid's wails had quieted, the little blond girl still out of sight. The woman was gone, too, Spud realized.

All was quiet. It struck him suddenly, too, that they'd taken a much less direct route coming in here than the one he recalled.

"But don't worry. I'm ready," the guy said quietly.

Ready? How could he be . . . Then, at a sudden cry of pain from somewhere out there in the snowy forest, Spud understood.

The snowshoes that Chevrier had rounded up for all of them felt like tennis rackets strapped to Lizzie's feet, and getting them out of each other's way was a puzzle needing to be solved at every step.

"Lift and slide," Chevrier had told her, but after a hundred yards she felt her more likely mantra was "Fall down and die."

Dylan wasn't doing much better, and from the way he held his injured arm tightly to his side, she knew this trip was most certainly not what the doctor ordered. Even Chevrier seemed less than practiced in the gear; only Missy Brantwell breezed along, one swift foot after the other into the woods.

Around them the night was silent, the snow falling in tiny flakes. "I hope you know where you're going," Lizzie managed to Chevrier, who was bringing up the rear.

"Yeah," he grated out. "I do." At Missy's direction he'd pulled over and left the Blazer by the road, then produced a GPS tracker with the flyover coordinates programmed into it and handed it to her.

"Here. You might think you know the way. But at night in the snow it's different."

He'd been right, though, about letting Missy lead. It was her kid out there somewhere, or at least they all hoped he was; moving along tirelessly, the desperate young mother's feet churned through the snow, and if not for the cops struggling behind her she'd have been making even better time.

Toward what, though? That was Lizzie's big question. The notion that her own dead sister's child might also be out here seemed merely a foolish fantasy, now that they were out here for real.

Crazy, you must be—What little illumination there was came from their flashlights, showing only snow plastered against huge trees and clumped in brushy thickets. The trail vanished quickly, the stub near the road becoming trackless wilderness in minutes.

Missy stopped. "I'm not sure," she said doubtfully, her head bent to peer at the GPS device's glowing screen.

Dylan clomped past her on his snowshoes, strobing the snowy darkness ahead with his flashlight.

"I think . . . ," he began as something huge flew out of the darkness at him. There was a heavy thud, then came his shout of surprise and pain.

"Damn," said Chevrier, running clumsily past Lizzie. "It's some kind of . . ."

But she already knew: *trap.* Hobbled by the damned snowshoes, she struggled forward to where Dylan lay in the snow, saw that he was—

Alive. Propped up on his elbow with one hand to his forehead, he swore a blue streak of the filthiest and most reassuring curses she'd ever heard.

Missy bent swiftly to him, pressing a paper

towel full of snow to his head. "Ouch," he uttered grimly, and then, squinting around, "What the hell was that thing? Nearly knocked my block off."

Cautiously Chevrier ventured toward the object, now hanging motionless, suspended by thick rope from a massive pine branch thrust out over their heads.

"Looks like a log, barbed wire wrapped around it," he said.

"Oh, great. That's just great." Lizzie clenched her fists at the darkness; if not for the clumsy snowshoes, she'd have kicked something. "So now this bozo's got the place booby-trapped?"

"Seems like." Chevrier looked unhappy. "And for all I know, we may have already missed a few. Which means . . ."

". . . that we could hit them on the way out," she finished for him. "Oh, this guy, when I get him, I'm going to . . ."

"It means something else," said Missy, looking up white-faced from where she was tending to Dylan's head wound. The pulse of terror Lizzie had felt when he'd been hit was fading now. But she still had a bad feeling.

A very bad one; this guy was smart and competent. And he'd known they were coming, somehow; you didn't climb way up there in that tree, make this hideous device, just on the off chance.

Missy thought the same. "He knows we're here. And this is just the beginning of his tricks. But how? How could he—"

Chevrier looked up from examining the rope the log hung on. "Yeah, this knot's fresh. So who knows? Maybe the flyover did put him onto us. If he's paranoid enough . . ."

"I don't know," said Missy again. "Maybe I was wrong, maybe we should go back and get more people, all the hunters around here, and—"

"Nope." Dylan got up, first to his hands and knees, then clumsily up onto his snowshoes again. The thing had only grazed him.

"Our guy's here now. But if he's as nervous as we think, then if we give him a chance he'll take the baby and run."

They were silent a moment, absorbing this. "Obviously we're going to have to be more careful," said Dylan, as calmly as if he hadn't just almost had his head removed.

"But we should go on," he said. "By the look of the GPS, we're already more than halfway there. And this might be our only chance."

Chevrier nodded reluctantly. "In for a penny," he said, his voice grim. "I don't know about you all, but I'm starting to feel like I've got a personal axe to grind with this son of a bitch."

"Me, too," Lizzie said. She took a breath of the cold, fresh air, feeling better suddenly. Anger could do that to a person.

And, after all, she'd done pretty well on that snowy road back there: using it, not letting it stop her. Not letting Roger Brantwell stop her, either.

But there was still something wrong. *You'd already decided how you wanted things to go,* Missy had said the other night after the dustup in Area 51. *To make things work out the way you want.*

And now here she was again, doing the same thing. *Trust me,* she'd told Missy. *I'll explain.* Only this time it wasn't just a matter of her versus some dope in a bar, brandishing a junky weapon.

This time, other people's lives were at stake, too. *We're all out here because I told Missy I'd come. If I hadn't, Dylan and Chevrier would never have gotten on board, they'd have talked Missy out of it, stopped her if need be. Instead—*

Lizzie looked around: deep woods, deep snow. Deep trouble, maybe, too. *Instead, here we all are. And she still thinks I just want to help her. That it's all I want—*

Maybe it was time to be honest about that. To earn Missy's trust instead of merely demanding it.

To deserve it, even. "Listen," she said. "You should know I've got my own reasons for being here. For wanting to go on."

Then she looked at Missy and told her about Nicki: who she was—*my only family in this world*—and that she might be here.

Emphasis on *might*. "So if you want to keep going, I'm in," Lizzie finished. "Just don't assume I've got your best interests at heart. Because it wouldn't . . . it wouldn't be the truth."

Damn, that hadn't come out the way she'd meant it. All she'd intended was to come clean on her own motives, but now from what she'd said, it must seem as if she didn't care about Missy's child at all, that all she cared about was her own family.

If I still have any. And Missy's reply made her feel even more foolish: "But, Lizzie, we've all got reasons."

Her voice—*even after I just arrested her father,* Lizzie thought; *man, that girl's made of something. Titanium, maybe*—was full of sympathy.

"Cody wants to arrest Daniel, I want Jeffrey back—"

She glanced toward Dylan, whose motives for being here were less clear to her. *To me, too,* thought Lizzie.

"Anyway, I'm glad for your help, all of you. For whatever your reasons," Missy finished simply.

Then Dylan spoke up. "Yeah. So don't worry, Lizzie. No one suspects you of any generous motives. Or whatever it is you're so worried about."

His voice was chilly. "By the way, since apparently it's truth-telling time, I lent my motel

354

room in Houlton to one of the Maine DEA cops last night; she got stuck late on that meth bust."

He stomped his snowshoes up and down, getting the feel of them again. "When we get out of here, somebody remind me to call her and tell her she can keep it, will you? Because I'm going back to Bangor. I've got a case of my own to work."

So that was it. He was a detective, for heaven's sake; it wouldn't have taken much for him to figure out that Lizzie had called his room, heard a woman's voice, and decided he was lying to her yet again. Probably the DEA cop had mentioned the hang-up, and he'd connected the dots. And now . . .

Now he'd had the nerve to get his feelings hurt about it. *Yeah, well, you bought that trip, buddy,* she thought at his down-jacketed back as he moved ahead into the darkness. *If you don't want to be figured for a liar, then don't tell . . .*

But he hadn't been lying, had he? Not this time. The truth was, she'd been wrong.

But before she could think any more about that, Dylan put a hand up. *Something up there,* the sharp gesture communicated. She hurried to join him, but as she reached him his arm thrust out suddenly, shoving her sideways into a snowdrift, and then he hurled himself after her.

An instant later the shooting started.

TWELVE

Spud crouched in the lean-to, holding the gun the guy had given him in both cold hands. Behind him in the gloom huddled the woman and the little blond girl, both of them swathed thickly in blankets.

The woman held Missy Brantwell's baby in her arms. She was spooning some kind of porridge to its lips, rocking the child gently as she did so. The little blond-haired girl looked on, her pale face serene as she rested against the woman.

It all looked so peaceful . . . or anyway it did until the woman turned her head. By the light of the oil lantern hanging from the lean-to's ridgepole, the scar on her face was a purplish ridge running diagonally from her right ear all the way to the corner of her mouth.

He tried smiling at the woman, wanting very badly to let her know that she wasn't in this alone, mostly so he could feel that way himself. But in response she only winced, turning away and pulling the blanket up to hide both herself and the baby while the little girl buried her face shyly once more.

So much for friendliness, Spud thought. Bad enough she had a face like that, but did she have to be a sourpuss on the inside, too? It just went to show what the guy must be like at heart, he thought; having her here, taking her in and caring for her when no one else would, probably; her and the girl.

Then came gunshots, somewhere beyond the clearing's edge. Spud's heart was still pounding anxiously when the guy appeared at the lean-to's mouth.

Wordlessly the guy jerked his head; Spud jumped up and clambered out of the shelter as if yanked by an invisible string. Overhead the wind thrashed the towering evergreen tops, but down here in the firelit clearing only the occasional icy gust of snow blew in, dusting the matted pine needles with white.

"Here." The guy led Spud toward the clearing's edge, past the end of a row of wooden pallets stretching back in among the big trees.

A heavy swath of clear plastic sheeting was pulled back from the pallets, which Spud felt sure had been stacked with plastic-wrapped packages last time he'd been here. But now all but one of them was empty.

"Hey." The guy spoke flatly. Spud hurried to where he'd been summoned; when he got there, the guy pointed at the ground.

"Sit. When they come through here, you shoot them." Without waiting for a reply, the guy turned and padded away.

Spud looked down again at the gun in his

hands: a pistol, heavy and foreign feeling. A hunting trip had been offered to him every autumn since he was nine—back then, his dad hadn't been such a loser—but he'd refused.

Hunting was too much work. Even at that age, he'd preferred first-person shooter games that could be played in the privacy of his comfortable room and that offered human figures as targets.

But as a result he'd never fired a real gun. Now he turned the pistol over in his hands, finding the trigger, lifting and aiming the gun experimentally. Cold, wicked looking, the thing had a lethal charm that enthralled him at once.

Shoot them, the guy had said. Admiring the seductive glint of the firelight off the weapon's dark metal, Spud let his left hand caress the gun barrel while his right clutched the grip.

Shoot them. Oh, yeah.

He could definitely do that.

Lizzie bucked upward, choking on snow, trying to get free of . . . "Get *off* me, dammit!"

Somewhere nearby, Chevrier cursed fervently and Missy was screaming something. Grabbing a snow-glazed sapling with both hands, Lizzie hauled herself free, then bent to turn the figure that had fallen on her.

"Hey," said Dylan, smiling weakly. "Crazy, huh? Twice in . . ."

Twice in three days. The hole in his down jacket was leaking a few feathers.

Whitely, innocently. "Oh," she heard herself say, dropping to his side. He was saying something else but she couldn't hear him.

"Missy, shut *up!*" Abruptly the girl obeyed, the silence afterward even more terrifying.

"Dylan?" No answer. "Dylan!"

Then Chevrier appeared, his hood's trim a wreath of snow. "Okay, this ends now," he said, pulling his phone out.

"But there's no—" *Signal way out here,* Lizzie was about to finish, then saw it wasn't a phone at all.

"Satellite phone," he said. "Pilot program, feds threw us a bone. We'd never have one otherwise; they cost a couple of grand each."

But it was paying for itself now, Lizzie thought. "Dispatch can get us some game wardens out here in twenty minutes or so," he added. "Good as deputies. Maybe better, in this environment."

He rattled off a string of commands into the device, then stuffed it away again as Lizzie found her voice.

"Missy, have you got a diaper in that baby bag you brought?" From Dylan's side she reached up blindly, felt Missy thrust the thick pad into her hand.

"Okay, now, you get down here and put pressure on this," she said, and the girl obeyed as the guttural pop of gunfire sounded again, small branches crackling as rounds whizzed through them.

She looked up at Chevrier, who nodded in understanding. "Oh, yeah, that's gotta stop," he said, unholstering his weapon.

"Stay here," he added to Missy, "until you hear the good guys coming." The wardens he'd summoned, he meant. "Then you run and guide 'em in, got it?"

Missy nodded. Dylan coughed, a wet, painful sound that left him gasping.

He'd dropped his gun somewhere in the snow. Lizzie held out her own. "You know how to fire this?"

Thinking that Missy wouldn't. But the girl took the gun confidently, checked the safety and magazine. "Dad showed me."

Yeah, he'd been handy with a firearm, all right. Lizzie banished the thought as Chevrier jerked his head: *You go that way.*

Nodding her understanding, she made her way past the trees to a shallow ravine, worked her way along it. The snow was much deeper here; battling through it, she first hit a hole that felt bottomless and hauled herself out, then slammed her knee into a rock masquerading as a snowdrift.

But eventually she found herself at the edge of a clearing. A campfire flared at the center of it; the perimeter all around the fire had been swept clean of the fallen pine needles carpeting the rest of the open area. Small sheds, lean-tos, and a long row of wooden pallets, most of them empty, ringed the clearing.

Then: "Hush. Keep still."

Like hell, she thought as her training clicked in automatically: *Crouch, pivot, and—*

Something touched her neck. Not a gun barrel. Cold, sharp . . .

"I want you to turn toward me. Slowly now."

Lizzie obeyed, thinking, *Duck, turn, head butt—*

Also, she had her own weapon. Gripped in her right hand, the HK semiauto she'd taken from Brantwell still had all ten rounds; the other three clips were in her pockets.

But as she turned, the sharp, pointy thing stayed pressed against her skin, drawing a bright stinging line around her neck until the point of it reached the soft flesh under her chin, and her captor stood before her.

Tall and smooth-faced, wearing a ragged fur hat that looked as if he'd made it himself . . . "Don't move," he cautioned calmly.

He carried a small battery lantern, so she saw clearly his rough costume of furs and . . . what was that, deerskin?

Great, she thought, *I'm being held prisoner by the Last of the Mohicans.* The blade touching her throat took most of the humor out of it, though.

Or all of it, actually. He moved the weapon away slightly: an arrow, she saw, its head a viciously barbed slice of metal that looked sharp enough to pierce steel.

"Show me the gun. Clips, too—you wouldn't have come without 'em." She held them up.

"Drop 'em in the pouch," he said, so she did that, too.

"That way," he instructed, gesturing with one hand. "Ahead of me."

She swallowed hard, still feeling the blade. "Listen, Missy just wants her baby back, so . . ."

Without warning, the arrow tip returned and struck, fanglike; a trickle of hot blood leaked down into her shirt.

"Just walk," the guy instructed, so she did, one step after another, into the firelit clearing.

"Oh, you're kidding me," she said when she saw Spud. The boy looked ridiculous with his frizzy blond hair, wild tattoos, and—the only non-ridiculous part—a gun in his hand.

"Over there," said the guy with the arrow tip still at Lizzie's throat; she followed his gesture to a lean-to made of logs, saplings, and pine boughs.

"You," the guy told Spud, "watch her." His wave seemed to levitate Spud up off the log he sat on, then send him lumbering toward the lean-to.

"God, Spud," she told him, "if I'd known all

you wanted was someone to boss you around, I could've done it."

"Shut up." Glowering inexpertly at her, he waved the gun at the lean-to's interior. "Just get in there."

Good, Lizzie thought. *He'll sit outside, and maybe I'll find something to hit him with from behind. Hit him hard . . .*

She ducked into the lamplit shelter, which had a thickly pine-needled floor. The fragrance of the evergreens mingled with the smell of campfire smoke. There were two low benches and at the rear what she thought at first was a pile of blankets.

Then the blankets shifted. A woman huddled in them, her face half hidden. And beside her, staring white-faced, was . . .

A little girl. Thin, unsmiling . . . The child wore a woolen hat, a few wisps of hair sticking out. Pale blond hair . . .

"Nicki?" Lizzie whispered it, her heart thudding.

"I said *shut up!*" Spud bellowed over his shoulder.

The child shrank back, burrowing against the woman. Then a wail came from deep within the blankets—

A baby's cry. The woman shifted, one white arm emerging from the coverings to retrieve a plastic baby bottle tucked in amidst a small cache of other baby items, piled against the lean-to's slanted wall.

The baby fell silent, faint sucking noises coming now from his warm refuge. The little girl, too, settled down by the woman again, her thumb in her mouth.

He's stolen himself a family, Lizzie thought. But the guy's motivations were the least of her interests now. Returning to the lean-to's entry, where Spud still hunkered with his weapon, she whispered insistently.

"You little idiot, what the hell are you doing?" If she could get him talking, then maybe she could distract him and—

"Shut up," he hissed. "Who asked you to come here, anyway?"

Half turning, he leaned in toward her. "And the next person who calls me an idiot gets a bullet in the fucking brain. I'm *done* being called things, get it?"

He aimed the gun at her, voice shaking with anger, but his hand terrifyingly steady. "I'm done," he began, "and—"

"Hey." Behind him, the guy appeared, blank-faced. Spud's went still, looking all at once devoid of emotion.

Like his new mentor, Lizzie thought, a thrill of real fright going through her at the idea. She'd seen it before, a young guy with no hope and no future finding direction in a gang, idolizing whoever was the ringleader.

They were always the most violent ones, at

least until they got killed by the cops or by some newer and even hungrier little savage.

"Yeah," Spud managed. "Sorry, I'll—"

The guy turned away without waiting for Spud to finish. He carried an armload of plastic bags now, and in the bags . . .

Something whitish was in them, like the crack cocaine she used to confiscate when she was back on patrol, when she first became a cop in Boston.

Or like methamphetamine. "Hey, Spud. Your guy's a freakin' drug dealer, you know that?"

No response from the teenager. Behind Lizzie, the woman and the little kids went on cowering in their blankets. Lizzie wanted badly to go back there. *Nicki, have I found you?*

Have I finally—"Yeah, he's pushing meth." A picture of the place the DEA had raided that morning—was it only this morning?—rose in her mind's eye.

"At," she added, "a nice profit for himself. Yeah, he's the lord of the forest, all right. If by 'lord' you mean 'slumlord.'"

"Shut up," Spud growled. He sat sideways with one eye on the lean-to's opening, the other on his fearless leader.

Back and forth, emptying the final pallet at the clearing's edge, the guy worked steadily. Finally he took off out through the trees with a big plastic garbage bag over his shoulder.

But his absence only increased her anxiety.

Probably he had a vehicle somewhere nearer the road; once he'd finished here, he could take off in it just the way Izzy Dolaby had predicted.

That's his plan. First, though, he'll have to finish us.

Minutes passed; she began thinking she was wrong. Maybe the guy had decided just to go while the going was good. But then, just when she thought he wasn't coming back, that they might get out of here without any more bloodshed once Spud figured it out, too, the guy came out of the woods again with Chevrier in front of him, marching the sheriff along.

Not with an arrow at the throat of his captive this time, though; this time, he had Chevrier's gun.

"Get out here." The guy gestured sharply with his free hand. Spud backed off as Lizzie exited the lean-to.

"Sit, both of you." Chevrier scowled furiously, obeying; at the guy's urging, Lizzie had no choice but to join the sheriff on the cold ground.

Inside the lean-to the baby began crying again, loud yells that sounded as if they must carry for miles in the silent woods. Lizzie's heart sank:

If Missy hears that, we're done for. She'll come running, and the wardens will never find Dylan if she's not out there to guide them.

And they'll never find us. Not until they find our bodies . . .

Because it was clear now what the guy must mean to do. He'd know he had to get away, that if they'd found him out here, then others would find him soon, too.

And he must know he'd have to go alone, not take his stolen family. Or not all of it; only the baby, Lizzie was willing to bet.

Only his own flesh and blood. As if to prove it, he shoved her aside, ducking into the lean-to and emerging with the child under his arm, wedged there like a bundle of rags. The woman scrambled after him, her arms stretched out imploringly. But then she stopped short, her face upturned in a mask of anguish.

The child whimpered as the guy hefted him a little higher under his arm, ignoring the weeping woman.

"Keep the gun on them," he told Spud. He eyed Chevrier and Lizzie flatly, then looked back at his helper, who by now seemed extremely nervous.

"But what if . . . ?" Spud began, an anxious whine creeping into his voice. The baby stopped crying, then coughed several times, a thick, wet hacking that Lizzie didn't like the sound of one bit.

The guy didn't seem to notice. "Don't worry," he told Spud. "You've got the gun, remember?"

He looked down at Lizzie, then at Chevrier. "So if either one of them moves one freaking muscle," he finished flatly, "just kill them both."

• • •

The two cops spoke quietly to each other. Spud didn't try to stop them; after all, what could they do?

And anyway, the guy hadn't said not to let them talk. So he watched silently, proud of the responsibility he'd been given, waiting for his newfound friend to return.

Around him the trees seemed to wait silently, too. The wind had dropped off, snow gusts no longer blowing into the campsite, and the fire's flames aimed straight up as if pointing out the clearing sky overhead, stars winking between the treetops.

But as the clouds thinned, the cold bit down hard. Spud's skin chilled down as well, wet from the snow that had melted into his clothes. The fire helped a little, but not nearly enough.

His feet throbbed miserably; he imagined how his toes must look. Red and swollen, as they had when he was a kid and stayed out too long sledding? Or was frostbite transforming them to dead flesh, blackened gangrene that would rot off and—

"Hey, Spud."

He grunted irritably. Why Lizzie Snow thought anything she said might interest him was beyond him. Didn't she know she was going to die out here soon?

"It's not that easy, you know," she said. "Killing

people, I mean. You'd better make sure you've got the stones for it before you try aiming that thing and pulling the trigger."

See? Right there she proved how ignorant she was, how much she misunderstood the whole situation. "Uh-huh," he said.

Let her chew on that, see how little effect anything she had to say could have on him.

Far away, the thin wail of a siren floated on the icy air. A cop car, Spud thought with an inner lurch of alarm. After the guy fired shots out there, someone must've called for help somehow. Now a bunch of reinforcements would swarm in and . . .

But no, Spud realized, relaxing slightly and sneering at the cops in front of him. First of all, they'd never find this place; the way in was twisty and hard to follow even without snow.

Anyway, the guy was out there; he'd take care of whatever—or whoever—needed to be dealt with. An arrow flying out of the darkness at some poor dope lit up by his own headlights . . .

Yeah, that would do it. Just like it had before. But Lizzie Snow wasn't finished blabbering.

"I guess you've got to be a little upset, anyway, at the way things are going."

Spud couldn't help himself. "Yeah, right," he replied. "I'm, like, totally shaking in my boots."

Actually he was. Damn, it was cold out here.

Still, he could keep it together for a little longer. Pretty soon the guy would come back.

"Good," said Lizzie Snow, unfazed by his attempt at sarcasm. "Because you should be. I mean," she added, glancing at the dying fire, "you've got to admit, things look pretty grim for you."

He glanced up at her. On the one hand, he knew she was only trying to mess with his head, provoke him into doing something or not doing something that she could take advantage of.

But on the other hand . . . "What d'you mean by that?"

Carelessly she shrugged. "I mean your pal there, the Lion King or whoever it is he thinks he's dressed up as—"

"Hey, don't make fun of him." Spud waved the gun, noting that his hand didn't want to unclench from around its grip.

Too cold. Too stiff. Could you even pull the trigger?

He brushed the thought away. "He's my friend," he went on stubbornly. "We're a team, him and me."

At that, Sheriff Chevrier spoke up. "Yeah, he's your pal, all right. That's why he's loading up his vehicle with his stash out there. What did he do, hide his van right near the road so he could make a quick getaway?"

Spud didn't know. The guy, he realized

suddenly, hadn't confided his plans, only given orders.

"Hey, he's probably got the heater running, too," Chevrier said, "while you're freezing your ass off here."

Spud shifted uncomfortably, stopped when he noticed Chevrier watching. "Shut up. He'll be back."

But it hadn't escaped Spud, either, that when the guy had left, he'd taken the kid with him. Lizzie Snow started in again:

"He's not coming back, Spud. All he wants is his own child, not you or any of us. You know that, Spud, don't you?"

Then Chevrier: "But hey, stick with him if you want. Believe whatever lie falls out of his mouth."

Enough . . . If he could, he'd have shot them both right then just to shut them up.

"I promise you," Lizzie Snow said, "that if he does come back, it'll only be to take that weapon from you. And before he leaves, he'll put a bullet in your head with it."

"Shut up." He was freezing now, really freezing to death. His feet ached all the way to his hips, his eyes burned, and his nose felt like it might crack and fall off his face.

Still she yammered on: "Because give me a break, Spud. I mean, think about it: what the hell does a guy like that need with you?"

"Shut up, shut *up!*" he bellowed. Where the hell was the guy, anyway? What the hell was he doing, lallygagging around out there in the warm van while Spud waited here, dying of cold?

He tried blowing his breath onto his fingers, to warm them. That way, they'd be all flexible and trigger-ready when the time came.

Noting this activity, Chevrier spoke. "Yeah, loosen up. He's going to get you to do it, see? And then he'll do it to you."

"I told you, shut up." Spud forced the words from between gritted teeth. But Chevrier only snorted dismissively.

"You think he wants a girl-killer riding shotgun with him?" Chevrier asked, sounding as calm as if he was sitting in a booth at Grammy's Restaurant.

Spud made himself remain still. Guessing, Chevrier was only guessing. There was no way anyone could've . . .

"Kid gave you a ride, didn't he?" Chevrier went on, wearing that look Spud hated, that I'm-better-than-you look. The girls had all worn it, too . . . until they didn't.

"Uh-huh," said Chevrier, either not noticing or not caring that Spud was ready to shoot him in the head right now, just to shut his freaking mouth for him.

But first he had to hear what that freaking mouth said.

"Dropped you in Bangor, on his way back to school," said Chevrier. "But after he dropped you off, he turned around and came back."

Didn't, thought Spud. No, he damned well . . .

"Yep. Forgot to bring along a term paper he wrote."

Chevrier turned to Lizzie. "Yeah, I never got the chance to get you up to speed on that part, did I?"

He went on. "I talked to the kid's folks. Turns out he had to have that paper, turn it in on time to keep his scholarship. But there was nobody home to email it to him, so he had to go back and get it himself."

"You're lying," Spud managed. Because for one thing, even if the kid had come back, how would—

Chevrier shook his head. "But then he rolled his car on the highway just outside of Bearkill. And when we got to the scene, guess what we found? That nose stud of yours, the one you don't have anymore. And that's why you don't have it, isn't it?"

Spud forced himself to shrug carelessly. "Lots of people have those."

But the sheriff had an answer for that, too, and where *was* the guy, anyway? By now he could've loaded up a tractor-trailer full of whatever it was he was hauling out of here.

"Yeah. They don't all have your DNA, though,

Spud. DNA that I swabbed off of your little nose doodad and that the lab down in Augusta is going to match with some of the spit I took off your coffee cup from Lizzie's office. Heck, results are probably back by now."

Now Spud knew he was lying. That wasn't even possible, was it? Or at least not so soon . . .

Surely it wasn't. But the cop's smirk broadened. "Yeah, we got you. So I just hope your pal left you some bullets to go with that little popgun you're holding, buddy."

Spud glanced nervously at the gun, realized he didn't even know how to tell if it was loaded.

Now Chevrier laughed. "Just funnin' with you, kid. See the clip sticking out of the bottom of the grip?"

Spud tipped the weapon slightly as Chevrier went on. "Yeah, there's bullets in it."

A brief pause, then: "So, listen, whyn't you just put one in your brain right now, save yourself and everyone else a whole lot of trouble? I promise," Chevrier added, "I solemnly promise you that if you do, it won't hurt a damned bit."

From the woods came the echoing report of a single gunshot, so near that Spud jumped and for an instant thought he had actually done it.

But he hadn't. "Shut your mouth," he told the sheriff, then sat back down on the log, reassuring himself again that the delay meant nothing ominous.

That a single gunshot meant only that the guy had abandoned the bow and arrow for a deadlier weapon, and when he came back, he and Spud could get the hell out of here.

And if the guy wanted Spud to shoot anyone first, like these two cops and the woman with the scar, too, maybe . . .

Hell, at this point he'd be *delighted* to do it.

The little girl was crying. "Get in there, tell her to shut that kid up," Spud ordered Lizzie irritably.

She slipped into the lean-to, now dim-lit by a battery lamp. The little girl's blond head popped up from behind the woman. *Blue eyes full of tears, that cornsilk hair . . .*

"Nicki?" The child's eyes widened, but she didn't answer.

Forcing herself to stay calm, Lizzie sat back on her heels and waited. The little girl wiggled free of the blankets.

"Hi. My name's Lizzie. What's yours?"

No answer. The little girl crept forward. By the weakening battery lantern's dim glow, her eyes gleamed blue.

But then the first unwelcome prickle of doubt came. Nicki's eyes were blue. But the bright aqua hue of this little girl's eyes wasn't a normal human eye color. And that cornsilk hair . . .

She forced herself to remain still even as sorrow hit her. The child gazed up at Lizzie, the part in her pale hair showing the dark brown at its roots.

Biting her lip, Lizzie smiled through her tears. The hair color on this child wasn't real. It had been bleached, the most recent application several weeks ago by the look of it.

Lizzie put her hand out, turned the little girl's face very gently to see the faint line of the blue contact lenses in her eyes, knowing now that the child had been deliberately disguised.

Dark hair, eyes some other color besides blue . . . it wasn't Nicki. "Lovely," Lizzie managed, caressing the pale hair lightly. "Now get back under those blankets, hmm? It's cold."

She didn't know how she got the words out past the lump in her throat, how she smiled again at the child.

So pretty, so sweet and obedient. And so not the child that she sought. *It's not her. It's just not.*

For a moment, disappointment overwhelmed her: *I came all this way, I gave up everything . . .*

But none of that mattered now. It was over, and it had all been for nothing.

"Are you a cop?"

Lizzie jumped startledly. The woman with the scarred face was looking at her; she'd been so silent that Lizzie had nearly forgotten her.

"Yeah," Lizzie answered. "That's the county sheriff out there. We're here to take your boyfriend into custody."

Outside, Chevrier tried another angle with Spud. "So who's the woman?" he asked. "In the lean-to, with the little girl. You know her?"

"Nah" came Spud's response. "She's with him." His tone was dismissive.

"I see." Chevrier sounded calm. "So what's the deal, then? You're all going to be one big, happy family? Or," he added insinuatingly, "do you think maybe you've got a chance with her?"

Spud made a sound of disgust. "You kidding? Jeeze, have you seen the face on that chick?"

Inside the lean-to, the woman looked down at her hands.

"She's like the Joker from the Batman movies," Spud went on as the woman listened.

Thoughtfully, turning some small object that Lizzie couldn't see over and over in her lap.

"Guy prob'ly took pity on her," Spud elaborated, "took her in when no one else'd have her, you know?"

The woman's lips pursed in a near smile. She seemed to be thinking hard about something. Then she got up, gesturing at the child to stay back while she crept toward the lean-to's mouth.

Lizzie moved, too, sudden suspicion seizing her. "Wait," she began. But it was already too late.

Chevrier turned, his eyes narrowing in surprise. Then Spud looked up, frowning.

"Hey," he objected, "you're not supposed to—"

Damn, thought Lizzie, *she's got a—*

"Gun," Chevrier said flatly, gathering himself to charge at the woman, but at her sharp gesture with the weapon he sank back.

"You," she said clearly to Spud. "You're a fool, you know?"

Her voice wavered on the edge of hysteria. But she kept it together long enough to finish what she had to say.

"You think he took me in. That I'm so ugly that nobody else would have me. So it's a kindness, him keeping me here." She jerked the gun at him. "Is that it?"

He looked around helplessly, seeming to realize he couldn't take back any of what he'd said.

Still, he tried. "Y-yes. I mean, it's nice of him, I—"

The woman laughed, a sound like ice breaking. "That's what I thought you said," she told him calmly, then paused, angling her head to give Spud a clear view of her face.

The scar, Lizzie thought, could probably be repaired by a good surgeon, or at least lessened somewhat. But right now it was a terrifying extension of her smile.

"Who," she inquired, "do you think did this to me?"

Spud got up, fumbling with the gun he held, and opened his mouth to answer or protest.

But before he could, she shot him.

Twice.

THIRTEEN

The guy entered the clearing again, this time with a rifle in his hands. Scanning around wildly, he searched for where the shots had come from.

Finally his gaze found Spud, who stood swaying. The woman's first shot had taken his left earlobe cleanly off, along with the ring that had been in it. Lizzie hadn't seen the second shot hit him. Now she watched as his eyes finally rolled up and he fell. How, the tattooed teenager's expression seemed to ask, could the universe have betrayed him so completely?

Turning, the woman got off a wild shot in the instant before Chevrier hurled himself at her, shoving her and Lizzie both into the lean-to where the little girl still huddled in terror, then following them in.

"What's this supposed to accomplish?" Lizzie hissed as he urged her toward where the child crouched.

"That back wall," he pointed out. "It's just pine boughs. We can—"

He'd snatched Spud's gun. Catching on to Chevrier's plan, Lizzie turned to the woman.

"Start pushing your way through. Not all the way, though, just so you can get out when I signal. And stay alert, we're only going to get one chance at this."

The woman nodded. Not stupid, Lizzie realized. You didn't have to be stupid to get into an awful fix like this. Just in love.

Or something. Lizzie turned to Chevrier. "He knows there's at least one gun in here. He must've left her with the one she's been firing, probably to use against us if it came to that."

"But then why didn't she shoot him just now?"

"I was afraid I'd hit the baby," the woman said dully as she pushed her way to the rear of the lean-to.

Which explained that. But it didn't explain why she'd sat there so passively afterward. Unless, like Spud, she'd hung onto the hope that the guy was coming back for her, too?

Stockholm syndrome, Lizzie thought. People could get pretty screwed up in how they felt about their captors, especially if the relationship had started out as something else. After enough time went by, they got confused, unable to tell friend from foe.

Now, though, it was clear that the woman had switched sides.

And they could figure out the why of that part later.

"He's probably thinking he'd better take us out quick," Lizzie said.

"Right," Chevrier began, then yanked her

380

down hard as a line of gunfire stitched through the lean-to's roof.

They scrambled to where the woman had already made good progress on pushing through the layered pine boughs. Cautiously Lizzie pushed her head the rest of the way out between the prickly branches and peered around the campsite, now fully moonlit.

With the clearing skies, bone-hard cold was setting in, too. Her breath made puffs in the frigid air; she pulled her face in as shouts came from a distance. Those reinforcements Chevrier had summoned were finding their way here, guided by the gunfire, probably, and they weren't being subtle about it.

So now the guy'd be in even more of a hurry, and Chevrier thought the same. "Good news, bad news," he uttered in a voice tight with pain, which was when she realized he'd been hit.

And meanwhile we're pinned down in a goddamned primeval forest by some meth-tweaking loony tune with a weapon . . .

Chevrier passed her the gun, but to use it she'd have to be able to see the guy. She tugged again at the woven-together pine boughs of the lean-to's rear wall.

Guy deserves a freaking merit badge, building this thing, she thought, the rough bark and sap-laden needles jabbing her hands mercilessly. She peered out and suddenly he was . . .

There. Forty yards, and he hadn't seen her. She braced her elbow, leveled the pistol . . . but now he'd moved, sliding behind a thick-trunked evergreen. Or . . . had he?

"Damn. He's circling around," she told Chevrier.

But which way? Meanwhile help was getting closer, by the sound of it, so maybe Dylan was getting help, too . . .

If he could be helped. With a pang of anguish, she turned from the thought as Chevrier pushed out alongside her, then angled his head sharply. She followed the gesture, and sure enough, there the guy was again. But she still had no good shot.

Besides . . . She gathered the woman and little girl close. "Okay, now, when I say so, you're going to go out this hole . . ."

She gestured at the gap in the lean-to's rear wall. "And then you're going to run. Just keep on running, don't stop. I'll come and find you afterward, okay?"

The woman's dark eyes were not quite focused. *Yeah, killing somebody will do that to you.*

"Okay?" Lizzie demanded again; this time the woman nodded, then grasped the child's hand just as footsteps sounded, faint creaks on the thin, cold snow.

"Get ready." Chevrier nodded. The footsteps stopped.

"Go." Lizzie shoved the woman and little girl

out the hole in the lean-to's wall, then felt Chevrier's hands doing the same to her. Gunfire lit the campsite in orange flashes.

"Run!" Lizzie ordered as the guy's weapon fired again, and a pain like a whip's lash stung her left thigh; she stumbled, cursing her left foot, now dragging instead of sprinting as she fought her way over a snow-covered fallen tree.

Then as she hunched behind it she saw that Chevrier wasn't with her. The snow all around lay silent and empty. No sound from the woman or the little girl, either, and she didn't see the guy with the gun.

She had a moment to wonder where he'd stashed the baby, or worse, if he'd—

"Psst." A tiny sound from right behind her. Slowly she put her head up out of the snowdrift.

It was the woman, standing in plain sight with the little blond girl peeping fearfully out from behind her, the moonlight slanting almost straight down through the tall trees picking them both out like targets in a shooting gallery.

Jesus. "Get down," Lizzie whispered, her words as loud as a shout in the forest silence.

But the woman only smiled enigmatically and shooed the child away from her toward the trees, and what was that all about?

Then Lizzie realized: *She's making herself a target.* So the little girl could get away . . .

Hurling herself at them, she grabbed the girl's

thin arm in one hand, the woman's in the other. "Run, dammit!"

The child obeyed, but the woman struggled free just as a shot whizzed past Lizzie's ear. Distantly, men's voices called to one another . . . too distantly. The guy's smooth face popped up, staring over the fallen tree at them in grim triumph: *Gotcha!*

But then his expression changed, first to a puzzled frown and then to a grimace. Lizzie glanced back. The woman still stood where she had before, but now she gripped the gun.

I never took it from her, in all the commotion I never . . .

And though her face was frightened, the woman's hand was steady, as if she braced it on some old inner strength that he hadn't quite managed to scare or brutalize out of her.

His face relaxed into a look of contempt. "You won't shoot me," he said softly. "You know you won't—"

The woman fired, the thwack of the hammer smacking down a bright sharp sound in the wintry darkness. But nothing happened.

The gun was empty. The guy grinned mockingly.

Focused on his victim, he didn't notice Lizzie gathering herself. *One lunge,* she told herself. *Hit the body midsection, carry him down and put a fist to his ear . . .*

But halfway over the fallen tree, her bad foot

gave out and the remaining one hit the tree's coating of ice. She fell hard, the impact knocking her breathless, and in the next instant he stood over her, his weapon aimed straight at her face.

I'll be darned, she thought wonderingly, *this is it. The time at the very end that we all wonder about, this is—*

A clap of thunder split the night. Clad in his skins and furs, the guy staggered uncertainly and fell backward into the snow, a dark stain spreading around his head.

Lizzie scrambled over and yanked his rifle away, as from behind the fallen tree Missy Brantwell appeared, gripping the handgun she'd shot him with and looking half-dead herself, her lips a bloodless-looking blue in her white face.

Behind Missy, three men in winter gear burst out of the woods. Lizzie struggled up and grabbed the arm somebody held out.

"Chevrier's over there," Missy managed, pointing, then paused to gaze down at the man she'd just shot.

The father of her child . . . Then she turned away decisively, leading Lizzie and the others to where the sheriff lay on his belly, one arm flung out as if trying to haul himself along.

In his hand was a chunk of firewood just the right size to use for a club. *Because he never gave up trying to stop the guy,* Lizzie thought sorrowfully. *He never quit.*

He's a cop, and that's his job. Or it was . . .

But then she saw that he was alive, his chest moving up and down stubbornly. A pair of cops gathered him up, hoisting him into a hurried chair-carry between them. Missy was leaving, too, with the woman and little girl, more cops shepherding them out along the trampled path they'd made through the deep snow, still others moving toward the campsite where they would find Spud. *So I don't have to decide whether or not to tell them he's there,* Lizzie thought. Fortunately for him. Finally only she still stood watching the little girl's small blond head vanish among the trees, something similar vanishing in her heart, as well.

It was never her. Nicki was never here at all.

It was all a . . . what? A lie? A misunderstanding?

Or more likely just a mistake. It happened; leads panned out or they didn't, and you had to accept that.

That was part of the job, too. "What about Dylan Hudson?" she called after one of the departing cops. "And . . . did they find the baby?"

"Yeah. Baby's okay, they found him in the guy's van out near the road. He was all loaded up and ready to go. I don't know what he even came back in here for."

But Lizzie did. *To kill us.* So he'd have a head

start, and so that if he did get caught, they couldn't testify against him.

"And there's another victim," he went on, "couple of the other guys are carrying him out, but I don't know who."

Dylan. Fatigue hit her, heavy as a boulder. But unless she wanted to stay here, she had no choice but to go on, didn't she?

The cop waited, gesturing for her to come along. Probably he was eager to leave, to go home to his wife and family.

Or whoever he had. She would be, if she did. Straightening, she followed his lead through the snow out of the silent woods.

A week later Lizzie pulled the Blazer to the curb outside her office in the northern Maine town of Bearkill.

She'd brought along a snow shovel, but to her surprise, the sidewalk was already cleared. With Rascal shifting impatiently by her side, she put her key in the lock.

"Hey, stranger." She turned.

"Hey, yourself." It was Dylan. "I didn't know you'd been let out of the hospital."

The other victim that night in the woods had been a passerby who'd stopped to help Spud when he'd first arrived and gotten bow-shot for his trouble. His truck hadn't been found for days, but during the next thaw his blood leaked down onto the road from a melting snowdrift.

His funeral was today. She meant to be there.

"Or," Lizzie added, struck by a new suspicion, "*did* they let you out?" The gunshot wound had nearly killed him. But he'd rallied, as he so often did.

"Yeah, well," he allowed. "Only so long a guy can take that foolishness."

Being in a hospital bed, he meant, from which she gathered he'd signed himself out against medical advice yet again. Now his shoulders looked thinner than she recalled under his topcoat, and his face was even leaner and sharper featured than usual.

But the glint in his eye and his wry, crooked grin were the same old Dylan. "Congratulations on those ex-cop deaths," he went on. "Sharp, the way you figured that one."

Lizzie shrugged. "Not really. It was just the way we said, that maybe two or three of the deaths were related, but not all of them."

So she'd looked at what the smaller number had in common, and bingo, there it was: border crossings. "Daniel wanted to move more product, but to do that he had to expand his supply territory and start bringing the drugs in from Canada."

And to do *that,* he'd needed a cooperative border guard or two. "The trouble was," she went on, "once he tried recruiting you, if you turned him down he'd have to . . ."

Dylan laughed without humor, following her inside, where it still smelled faintly of paint and new carpet. "Yeah, it really was an offer a person couldn't refuse, huh?"

Because if you did . . . well, Clifford Arbogast from Caribou and Michael Fontine from Van Buren had refused Daniel's corrupt job opportunity.

And had suffered the consequences. Dylan made an unhappy face. "And the rest of Chevrier's pals did kill themselves?"

She shook her head. "Dillard Sprague, the guy whose wife found him dead at the bottom of his porch steps? He really was an accident, I'm pretty sure. As for Bogart and Sirois—"

"The two who shot themselves, supposedly."

"Right," she said. "Officially, they were suicides. But I was able to get the medical examiner to reopen their cases and start getting them reclassified."

Dylan looked impressed. "And how did you do that?"

"One"—she held up a finger—"when I dug into his history a little, I found out Carl Bogart had super-high blood pressure in addition to his other problems. Perfect candidate for a stroke. Which if he'd suffered one while he was carrying that pistol of his and fell with it—"

Dylan's eyebrows went up skeptically. "Pretty good trick, Lizzie. Gun went off when he fell? You really think—"

"No. Personally I think he got fed up, decided on impulse to get it over with. But I didn't have to show that it was certain, only that it was *more* likely than him doing it on purpose."

Rascal sniffed Dylan judiciously, decided he was okay, and lay down with a sigh.

"And Chevrier's testimony about Bogart's plan for an actual suicide," she went on, "combined with the MD's sworn statement on Bogart's blood pressure . . ."

She took a breath. "When you looked at the whole picture, it was clear that it could've been accidental."

It hadn't hurt, either, that the medical examiner had known and liked Carl Bogart. Dylan laughed.

"Okay, okay. So you got over on an insurance company instead of the other way around for once. Nice going. But what about—"

"Yeah, funny thing about Sirois," she cut in. "He had all those medications and vaporizers, little oxygen tanks and so on. And," she added, "one tank that *wasn't* oxygen."

Dylan tipped his head questioningly. "Because it was . . . ?"

"Helium. There was one tank that was different in there, not green like the oxygen tanks. Brown. It bugged me, so I looked it up, and it turns out there's a color code for those tanks."

"Brown is helium?"

"Right. Simple, painless . . . and deadly, actually."

"Really. So it's not just for party balloons?"

"Um, no. There's a little more to it than just breathing it through a mask, but not much. And it's not, you know, violent. A big plus, lots of people would say."

He nodded in agreement. "But instead the guy got into the bathtub with a long gun, made an awful mess for people to find."

"Correct. So you tell me," she added, "what's wrong with this picture?"

He looked convinced. "Yeah, you wouldn't shoot yourself if—so you think someone staged his death? Made it look like suicide, but they didn't know he had a better method than . . ."

"Uh-huh. They made him shoot himself. By threatening his kids, maybe? I don't know yet. It's an open case. But my point isn't how, it's that if someone forces you to, it isn't suicide anymore, is it?"

"And that someone was . . . ?"

She shrugged. "Like I said, I don't know yet. I didn't have to solve the case, though, just get the ME to reopen it. It was probably Daniel—he'd have known Sirois would be a big help in finding a remote campsite in the woods—but we'll have to see."

She looked down the street toward Saint George's, the church where the funeral was scheduled. No cars had begun gathering yet.

"Anyway," she went on, "what I do know is that

if Sirois threatened Daniel's operation in any way, Daniel wouldn't have hesitated to get rid of him, just the way he did the other two, Fontine and Arbogast."

Rascal came and sat beside her. "Meanwhile, Brantwell has started talking. Feds've got him on account of he crossed state lines. From what I hear, he's trying to get a deal, blaming it all on Daniel. But he'll still be going away."

She sighed, imagining it. "Too bad for Missy."

"Yeah, huh?" he said, and frowned. "Listen, I'm really sorry it wasn't Nicki out there."

"Me, too. Not your fault, though," Lizzie added. "Thinking it was her, I mean. Her mom had disguised her so her ex-husband wouldn't recognize the kid if he came looking."

She reached down to smooth Rascal's glossy fur. "Well, he'd have known if he saw her close up, of course," she amended. "But the mother was doing the best she could."

Like all of us, Lizzie thought clearly. *But sometimes things don't work out anyway.*

"It's no wonder you thought the hair was natural," she went on. "Woman's a professional hair colorist, back in her old life. And he's a real prize, the ex-husband she ran away from in the first place. He's got a sheet a mile long."

Of criminal offenses, she meant. Dylan shook his head tiredly. "So this woman, she gets away from one abusive guy and then she runs into—"

392

"Uh-huh. The weirdo in the woods. Bad luck, huh?"

Lizzie sighed, remembering her interview with the woman; for a while there, no one else had been able to get near her.

"I guess our pal Daniel was a real charmer at first. Missy says that's his way. But the first time this new woman tried to leave him, he cut her face," said Lizzie.

The second time, he'd threatened to use the knife on the little girl; yeah, he was charming as all hell.

Dylan looked puzzled. "So why'd she have a gun, then? Seems to me he'd have taken away any—"

Lizzie nodded. "He did. We were wrong about that, he didn't leave her with it. But the little girl saw where he'd put it." The child's name was Ashley. "So before Spud arrived, while Daniel was busy stashing meth in his van so he could get away—"

It was the only part of the story that had made the woman smile. Dylan, too: "She scampered out and found it?"

"Yup. Daniel was smart, and he was good at his backwoods survival thing, but not infallible. He could make mistakes."

Dylan made a face. "Fortunately, huh?"

"Yeah. And speaking of luck . . ."

Lizzie gestured at the papers on her desk. Atop

the nearest stack was a notice of Spud Wilson's first court appearance.

The woman's second shot had missed him entirely; he'd simply fainted, apparently in fear. "He'll be in court this morning."

"Yeah, I know. My case, remember?" The three dead girls in Bangor, he meant. "I'm the one who's driving him back to jail afterwards," Dylan said, not sounding eager.

Or more accurately to prison; the hearing wasn't for any material reason, only to transfer the young man to state custody.

The bartender from Area 51 stuck his head in the door.

"Lizzie, can you come over when you get a chance? They're gonna serve papers on poor Henry, his wife's gonna try an' divorce him again, and it'll go better if you're there, you know?"

Henry was the guy who'd had Missy Brantwell trapped in a stranglehold Lizzie's first night here. She sighed again.

"Gimme a minute, I'll run over." It was a bit of a chore, but if it made things easier for everyone, why not?

"So anyway," said Dylan, "I just came by to—"

She faced him. "Why did you come to my place that night? The night Missy's baby went missing, you were hurt and you could have just gone to your motel room. It was closer. But instead you drove all the way back up here."

She'd been wondering about it ever since. He could've shared the motel room with the woman DEA cop. So why hadn't he?

He shrugged. "Yeah, well, you said it. I felt like hell, I didn't want to be with some stranger."

Then he looked straight at her. "I wanted to be with you, Lizzie. That's all. Just . . . anyway, that's the reason."

Silence while she absorbed this. Then: "I see. I'm sorry I misjudged you."

There, she'd said it. "I never should've been checking on you in the first place. And when I did, I should have known—"

"No," he interrupted flatly. "No way should you have thought anything but what you did."

He studied the floor. "It's not so easy getting over a thing like I put you through, Lizzie. Maybe you never will."

Looking up, he added, "But what I came to say right now is that I'm on the team getting the case against Spud together."

"Oh." She let the news sink in. "So you won't just be driving to Bangor but staying? And you'll be busy, I suppose."

He nodded, a lock of dark hair curling down over his pale forehead. "Right. But Bangor's not so far, Lizzie . . . If you ever wanted to we could still . . ."

Right, they could. It would be easy.

Too easy. "Yeah," she said. "You know what,

though? I think I'm going to just focus on the job here for a while."

From across the street, an angry yell from Area 51's general vicinity said Henry's divorce papers had arrived, courtesy of some hapless process server who hadn't known what he was in for.

Also, Lizzie was scheduled to take that long-delayed physical this afternoon: sit-ups, pull-ups, et cetera.

But there was one last thing she needed to know. "Dylan, the photographs. Of Nicki. You didn't—"

"Make the whole thing up just to get you here to Maine?" He frowned at his shoes. "I deserve that, don't I? But no."

He met her gaze. "I don't know where they came from. But I didn't fake them. And I still think she's out there."

She thought about it a moment. "Okay." Then she moved toward the door. He caught her as she went by, folding her into his arms and holding her close.

"Take care of yourself," he said.

"You, too." She bit her lip hard. Finally:

"Don't let Rascal out when you leave," she told him, backing away, then turned to find the burly veterinarian Trey Washburn standing just out-side the front window, looking in.

Not at Lizzie, but past her; glancing from Trey to Dylan and back again she saw the two men's eyes lock briefly, neither man betraying any expression; they didn't need to. Then as Trey's gaze met Lizzie's he smiled, tossing her a little wave like a salute before turning and striding away. From the few faint birdcall notes that filled the air, she thought he might be whistling.

"Hmph. Guess you'll be seeing plenty of him while I'm not around," said Dylan.

"Oh, I don't know," she replied airily, and was about to add some light, jealousy-provoking taunt; that is, until she saw Dylan's face.

"Don't," she repeated gently, "let Rascal out." Then she went out herself into a bright, bone-chillingly cold winter day in the little town of Bearkill, Maine.

Across the street, a car in the Food King's icy lot skidded and banged, horn blaring, into a parked one. A snowmobile shot fast and absolutely illegally uphill on the library lawn. And the fire siren atop the cupola on the potato barn went off, signaling a blaze somewhere.

So much for the funeral; on the street outside Saint George's the long, black hearse was just now pulling up. She'd never get there in time, not that anyone would miss her.

Instead she headed for the fender-bender; after that came the snowmobile, a check on the fire siren, which turned out to be for a shed blaze somewhere, and finally a visit to Area 51. There her old pal Henry, after an initial tantrum, had settled down and taken the divorce papers stoically, although with a gleam in his eye that she thought boded ill for later when he'd had more beer.

All of which took half the morning; by the time she finished sorting it out, she had barely enough time for the sixty-mile drive to Houlton and Spud's court hearing.

But she made it.

FOURTEEN

As Cody Chevrier crossed the parking lot between his office and the dome-topped, red-brick edifice of the Aroostook County courthouse, he felt his mood darken. Inside, Spud Wilson's folks would be waiting to hear what came next for their son, still hoping that there had been some kind of mistake, and Cody meant to be there with them when they learned that there hadn't, that the boy they'd raised was to be tried as a killer.

It was his duty. But he didn't like it. Inside, he climbed the polished stairs to the courtroom level, read the schedule posted on the wall across from the stairwell, and found the room with its varnished wooden wainscoting, heavily ornate wooden bench flanked by the State of Maine and American flags, and the prosecutor and defense desks of brightly polished wood, sitting at right angles to the witness stand.

All the hearing participants had already arrived: Al Bacon, the county judge; the prosecutor, Marion Brandt Daly; defense attorney Hamilton Bell; and Spud himself, with a white padded bandage covering his injured ear.

His folks were there, too, his father and mother looking stunned in their Sunday clothes, as if being well dressed might somehow be of help to their boy. His mom wept quietly into her tissues while his father, eyes bleary as if recovering from a hangover, sat with his hands stuffed in his pockets.

Behind them sat Lizzie Snow, waiting like the rest for the proceedings to begin, which shortly they did, and almost as soon as they had begun, they were finished: the complaint was read, Spud was asked how did he plead, and he replied, "Not guilty."

All of which had been expected. Cody shifted, trying to ease the ache in his wounded shoulder, and wished the heat in here wasn't always turned up so damned high. But he wouldn't be here long; there might ordinarily have been a defense argument on why Spud Wilson ought to be let out on bail.

There was no bail for murder charges in Maine, though, so all that remained was for the judge to speak.

"Prisoner is remanded to the custody of the state." The transfer had already been arranged and agreed to.

But Spud still looked puzzled. "Jail?" he queried shakily. He'd been in a cell downstairs; the county lockup was right here in the building. "Does he mean I'm going back to—"

But his father understood, all right. "No!" he shouted, his face reddening as he yanked his right hand out of his pocket.

A hand with a gun in it. Not for the first time, Cody cursed the absence of metal detectors in the courthouse building; every year he argued for them, and every year there was simply no money for it.

"No, you ain't takin' my boy," the old man yelled, "this ain't fair, this—"

"Marty!" Spud's mother cried, but he shoved her roughly away.

"—this ain't *right!* And it's your fault! You . . . you always *coddled* him so, you made him that way!" He grabbed his wife, held the gun to her head, then waved it around.

"Don't come near!" he threatened as Cody jumped up.

For an instant the courtroom was still, even the deputy who'd run in when the judge hit the panic button under his desk froze in place. Only Lizzie Snow stood slowly, her face a smooth mask of intent, right behind Wilson so he didn't see her.

Then she was on him, her hand plucking the weapon from his in a quick, deft motion, his arms seized and yanked behind him. Another moment and he was on the floor with her knee in his back.

Spud stared slack-jawed. Cody wondered again if the boy was on some kind of medication, or if he'd suffered a brain injury in the shooting.

But that didn't matter now, or at any rate it couldn't be helped. Al Bacon concluded the hearing and they all left the courtroom, Spud and his father in custody, leaving only Mrs. Wilson in her worn coat and run-down shoes, looking confused.

Before Cody could reach her, though, Lizzie was with her, offering the woman a tissue and a ride home. "We can come back to check on your husband later," she added kindly.

Cody paused in the doorway as Mrs. Wilson went out into the hall. "After you get her home, you want to go get lunch?" he asked.

Lizzie shook her head. "Can't. I told Missy I'd stop by, talk to her about working in my office. I need—"

He waved tiredly. "Yeah, a replacement for Spud. Fine," he told her, and with a grin at him she was gone.

A grin, by God, after what she'd been through. *Ain't she a pistol, though?* old Carl Bogart would've said, and she was; Cody watched from the second-floor window as she guided poor Flora Wilson across the parking lot. With that spiky black hair, red lipstick, and elaborate eye makeup, she hardly resembled a cop at all . . .

But she was his new deputy, just as he'd been Carl Bogart's; watching her help Flora Wilson into the Blazer, Cody thought that on balance he'd done as well as Carl had, picking one out.

Better, even. Meanwhile, though, his shoulder still hurt like a son of a bitch. Sighing heavily, he decided to take one of those pain pills they'd given him after all, call dispatch and tell them he was going on home to bed.

Lizzie and the other deputies could handle things without him, he thought.

So he did.

"Missy? Missy, what happened?"

Lizzie hurried across the driveway toward the Brantwells' back porch, where the girl stood watching the fire crew finish putting out a smoldering heap, one that had been a shed.

Missy shook her blond head sorrowfully. "Mom thought that she was in the kitchen and tried to light the stove out there."

The girl turned. "Oh, Lizzie, we can't leave her for even a minute now."

They'd already put the fire out once, earlier, but some hot embers had blazed up again; now the fire crew soaked the ruins carefully a final time before packing up at last.

"I'm so sorry," said Lizzie. "Is the baby okay?"

He was still recovering from his time in the woods; for a couple of days they'd thought he might be coming down with pneumonia.

Missy brightened. "Oh, much better. Having his morning nap. But—"

She bit her lip, staring across the driveway. "Lizzie, I don't know what I'm going to do. I mean, with Dad gone."

In federal custody, she meant, which he probably

would be for a long time. "Isn't Tom Brody in charge when your dad's been away in the past?"

Missy nodded uncertainly. "Well, yes, but that was only for a few days at most. And anyway, Tom's not around."

"Really?" Across the drive, the firemen inspected the shed wreckage, looking for more hot spots. "You mean on vacation?"

"No, I mean no one knows where he is. He didn't show up for work the day after Dad got arrested and no one's seen him since. I'm getting worried about him."

Missy turned, her expression troubled. "You don't suppose . . ."

Damn, Lizzie thought. She'd known it must be someone; Daniel wouldn't have approached a respectable guy like Brantwell just on a whim. But she'd been hoping it wasn't the pleasantly ferret-faced foreman, the only one who knew how this farm ran besides Roger Brantwell himself, who'd been the link.

"I'm sorry, Missy. But Brody must've known your dad had money problems. He saw the accounts, what came in and what money was owed."

Missy's shoulders slumped. "You think he told Daniel that Dad might be open to a deal? To getting paid for carrying drugs?"

Lizzie shrugged. "Something made Daniel think your dad was a candidate."

And now Brody was gone. Lizzie made a mental note to check in with Chevrier about it, as Missy replied.

"Great. Something else for me to feel paranoid about. After Spud just walked right into the house and took Jeffrey, it's like I can't trust anyone. And this just makes it—"

"You know that's what happened?" It had been another thing Lizzie kept wondering about, how Spud had gotten inside and taken little Jeffrey without being noticed.

Missy nodded ruefully. "Mom remembered. I mean, not in an accurate way, that Jeffrey was kidnapped. And not soon enough to help. But when I was helping her get ready for bed last night"—the girl's face crumpled suddenly; she struggled for control and gained it—"she told me about the nice boy with the pretty pictures on his arms who took Jeffrey outside to play."

Lizzie couldn't help but laugh. "Oh, man. So she saw Spud? But he must not have seen her or . . ."

Missy nodded, smiling through her tears. "Right. Daniel had told Spud to steal the baby for him so he could get away. I guess because you were looking for that little girl?"

"Well, partly," Lizzie allowed. "After the bust at Izzy Dolaby's, though, he must also have realized the authorities were getting closer to him, too."

The last of the fire department vehicles pulled out of the driveway. The smell of smoke still hung in the air.

"But it was getting too cold for them to stay outside much longer, and if they came into town, he was worried I might see the little girl. Or that's what Spud said, anyway."

Missy was silent a moment. Then: "He knew all along. About Jeffrey, I mean. Daniel knew about the baby, he'd been watching me secretly since right after I left him, he took *pictures* . . ."

Her voice broke. "I know," Lizzie said gently. The photos had been found on Daniel's computer, which he had powered via solar panels. "He was big on watching people, wasn't he?"

It was the same laptop that Daniel had been using to monitor Lizzie's office via his bugging gadgets. Lizzie felt unclean just knowing the guy had spied on her for a few days; what Missy must feel after a year of being stalked was . . .

Well, it couldn't be good. "It turned out not to be her, by the way."

Lizzie looked out across the valley through the lightly falling snow, toward the forested hills beyond.

"The little girl out there, she turned out not to be the one I'm looking for."

She bit her lip. The disappointment was still very fresh. "And now she and her mother have taken off again."

Missy looked stricken. "Oh, the poor things. You couldn't keep them here just to help them somehow?"

Lizzie shook her head. "Social Services tried. But there turned out to be a sister in Bangor who said she'd take them in."

She brushed off the unhappy memory of the stiff, blond-helmeted relative grimly ushering the two unfortunates into her plush SUV. Watching them go, Lizzie had wondered how long the arrangement would last.

But like so many things, it was beyond her control. "And there was nothing to hold them here for. Mom was a victim, shot Spud in self-defense. They were free to go. So sayeth the court."

End of story, at least for now. But she could still do something about someone else.

"Listen," she began, and described what she had in mind. But when she'd finished, Missy looked doubtful.

"Oh, I don't know, Lizzie. There's still the whole farm to try getting a handle on. And if Mom can't be left alone at all, I don't know how I'd—"

Lizzie put a hand on the girl's arm. "Look, I realize you need to care for your family, and I respect that. What you've told me about wanting to live here in Bearkill, too . . . well, let's just say I understand better now."

Cody Chevrier, for instance, had lived a great

life here, and so had Carl Bogart's wife, Audrey; the more Lizzie heard of her, the more she admired the wise old sheriff's spouse.

"But, Missy, is a twenty-four-hour-a-day nurse's aide job taking care of your mom really what you want?"

Even aside from the problem of running the farm, she meant. Missy studied her hands.

"No. And that's what it would be, too." But it wasn't what worried Missy the most. "Oh, Lizzie, how could he have done it? Dad, I mean, and not just the drugs. He meant to kill you all!"

"Yeah." Lizzie had thought about this, suspecting that the question was coming. "Or he said he meant to. Who knows if he'd have been able to."

Missy looked mutinous. "He was making pretty good progress toward it."

She hadn't forgiven her father. But everything would get easier for her if she did, Lizzie suddenly understood somehow.

"Look, Missy, think about what you'd do for Jeffrey."

No reply. But Missy was listening.

"I mean, your dad didn't start out planning murder," Lizzie went on. "All he wanted was for you and your mom and Jeffrey to be okay, and moving the drugs looked like the only answer to him. He didn't know things were going to get so crazy, and by the time they did . . ."

She paused, wondering if she should say the next thing. "By that time, he'd started using the product."

Missy looked up, shocked. "Dad? Was doing meth? Lizzie, I don't—"

Believe it, she'd been about to say. But after his arrest, he'd been taken to the hospital to be checked out; he had, after all, been in a vehicle accident—and blood tests had been done.

"Missy, he'd been driving a lot, to and from New York. On the road late at night, I guess he felt he needed something to stay awake. Something," she added, "industrial strength."

She touched the girl's shoulder. "All I'm saying is, one thing led to another. He didn't know how badly it would all go. And once it did, he must've known what a pickle you'd be in here, without him. He just wanted to protect you."

Missy smiled through her tears. "Thanks. You'd make a good defense attorney."

Lizzie managed a laugh. "Yeah, well. He's lucky he's got a real one." Which was going to be another problem, she realized, paying for the attorney Brantwell needed.

Then a thought struck her. "You know, Trey Washburn already knows how to run a farm. You should call him."

The veterinarian, who after a frightening twenty-four hours in the hospital had now recovered completely from his knock on the head, had big tracts of land, some with crops on them.

Missy blinked uncertainly. "But doesn't he already have his hands full with—"

"No doubt he does, with his veterinary practice. But I'll bet he could help you find another foreman, someone trustworthy. I'll bet he'd help you keep an eye on things, too, make sure it's all being done right."

Missy looked hopeful. "Maybe. And . . . you know, they have a day-care program at the nursing home. It's right down the street from your office and it doesn't even cost much, so if I had a job I might be able to afford having someone here at night."

She looked questioningly at Lizzie. "So if I could bring Jeffrey to your office with me . . ."

That hadn't been in Lizzie's plan, but it could work if she wanted it to. "I'll be needing some-one to help me with Rascal, too," she said.

The dog deserved more attention than she'd been able to give him. "So you could all get out for a walk every day," she went on, "when the weather gets better."

Possibility lit Missy's face. "Or even now. I like walking in the winter." But then her face fell.

"I might still have to sell the farm, though. Or it might just get taken, if part of Dad's sentence ends up being not only jail time but also a big fine."

Both of which were likely. "Look, let's just take one thing at a time, okay?"

In the back of her mind, Lizzie thought that Trey Washburn's large appetite for acreage might solve Missy's problems. But that was a conversation best left for another day.

"Okay," said Missy. "You're right, for now I've got enough on my plate." She took a deep breath, steadying herself.

"Anyway, I'm sorry that you didn't find what you wanted out there. Who, I mean."

Lizzie turned to go. "Yeah. Thanks. Me, too."

There'd be time enough later to dwell on her next step in trying to find Nicki, and she should get back to work. But she did have a final question.

"You threw the rock, didn't you? My front window that night, when it got smashed . . . you put the note on the rock and you snuck up and—"

The pink flush creeping up Missy's neck gave Lizzie her answer. "But why?" Lizzie persisted.

"I was worried about you, and I guess I panicked. I didn't know yet, but I already had a feeling about what might be going on. And I knew that if Dan was involved at all, things could get ugly quick."

Missy looked up. "You'd been so nice to poor

411

Henry in the bar that night. So humane, I guess is the word. I wasn't sure you were . . ."

"Ready for it?" Lizzie finished. She thought for an instant about a man clad in furs and skins, heavily armed and holding a woman and child prisoner.

Descending the porch steps, she replied, "Yeah, maybe you were right. But listen, next time, give me a heads-up in person, okay? I can't go on replacing those expensive windows."

She got into the Blazer. On the way out, she passed one of Brantwell's farm workers; with a roaring chain saw he was cutting up a charred beam from the incinerated shed.

His expression didn't change as she went by. She wondered if the missing foreman was the only farm employee involved in luring Brantwell into a deal with the devil.

But there would be time enough to find that out, too, she thought; meanwhile Missy could use a friend.

And so could I, Lizzie thought. *So, absolutely, could I.*

Heading back to the office in Bearkill, she passed children out sledding, their snowsuits bright as gumdrops as they zipped downhill.

A man trudging across an open field shouldered a shotgun. Dogs romped by a fence. A red tractor pulled a long wagon with hay bales stacked on it.

And over it all loomed the Great North Woods: vast, silent. As she swung around the long curve into town past the old potato barn, her radio sputtered.

"All units . . ."

She pressed the handset button and answered.

ACKNOWLEDGMENTS

Thank you to all of you who helped: Ken Brown, "Cur" Soucy, Cathie Pelletier, and Lise Pelletier.

ABOUT THE AUTHOR

SARAH GRAVES lives with her husband in Eastport, Maine, in the 1823 Federal-style house that helped inspire her books. This series and the author's real-life experience have been featured in *House & Garden* and *USA Today*. She is currently at work on the next novel in her new mystery series, to be published by Bantam.

www.sarahgraves.net/
Facebook.com/SarahGraves2011
@sarahgraves2011

Center Point Large Print
600 Brooks Road / PO Box 1
Thorndike, ME 04986-0001 USA

(207) 568-3717

**US & Canada:
1 800 929-9108**
www.centerpointlargeprint.com